"Let us welcome o
Dame du Miroir aux F[...]
Lake. Priestess of the Tri[...]

Smiling faces beame[...]
Tribe applauded and cheered.

The voices subdued as Laudine raised her hands. "When a warrior is inducted, a priestess—representing the embodiment of the Goddess—welcomes him into Her Tribe." Smiling at Issylte, the newly welcomed priestess, Laudine cast her grin toward Tristan. His hungry eyes devoured Issylte, his feral face ravenous and fierce.

"When a new priestess is inducted, a warrior is selected to worship the Goddess within her." Laudine beckoned Tristan, who rose to his feet, all the while staring expectantly at Issylte, his intense eyes aflame. Issylte's legs trembled under her gown. Laudine, her auburn hair glowing in the firelight, announced, "Tristan will complete the final step in your induction into our Tribe."

Holding her gaze with his mesmerizing blue eyes, Tristan strode confidently up to Issylte. The warrior who would welcome her into the Tribe of Dana. Issylte's mouth went dry, her legs quivering at his approach. Power emanated from him, a magnetic aura that beckoned with promise. And made her magic sing.

Praise for *The Wild Rose and the Sea Raven*:

"A sensational, well-crafted, fantasy fiction novel, with a perfect blend of magic, mysticism, romance, tragedy, drama, and suspense."
~ *Finalist Award from Reader's Choice Book Awards*
~*~

"The Wild Rose and the Sea Raven is everything I would expect a novel of Arthurian times to be and more. The battle scenes are realistic and bloody as one would expect in any knight's tale, but the romance and the passion of the characters are developed superbly and will have readers turning pages relentlessly to discover the next thrilling chapter of this story."
~*Grant Leishman for Readers' Favorite Book Reviews*
~*~

"I highly recommend The Wild Rose and the Sea Raven by Jennifer Ivy Walker. Congratulations on writing a very enchanting story filled with magic, knights, an evil queen, and people with hearts so pure that nothing can break them. I am now a fan!"
~ *Teresa Syms for Readers' Favorite Book Reviews*
~*~

"Her world building skills are masterful, and Avalon, though hidden in the mists, is brought to life as a place both fragile and powerful. Her rich storytelling and blending of genres will delight readers and fans of paranormal, historical, romance alike."
~*Avis Adams*

~*~

"This beautiful fantasy novel captured my full attention from start to finish. Jennifer Ivy Walker infuses espionage, betrayal, love, magic, and danger throughout the story. The end of the story left me yearning to read the sequel."

~*~

"The Wild Rose and the Sea Raven by Jennifer Ivy Walker is an epic novel that drew and kept me locked in. It was intense, delving into magic, royal politics, deceit, treachery, betrayal, fate, courage, and survival. I loved the beautiful plot, sound character development, and riveting storyline."

The Lady of the Mirrored Lake

by

Jennifer Ivy Walker

*The Wild Rose and the Sea Raven,
Book 2*

The Lady of the Mirrored Lake

Cover Art by *Rae Monet*

The Wild Rose Press, Inc.
PO Box 708
Adams Basin, NY 14410-0708
Visit us at www.thewildrosepress.com

Publishing History
First Edition, 2023
Trade Paperback ISBN 978-1-5092-4683-0
Digital ISBN 978-1-5092-4684-7

The Wild Rose and the Sea Raven, Book 2
Published in the United States of America

Dedication

To Madeleine Ivy, my youngest,
for your youthful exuberance, enthusiastic
encouragement, and endless support as I realized my
lifelong dream.

Chapter 1

La Joyeuse Garde

The salt air was tangy and crisp, the white sails billowing in the strong ocean winds under a warm summer sun as the cog ship sailed south from Avalon toward the craggy coast of *la Bretagne* in northwestern France. Tristan leaned over the taffrail from the deck of the ship to watch the white capped waves lick the sides of the vessel as they skimmed across the Narrow Sea. He had to get Issylte out of that desolate room below deck. He'd heard her heaving and sobbing for two days now. She needed fresh air, fresh water, and sunlight to ease her queasy stomach—and her broken spirit.

He'd felt her pain—just as she had felt the Morholt's blade slice open his flesh in the battle of Tintagel. Tristan knew she loved the Elf Ronan, and the thought made him sick with jealousy and rage. He wanted to *kill him*—but that would hurt her, something he could never do. No— he'd be her champion, as promised, and lead her army. He would fight for her and help her challenge the evil Black Widow Queen. If the Goddess granted them a victory—and Issylte were finally able to reclaim her father's Irish crown—then even if she decided to return to her Elf, Tristan would support her. She'd saved his life. And now he wanted to save hers.

Even if it meant she loved another.

1

He knocked on the wooden door of her quarters.

"I'm sick! Please go away!" she whimpered from inside.

Tristan knocked again. "Issylte, please come up on deck with me. The fresh air will do you good."

"No, I'm sick. Go away."

He opened the door and the stench of vomit assailed him. She was lying in her cot, a bucket on the floor beside her. Yet, with the rocking of the boat and the small size of the container, she had missed, and the floor was covered with it. She was whimpering, wounded, and wretched.

Tristan walked to the bed and pushed the bucket aside with his boot. Taking her by the arm, he gently insisted that she come with him. Although she resisted at first, he finally removed her from the dark cabin and motioned to a couple crew members who went in to clean her quarters. Tristan brought her up onto the deck, into the sunshine and salt air, where Lancelot was leaning against the taffrail.

The White Knight's eyes widened in shock at the sight of her struggling to walk, tightly clutching Tristan's arm. Issylte's beautiful long hair was stringy and knotted, stuck to one side of her face, which was pale and tinged with green. Dark circles brimmed her red, swollen eyes, and her lips were cracked and dry with thirst.

"Good day, Issylte! I am glad you are joining us here on deck. The fresh air will restore you." Lancelot smiled reassuringly as Tristan guided her to the balcony. "Stare at the horizon. It helps against *le mal de mer.*" He poured something into a cup and swirled the contents. "Before we left Avalon, I asked *ma mère* for a remedy for sea sickness." He handed her the beverage. "Drink this. It will settle your stomach and revive you."

Issylte sipped the herbal water, a blend of fresh ginger and a trace of mint. She gazed off into the horizon and drank slowly, whispering soft words of gratitude between swallows.

"We'll reach the coast of Bretagne soon," Lancelot said brightly, offering a bit of encouragement and distraction. "I sent a messenger ahead of us, a few days before we left Avalon." He smiled, as if to ease her discomfort. "I keep a stable at the port, so horses will be ready for us when we arrive. From there, it will take three days to reach my castle." Lancelot shot a glance at Tristan. "We'll stop along the way, to rest and water the horses. Set up tents at night to sleep." His warm smile seemed to cheer Issylte. "We'll be there soon, you'll see. I am anxious to show you my *château*," he said proudly. "It is made of white limestone, which glistens in the sunlight. It's truly beautiful." His face beamed with a youthful exuberance that brought forth a hint of a smile from the seasick and heartsick Issylte.

"I have asked the servants to prepare the Rose Room for you. You'll have your own bath. A luxurious bed with silken sheets. And enormous windows overlooking the river Élorn." Lancelot grinned at Tristan on the other side of Issylte. "The woodland is abundant in game. Tristan and I can do a bit of hunting, and you, my princess, will have a magnificent view of the forest that you hold so dear."

Sipping her herbal brew, Issylte smiled at the White Knight. "You, dear Lancelot, are a wonder. Thank you...for everything." Squeezing his arm affectionately, she murmured, "It will be lovely to see your castle." Turning to Tristan, she added, "And I look forward to meeting the Tribe of Dana."

Lancelot shifted uneasily against the taffrail. "When we left Avalon, we told everyone that you were returning to Anjou, to throw the clairvoyant dwarf off your trail, should he and the Black Widow Queen try to track you." Meeting her gaze, his tone became serious. "Frocin and his band of dwarves have spies throughout the realm. It would be best if we did not announce your reason for coming to Bretagne, nor reveal your true name."

With a glance at Tristan, he said, "We'll tell the innermost circle of the Tribe—those we trust implicitly—her identity and purpose in joining us." Twisting to face Issylte, he remarked, "It will take months—likely a year—to recruit and train an army large enough to challenge the queen. That would give ample time for word to reach her, should we use your real name. I suggest instead that we say you're a lady from Camelot, the sister of a fellow knight. That you wished to sojourn in Bretagne, so Tristan and I have escorted you to my castle. Where you shall be our honored guest." He flashed Issylte a dazzling grin, eliciting a weary smile from her in return.

She nodded, as if agreeing to a new name and identity, enabling her to remain hidden from her wicked stepmother. The ruthless Black Widow Queen whose relentless pursuit of Issylte was the reason they were fleeing Avalon, headed to Lancelot's *château, la Joyeuse Garde*.

Lancelot suggested, "In Ireland, you were Églantine, a flower of the forest. In Avalon, you were Lilée—a flower of water. I propose that, in Bretagne, you should be named for the third sacred element of the Goddess—a *stone*—and be called Opale. A luminous

4

pale gem that sparkles with golden highlights, like your glorious blonde hair."

He raised his eyebrows inquisitively at Tristan, who grinned and ducked his chin affirmatively. "I like it. It's perfect." Then, casting a soft gaze at Issylte, he murmured, "Just like the golden light of the Goddess I saw in you when I first opened my eyes in Avalon."

"Opale…" Issylte whispered. "The same pearlescent color that your mother prefers." She grinned at Lancelot. "I like it. Opale I shall be."

"Tristan or I shall always be at your side," he replied cautiously. "If anyone should question your family background, we can offer snippets of life in Camelot— as members of Arthur's court." Then, perhaps to give them some time alone, Lancelot said cheerfully, "And now, I must excuse myself, for I need to check the riggings of the sail and the supplies we have stored." Kissing Issylte's hand and winking at Tristan, the White Knight of Avalon left them leaning against the taffrail, gazing out at the Narrow Sea.

****

Issylte stared at the expanse of blue all around them. Sea gulls cawed in the endless sky; the tangy brine of the sea filled the salty, soothing air. The sun was warm on her face, a summer breeze caressing her skin. The ship was sailing at a good speed, for the wind was with them. The vessel parted the white-capped waves as they flew toward the craggy coast of Bretagne.

Tristan fetched a bucket of cool, fresh water and dipped a clean cloth into it, squeezing out the excess. Carefully, gingerly, he wiped her brow, then the hair which was stuck to the side of her face. He washed her cheek, the side of her face and neck, wiping away the

5

sadness and sickness with tenderness.

When he finished, he emptied the bucket, tossing the contents over the rail into the ocean. He replaced the pail, spread the cloth over its top to dry in the sun, and returned to her side, placing his arms against the taffrail to gaze at the sea.

Tristan spoke first. "You loved him."

A tear streamed down her cheek. "Yes."

"He wanted you to stay in Avalon."

Again, she replied, "Yes." Her eyes brimming, she turned to Tristan. "But I could not. I *had* to leave. To follow this path that the Goddess has set before me." She looked down at the cup still in her hands. "I don't know where it leads, but I knew I had to take it."

His intense blue gaze bore into hers. "I don't know where it leads either, Issylte. But I will be at your side. I will *fight* for you." Taking her hand, he raised it to his warm lips. "I'll lead your army. And be *your champion*." He lifted her chin gently and locked his gaze with hers. "You saved my life, Issylte. Now *I* will save *yours*."

As she stared into the cerulean depths of his eyes, Issylte saw the black bird again. The Cornish *chough*— the royal sea raven of Cornwall. She glimpsed the amber eyes of a wolf. A fountain in a forest. The still lake she'd seen in the *sighting*—the mirror of water which held a secret she had yet to discover.

A treasure she was meant to protect.

Dozens of images emerged in the limpid pools of Tristan's gaze.

A white castle overlooking a courtyard with a pair of swans floating on a dark lake. *Swans mate for life,* Viviane had whispered. A stone altar in a thick forest, with warriors—*the Tribe*—gathered around a fire. A cottage in a forest, with a fountain and waterfall nearby. A pink stone castle high on a cliff near the sea. A tattoo—not the one on his wrist, but similar—with a Celtic trio of delicate swirls. The bubbling spring within the sacred cave, the sparkling star shimmering at its center.

La Grotte de l' Étoile.

Ronan brought me there. Why do I see it in Tristan's gaze?

In the breadth of an instant, the images drew her to him, joining her essence to his, an *otherworldly* bond far beyond the mortal realm.

Have you not felt the truth of this when you look into his eyes? Can you not sense a spiritual bond between your soul and his? Viviane's prophecy flashed into Issylte's mind as she soared within Tristan's gaze.

She pictured Ronan, alone and suffering in Avalon. Viviane, who had been like a mother to her. *Tatie,* who had taught her the verdant magic of the forest and who had died to protect her. Her father, whom she'd been unable to save from the poison of the Black Widow Queen.

She remembered Luna and Noisette, her beloved horses. She thought of Lancelot and his kindness, and of this knight before her, who had promised to save her life. Lead her army. And help her reclaim her throne. Overcome with emotion, tears spilling down her cheeks, legs trembling under her ruined gown, she whispered simply, "Thank you," as the blue waters of Tristan's eyes soothed her spirit in a wave of calm.

After a few moments, he looked back at the sea, extending his gaze out to the horizon. He emitted a loud sigh, his mood darkening with his thoughts.

Issylte sensed his rage at the betrayal by Indulf. The

fellow knight who had claimed Tristan's victory over the infamous Morholt, the Viking warrior he'd slain in the battle of Tintagel. Indulf—the traitor who had usurped Tristan's position as First Knight of Cornwall and champion to his uncle Marke, the king. She shared his anguish at the injustice of being called a *traitor* and *coward*—he, the hero who had slain the Black Knight and saved his uncle's kingdom! Issylte knew of his past—how he'd always punished himself with guilt for being incapable of defending his family. And now Tristan found himself banished from the kingdom he had nearly died to defend.

Once again unable to protect the only family he had left.

His uncle.

His king.

She tried to soothe his suffering, as he had done for her. "Perhaps we can reach King Marke somehow. Before he marries the Queen. Find a way to convince him of the truth. That *you* were the one to slay the Morholt. That Indulf is a liar and traitor. And that Frocin is allied with Queen Morag. The Black Widow who poisoned her first husband. *My father*."

She touched his arm, offering encouragement and companionship in the simple gesture. "Although you are banished, perhaps one of King Marke's allies—a lord from another kingdom—might convince him of your true valor, restoring your name and position in Cornwall." Tristan continued to stare out to sea, but she knew he was listening. She hoped her words would reach him, inspire him, soothe him. "If we could expose Indulf's lies, Frocin's treachery, and the danger the Queen and her dark wizard pose to his kingdom, perhaps your uncle would join us. To fight against the evil which threatens us all."

He moved toward her, a shred of hope—and the blaze of fury—burning in his eyes. *Once he regains his full strength, he will be more fearsome than the Morholt he defeated. The champion who will lead my army. The knight who will help me reclaim my throne. The prince who will become King of Lyonesse and heir to the crown of Cornwall. After six long years, the Goddess has finally revealed my fate. And it is entwined with his.*

****

For the next few days, Issylte spent as much time as possible on the deck of the ship, avoiding her dark cabin and the nausea it evoked. Today, the final day of their voyage, the rocky coast of Bretagne appeared in the distance as sunlight streamed through the scattered clouds and sparkled on the whitecaps breaking against the hull. As she, Tristan, and Lancelot stood together on the prow of their vessel, the White Knight spoke of the reception he'd planned to welcome her as the Lady Opale.

To entertain the distinguished guest they were escorting from Camelot, Lancelot had ostensibly requested the presence of several lords and ladies for a month-long *séjour* at *La Joyeuse Garde*. Yet, in reality, he'd invited powerful allies whose military support he hoped to obtain in the challenge against the wicked Black Widow Queen.

"Prince Kaherdin is the son of King Hoël of Armorique," Lancelot began amicably. "The monarch who placed several orders with Ronan for Elven armor and weapons. For *hundreds* of knights." At the mention of the Elf's name, Tristan spun away, his lip raised sullenly. Issylte stared straight ahead at the horizon, swallowing a wave of grief and guilt. "Kaherdin and the Lady Gargeolaine, whom I believe he intends to marry, will arrive with his sister, the Princess Blanchine." With a glance at Tristan, who had looked at him, Lancelot suggested, "Perhaps Armorique will join our cause."

Tristan nodded, as if mulling over the implications of another monarchy on their side. "Lord Bénézet might ally with us, with Viking slave raids now directed at Anjou." His fierce gaze locked with Lancelot's.

"Indeed. I have invited Bénézet, Abélard from Poitou, and Audric of Aquitaine." Lancelot glanced at Issylte. "Abélard and Bénézet are married; their wives will accompany them, so you'll have some female company for a change." With a conspiratorial chuckle, Lancelot smirked to Tristan, "Audric is single and quite *dashing.* I thought perhaps he could entertain the Princess Blanchine." Dazzling Issylte with his famous boyish grin, Lancelot's tone became more serious. "Lord Esclados—the Red Knight—and his wife, the Lady Laudine, will be among the guests. He is a warrior of the Tribe of Dana, and she is one of the priestesses. They are the Lord and Lady of the sacred Fountain of Barenton, in the enchanted Forest of Brocéliande."

"Esclados was the one who invited me to join the Tribe," Tristan told her. "When I killed the dwarf Bédalis and freed his wife Laudine, he arranged for the Druid to give me the magic of the golden herb."

As Tristan stared into her eyes, her verdant magic stirred. His presence was enticing, beguiling, bewitching. With considerable effort, she redirected her thoughts and forced her attention back to Lancelot, who was still speaking.

"I have planned a celebration to welcome you as our guest, the Lady Opale, complete with a feast and a ball," he grinned, kissing Issylte's hand. "With plenty of opportunity to hunt, train with my knights, and restore your warrior's body to battle condition, my friend," he chortled, slapping Tristan on the back. Tristan shot her a breathtaking smile. "There will also be the opportunity to privately solicit the support of potential allies," Lancelot added, his tone more serious as his gaze darted between them. "Each of the lords I have invited has earned my trust. I'll convey the importance of discretion—that we do not wish to announce our intentions until we have acquired sufficient forces to challenge the queen." He stretched his back as he shifted away from the railing. "I have planned for my guests to stay for the month of September. The Goddess willing, we'll have obtained their commitment to our unified cause and count them as allies prior to their departure."

The wings of a white dove fluttered hopefully in Issylte's verdant heart.

****

The ship docked at the seaport on the rocky coast of Bretagne where they disembarked, loaded supplies, and prepared to ride south to *la Joyeuse Garde*. Lancelot concluded, "Once you've fully recovered, Tristan— we'll ride to the Château of Landuc and summon the leaders of the Tribe. Finalize our strategy, confer with our allies. Recruit and train an army. Prepare for battle." His encouraging words sent a wave of hope through Issylte's weary bones. The three friends mounted the horses brought to them by Lancelot's stable grooms. The White Knight grinned at the two of them. "Let's hope the next few weeks will be fortuitous indeed."

After three days on horseback, stopping periodically to rest and water the horses, pitching tents at night as they headed south, Issylte, Tristan, Lancelot, and his entourage finally arrived at the glorious *Joyeuse Garde.* The magnificent castle, which faced south, sparkled in the afternoon sun, the brackish waters of the Élorn river casting a salt spray in the breeze, the thick, pine-scented forest around the palace encasing it like a luminous gem.

The travelers dismounted, leaving their horses to be groomed by stable hands who would also unpack the saddle bags. Lancelot—the *châtelain*—and his guests were received by smiling servants who welcomed and ushered them into the pearlescent limestone *château.*

"Issylte, my attendants will show you to the Rose Room, where they will draw your bath and help you refresh from your journey." Lancelot's eyes twinkled, despite his fatigue. "Rest for the afternoon. Tonight, we shall have a quiet supper, with just a few of my higher-ranking knights joining us on the terrace near the lake. Just under your balcony." He flashed her a heartwarming smile. Kissing her on each cheek—*la bise* that reminded her of Viviane and *Tatie*—he murmured, "*À bientôt, ma belle*," heading off with Tristan, whose gaze lingered on her as she followed the servants to her room.

The Rose Room was exquisite, situated in the rear corner of the second floor of the castle, with a magnificent view of the deep lake, the distant Élorn river, and the thick, abundant forest to the north and west. The walls were plastered a creamy white, the polished wooden floors fragrant with pine oil, gleaming in the soft glow of the setting sun. Issylte smiled dreamily as she entered the chambers which would be hers for the next few months. *Peaceful and serene. With a magnificent view of the forest.* Verdant magic thrummed in her veins.

The enormous sunlit windows were adorned with mauve silk draperies, the same rosy color of the tufted coverlet upon the sumptuous bed. A stone fireplace, made from the smooth gray rocks of the roaring river, graced the western wall, flanked by a large, intricately carved wooden armoire, matching table, and pair of mauve velvet chairs. To her delight, there was a pitcher of cool water, a goblet, and an enticing platter of fresh fruit on the table. The sweet aroma of lush, ripe melon slices and succulent strawberries made her mouth water. She slurped a fat, juicy strawberry as she admired her beautiful new bedroom.

Two embroidered tapestries embellished the pale walls—one of a lady and unicorn; the other, a floral depiction of mauve roses in the same deep pink hue as the draperies. *The Rose Room. Perfect for Églantine— the Wild Rose of the Hazelwood Forest.* She smiled contentedly as she devoured the savory strawberries.

The tall, windowed doors leading out onto the balcony were opened wide, the tang of brackish spray from the river mingling with the rich pine scent of the forest as the late summer breeze perfumed her room with the fragrance of nature. Her heart sang as she gazed at the lovely view of the dense forest, shimmering lake, and sparkling river, glistening in the late afternoon sun.

Issylte strolled out onto her balcony, which extended out over a private courtyard and terrace, enclosed by a stone wall, covered in vines of heady pink roses in full bloom. A small waterfall cascaded from a fountain in the center of the terrace, fed by a stream which flowed from the lake behind the castle to the river in the east. *Incredibly beautiful,* thought Issylte, inhaling the floral fragrance of roses and the crisp saline breeze while savoring the soft kiss of the sun on her cheeks.

"Your bath is ready, my lady," the older of two solicitous attendants announced cheerfully from the adjacent bathing area. "There is perfumed rose soap, a clean towel, and a lovely deep green gown which we unpacked from your bags. Our *châtelain* said it is your preferred color." With a pleasant smile, she asked Issylte, "Shall we assist you?"

"No, thank you. I will be fine on my own," Issylte replied gracefully to the courteous servants.

Bowing their heads, the two women dipped into a slight curtsey. "We shall return a bit later to escort you to the terrace for supper. Enjoy the rest of the fresh fruit…and your bath, my lady."

Issylte heard the door close softly behind them. She finished the rest of the strawberries and melon slices, savoring the sweet juice, then drank the cool water from the pitcher before heading into the bathing room, where billowing steam luxuriated from a lovely white porcelain tub. Sinking slowly into the warm water, Issylte hummed with pleasure as the heat soaked the strain of the voyage from her seasick weakened body.

As she washed the brine from her hair with the sweet-smelling rose soap, she remembered the mineral rich bathing pool in Avalon, when she'd first washed away the salt of the sea voyage from Ireland. Memories flooded her. Viviane, Nyda, and Cléo. Gwennol and the victims of the horrid Viking slave raids who had tremulously learned to love again. Her patients. The apple blossoms and *aubépines*. The *Fontaine de Jouvence,* the lilies on *Lac Diane.* The delicate white

swans.

And most of all, Ronan. Her beautiful blond stallion and his cozy stone cottage in the woods. Maëva, Marron, and Noisette. His magnificent stallion Noz. Issylte's heart clenched, and the tears began anew. It was a long time before she finally emerged from the bath.

****

The setting for the intimate dinner was lovely, with a table for six on the cobbled stone terrace below Issylte's Rose Room chambers. The small courtyard under her second story balcony was enclosed by a wall made from river stones, covered with deep green ivy replete with fragrant pink roses under the starry night sky. Beyond the stone wall lay a grassy courtyard which led to the deep lake and thick, dense forest to the north and the shimmering waters of the swift flowing river to the east. Moonlight reflected on the rippling surfaces under the brilliant stars as Issylte followed Lancelot's servants through the windowed doors leading from the *château* to the charming terrace where three of his most trusted knights sat waiting with Tristan and the *châtelain* himself. All rose when Issylte stepped out into the fragrant night air to join them.

Judoc—the First Knight of *la Joyeuse Garde* and commander of Lancelot's regiment—as well as Darius and Gaël, the next two highest-ranking knights, kissed Issylte's hand in greeting as they seated themselves under the canopy of stars. As Lancelot's most trusted men, the three knights had been told the truth—that Issylte was assuming the false identity of the Lady Opale, a guest from Camelot enjoying a *séjour* at *la Joyeuse Garde*. They knew she was fleeing the wicked queen who had ordered her death, for Issylte—as the rightful heir to the Irish crown—posed the sole threat to her stepmother's claim to the throne. They knew Tristan well from his intensive training last summer, when Lancelot had first introduced him to the château as his *protégé.* Issylte sat at the table, sipping the wine that Lancelot offered, smiling at his most loyal knights.

Judoc was tall and muscular, with long black hair that reached the top of his broad shoulders. A jagged scar sliced across the left cheek of his rugged warrior's face, his deep green eyes shining with intelligence as they met Issylte's esteemed regard. Darius was quite handsome, with light brown hair pulled back with a leather cord. His chestnut brown eyes gleamed in the candlelight, friendship and trust glowing in his steadfast gaze. Gaël was the tallest of the three—though not as tall as either Tristan or Lancelot—with curly red hair, twinkling hazel eyes, and a thick, bushy red beard that hid most of the freckles dusted across his grinning face.

Ever the amiable host, Lancelot discussed the upcoming reception he had planned, the guests who would be arriving, the dancing, feasting, hunting and falconry he had planned to entertain everyone. With Issylte, he chatted about his extensive library, which she was welcome to browse, suggesting lovely areas on his castle grounds where she might stroll, accompanied by his servants—who would be her attendants while she remained at the *château*—and always guarded by six of his trusted armored knights.

On a more somber note, Lancelot mentioned the threat of renewed Viking slave raids and his desire to increase the number of knights and weapons in *la Joyeuse Garde* to prepare for a possible attack. He charged Judoc, Darius, and Gaël with recruiting, training, and equipping a hundred additional knights, with orders to provide accommodations for the expanded army.

As the sumptuous dinner concluded with a marvelous cherry dessert—a delicious *tarte aux cerises*—Lancelot addressed Issylte. "Tristan and a few of my knights will travel to the nearby village of Kerléroux to place the order for weapons and armor for my additional knights. They'll be gone for a few days, returning in time for the welcoming celebration that I have planned for next weekend. With *you* as the guest of honor." He kissed her hand gallantly and flashed her his famous boyish grin. Issylte's cheeks flushed as she ducked her head and smiled.

Lancelot shot a sly grin at Tristan. "The Blue Knight of Cornwall needs a new sword, for his was broken in the Morholt's skull!" Laughter rippled among the knights as the servants refilled their goblets of wine and cleared away the empty dessert plates. Issylte inhaled the fragrant scent of roses on the vine and looked appreciatively at the lake, glistening and gleaming under the opalescent moon. The forest called to the verdant magic in her veins. "I shall remain here, to prepare for the arrival of my guests later this week," Lancelot informed her, drawing her attention away from the enchanting woods. He spoke to his three most trusted knights. "Prince Kaherdin, the Lady Gargeolaine, and the Princess Blanchine—Kaherdin's sister—will be journeying from Armorique to remain with us for the month of September." Lancelot paused and raised his goblet of wine, inhaling the fragrant bouquet. He took a large mouthful, savoring the exquisite white burgundy that he loved so well, his exuberant gaze twinkling in the light from the fragrant beeswax candle on their linen covered table.

Issylte gazed at the glimmering waters of the river, looked up to the stars twinkling in the dark sky. The fragrant roses on the vines enclosing the small courtyard and the crisp green notes of the pine forest in the near distance enveloped her in the loving embrace of nature. Her forest fairy essence hummed contentedly as she smiled softly, returning her focus to Lancelot.

"Lord Esclados and Lady Laudine will arrive from Landuc," he said to Judoc. "The men will want to train with you during their stay, as Tristan recovers his strength." The White Knight turned toward Issylte, his face exuberant. "And the ladies will entertain the charming *Lady Opale* as we welcome her to *la Joyeuse Garde.*" Lancelot gestured to a servant, who quickly refilled the wine goblets. "Lord Bénézet and his wife will voyage from Anjou, on the Loire River. Abélard and his spouse will arrive from Poitou, near the port of La Rochelle. Audric of Aquitaine is expected by the week's end as well. All are eager to defend against the impending Viking attacks and will likely be eager to join our cause." After a brief pause, he added—locking eyes with Tristan—"I have also invited Lord Kjetil, a powerful knight from Normandy."

Issylte noticed how Lancelot eyed Tristan warily. "Kjetil is the son of a Viking who married a French *marquise* and settled in Normandy. They have vast pastures where they raise cattle and produce cheese. They also own apple orchards which are famous for cider and *Calvados,* an exquisite *liqueur* which is their *spécialtié régionale."* He shot Tristan a commanding look. "As a Viking, Kjetil will be a most valuable ally.

His familiarity with Viking ships, warfare tactics, and battle strategies will help us improve our defenses against the renewed attacks."

Tristan returned Lancelot's hard stare, his countenance an equal blend of disbelief and disgust. Issylte shivered at the intensity of Lancelot's gaze, fixed on Tristan, who was simmering with barely controlled rage.

When dinner concluded, the three knights of *la Joyeuse Garde* bid them goodnight, thanking their host for the enjoyable dinner, kissing Issylte's hand in parting, and returning to their quarters. Lancelot's two female attendants arrived to escort her back to the Rose Room. As she thanked Lancelot for his gracious hospitality, he rose to kiss her on both cheeks—*la bise*—as his mother had always done in Avalon and *Tatie* in Ireland. "*Bonne nuit, ma belle,*" he whispered softly.

Tristan kissed her hand and whispered, "Goodnight, Issylte. Sleep well." A glorious wave of blue washed over her as she swam in the depths of his limpid gaze. Her magic stirred in response. Bidding them both goodnight, she followed the attendants back to the Rose Room, leaving the two men alone at the table to finish their wine.

****

Livid, Tristan spun toward his implacable host. "I cannot believe you invited a fucking *Viking*! By the Goddess, Lance, you truly expect me to be *civil* with a *bloody Viking* living under our roof?"

"I do," Lancelot said unequivocally. "And I expect you to remember that he is a *potential ally*—and a valuable one at that." Lancelot took a large swallow of wine and keenly observed Tristan. "In the morning, after you and the men break your fast, my knights will escort you and Darius into Kerléroux. I had a female attendant place an order there for several dresses for Issylte to wear as the Lady Opale, including an elegant gown for the upcoming ball. Darius knows the dressmaker's shop. He'll pick up the packages."

Rising from his chair, Lancelot downed the rest of his wine and stretched lazily. "I know it will take several months for the blacksmith to complete my order for weapons and armor for all the new knights we'll be recruiting. But you should be able to remain in the local inn for a few days until your new sword is ready. I'm sure the blacksmith will hurry the order for your blade— for an extra bag of silver." He placed a velvet pouch on the table before Tristan and shot him an impish grin.

Lancelot clasped Tristan on the shoulder with a deep chuckle. He then disappeared into the recesses of the *château*, leaving Tristan to curse under his breath, wondering how he could possibly restrain himself from killing a most honored guest of the legendary Sir Lancelot of the Lake.

Chapter 2

La Demoiselle Aux Mains Blanches

Blanchine of Armorique sat at her elegant, mirrored vanity, staring at her own reflection. Although most young women of twenty would consider her exceptional looks a true blessing from the Goddess, Blanchine thought of it as a curse, for it made her the victim of unwanted, amorous attention from every foppish noble and vapid *viscomte* whom her father, King Hoël, invited to *le Château Rose* as a potential husband for his cherished daughter.

Tall and slender, with black wavy hair that cascaded to her waist, Blanchine was called *la Demoiselle aux Mains Blanches*—the Maid of the White Hands—for her porcelain skin, delicate hands, and adequate skill as a healer. Having lost her mother when she was just four years old, the Princess of Armorique had been raised by her doting father, older brother Kaherdin, and a strict, cold governess whose only real contribution to the child's upbringing had been a modest knowledge of the art of natural medicine.

Yet, most of Blanchine's "patients" were lecherous old men, such as *le Comte de Riol,* whose filthy beard, yellowed teeth, and putrid breath sent a shudder of revulsion at the memory of his lustful gaze when she'd treated his wound. Thank the Goddess her father—

perhaps in compensation for the loss of her mother at such a tender age—had promised his princess that she would have a say in the husband he chose for her. And Blanchine had firmly and irrevocably refused Riol's urgent and recurrent proposals of marriage. She shivered again in disgust.

Kaherdin, her older brother, had found the love of his life, the Lady Gargeolaine, who had recently agreed to become his royal wife. When Kaherdin eventually became King of Armorique as their father's heir, Gargeolaine would become his queen, a prospect which thrilled her family as much as the auburn-haired beauty herself.

Sighing heavily at the thought of two entire days riding in the royal carriage with her overly exuberant, soon-to-be sister-in-law, Blanchine admitted that the trip to *la Joyeuse Garde* would at least be a welcome change of pace from the monotony of life in *le Château Rose*.

For, although Gargelaine had been accompanied by a chaperone who was staying at King Hoël's castle—ostensibly to preserve the young woman's royal reputation—the governess was old and seemingly deaf. Blanchine had heard Kaherdin and his enthusiastic fiancée *every night*—and most mornings and afternoons, too—loudly and passionately expressing their love in the adjacent room. Yes, a trip to another castle would be most welcome indeed.

As she prepared herself for the pending departure, Blanchine pondered her own future. Her brother and his wife would become King and Queen of Armorique, and she, as a royal princess, would be expected to marry a prince—or at least a high-ranking noble, such as a duke or count. *But not le Comte de Riol!*

Blanchine had met many suitors, all of whom she'd rejected, for none made her heart flutter. She refused to marry an insipid noble who just wanted her for her pretty face—or her father's generous dowry. She longed for a man to inspire the same passion she felt whenever she spotted the handsome knight Cédric, whose charming smile and muscular physique made him all the more dashing. Unfortunately, she could never marry a knight. As a princess, her future husband would have to be a monarch. She exhaled audibly just as Kaherdin popped his head around her chamber door.

Her brother's voice interrupted her doleful reverie. "Blanchine, the carriage is loaded, and all your bags have been stored. Are you ready to leave?"

"Yes, Kaherdin. I'm ready." Her lady-in-waiting, Marolle, would ride with her in the carriage, along with Gargeolaine and her deaf chaperone. It would be a *very* long ride indeed.

"I've heard that Sir Lancelot is incredibly handsome," Gargeolaine was now babbling, as they were at last *en route*. "And the finest knight in the land! Did you know that his mother, the Lady Viviane, is a *fairy?!* I have heard tales of his childhood with the Lady of the Lake, in the enchanted Forest of Brocéliande! I cannot wait to meet him!"

Blanchine stared out the window. *Maybe if I do not listen, she will stop talking.*

"There will be several other royal couples staying along with us," Gargeolaine continued exuberantly. "Sir Lancelot is hosting a feast, and a ball! It will be so exciting! What color is your gown, Blanchine? Mine is a rose gold silk, to highlight my hair."

The *Demoiselle aux Mains Blanches* felt obligated

to be at least somewhat cordial to her future sister-in-law. After all, she would one day become the Queen of Armorique. "An icy blue, like my eyes."

"Ooh, that sounds exquisite! And do you have jewels to match as well?"

"Yes, Gargeolaine. I have a necklace of aquamarine gemstones, in the same pale blue color as my gown." Blanchine stared in exasperation at the rosy cheeked beauty that her brother absolutely adored.

"Oh, Blanchine! You will look like a goddess! Perhaps the handsome Lancelot will fall for you, just like all the other noblemen you have met. You are so lovely, Blanchine. I envy your delicate beauty."

Blanchine flashed an insincere smile that she hoped would silence Gargeolaine. Unfortunately, the attempt failed.

"The handsome Lord Audric, the *Viscomte de Sauterne*, will be one of the guests, Kaherdin told me. He is very good-looking...and *unmarried*." Gargeolaine flashed a bright smile from her full, sensuous lips. Blanchine inwardly rolled her eyes.

Although she talks too much, I can at least appreciate why my brother fancies her looks. Blanchine took in the sparkling amber gaze, the thick, reddish-gold curls, the delicate rosy complexion, and ample bosom of her brother's fiancée. She does make him happy. No, more than that. Wildly exuberant. With a perpetual smile on his face. Blanchine sighed audibly and feigned a yawn.

"I'm feeling a bit sleepy, Gargeolaine. I will just close my eyes for a while, if you don't mind." *That should keep her quiet*. Much to Blanchine's delight— this time, it did.

When they finally arrived at the *château,* having stopped along the way to rest the horses, and having spent one night at a pleasant inn, Lancelot's servants greeted the royal travelers with pampered attention, escorting them into the reception hall where the joyous host welcomed his guests to *la Joyeuse Garde.*

"Kaherdin, welcome! It is good to see you again, my friend," the White Knight beamed, clasping the arms of the Prince of Armorique in a warm greeting.

"Lancelot, you are looking well. Thank you for your gracious invitation. May I present the lovely Lady Gargeolaine, daughter of *le Comte de Pontrieux*, who has filled me with incredible joy by consenting to become my wife."

Lancelot bowed gallantly at the waist to kiss Gargeolaine's hand. "It is a pleasure to meet you, my lady. *Bienvenue à la Joyeuse Garde.*"

Kaherdin placed his arm around Gargeolaine's waist as she smiled effusively, cheeks flushed at the attention from the chivalrous Lancelot of the Lake. "And may I present my sister, Princess Blanchine. You may remember her from your visit several years ago, when you accompanied King Arthur to *le Château Rose.*"

Lancelot bowed even more deeply at the waist to honor her royal standing as he kissed her hand. "Welcome, Princess Blanchine. It is a pleasure to see you once again. I do remember that you were very lovely as a young girl, but now, as a woman, you are *ravissante.*"

Blanchine smiled coolly at the eager host. *He is quite handsome, but just a knight. Not for you, Blanchine. Not for you.*

"And may I introduce the Lady Opale, a guest of mine from the court at Camelot, and Sir Tristan of

Lyonesse, nephew and heir to King Marke of Cornwall." Kaherdin shook hands with the handsome guest, whose enormous height and massive bulk reminded Blanchine of the Elf Ronan, who had recently delivered weapons and armor to her father's castle. *If he is heir to his uncle's throne, then he will become King of Cornwall!*

As Sir Tristan bowed respectfully before her, Blanchine extended her elegant white hand for him to kiss, noting the width of his warrior's neck and the dark brown waves of his thick, glossy hair. Power emanated from him, and for the very first time in her life, the Princess of Armorique was immensely attracted to a potential suitor.

"It is a pleasure to meet you, Your Majesty," the Lady Opale murmured as she curtsied politely. Blanchine examined the young woman's blonde hair—unbound, in the style of a maiden. The courtier's golden locks were as long as her own, extending past her waist, to grace her hips. The dark green dress enhanced her fair skin, and when Blanchine looked into Opale's eyes, she was stunned by the emerald beauty she beheld and the aura of power which emanated from her.

"*Enchantée, Mademoiselle*," she replied, in the cold, regal voice of the Princess of Armorique.

Sir Tristan seemed to linger by Opale's side, Blanchine noticed. He also seemed to follow her every move, she remarked with disappointment. *Perhaps tonight, at dinner, you can entice this most handsome heir of Cornwall. If you can swat away that pesky fly, the Viscomte de Sauterne,* Blanchine thought, as she recognized Lord Audric of Aquitaine, who now approached their royal entourage.

"Prince Kaherdin! Lady Gargeolaine! What a

pleasure to see you again!" Audric sputtered cheerfully, bowing to the Prince of Armorique and kissing the hand of his lovely companion. Then, fixing his full, arduous attention on her, he exclaimed, "And Princess Blanchine! I look forward to the pleasure of your *delightful* company for the next four weeks." He held her hand a bit too long and kissed it a bit too affectionately, annoying the lovely *Demoiselle aux Mains Blanches* with his overly amorous intentions. She withdrew her hand and surreptitiously wiped off the wet vestiges of the unwanted affection of the foppish *Viscomte de Sauterne*.

Ever the gracious host, Lancelot motioned for his servants to come forward. "Please, allow my *domestiques* to escort you to your chambers. I am certain you would like to refresh and rest a bit after your long journey."

Leading his royal guests toward the staircase, he placed his right arm across his chest and bowed humbly. "Dinner will be served at seven this evening. We shall feast on oysters, divine seafood, fresh vegetables from the garden, and…" with a dashing grin at Lord Audric, the *Viscomte de Sauterne*, he added, "some exceptionally fine dessert wines to accompany our delicious pastries. *À ce soir!*"

****

The banquet hall was lavishly decorated, with bouquets of fragrant flowers atop each of the two rectangular tables, which were set with white linens, sparkling glassware, and polished silver, glistening in the candlelight of the crystal chandeliers. The windowed doors leading out onto the private courtyard were opened wide, offering the royal guests a magnificent view of the wisteria in bloom and the lovely water lilies on the surface of the lake where a pair of swans floated gracefully. *This is the courtyard with swans on the lake that I glimpsed in Tristan's eyes,* Issylte realized, as she followed her attendants into the elegant room. *It is magnificent!*

Lancelot's guests were introduced to one another and seated, with Issylte placed between Tristan and *le châtelain,* opposite Kaherdin, Gargeolaine and Blanchine. Lord Audric seemed delighted to be seated beside the haughty Princess of Armorique, who pointedly ignored his repeated attempts to catch her eye. Issylte stole a glance at Kaherdin's lovely fiancée. *She is the pregnant woman I saw in the tower with the dwarf Frocin!* A shiver crept up her spine. She took a sip of water to hide her distress.

The second table of guests, set for seven, seated Esclados and Laudine, Lord Kjetil from Normandy, Abélard and Odette from Poitou, and Bénézet and Sidonie from Anjou. The elegant wives chatted amicably amid the festive ambience, the smiling faces indicating everyone was thoroughly enjoying the White Knight's gracious hospitality.

As oysters were being served, along with the host's preferred white burgundy wine, Lancelot commented to Kaherdin on the recent order for additional armor and swords that King Hoël had placed with Ronan.

"Your father the king recently requisitioned armor and weaponry for several hundred knights, Kaherdin. Is he preparing for battle?"

Savoring the succulent oyster, then wiping his mouth with the white linen napkin, the Prince of Armorique replied, "He wishes to defend against potential Viking assaults, which are expected to

28

recommence. Rumor has it that Ireland is now focusing on the northern and western coastlines of France." Kaherdin sipped his wine and exclaimed with a heartwarming grin, "An extraordinary vintage, to perfectly complement the delectable seafood. My compliments, Sir Lancelot of the Lake."

Lord Audric, the *Viscomte de Sauterne*, added cheerfully, "Truly a most splendid burgundy. And I look forward to sharing with you the delicious *sauternes* I have brought, as a gift from Aquitaine." Audric gazed pointedly at Blanchine as he sipped his wine. In a sultry, seductive voice, he hummed, "A sweet, rich, *sensual* flavor. Most exquisite indeed." The Princess of Armorique quickly diverted her attention to her place setting.

Lancelot resumed the topic of the conversation. "I do believe it is wise to prepare for renewed Viking attacks. Especially given the recent alliance between Ireland and Cornwall, with the upcoming royal marriage between Queen Morag and King Marke." Gasps rippled among the guests from Armorique and Aquitaine. "It appears that a certain Lord Indulf—one of the Knights of the Round Table from Cornwall whom I trained—has allied with the infamous dwarf Frocin, who serves the powerful Queen of Ireland and her dark wizard, Lord Voldurk. They plan to resume the profitable Viking slave raids, focusing on the coast of France. Your father is wise to defend against a likely attack. I plan to follow his fine example."

Princess Blanchine addressed Tristan. "A royal marriage and alliance between Ireland and Cornwall, united against the kingdoms of France, would put you in a compromising position, would it not, Sir Tristan? You would be forced to side with your uncle and his new wife, against your friends seated here at our host's lovely dinner celebration. Most distressing, it would seem." Unease swept over Issylte as Blanchine's icy blue stare challenged Tristan. Her verdant magic stirred in response.

Lancelot intervened. "The knight Indulf is a traitor, Princess Blanchine." He glanced at Kaherdin, then Audric, drawing them into the conversation. "Indulf has proclaimed himself the victor in the Battle of Tintagel against the deadly Morholt—the Black Knight of Ireland who weakened the kingdom of Cornwall with relentless Viking attacks." Meeting Kaherdin's stare, Lancelot smirked, "But *Tristan* is the warrior who slew the Morholt. I was there on the battlefield. I witnessed it myself."

Tristan spoke, his expression a mask of barely contained rage. "Indulf is not only a traitor, but a close ally of the dwarf Frocin—a ruthless mercenary known for brutality, revenge…and murder."

"Queen Morag—King Marke's newly betrothed," Lancelot continued warily, "is rumored to have poisoned her first husband, King Donnchadh of Ireland." The White Knight eyed each of his royal guests. "The Black Widow Queen has a powerful dark wizard at her side, a Lord Voldurk. The *healer* who helped her poison the king." Lancelot observed his companions over the rim of his wineglass as he sipped his white burgundy.

Kaherdin, Gargeolaine, and Audric exchanged surprised glances. But Princess Blanchine stared at Tristan. A chill crept up Issylte's spine. And something else. *Are you jealous, Issylte?* She took a sip of her wine to steady herself as she averted her gaze from the

Princess of Armorique.

Tristan spoke again. "We fear that my uncle has been deceived by his betrothed and is in grave danger. The Black Widow Queen may plan to poison him as well. Perhaps we should attempt to convince him of the truth. Dissuade him from marrying a queen enshrouded with rumors of murder. Yet, an attempt to warn King Marke might very well incur the wrath of Queen Morag and her allies. Provoke them into attacking France. What say you, Prince Kaherdin?"

Kaherdin stared into his goblet for a moment before responding. "Let us reflect during our visit. We'll consider all possible outcomes. Although it would be ideal to prevent this royal wedding and powerful alliance between Ireland and Cornwall, we must not draw their fire upon Armorique or *la Joyeuse Garde.* Let us reflect, deliberate, and decide wisely." Tristan nodded, raised his goblet, and drank, his deep blue gaze pensive and solemn.

Lancelot, with his keen eye as a host, seemed to observe that his guests had finished dining and would welcome some entertainment. "In the meantime," he piped jovially, "now that we have finished our delectable meal, let us enjoy some fine music. And a bit of dancing." He gestured to the musicians who had installed themselves at the far end of the adjacent ballroom. Lancelot's voice rose above the din of lively conversation and clinking silver. "*Messieurs dames*, I thank you all for accepting my invitation to celebrate as I welcome my guest, the Lady Opale of Camelot, to *la Joyeuse Garde*." Issylte smiled softly, bowing her head at the attention of the many nobles who applauded her as the guest of honor.

"I propose that we now sample the delicious pastries, courtesy of my talented *pâtissier*. That we imbibe upon the magnificent *sauternes* dessert wines, a gift from the most generous Lord Audric, *le Viscomte de Sauterne*." Audric positively beamed at his magnanimous host. "And that we regale with dancing to the fine music of my accomplished musicians. Enjoy yourselves, *mes amis*. After all, this is...*la Joyeuse Garde!*"

The fiddlers and flautists began playing, the lively melody enticing. Lancelot's guests, delighted with the fine pastries and dessert wines, sauntered out to the dance floor and began twirling like brightly colored jewels, sparkling in the candlelight. Gargeolaine, resplendent in a mauve silk gown, seemed to bask in the love light of Kaherdin's gaze. Issylte watched as the Prince of Armorique held his love against his chest, eliciting ripples of delighted laughter as he swirled her in his arms.

****

Gargeolaine, dizzy with excitement, spoke breathlessly to her fleet-footed fiancé. "Kaherdin, I have an idea." He was kissing her throat, anxious to get her alone upstairs. She knew he was hoping that her governess had already retired for the evening. "What if you traveled to Tintagel, perhaps with your father or Blanchine—to congratulate King Marke on his upcoming royal wedding? You could present a royal wedding gift. Perhaps seek an alliance with Cornwall. And prevent an assault on Armorique."

Kaherdin, focused intently on her voluptuous curves, seemed barely able to concentrate on her words. "Kaherdin, are you listening to me?" Rebuffed slightly, he looked sheepishly at her.

"Of course I am, *mon petit chou*. I plan to discuss it with father upon our return." Then, as if to ingratiate himself a bit, knowing what delights she would bestow upon him in the bedroom, he whispered in her ear, "Your idea is splendid, Gargeolaine. You will be a most brilliant queen."

She beamed at him, positively glowing with his praise. His face revealed an insatiable hunger, as if she were a fresh, juicy peach to devour. Kaherdin moaned, "Let's retire now. You're driving me wild in that dress. I cannot wait to slip you out of it…"

His face shone with delight when she whispered back, "Nor can I." Unfortunately, just as the two lovers were about to disappear into the stairwell, Blanchine approached her brother, her expression aghast.

"Kaherdin, would you do me a favor?" She glanced longingly at Tristan. "I'd really like to dance with the knight from Cornwall. Could you perhaps ask him for me? I'll go sit at the table. Thank you, dear brother." She smiled at Kaherdin and returned to her seat, her shimmery dress a sea of icy blue silk.

****

Issylte, from her perspective at the table, observed Lancelot chatting with Tristan and Esclados against the wall near the windowed doors. The jubilant music and revelry continued all around as Lord Audric ventured to the table, insisting that the Princess of Armoroique dance with him. Blanchine, perhaps realizing that the *Viscomte de Sauterne* was an indispensable French ally, reluctantly allowed Audric to lead her onto the dance floor. Issylte did not miss the discomfort and disdain written clearly across the pinched, lovely face of the

Princess of Armorique.

Alone at the table with Laudine—the Lady of the Fountain of Barenton—Issylte wondered what possible topic of conversation she might begin as the Lady Opale. Fortunately, she was spared that awkward decision when Tristan and Eslados returned to the table. Lancelot mingled with his other guests.

"Laudine, my love, come dance with me." The chivalrous Red Knight, superbly attired in a red brocade tunic embroidered with gold thread, kissed his wife's slender hand.

Laudine, her ruby red gown clinging to her curvaceous form—still attractive in her middle years—rose graciously from the table to accept her husband's invitation to dance. Together, they made a splendid couple, magnificently clad in scarlet. Issylte watched them with wondrous delight.

Tristan smiled at them as the couple strode away, arm in arm, and began to dance. He approached Issylte and bowed before her like a gentleman. Extending his hand, he asked gallantly, "Would you do me the honor of dancing with me, my lady?"

At his touch, a thrill of pleasure flowed up her arm and spread throughout her entire body. Lifting the folds of her deep green gown with her other hand as she stood, Issylte followed him to join the revelry. The wings of a white dove fluttered wildly in her breast.

Tristan walked backward, facing her, grinning from ear to ear, as he held her hand in his outstretched arm. He pulled her seductively to the dance floor without ever removing his intense eyes from her smile. Blanchine stared openly, jealousy written clearly across her haughty, beautiful face.

In Tristan's embrace, Issylte's breath felt shallow, her heartbeat rapid, fully aware of the hulking shoulders and enormous arms that held her close. His scent was the salty tang of the ocean, mingled with evergreens of the forest and an earthy, musky, distinctly male essence that called to her. Despite the open doors, the room was very warm, and the heady fragrance of him, combined with the sumptuous food and superb wine—Issylte swooned and lowered her face to his chest, longing to touch the dark hair she knew was hidden under his deep blue tunic. She was undeniably attracted to Tristan, yet guilt and grief flooded her at the thought of Ronan. The beautiful blond stallion she'd left behind. Issylte swallowed a lump in her throat and tried to quell her quivering legs.

****

Tristan felt her tremble as he held her protectively in his arms. He, too, inhaled her scent—a blend of wild roses and the green notes of the forest, enhanced with the fecund richness of loam and the full body of the earth. His spirit stirred.

He longed to touch her golden hair, her pale skin, her rounded curves. But he knew she was not ready. That she still grieved for the Elf. He had to be patient. And let her lead the way.

So, he contented himself to simply hold her. A rare flower, her nurturing essence soothing his savage soul. He smiled down at her. "You look lovely, Issylte. A forest fairy, adorned in deepest green." Subtly, he inhaled the fragrance of her hair as she nestled her head below his chin. A peaceful, verdant calm caressed him.

"I am fortunate that Lancelot had the foresight to order a few dresses for me," she mused. "The Lady Opale could not have worn the blue robes of a priestess

35

of Avalon to this elegant reception." She flashed him an achingly beautiful smile. "Our wonderful host thinks of everything, doesn't he?"

The song ended, and they returned to the table to rejoin Lancelot and his guests. Kaherdin approached Tristan and said quietly, "Would you please ask my sister to dance? She is tired of the relentless Lord Audric and would welcome a respite."

Darting an apologetic smile at Issylte, Tristan replied, "Of course." He then walked over to Blanchine and requested a dance, which she accepted willingly. In her aquamarine dress, which accentuated her regal stature and icy blue eyes, the Princess of Armorique looked positively stunning. A thrill rippled through him as an unmistakable wave of jealousy crashed upon Issylte's pale face as she watched them dance.

****

Kaherdin, seated with Gargeolaine at the table, spoke amicably to Issylte. "My sister has rejected all of the suitors who have courted her, much to our father's chagrin," he chuckled. "Yet, this Tristan, the heir of Cornwall, seems to have caught her eye. Who knows? Perhaps she has finally found someone who meets her impossibly high standards!" Gargeolaine and her fiancé laughed heartily, and Issylte's heart sank at the thought of Tristan marrying Blanchine.

Why, Issylte? Do you want him for yourself? Have you forgotten Ronan so quickly? Are you that heartless?

The two dancers were enjoying themselves; it was obvious. Tristan held Blanchine with one arm placed gently behind her back, the other holding her hand as they twirled on the dance floor. The Princess of Armorique tossed her head back to laugh at something

Tristan had said, exposing her elegant white neck. The beautiful black waves of her hair cascaded down her slender back over the elegant gown that molded to her graceful body and drew attention to her slender hips. A dainty silver tiara adorned with aquamarine gems and diamonds glinted amidst her glorious *chevelure*. Issylte felt positively ill.

They returned to the table, laughing gaily. Tristan gallantly withdrew Blanchine's chair to seat her regally before returning to his place at Issylte's side. She sighed in relief as he sat down next to her, a grin on his handsome face.

"You are a wonderful dancer, Sir Tristan," Blanchine cooed. "I look forward to the ball in two weeks. You must promise to dance with me all night. I have not enjoyed myself this much in a very long time!" Her icy blue gaze devoured Tristan, who—to Issylte's dismay, seemed delighted at the display of royal feminine attention.

Blanchine cast Issylte a triumphant and dismissive look, as if the Princess of Armorique considered the lower-ranking Lady Opale to be an insignificant competitor for the affection of Sir Tristan of Cornwall.

As she reached for her goblet of wine, Issylte's fingers accidentally brushed against Blanchine's hand, placed flat upon the table. In the breadth of a moment, she saw a flash—the snakelike wizard and the wicked queen—seated near a black velvet curtain in a darkened room with Blanchine. Conspiring against Tristan. A shiver of dread crept up Issylte's spine as her magic thrummed in warning. *The Princess of Armorique exudes evil. She plans to harm Tristan. I must be watchful. And ready.*

The musicians stopped playing; the revelry was winding down. Lancelot addressed his guests once again. "I am most pleased that you enjoyed our welcoming reception this evening. As we part company, I wish you all a restful sleep and look forward to seeing you in the morning. I have arranged a hunt for us tomorrow, and in the afternoon, the lovely Laudine will entertain us with the glorious melody of my golden harp." With a gallant smile, he offered, "Throughout your stay, you are free to enjoy my library or take advantage of my stables, should you wish to ride in the forests to the west of the *château*. Stroll along the lake behind the castle, perhaps observe my knights training. Enjoy a game of chess or even a hand of whist in my *salon*. For now, I bid you all goodnight. Sleep well. *À demain*!" Lancelot bowed to the crowd as it dispersed, his guests retiring for the evening.

As she settled into the sumptuous bed in the beautiful Rose Room, her attendants having helped her undress before retiring themselves, Issylte was plagued with unease. Menace lurked in Blanchine's frigid stare. The touch of her icy fingers reminded Issylte of her stepmother's dreadful hands. Somehow, Blanchine posed a threat to Tristan.

Issylte would be observant. Watchful. Alert. As she finally drifted off to sleep, she vowed to keep a close eye on the mysterious and foreboding Princess of Armorique. And prevent Blanchine from harming the sea raven warrior who would lead her army against the Black Widow Queen.

Chapter 3

Kjetil of Normandy

Lancelot had wisely seated Tristan and the Viking Kjetil at different tables throughout the four weeks of merriment at *la Joyeuse Garde.* He'd been careful to arrange alternate hunts, training sessions, and equestrian outings so that the two were always kept well separated. Friday evening—just two days from now—marked the culminating event: the feast and ball which he'd organized, with fifty of his highest-ranking knights and their ladies joining the other guests, adding to the excitement and revelry in entertaining the lovely Lady Opale from Camelot.

Tonight, however, Lancelot had observed Tristan glowering at the Viking all through dinner, drinking more wine than was his custom. Kjetil had been returning Tristan's stare with an equally hostile regard, as heavily into his cups as the Knight from Cornwall.

Fortunately, the musicians now began playing, and his guests mingled—some dancing, with others strolling out into the fragrant courtyard to sit upon a stone bench under the wisteria blossoms, or gaze upon the moonlit lake. Lancelot sat down at the table beside Tristan. He motioned to a servant to refill their goblets of wine. "You are in a most sullen mood tonight, my friend. Lighten up and enjoy yourself."

Tristan scowled as his gaze followed Kjetil, who had strolled over to chat with Issylte and Laudine by one of the windowed doors overlooking the courtyard. His frown deepened when he noticed that Laudine had accepted her husband's invitation to dance, leaving the Viking alone with Issylte.

"Abélard and Bénézet have committed to join us, should Ireland attack France. Abélard plans to train an army of at least two hundred knights. And Bénézet, with his close ties to *le Duc d'Anjou,* hopes to recruit twice that amount."

Tristan wasn't listening. He was glaring at Kjetil, who was laughing and chatting amiably with Issylte. The Blue Knight was seething, his muscles taught, perched on the edge of his chair, a lion ready to pounce. Lancelot tried again to distract him. "Audric promises two hundred from Aquitaine, and Kjetil has offered the same."

At the mention of the Viking's name, Tristan cast his scowl to Lancelot. "I am trying to restrain myself, Lance, but if he touches her…"

Lancelot decided to intervene before Tristan lost his temper. Leaving his sullen friend at the table, he approached Kjetil and Issylte. "Ah! My lovely Lady Opale, would you do me the honor of dancing with me?" Taking Issylte's hand, Lancelot said amiably to Kjetil, "Please forgive the brashness of your host, but I have yet to dance with this lovely lady, my honored guest." Then, smiling at Issylte, Lancelot led her away from the Viking and into the ballroom.

****

Blanchine took advantage of this rare opportunity to sit beside the unaccompanied Tristan.

"Lancelot is such a fine host," she exclaimed jovially, positioning herself at his left, so that she faced the knight from Cornwall and partially obstructed his view of Kjetil, who was now chatting with Esclados and Laudine.

"I have not enjoyed myself this much in *ages*!" she effused, edging her chair closer to Tristan and leaning toward him, hoping to entice his attention with her lovely *décolletage*. But he seemed impervious to her feminine wiles, still glaring at Kjetil, his eyes dark and brooding. "My brother tells me that you are the son of the late King Rivalen of Lyonesse, the kingdom at the southern tip of Cornwall. Is that correct, Sir Tristan?"

He seemed to realize that he was expected to respond, for she was after all the Princess of Armorique and sister to Lancelot's close ally. Tristan averted his stare from the Viking to look at her. "Yes, Your Majesty. That is correct."

Excellent! Perhaps father would approve of the Prince of Lyonesse as a potential suitor!

Unfortunately, Tristan's attention had returned to Lord Kjetil, who was smiling at the insipid Lady Opale in the arms of Sir Lancelot, twirling on the dance floor.

Blanchine decided to try a more direct approach. "My father, King Hoël, has been amassing an army of knights to defend against a Viking attack. But Sir Tristan, instead of preparing for war...perhaps an *alliance* might be a better solution."

At that moment, Lancelot and the Lady Opale returned to the table, breathless from dancing and smiling with sheer joy. The *châtelain* seated his guest directly across from Tristan, then sat down beside the Lady Opale, opposite Blanchine. As if intrigued by the last bit of conversation that he'd heard upon approaching the table, the host inquired, "An alliance instead of a war? Please elaborate, Princess Blanchine. I am anxious to hear more."

Blanchine did not wish to reveal her proposal before the Lady Opale. No, she would wait for a more opportune moment. Perhaps she could find Tristan alone... "An alliance with Armorique, Sir Lancelot," Blanchine replied, leaving out the essential component—her hope for a betrothal to Tristan. "My brother has committed to five hundred men to join forces with yours, in the event of an attack on Bretagne." Sipping her wine, Blanchine shifted her gaze from Lancelot to the young blonde beauty at his side. She smiled slyly as an idea dawned.

I'll push them together. Then Tristan will be mine.

"You two make a most handsome couple." Her expression coy, Blanchine flashed a coquettish grin at Lancelot and Issylte. Tristan raised his eyebrows in disbelief as he shot Lancelot an incredulous look.

****

Lancelot locked eyes with Tristan, his gaze speaking volumes. *You know my heart, Tristan. She is in Camelot.* He had noted Blanchine's amorous interest in his friend. He also sensed the innate attraction between Tristan and Issylte, a yearning that exuded from them both, apparent for all to see. He would diffuse this tension and foil Blanchine's obvious attempt to ensnare Tristan. With his famous boyish grin and irresistible, chivalrous charm.

"Your Majesty, would you please do me the honor of dancing with your host?" Lancelot stood, one arm folded across his stomach as he bowed before the Princess of Armorique, his other extended as he gallantly

42

offered her his hand. *There is no way for her to refuse,* he smirked triumphantly as he flashed her a dashingly handsome grin.

"It would be my pleasure, Sir Lancelot," Blanchine replied in a voice that conveyed quite the opposite emotion.

****

Finding himself delightfully alone with Issylte, Tristan still scowled with jealousy. "You certainly enjoyed the Viking's attention. Did you like being in his arms, too?"

Issylte smothered a smile. "You are jealous."

Glowering at her, he spat, "I am."

Just as Tristan was about to ask Issylte to dance, Kjetil swaggered up to the table.

"My lady, might I request another dance?" he asked, his deep voice oozing with Viking charm.

Tristan glared at the enormous blond knight, who stood well over six feet tall, his long hair pulled back like the Elf Ronan's, his beard forked and braided, evoking the memory of the Morholt. Kjetil glowered at Tristan, his Nordic face hostile and challenging. "She does not wish to dance," Tristan growled in warning.

"I did not request *your* permission, Tristan of Cornwall." Kjetil flared his nostrils defiantly, a bull ready to charge.

"*Leave her alone.*" Tristan's voice seethed with hostility; his jaw clenched with fury.

Ignoring him, Kjetil reached for the princess' hand.

Tristan shot out of his chair—which crashed to the floor—and sprinted around the table, hurling his bulk through the air to tackle the Viking. Kjetil threw Tristan off as he deftly regained his footing. His bearded face was livid, his breath ragged and heaving. Memories of impotent rage flooded Tristan. The Viking who had beheaded his father and impaled his mother. The Nordic beasts who had raped and killed his sister. And the fucking Morholt who had tried to conquer his uncle's kingdom. Tristan released his long pent-up rage.

****

Issylte's heart hammered. Kjetil and Tristan were hulking brutes of the same massive size and apparent strength. But Tristan was not fully recovered from his nearly fatal injury against the Morholt. Her stomach dropped as she saw Tristan hurl himself at Kjetil, who threw Tristan to the floor and jumped effortlessly to his feet. Kjetil was a powerful, adroit warrior. *A Viking!*

In the blink of an eye, both men were brawling, landing punches to the chin, savage blows to the torso, grappling each other to the ground in a whirlwind of testosterone laced fury. To Issylte's horror, Lancelot was not only doing nothing to break up the fight—but was even *taking bets!* Her mouth agape, she watched as the White Knight chuckled with Esclados, Kaherdin, Abélard, Bénézet, and Audric, all of whom seemed to find the conflict most entertaining, bags of silver being waged on the winner.

When Kjetil finally emerged victorious, having flattened Tristan on his back with a perfect blow to the jaw, the Viking accepted the congratulations bestowed upon him by those who had won Lancelot's silver. The Lady Laudine led Kjetil to a chair, seated him, and was now dabbing at his bloody lip and facial contusions. The Viking grinned wickedly as he watched Lancelot help a subdued and obviously injured Tristan to his feet.

Lancelot ribbed Tristan in a hearty jest. "We need to

train you *harder*, my friend. You just cost me four bloody bags of silver!"

Battered, his face bleeding and a swollen eye becoming sickeningly black, Tristan burst out laughing. Kjetil, dodging Laudine's ministrations, strode over to the knight, extended his hand, and bellowed, "Tristan of Cornwall, if you fight like that when you're injured, I'd hate to go up against you when you're at your best! By the Goddess, man...you're a beast. *Like me!*"

Tristan accepted the outstretched hand and guffawed, wincing at his injuries. Fixing Kjetil squarely in the eye, he roared, "And you, Kjetil of Normandy, are the best I have *ever* fought." Shaking the Viking's scarred, outstretched hand, Tristan smirked, "Maybe we can have another go—after Lancelot has *trained me* to meet his expectations." He shot a mischievous grin at his bemused host.

Chuckling heartily, Kjetil put his arm around Tristan's shoulder and muttered something under his breath. As the two men strode back toward the table, Kjetil's arm atop Tristan's shoulder, Issylte heard the Viking boast, "I wasn't trying to steal your lady, you know. I've got my own...back in Normandy. My Cosette." Grinning ear to ear, he beamed, "We're to be married this Yuletide." At Tristan's raised eyebrows and expression of pleasant surprise, the Viking added, eyeing Issylte wickedly, "Besides, the Lady Opale...she's *yours*. Anyone with a pair of eyes can see that." Tristan locked his possessive blue gaze on hers. A white dove fluttered wildly in her heart.

Kjetil wandered over to Audric and Abélard, who congratulated him on the victory, thanking him for winning them the bags of silver. Tristan's eyes held hers as she watched him. She knew her face reflected wonder. Undeniable attraction. And reproach.

He strode quickly over to join her; she motioned for him to sit so that she could cleanse his wounds as Laudine had done for Kjetil. With a cool, clean cloth, she wiped the dried blood from his face, wincing at the sight of his left eye, which had blossomed into a hideous shade of violet and was nearly fused shut. Her pulse quickened as she touched his warm skin. "I have fetched some herbs which reduce swelling and inflammation. I've made a poultice for your eye." Quietly, with her gentle healing touch, she placed a cool compress on his face. Tristan sighed with obvious relief at the touch of her hand.

"You provoked him." She took one of his hands, guiding it into place to hold the compress against his eye as she carefully wiped the blood from his torn lip.

"I did." He inhaled deeply as he turned his face to kiss her hand, so close to his lips. "I did not want him to touch you." The intensity of his deep blue stare bore into her soul.

The music played in the background, the dancing and revelry having resumed all around them. Tristan let go of the compress to his eye and pulled Issylte down onto his lap. Feeling the hardness of his body pressing against her bottom, she imagined for a moment simply lifting her dress and straddling him right here in the chair. Her cheeks flushed with desire, she stood back up to regain her composure as she replaced the compress against his eye. Her heart was pounding furiously.

"I do need *healing,* Issylte. My entire body does. I *yearn* for you. Please come to my room tonight."

In the longing of his deep blue eyes, she saw the magnificent naked body he had offered her in the bathing pool at *Le Centre*. As she imagined his lips caressing them, her breasts tingled; at the thought of him between her thighs, her legs quivered. A painful, hollow ache in her longed to be filled—yet, though her body was more than ready, her heart was not.

"I cannot, Tristan." His face fell; he spun away to stare at the lake outside, sparkling in the moonlight. Gently twisting his chin toward her so she could recapture his gaze, she whispered, her voice full of promise, "*Not yet.*"

****

The evening was ending, for the musicians had stopped playing. The guests were retiring to their respective chambers. Tristan watched Issylte ascend the stairs to the Rose Room, his gaze caressing her beautiful curves, the long blonde hair cascading down her back. He longed to kiss her luscious lips, stroke her soft skin… His entire body ached and throbbed with desire.

He envisioned the upcoming ball, which would take place in two days' time. He'd hold her close, inhale her intoxicating scent of wild roses, absorb the verdant magic which soothed his savage soul.

They would have *months* together, once Lancelot's guests departed.

And he couldn't wait to surprise her with his gift.

Chapter 4

Morgane la Fée

The dwarves were getting closer. She'd seen the vile creatures Bothor, Malvon, and Thigruc sniffing around the Forest of *Brocéliande*. They were desperate to find it. Morgane prayed that she had hidden it well enough. That her enchantments could protect it. Everything depended upon keeping the orb out of Voldurk's evil grasp. The entire Celtic realm was at stake.

Thank the Goddess Esclados had summoned the storm and the Blue Knight had slain the wretched creature Bédalis. The dwarf had very nearly captured the Lady Laudine, guardian of the sacred Fountain of Barenton. If Voldurk had gotten his hands on her...

Indeed, all the priestesses of Dana were vulnerable now, for they were the guardians of the sacred waters of the Goddess. And Voldurk, through his recent alliance with the infamous Frocin, the leader of the dwarves, had found a way to penetrate the sanctity of the sacred forest and its holy waters.

Although the dark wizard himself could not enter the enchanted realm of the Goddess, which was protected by powerful magic against his evil, the dwarves—as *otherworldly* creatures, much like the Little Folk or the Elves—were natural inhabitants of the sacred forests. And now that Frocin had committed his entire legion of dwarves to Voldurk's quest to capture the priestesses of Dana, the foul cretins were actively hunting the members of Goddess Tribe.

For Voldurk had discovered that *Morgane*—a fairy as powerful as the Lady of the Lake—had hidden the orb in one of the sacred waters of the Goddess. His servant Frocin, with the gift of clairvoyance, had traced Morgane's trail of magic to the Forest of Brocéliande. The dwarf knew she had hidden the orb in one of the bodies of water within the sacred forest. But, because of the triple layers of enchantment with which she had protected it, the hideous dwarf had been unable to pinpoint its precise location. Thank the Goddess, he did not know.

Not yet.

But he was determined to find it.

And Frocin never failed.

If the dwarves managed to capture a priestess of Dana, they would deliver her to Voldurk. Through dark magic and torture, the wizard would force her to surrender to him the sacred power of the water she defended. Making him infinitely more dangerous.

And evil.

And if that sacred water held the hidden orb, then the dark wizard could force the priestess to retrieve it. Providing him a priceless talisman of inordinate power. The magnificent orb that she had foolishly and naively crafted for him. Because she had been blinded by love.

Morgane la Fée—one of the trio of fairies studying with the famed wizard Merlin—had fallen in love with Voldurk, a colleague and close friend of her mentor whose exceptional talents had rivaled those of the famed Druid. But unlike Merlin, who had sought divine

49

knowledge for the benevolent purposes of healing and protection, Voldurk had been seduced by the alluring power of darkness.

Morgane had found him irresistible, charismatic, and passionate—a tall, dark, handsome, fiery lover whose amorous skills drove her wild. She'd been besotted, smitten by the enticing Druid, more than willing to please her dark lover, who had learned of her extraordinary skill in channeling the divine power of gemstones. *La Fée Blanche des Rochers.* The White Fairy of the Sacred Stones.

He'd discovered that Morgane had created the sacred scabbard of King Arthur Pendragon. That she had infused the gemstones in the enchanted sheath with the divine protection of the Goddess, rendering the young king invincible in battle. Longing for such invulnerability himself, Voldurk had recently seduced Morgane, rekindling the old flame which still burned in her lonely heart despite the passage of years.

To manipulate her into crafting an object of immeasurable power for himself.

And she had foolishly fallen for his wicked lies.

The seductive wizard had learned that in the enchanted realm of Avalon—where Morgane had helped Viviane establish a center of healing—there was powerful magic. It flowed in the sacred waters of *La Fontaine de Jouvence.* It emanated from the celestial ore of the fallen star that Morgane had discovered in the hidden sea cave of *la Grotte de l' Étoile.* And it lay within the preternatural skill of the Elves who forged weapons of unsurpassed excellence. Like Excalibur, the unparalleled, legendary sword of King Arthur Pendragon.

Voldurk had discovered that Viviane's lover, the Elf Gofannon—the blacksmith of the god Lugh himself—had forged the famed Excalibur from celestial ore mined on the island of Avalon. He knew that if he were able to obtain an armament of magic crafted by the fairy Morgane, derived from the raw material on Avalon and imbued with magic through her supreme skill with sacred stones—the power he could obtain was unimaginable.

So, he'd seduced her. Made her believe he loved her. Drove her wild with passion and promises. And asked her to craft him a talisman of protection. A gemstone which would make him as invincible as Arthur and his sacred scabbard.

Beguiled by his false affirmations of love, blinded by his alluring charm, besotted by his amorous skill, Morgane had foolishly promised him a talisman of unparalleled power. Into which she would imbue her very heart and soul. And all her otherworldly skill as *la Fée Blanche des Rochers*. The White Fairy of the Sacred Stones.

So, she'd returned to the island of Avalon, where she had once discovered the hidden cave of *la Grotte de l' Étoile*. Where, within the bubbling fountain, a star-shaped pattern of light radiated from a bed of crystals beneath the sacred spring.

She'd extracted the celestial crystal from the depths of the spring, selecting the most enormous, exquisite gem to create the protective talisman. As magnificent as a perfect, flawless diamond. Blinding in brilliance. And pulsing with power.

Morgane had taken the treasure to her hidden castle in the enchanted forest, where she kept a vast collection of precious gems, sacred crystals, and rare minerals in the second story workshop of her limestone tower. In the *atelier*, she'd infused the celestial crystal with the essence of pure merlinite and pearlescent moonstone, crafting a magnificent orb, channeling the divine power of the Goddess into its luminous depths. Whispering spells that she'd learned from her incomparable mentor, infusing layer upon layer of magic, *Morgane la Fée* had poured all the love in her heart and all her *otherworldly* essence into the talisman of inordinate power.

Eager to offer her priceless gift to the man she loved, Morgane had examined her radiant creation—an enormous, faceted, oval gemstone—the size of a dragon's egg—lying in her hand. Pearlescent and glowing, like the moon, it had sparkled like a diamond and twinkled like the celestial orbs in the starry night sky.

Yet, as it glowed in her palm, a vision had emerged within its magic depths. Transfixed with horror, she had observed her beloved Druid, enthralled in an amorous embrace with a raven-haired beauty. Beside the bed in which the mysterious brunette held Voldurk wrapped within her long white legs, Morgane had spotted a crown atop a black gown, carelessly thrown over a velvet tufted chair. *A queen! The faithless bastard is bedding a bloody queen!*

Livid with rage, Morgane had taken the precious orb and cast a powerful spell, warding it from evil. Then, hiding it within her cloak, she'd ridden deep into the Forest of Brocéliande to the lake with water as still as glass. *Le Miroir aux Fées.* Mirror of the Fairies.

Casting aside her clothing, clutching the priceless orb, she had swum naked to the bottom of the lake, into the entrance of the sacred cave, *la Porte du Dedans*—the Portal from Within. She'd placed the orb within a carved wooden box and had hidden it among a trio of rocks at the entrance to the cave, casting another spell of protection against evil. She'd then returned to the surface of *le Miroir aux Fées,* enshrouding the entire lake with a third layer of magic for defense.

To prevent Voldurk from ever finding it.

The three sacred elements of the Goddess, for a trinity of divine protection.

The forest—*la Forêt de Brocéliande.* The element of water—*le Miroir aux Fées.* And stone—the cave portal of *la Porte du Dedans. With my three spells of protection, and a trinity of sacred elements of the Goddess Dana, this magic orb must never fall into the hands of the wicked, deceitful, and unfaithful wizard who betrayed me. Voldurk. Damn him for all eternity!*

Morgane donned her deep purple gown, her soul still simmering with rage. She rode her white horse to a nearby valley, where she spotted two enormous stones high upon the forested ledge. *Les Faux Amants*—the False Lovers—she reflected, selecting them to represent the treacherous Voldurk and his paramour queen. Shrieking with rage, tears of anguish staining her cheeks, she cast a tempestuous spell of bewitchment, enchanting the entire vale. *Any faithless lover will become entrapped here, destined to die in this destitute Val Sans Retour. The Vale of No Return.*

Her broken heart shriveled with hatred, Morgane *la Fée* retreated into her enchanted castle within *le Val Sans Retour.*

To keep a watchful eye on the hidden, priceless orb.

The deliciously wicked web she had woven to trap

knights as faithless as the wanton, heartless wizard.

And the withered, wizened dwarves who served him.

Chapter 5

Le Bal

"You are most handsome, Sir Tristan of Lyonesse," Princess Blanchine cooed. "The blue of your elegant tunic is a most becoming color. I must admit, I find you captivating. Even with a blackened eye." Flashing him a sultry smile, she savored the good fortune of finding him alone.

Music filled the air as Lancelot's guests twirled on the dance floor of the elegant ballroom where the sweet scent of jasmine and wisteria wafted in from the courtyard. In the distance, the lake shimmered in the moonlight where two white swans floated peacefully among the water lilies. Blanchine eyed Tristan from enticingly lowered eyelashes, grateful to have found him alone. Her stomach fluttered in anticipation.

He'd been standing near the windowed doors, watching the Lady Opale dance with Lord Audric of Aquitaine, leaving himself vulnerable to her amorous attack. Taking full advantage of the rare opportunity to beguile him with her ravishing beauty, Blanchine was crestfallen to note that his eyes never left the dance floor, nor the golden-haired beauty in the emerald-green gown.

"You look as if you might like to dance. I would be delighted to accept an invitation, Sir Tristan." Sliding gracefully before him, Blanchine attempted to block his view of the Lady Opale. Unfortunately, because he towered over her, her subterfuge failed. He seemed deaf and blind to her seductive wiles, a frustrating disappointment that she—the exquisitely beautiful princess—had never yet encountered. Her heart fell when Tristan excused himself politely and rejoined Lancelot at the table where they had recently feasted quite lavishly. *I must do something. Perhaps Kaherdin can help.*

Although Kaherdin looked as if he were ready to devour Gargeolaine, Blanchine nevertheless sauntered over to her brother and his buxom fiancée, resplendent in the rose silk gown which she had described so tediously in the carriage while en route to *la Joyeuse Garde.*

"Kaherdin, might I have a word with you?" Blanchine smiled blankly at Gargeolaine, extricating her brother from the enchantment of the auburn-haired beauty, whose petulant pout held his gaze as he was reluctantly pulled away.

"Father has been trying to find a potential husband for me for quite some time now." Blanchine tried and failed to capture her brother's attention, which was still fixed on the curvaceous redhead who held his heart. "Kaherdin, are you listening to me?" Blanchine stepped in front of him, cutting off his view of Gargeolaine.

"Of course I am. What is it, Blanchine? I do not want to leave my gorgeous fiancée unattended. There are quite a few predatory knights ambling about, and I am anxious to return to her."

"As you know, dear brother, not one of the suitors that father has introduced to me was the least bit attractive or tempting." Pausing for a moment until his gaze met hers, Blanchine added, "But now I have finally met someone who interests me *very much*."

Kaherdin raised an eyebrow, intrigued.

"Sir Tristan, son of King Rivalen of Lyonesse and heir to his uncle Marke, the King of Cornwall." Smoothing the iridescent gown that matched her icy blue eyes, she added, "Or at least, he *will* be, once you sail to Cornwall on his behalf."

Kaherdin placed his hand atop his dark head, raised his face toward the high ceiling of the ballroom, and laughed out loud at her preposterous idea. "Blanchine, we cannot simply sail to Cornwall and insist that King Marke reinstate his nephew as heir to the throne! Not only is it none of our concern, but we do not wish to provoke a king, recently allied with Ireland, who looks to our own coast for a potential attack!" He took her hands, speaking softly into her beseeching eyes. "Although I cannot sail to Britain, dear sister, I certainly can—and will—speak to Father on your behalf." Kaherdin kissed her hand. "I am certain that Father will find Sir Tristan, *the son of a king*, a most suitable match for his beautiful, impossible to please daughter."

Blanchine smiled exuberantly at the older brother whom she adored.

"And perhaps, after the royal marriage of his exquisite daughter to the *Prince*," Kaherdin grinned, "Marke might decide to crown Tristan *King* of Lyonesse. With you as his *queen*." She was as gleeful as a child at Yuletide. "Now, please excuse me, dear sister. I wish to return to my bride-to-be."

Blanchine watched her brother return to the woman who would one day be his own queen. She was thrilled by Kaherdin's words, filled with hope at the prospect of marrying the man of her dreams. Her face bright with endless possibilities, she searched for Tristan, and found him—with the Lady Opale, swirling on the dance floor.

One of his arms rested on her back, cocooning her protectively, while he held her slender hand in the other. They were locked in an expression of wonder and longing, their smiles reflecting the joy of an intimate conversation. Jealousy surged through Blanchine, heartsick with envy and anger.

Lancelot appeared at her side, dashingly handsome in a white tunic embroidered in gold, his thick brown hair dusting his shoulders. "Might I have this dance, Princess Blanchine?"

Although the music was lively, and the guests—more numerous this evening, for the host had invited many of his knights and their ladies—were joyous, Blanchine was sullen and cold as she watched the Prince of Lyonesse dancing with another woman. A lesser noble!

As she danced with Lancelot, her mind wandered. She would have to plead with Father and enlist his royal aid in her quest to marry Tristan. Perhaps Father would be amenable to an alliance between Cornwall and Armorique through a royal marriage of his daughter to King Marke's nephew.

Perhaps Father could persuade King Marke to restore Tristan's birthright and crown him King of Lyonesse. After all, Tristan was the son of King Rivalen and the rightful heir to his father's throne. Even if Marke refused to give up Cornwall, she and Tristan could rule as King and Queen of Lyonesse. The thought exhilarated her, sending a chill of excitement throughout her elegant body, lifting her spirits brightly. Her spirit sparkled like the brilliant aquamarine gems in her glittering, golden coronet.

They were leaving tomorrow, returning to *le Château Rose*. She couldn't wait to tell Father she had found the perfect husband! Now, she needed him to act and arrange the royal marriage on her behalf. Perhaps she and Tristan could be married at Tintagel, along with King Marke! The excitement was nearly too much to bear.

When the song ended, Lancelot escorted her back to Kaherdin and Gargeolaine, who were chatting and sipping wine with Abélard and Odette of Poitou. Kissing Blanchine's hand and thanking her for the dance, the White Knight sat down beside Lord Esclados, the Red Knight, and his pretty wife, the Lady Laudine. "We can count on Audric, Bénézet, Kjetil and Abélard," he announced to Esclados. "Each will recruit, train, and equip at least two hundred knights. How many can we expect from the Tribe?"

"I will summon the leaders to meet at the *Château de Landuc* in late October. We can confer, discuss our options, and plan how best to proceed. Perhaps two or three hundred as well." The dark, intelligent stare of Sir Esclados held Lancelot's assessing gaze. The White Knight nodded, glancing around the elaborate ballroom, taking in the revelry and jubilant dancing all around them. "Queen Morag has the entire Irish army at her command. It would be foolish to challenge her until we are well prepared." Raising his goblet of wine to his lips, Esclados swallowed a mouthful of Lancelot's delicious burgundy. "*For war.*"

His ominous words hung in the air as Tristan and Issylte sat down to join them, the gaiety in their youthful exuberance disappearing at the somber atmosphere of the table.

"We were just discussing preparations for inevitable war with Queen Morag," Esclados said solemnly in greeting, ducking his head to Tristan and rising to kiss Issylte's hand before returning to his seat at his wife's side. "We'll convene in late October at Landuc, where I will summon the leaders of the Tribe. Once we have a fixed strategy, and sufficient forces for a challenge, we shall meet again with the allies who are here tonight. Perhaps next spring." He sipped from his silver goblet. The Red Knight bowed his head to Lancelot before raising his goblet once again.

"In the meantime," Lancelot announced, his warrior regard fixed on Tristan, "*we train.*"

****

Tristan shot Lancelot a feral grin, remembering the intensive formation of the White Knight's armed men and the techniques learned at the hands of the Avalonian Elves. At the thought of Ronan, Tristan felt a surge of jealousy and glanced quickly at Issylte, who was staring at him with her luminous, dark green gaze. *Give her time, Tristan. Be patient. Perhaps tonight.*

Audric, who had been dancing with the Princess of Armorique, joined their table, as did Kjetil, whose beastly grin Tristan returned with a sly smirk. *Next time, you're mine,* thought Tristan as he savagely shook the Viking's extended hand, the two warriors locking eyes in a fiery challenge.

Kaherdin, Gargeolaine, and Blanchine bid them all good night, for they were departing early for the return trip to *le Château Rose.* Abélard and Odette, then Bénézet and Sidonie soon followed. The high-ranking knights who had been honored by Sir Lancelot's invitation to the feast and ball began to exit their lord's castle, their elegantly attired ladies on their arms. Soon, the servants were tidying up the empty ballroom.

Esclados and Laudine retired to their guest chamber, and Lancelot bid everyone goodnight as well. Tristan escorted Issylte to the Rose Room, hopeful and expectant. They lingered in the dim hallway where moonlight shone through the window at the end of the corridor.

"It was a marvelous ending to a magnificent *séjour*," Issylte whispered. *Is that anticipation I hear in her breathless voice?* Tristan hovered over her, her scent beckoning, her emerald-green eyes bewitching. "The feast was incredible, and the dancing…"

His torn lip was barely mended, yet he longed to claim her lips with his own. Leaning down to graze the top of her head, he brushed a gentle kiss in her hair, which smelled of roses.

"Your eye is healing nicely," she murmured, touching his cheek. He turned his face and kissed her palm, then met her eyes as he slowly lowered his lips to linger just above hers, waiting for permission to continue.

Her breath caught as she parted her lips slightly.

Tristan enveloped her with his strong arms and kissed her gently, caressing her lips with sensual softness. She emitted a slight moan—which stirred his passion—as he took her lips into his, parting them with his tongue, tasting her, wanting more.

Don't frighten her, Tristan. Go easy…slowly… gently.

So, he did. He kissed her lips, her cheeks, her neck.

He stroked her hair, her face, her shoulders. He held her body close to his, knowing that she could feel his desire, the need for her which was throttling him.

He longed to sweep her up in his arms, carry her inside, lay her gently on the bed, and worship this golden goddess who had healed him. And now held him spellbound before her, suspended at the entrance to the room where he could finally make her his own.

"Good night, Tristan. Sleep well." Quietly, she withdrew from his embrace, her eyes conveying the same yearning that he knew shone in his, and retreated into her room, closing the door softly behind her.

Wounded by her rejection, his body aching with unfulfilled need, Tristan slunk away from Issylte's door and silently shuffled down the dark corridor to his own lonely room.

****

From the crack in her open door, from which she had observed Tristan's failed attempt to bed the Lady Opale, Princess Blanchine smiled triumphantly. She was even tempted to slip down the hall, knock on his door, and alleviate the pain of his lust herself.

No, that is not the behavior of a princess, Blanchine. You are not a slattern! You shall be his queen, not his whore. Be patient. Father will arrange everything.

****

As the moon shone through the silky curtains of the Rose Room, Issylte wondered if she should have invited Tristan into her room. But she just couldn't. Although he stirred her passion, she still grieved for Ronan. She even felt guilty, as if she were betraying the Elf in her attraction to the Blue Knight. But her relationship with Ronan was over. She couldn't have stayed in Avalon; he

62

wouldn't have been able to come with her to Ireland. Still, her heart grieved for the loss of what they'd had. And what they might have shared in the future.

Yet, Tristan's kiss had awakened more than just her body. The taste of him called to her; the masculine scent of his flesh lured her; the deep pools of his eyes beckoned like cool, refreshing waves which would cleanse her broken spirit and refill her empty soul.

Her body trembled from his kisses; her spirit longed for him. Torn between desire and guilt, Issylte found sleep elusive as she tossed restlessly in her empty, lonely bed.

****

Tristan, equally aroused and longing for her, stared at the moon from the opened windows of his chambers. Would she ever stop loving the Elf? His desire for her was all-consuming, tormenting him body and soul. He— the sullen, angry knight whose only interest had always been in battle—now found himself seeing her face, longing for her touch, eager to be near her, as if absorbing the healing power of the Goddess that emanated from her spirit.

He thought fleetingly of Lancelot and his impossible love for Queen Guinevère. Was he, like the White Knight, also destined to suffer *un amour fou—a* love so intense as to drive him mad?

Tristan crawled into bed and pulled the blanket over his shoulder, trying to settle down so that he could sleep. He closed his eyes and saw Issylte's face, felt the softness of her lips, her hair, her skin…the luscious body he longed to worship. When at last his hand abated the unbearable ache for her through blessed release, he drifted off to restless sleep, tormented by tantalizing dreams of his green and golden goddess.

Chapter 6

Emeraldfire

Chilly winds blew scattered clouds over the choppy surface of the Élorn river as Issylte gazed at the red and gold leaves strewn across the courtyard. A flock of brown geese honked as they flew overhead in their annual migration south. The regal guests had departed *la Joyeuse Garde* in carriages and on horseback. The knights had returned to their training, and Lancelot had just left the table where Tristan and Issylte now sat within the walled terrace beneath the bedroom window of her Rose Room. The fresh tang of the estuary and the green fragrance of the forest filled the crisp autumn air.

The three of them had broken their fast together here on the terrace, reminiscing about the highlights of last night's ball and the joyous festivities of the month-long *séjour*. They'd reflected about their good fortune in obtaining French allies and had discussed the upcoming trip to the Red Knight's castle of Landuc to meet the Tribe in late October.

Now, alone with Tristan amidst the fading rose trellises, the lush forest perfuming the air with pine and evergreen, and the flowing river sparkling in the distance, Issylte noticed he seemed preoccupied. Jumpy. Tense.

Taking the pitcher that the servant had left for them,

she poured some of the cool water laced with fresh mint into their glasses and handed one to Tristan. "You seem especially pensive, Tristan. Is something troubling you?"

He rose to his feet, grinned down at her, and motioned for her to remain seated. "Stay here. I have something to show you. I'll be right back." He disappeared into the castle, leaving Issylte to wonder what he was so eager to share. A curious smile dawned as she sipped her mint water in amusement.

A few minutes later, he returned with a bag slung over his shoulder and carrying two swords, encased in sheaths, which he stood against the stone wall enclosing the terrace. Placing the bag down upon the cobbled stone floor of the terrace, he spun to look at her, his eyes wide with delight. Her pulse quickened. *What is he up to?*

Tristan took the larger of the two swords, unsheathed it, and slashed through the air as if striking an opponent. Showing off his exceptional swordsmanship. Issylte smiled at his chivalrous display.

"This is the sword I had forged last month when I went into Kerléroux with Darius and a few of Lancelot's knights." Demonstrating a few more jabs and lunges, he grinned at her and exclaimed proudly, "I am extremely pleased with its quality. I've named it *Lamdefer*— Ironblade. It's an even better weapon than the sword *Tahlfir* that I broke in the Morholt's skull."

Curious as to where he was leading with this impressive display of knightly skill, Issylte watched him, rapt with attention. He replaced *Lamdefer in* its sheath, stood it against the wall, then selected the smaller sword, which he unsheathed before her.

It was more slender than his sword, with a dark, sparkling emerald in its pommel. Tristan swept the air with the magnificent blade, then displayed it before her, the deep green gem gleaming in the morning sunlight.

She looked up at him in wonderment.

"When I had *Lamdefer* forged, I also had this beautiful sword crafted for you, Issylte. I have named it *Emeraldfire*. Forged in flame, adorned with the deepest green gemstone to represent *you*. The Emerald Princess of Ireland." He extended his hand to her, into which she placed her own, rising from the table to stand before him. He then offered her the sword—extending the grip for her to grasp. "Take it, Issylte. It is *yours*."

Placing himself behind her, Tristan instructed her how to hold the weapon. Then, guiding her arm with his, he helped her to sweep and slice through the air as she became familiar with its feel. "I plan to train with Lancelot's finest knights, honing myself back into battle condition." Circling in front of her to meet her gaze, he grinned, "And I plan to train *you*, my princess. To become a warrior, like me."

She shot him an incredulous look. He elaborated, a twinkle in his eye. "You already have excellent equestrian skills. That is most important. We'll begin by having you ride toward a target, striking it with a wooden sword, like I once did as a squire. When you have perfected that skill, we'll graduate to using *Emeraldfire*—sheathed at first—until you learn to strike with deadly accuracy."

He took the sword gently from her, sheathed it, and stood it beside his own weapon. Taking her hand, he drew her to him. "I will also teach you self-defense techniques. How to break free from an assailant's grasp. How to fracture a rib with your elbow. You'll learn a man's weaknesses—how to kick or knee the groin, deliver a sharp blow to the windpipe, gouge eye sockets, or stomp a foot to loosen a hostile grip."

He wrapped his arms around her neck, as if he were an assassin, and showed her how to thrust her arms up through his, in order to escape. Pinning her against him in a different hold, he pulled her elbows into his ribs to show her the maneuver to break free. Releasing her, he twirled Issylte to face him as he continued outlining the training he had designed. "Every morning, after breaking fast, we'll do target practice on horseback. Then, we'll return here, and I will teach you self-defense. Hand-to-hand combat techniques. And how to wield *this*."

Tristan reached into the bag and removed a belt containing a sheathed knife, which he placed into her hands. He then withdrew the slender blade which, like her new sword, held an emerald in its pommel. "*Émeraude*. Emerald. A dagger made just for you."

Replacing the blade in its sheath, he strapped it to her ankle under her gown, a shiver of pleasure rippling up her leg at his touch. She thought of the dagger Cian had given her years ago, when he released her in the Hazelwood Forest. She still had that weapon. Now she would have her very own blade as well. *Made just for me.*

Returning to the bag, Tristan removed three tunics, two pairs of breeches, and a pair of soft leather boots, which he laid on the table. "This clothing belonged to one of Judoc's squires—a boy of thirteen, who is about your size." Holding up one of the tunics for her to inspect, he added with an impish grin, "Much more practical for training than a long gown."

Beaming at him in astonishment, Issylte remarked, "Never before has anyone offered to train me. I have always been treated as a fragile princess who needed protection and pampering. But this…" she said, gesturing to the weapons and clothing, "is the first time anyone has taken me seriously in my desire to challenge the queen. No one else has ever considered the importance of developing my strength…and the ability to *fight*."

Issylte walked up to him and placed a hand on his broad chest. His heart pounded under her trembling palm. Filled with gratitude and joy, she raised her eyes up to his. "You have promised to lead my army. To fight at my side. But Tristan, training me to become a *warrior queen* is the best gift you could ever offer. Thank you, from the bottom of my heart."

She stood on her tiptoes to kiss him lightly on the lips. He pulled her to his chest and held her close. She could feel and hear his thumping pulse. Verdant magic roared in her veins.

After a few moments, he released her and stepped back, his brilliant blue eyes alive, his handsome face eager and exuberant. "Each morning, you and I will develop your skills with *Emeraldfire* on a charging horse. Then, we'll practice the self-defense and combat techniques. After that, I'll be training every day with Lancelot's knights. But I'll also teach you a routine for strengthening that you must practice on your own. In the evening, you and I will run together at the edge of the forest, along the river, and around the lake. By the time we go to Landuc to meet the Tribe, you'll be in prime condition, which we must maintain with ongoing, vigilant training—as you prepare to challenge the queen for your throne."

Tristan whistled toward the side of the castle, where

two stable hands emerged, each leading a magnificent horse. One was a deep brown stallion, with black mane and tail; the other a glossy, solid black mare with extraordinary fire.

"This is *Aiglon,* my warhorse—a *destrier,*" Tristan said, bringing the brown stallion toward her. She approached him slowly, letting the animal sniff her hand, then stroked his shoulder as she murmured hello in a soothing voice. The smell of his warm, glossy coat reminded her of Luna. Maëva. Marron and Noisette. Noz. She swallowed an enormous lump in her throat.

"And this," Tristan said, as the groom approached, leading the black mare to Issylte, "is *Minuit. Your* horse."

Issylte was dumbfounded. She gaped at Tristan, widening her eyes in astonishment.

He nodded and grinned. Her heavy heart melted. "She's *yours,* Issylte. Isn't she beautiful?"

Tears blurred her vision as she took in the splendid creature who regarded her with large, expressive eyes that evoked both intelligence and spirit. *Minuit* was beyond magnificent. Midnight fire. Issylte's heart burst with love. She glanced up at Tristan, tears glimmering. Brilliant blue waves of calm washed her as she swam in his intense gaze.

She let the mare smell her trembling hand, to become acquainted with her scent. Issylte crooned, her voice gentle and loving, "*Bonjour, Minuit. Tu es tellement belle.* You're so beautiful." She then slowly stoked *Minuit's* neck, shoulder, and finally, her muzzle. Memories of Luna flooded through her. And of Noisette, the chestnut foal that Ronan had given her. Now Tristan had given her *Minuit.* She was overwhelmed with joy.

Tristan seemed delighted by her obvious love for

Minuit. "Would you like to go for a ride?" he asked enthusiastically. His dashing smile stirred her soul.

"I would *love* that!" she exuded, a tear rolling down her cheek. She wiped it away with a brisk flick of her hand and accepted Tristan's boost into the saddle. She stroked *Minuit's* neck, cooing softly to her beautiful new horse. Tristan mounted *Aiglon* and waved appreciatively to the grooms. And, under the cloud-streaked autumn sky, the brisk wind whipping her hair in glorious freedom, Issylte galloped with Tristan across the open plain toward the dense forest burnished red and gold.

Each morning, Tristan taught her how to wield *Emeraldfire,* demonstrating lunges, strikes, and defensive blocks. He trained her to race *Minuit* toward the target he created—a tall, wooden tree trunk with a strike zone area outlined in the center.

Beginning with a wooden sword, she progressed to hitting the target with her sheathed sword. After the target drills on horseback, Tristan helped her learn to break free of various strongholds, demonstrating how to maximize the blows she would use in self-defense.

He designed a strenuous calisthenic routine to strengthen her body and instructed her on how to handle—and inflict potentially lethal strikes—with her new dagger, *Émeraude.*

And every evening, they ran together on various paths along the river Élorn, through the thick forest, or around the lake behind the *château.* At first, Issylte could barely run at all, but after nearly two months, she had improved enough to keep up with Tristan and had greatly increased her pace.

The autumn weather was still quite warm in the direct sun, and Issylte found the squire's woolen tunics too hot for training practice. So, for a much lighter attire, she cut off the bottom of a couple of the white *chemise* dresses that she wore under her gowns, tying them at her waist for freedom of movement.

The perspiration of her strenuous routine made the thin white cloth adhere to her body, and she often found Tristan gazing longingly at the clear outline of her breasts. He, too, perspired in the heat, and frequently removed his shirt during their training sessions.

Sometimes, when he held her pinned against him in her self-defense lessons, she wanted to turn toward him, devour his sensuous mouth, and wrap her legs around him, welcoming him into her body instead of resisting, fighting, and breaking free.

The sight of his naked chest, the strength of his chiseled arms around her, the scent of his fresh sweat…he was becoming increasingly difficult to resist. Still, frequent thoughts of Ronan plagued her with guilt.

But…perhaps just a little less.

Tristan, like Issylte, was making tremendous progress in his training, having fully recovered from the wound inflicted by the Morholt's poisoned blade. He had regained the weight he'd lost during his convalescence and had increased the mass of his enormous body to its peak warrior condition. Issylte had noticed that he, as well as Lancelot and the other knights of *la Joyeuse Garde*, consumed large quantities of food—especially meat, cheese, and grains. Indeed, the *châtelain* fed all his men exceptionally well, for they trained continuously for battle. And many would go to Landuc soon when they brought her to meet the Tribe. Issylte was both terrified and thrilled.

One morning in early October, she and Tristan were

practicing her self-defense training when he abruptly released her and stood at attention, his gaze focused intently on the edge of the forest. As Issylte watched in astonishment, an enormous gray wolf—perhaps twice the size of an ordinary wolf—emerged cautiously, stealthily approaching Tristan, who did not appear frightened in the least. On the contrary, he rushed forward to greet the massive beast, nodding as if in comprehension. *He is communicating with the wolf through his Druidic gift of l'herbe d'or!*

Tristan spun toward her, his face urgent. "The wolf has come to request our aid. The woodland creatures told him that the forest fairy *Églantine* lives here. A gifted healer who might be able to save his mate. He wants us to follow him. But we must hurry. She is gravely wounded."

Issylte raced into the château, up the stairs, into her Rose Room. She fetched her basket of healing herbs and sacred stones from the wooden armoire, wrapped a cloak around her shoulders, and dashed back to Tristan, who was saddling their horses with the help of a terrified groom.

Once they were seated atop their mounts, the huge wolf dashed into the forest, with Tristan and Issylte close behind. He led them deep into a hamlet where heavy branches from gigantic oaks hung low, forming a natural protective shelter against the backdrop of rocky, forested ledge. On a bed of thick leaves under the dense oak branches lay a large gray wolf, smaller than her mate, yet still enormous in size. The shaft of an arrow protruded from her left hind flank. She was trembling, whimpering, and bleeding from the wound.

The male wolf approached his mate, who moved her

head weakly toward him. *He must be telling her I am here to help,* thought Issylte, who waited for Tristan to nod in assent before crouching beside the injured female.

"He says they were hunting when the arrow pierced her. They managed to elude the archer, but she is in great pain. He begs you to save her."

The female wolf was panting desperately, in obvious agony. Issylte stroked her fur to reassure her. As she touched the wolf, the familiar tingling sensation of numbing chill crept up her hand. Wolfsbane!

Issylte fumbled through her supplies and found the vial which contained the same foxglove tincture she had used to save Tristan. But how much to give a wolf? She was huge, but not as bulky as Tristan. One drop might not be enough. Her magic would tell her the right dose. Issylte held the vial in one hand as she placed the other on the wolf's ribcage near her faltering heart. *Two,* her magic hummed. This wolf needed two drops to survive. Just like Tristan.

As she had done back in Avalon, Issylte placed two drops under the lolling tongue of the wolf, eyeing the enormous canine teeth that could so easily tear open her exposed throat. As she felt the wolf's heartrate increase steadily, Issylte suddenly glimpsed an array of startling images with her gift of *sight*.

A stunning sea creature with deep green scales and tailfin like a fish, yet with the head and torso of a human female. Long blue hair rippling like the turquoise waters of the Narrow Sea, floating in the ocean breeze. And the brilliant star pattern of light from *la Grotte de l' Étoile.* Issylte's magic soared. *I need to use the star crystals to heal her, too. Just as I did Tristan.*

Issylte made three crystal grids of healing stones

around the body of the injured wolf. Her gift revealed that this wolf was somehow linked to the sea, so Issylte formed a droplet shaped outer grid of ocean jasper stones around the wounded lupine body. For the inner grid, Issylte chose blue turquoise stones to symbolize the ocean, the color of the creature's hair in the vision, and the curative essence of water. And closest to the wolf's body, she made the five points of a star to channel the celestial healing energy of the Goddess into her critically wounded patient.

Issylte murmured the spells of healing she'd learned from *Tatie* in the heart of the Hazelwood Forest. The enchantments from the ancient manuscripts of the wizard Merlin that she'd studied in Avalon and had used to heal Tristan. With her hand over the wolf's heart, Issylte summoned the verdant healing magic of the foxglove plant circulating through the lupine blood. With her other hand, she channeled the divine curative power of the Goddess through the sacred crystals into the body of the injured wolf, pouring her essence into saving her. For Issylte knew that the Goddess had entwined her fate once again.

With this magnificent wolf.

She removed the arrow and stanched the bleeding, cleansing the wound with yarrow and turmeric, bandaging it with raw honey. She remained at her patient's side for several hours, uttering incantations, channeling her verdant magic into the sacred stones and herbs. Finally, as the sun began to set and the autumn chill made her glad she'd brought her cloak, the female wolf stirred, raising her head to look directly into Issylte's eyes. Intuitively, she knew the wolf was thanking her, but Tristan voiced it aloud.

"She is grateful to you for saving her life," he said as he crouched down next to her and stroked the wolf's furry head. He looked at Issylte, his expression full of wonder. "She also says that one day, you will need her help. And that you will find her through the Cave of the Fallen Star."

Issylte's heart pounded with adrenaline. This wolf, whose destiny was somehow entwined with hers, was linked to the sea. To an *otherworldly* creature with magnificent green scales and long turquoise hair. And to *la Grotte de l' Étoile* on Avalon. The Goddess had brought them together. For a fate yet to be revealed.

The male wolf approached them and communicated briefly with Tristan, then began licking his mate's face. The two humans rose to their feet and brushed the leaves and twigs from their clothing as they locked eyes in gratitude and prepared to leave.

"He, too, thanks the forest fairy Églantine for saving his mate. In return, he promises that his pack will protect us. The wolves will patrol the forest around *la Joyeuse Garde* and eliminate any danger. He is deeply indebted to us both."

Issylte stroked the fur of her patient, then the male wolf. "You are most welcome. But please, before we leave, tell Tristan your names. We are honored to have met you both."

The wolf seemed to confer with Tristan, who then raised his head to look at Issylte, his eyes widened in astonishment. "His name is Garou, from *Le Vallon de la Chambre aux Loups*—the Valley of the Chambre of Wolves. Near the enchanted forest of Brocéliande. And his mate's name is Ondine." Tristan took hold of Issylte's trembling hand. "He promises they will help us

76

when we need them." He shook his head in disbelief. "Garou says I can summon the wolves. Anytime. Anywhere. *With my mind.*"

Issylte's breath hitched. A chorus of magic sung in her heart as she locked onto Tristan's ocean blue gaze. They shared the same breath of wonder, then turned to say goodbye. At least a dozen wolves had come from the woods to hover protectively around Ondine. Garou stood proudly at his mate's side, his amber gaze glowing as he lowered his head in respect and gratitude.

Issylte returned the bow, then strapped her bag of herbal supplies to *Minuit*'s saddle. She and Tristan mounted their horses and rode back through the forest to *la Joyeuse Garde*, escorted by several massive wolves from Garou's loyal pack.

The white limestone *château* gleamed in the crepuscular light, the chilly autumn wind blowing her long, loose hair as she and Tristan emerged from the forest onto the castle grounds where Lancelot and his knights welcomed them home. As the enormous gray beasts disappeared into the forest, she knew the Goddess had entwined their fates with these wolves.

And Issylte couldn't wait for Her to reveal how.

Chapter 7

Darius

A late October wind whistled through the dense trees as the group of riders approached a clearing in the heart of the Forest of *Brocéliande*. Issylte, atop *Minuit*, rode alongside Tristan and Lancelot as they arrived at the Fountain of Barenton. A preternatural stillness surrounded them, a thrum of energy in the air, as if the entire forest were protected by powerful enchantment. Issylte's magic soared in her veins.

This is the fountain and well that I saw in Tristan's eyes. And there is the tall pine tree, next to the well. The Mirrored Lake is near here, too. I can sense it.

"This is the sacred fountain where Esclados summoned the storm," Tristan told her. "There is Merlin's stone where he poured the water from the well, using the golden basin you see hanging on that pine tree." As Issylte looked, a memory surfaced—the image of warriors seated around a fire.

The Tribe of Dana met here. The lake is nearby. With the hidden object a dwarf seeks. A sacred object I must protect.

"This is where I was inducted into the Tribe of Dana." Tristan stopped his horse, as did the other knights who were accompanying them to the *Château of Landuc* for the meeting with the Tribe. "The Druid gifted me with *l'herbe d'or* before the campfire right here, in this clearing." He gestured to the area in front of the well which stood before them. Issylte had glimpsed this entire setting in Tristan's gaze.

"Lancelot," she inquired, as she stroked *Minuit's* neck, "Is there a lake near here?"

"Yes, *le Miroir aux Fées*—the Mirror of the Fairies. It's not far. Come, I'll show you."

Issylte and Tristan, along with their armed guards, followed Lancelot on horseback to a large, still lake whose surface was as smooth as glass. Lush forest surrounded it; large rocks and tree-covered ledges protected it. The fragrance of deep, rich earth and the green notes of pine mingled with the lush, freshwater scent of the lake. An *otherworldly* aura heightened all her senses. *Something sacred lies within this lake. A treasure that I must defend.*

"*Le Miroir aux Fées* is so well protected by this thick forest that no breeze touches it. The surface is smooth and still as glass—a mirror which reflects the natural beauty which surrounds it. *C'est magnifique.*" Lancelot gazed in awe at the crystalline surface.

Issylte agreed, breathless with wonder. "Lancelot... is something *hidden* within this lake?"

"Not that I am aware of." The White Knight glanced at her, an eyebrow arched in curiosity. "But Laudine might know. Come, let's continue to the castle. It's not far. You can ask her when we arrive."

When they at last reached *le Château de Landuc*, Issylte was impressed by its size and strength. Two barbican defense towers flanked each side of an enormous drawbridge over a moat at the entrance to the castle. A large outer stone wall surrounded the building, with an inner curtain wall for a second level of defense.

The castle itself was much larger than *la Joyeuse Garde*, with turrets and towers reaching high above the thick trees of the forest. Built upon a rocky plateau, surrounded by dense woods, with a lake and stream flowing nearby, *le Château de Landuc* was a magnificent, imposing fortress in the middle of *la Forêt de Brocéliande*.

"*Bienvenue.* Welcome to Landuc!" Esclados boomed, as the riders dismounted and handed their horses to the grooms.

Laudine approached Issylte and kissed her on both cheeks—the French *la bise* which reminded her of *Tatie* and Viviane—as she escorted her guests inside the castle. "The servants will see you to your rooms so that you may refresh. Then, please join us in the banquet room for a light supper. We have *potage*—a lovely vegetable soup—as well as fresh bread, and of course, plenty of delicious wine. *À bientôt!*" she beamed to her guests.

Esclados directed the servants toward Tristan, Lancelot, and the knights who had escorted them from *la Joyeuse Garde,* while Laudine led Issylte to a lovely room on the second floor with windows which opened onto a balcony, offering a splendid view of the dense forest which enclosed the castle.

"There is a pitcher of fresh water on the table, and an armoire for your clothing, which my servants will unpack and store for you. If you wish to bathe, there is a porcelain tub on the lower level, which they will be happy to prepare for you. Is there anything else I can do to make you more comfortable?" Laudine asked graciously, her lovely smile twinkling in her golden-brown eyes.

"No, thank you, Laudine. But I do have a question, please."

"Of course, Issylte. What would you like to know?"

She looked down at her feet, then met Laudine's curious gaze. "Lancelot showed us *le Miroir aux Fées*. I have seen it before, in one of my *sightings*."

Laudine appeared intrigued as Issylte asked breathlessly, "Is there something sacred, hidden in the lake? In my vision, a dwarf was searching for something, but I don't know what." She searched Laudine's curious face. "I sensed that I am supposed to protect it. To prevent a dwarf from obtaining it. Do you know what it might be?"

The Lady of the Fountain replied hesitantly, "No, I don't know of anything hidden in the lake. I'm not aware of any sacred object there. But the dwarves have been prowling through our forest recently. We must be extremely cautious. I'm sure Tristan told you about Bédalis and his attack."

"Yes, he told me about summoning the storm to defend the sacred fountain. And how he killed the dwarf to save you."

"Exactly. And that's why my husband Esclados had the Druid give him the magic of *l'herbe d'or*. Now Tristan can communicate with birds and wolves. A valuable skill for a valiant warrior of the Tribe of Dana." Laudine's warm smile lit up her pretty face. "I'll leave you to freshen up for *le souper. À bientât, ma belle.*" Kissing Issylte's cheeks once more, *la châtelaine* retreated, returning to her other guests as Issylte settled into her new room.

****

81

The potage was delicious, a blend of fresh vegetables from a late harvest in the garden, enhanced with savory fresh herbs, complemented by the full flavored, rich body of the fine red wine that Esclados was serving quite generously.

As the guests were finishing the meal, and the servants were clearing away the dishes, Issylte observed the members of the Tribe of Dana who were seated at the table with her.

Kirus, the well-respected leader of the Tribe, was an enormous man with thick brown hair that touched his broad shoulders. Intelligent hazel eyes shone in a ruggedly handsome face marred by a long, vicious scar that extended from just under his left eye vertically down his prominent cheekbone. Beside him sat an exquisitely beautiful priestess named Nolwenn, with long, glossy black hair and astonishing violet-colored eyes. She wore an intricately carved silver pendant with a large amethyst gemstone that radiated energy which thrummed to Issylte. *She is skilled with the healing powers of the sacred stones.*

Dagur had curly black hair, a full beard, and an astute brown gaze. Though not as tall as Kirus, he was equally burly and muscular, with arms like a tree trunk. *A powerful bear,* Issylte thought, smiling as she met his dark gaze.

Solzic was enormous, blond, and bearded, with brilliant blue eyes. He sat beside a petite brunette priestess named Lysara who smiled warmly, snuggled beside the warrior who was obviously her lover. The two made a striking couple, a blend of opposites in both coloring and size. Issylte smiled warmly at them both. Lysara's brown eyes sparkled, simmering with power as she returned Issylte's friendly gaze.

A meaningful glance and knowing smile shared between Tristan and Nolwenn sparked a disturbing and surprising wave of jealousy in Issylte. Nolwenn, who seemed to be romantically involved with the leader Kirus—for his arm was wrapped around the back of her chair—was tall and lean, with a muscular physique which displayed tremendous strength. *A warrior as well as healer skilled with sacred stones.* Issylte read friendship and trust in Nolwenn's amethyst gaze. She smiled at the beautiful priestess. *We will become close friends. I am glad to meet her.* Her magic sung in kinship.

All three of the priestesses at the table—Laudine, Nolwenn and Lysara—shared the same tattoo on their inner right wrist.

Like the mark that Tristan and Lancelot shared with other male warriors of the Tribe, the tattoo of the priestesses revealed three arms of a Celtic triangle which curled downward into a spiral. Yet, the mark of the Priestesses of Dana was more slender and feminine, with the trio of spirals swirling into delicate, curled scrolls. Verdant power quickened in Issylte's veins.

Esclados addressed the group seated at the table and gestured to Issylte. "Not only has the Emerald Princess been denied her right to the throne of Ireland by the Black Widow who poisoned her father, but now the same wicked queen threatens Tristan's uncle, King Marke of Cornwall."

Whispering spread around the table as the Tribe exchanged concerned glances.

"Queen Morag of Ireland has allied with the dark wizard Voldurk. She has also allied with Frocin, leader of the dwarves, and a traitorous knight named Indulf."

The Red Knight leaned back in his chair and locked his regard on Kirus, whose fierce gaze blazed with power. "A coalition between Ireland and Cornwall, with attacks and slave expeditions that target the entire coastline of France—is a threat we must face as a unified front." Kirus nodded gravely, as did the other leaders of the Tribe of Dana, all concurring with the Red Knight. "It is essential that we prepare to defend against the Irish threat. And ready our army to sail with Tristan—a member of our own Tribe—to liberate King Marke and Tintagel from the Black Widow Queen."

Lancelot addressed the assembled group. "Queen Morag of Ireland poisoned her first husband, King Donnchadh. Issylte's father." His deep blue eyes—so like Tristan's—blazed with fire. "The Black Widow Queen is now betrothed to Tristan's uncle, King Marke of Cornwall. Not only does she threaten the coast of France, but Tristan's inheritance. And Issylte's right to her father's throne."

Kirus glanced pensively at the warriors seated around him. Forming strategy. Assessing strengths and weaknesses. He spoke firmly to Lancelot, his deep voice simmering with power. "We'll summon the leaders of the Tribe of Dana throughout the entire Celtic realm. Amass an army of three or four thousand. Our warriors, their feudal lords, men-at-arms. We'll train and equip new men, build ships, forge weapons and armor." He took a long pull from his goblet of wine and locked his fierce gaze upon Dagur. "We'll prepare to defend our coasts. Be ready to sail to Cornwall. But…" he said, eyeing Tristan warily, "it will take months—more likely a year—before we're ready."

Lancelot gazed at Tristan and nodded solemnly.

"Then we begin now."

****

Tristan, Issylte, Lancelot, and his knights spent several more days at Landuc, enjoying the hospitality of Esclados and Laudine. They parted ways in early November, with plans to reconvene again in June with the leaders of the Tribe for an update on progress. Issylte hugged Laudine, Nolwenn, and Lysara, her new Priestess of Dana friends, looking forward to seeing them again in the summer. The men clasped shoulders and shook hands as they said their goodbyes, and the riders returned to *la Joyeuse Garde* for the upcoming Yuletide season.

And preparation for war.

November passed quickly, with Issylte training every morning with Tristan, practicing self-defense, developing her skill with the sword *Emeraldfire*, honing her accuracy atop *Minuit*. Tristan trained hard each day with Lancelot, Judoc, Darius and the knights of *la Joyeuse Garde,* returning to run with her every night. He complimented her improved strength, stamina, and speed, his praise and steadfast presence comforting and encouraging.

And undeniably appealing.

The Yuletide season was delightful. Issylte joined Lancelot's servants and several of the knights' wives in decorating the castle with evergreen boughs and hellebore blossoms. The entire castle feasted on fresh fish, venison, and pheasant; they spent many evenings playing cards or chess, dancing to lively music, and enjoying the festive ambiance of *la Joyeuse Garde*. And much to her surprise and delight, Tristan offered her a bow and quiver of arrows as a Yuletide gift.

"It is essential that you learn archery as well as swordsmanship. We'll add this to our daily training," he grinned as she received his gift and looked up at him in astonishment.

The quiver was made of gleaming brown leather, with thirty arrows fletched with four feathers each. As she examined the magnificently curved wooden bow, Tristan said proudly, "It's made from the wood of the yew tree. Flexible enough to bend without breaking. Resilient, so that it snaps back into shape with speed and accuracy when the arrow is released. And the grain of the wood can compress and stretch without splintering or fracturing." His brilliant grin took her breath away.

And so, every morning, before he left to train with Lancelot's knights, Tristan taught her to use the bow and arrow.

"Stand at an angle, with your feet placed like this," he demonstrated, positioning her perpendicular to the target. "Hold your body like this," he urged, guiding her torso into proper form. As he placed his hands on her hips to align them correctly, Issylte's face flushed as she imagined him positioning her hips for a very different reason. He wrapped his arms around her, showing her how to nock and tightly draw back the bowstring, keeping her collarbone parallel with the arrow. The alluring scent of leather, pine, and the salty tang of the ocean in him made her nearly swoon.

"I gave you this gift for another reason, you know," he whispered teasingly into her left ear. "So I could hold you close. And do this." He kissed the nape of her neck where it touched her shoulder. A soft moan escaped her lips as he pressed his hardened body against hers. A hollow emptiness ached deep inside as he twirled her to face him. She swam in the sea of his deep blue gaze as his lips tenderly sought hers. He pulled her close, the kiss deepening, the intensity mounting, the pressure increasing. Her quivering legs could barely support her weight.

She pulled away, gasping for breath. His fierce eyes blazing with desire, he stepped back and lowered his head slightly, steadily holding her gaze. The sonorous timbre of his deep voice vibrated in her bones as he whispered in promise. "When you're ready, my princess. I am *yours*."

Issylte, her legs shaking, could barely walk as she backed away, wobbling unsteadily toward the shelter of the castle. At the entrance door, she spun to take one last look at him, standing at the edge of the forest, his handsome face filled with longing. The white dove in her heart fluttered wildly, her magic soaring in the intensity of his gaze.

****

One morning, Issylte was practicing archery while Tristan and Lancelot were training with Darius and Judoc nearby. Winter's snow was melting, and the crisp scent of spring hung in the cool air. Inhaling the delightful scent of pine, snow, and rich earth, she positioned herself, nocked her arrow, and took aim.

Just as Issylte raised her bow to fix upon the target, Darius burst from the woods on her deaf side, breathless with exertion, simultaneously battling two enemy knights. Her arrow still nocked in the bow, Issylte aimed at one assailant, but with the rapid blows, blocks, and maneuvers of the embattled knights, did not dare release it for fear of hitting Darius. Adrenaline raced through her veins as an ambush unfolded before her.

A dozen armored knights emerged from the words, engaging with Lancelot's knights who stormed from the castle to defend against the onslaught. Within moments, swords were clashing as Tristan, Lancelot, and Judoc battled other assailants who rode out from the thick forest to attack the castle. Clad in practice gear rather than full armor, Darius took a brutal slice in his shield arm from one attacker as he slew an enemy knight and engaged a third who charged from the woods, followed by several more heavily armed men. Shrieks of pain and shouts for reinforcements flew across the castle grounds as more of Lancelot's knights arrived on horseback from the training field to enter the gruesome foray. The coppery tang of spilled blood, the thick aroma of churned mud, and the pungent stink of sweat and gore swirled in the turbulent breeze.

Darius had slain his opponents but was bleeding furiously. He'd collapsed near a tree and needed immediate medical attention, yet with the chaos of Lancelot's knights emerging from the castle and the steady stream of warriors flowing from the forest, all Issylte could do was tear the sleeve of her gown and use it as a makeshift bandage to slow the loss of blood. Her heart hammered in her chest as she applied pressure to his profusely bleeding wound.

An eerie, unearthly howling bellowed from the bowels of the dense forest. A shiver ran up Issylte's spine as dozens of massive gray wolves slunk from the shadowy woods and, in a sudden frenzy, lunged at the enemy knights. She watched in horror as men died in agony, their throats viciously ripped open by bloody fangs, limbs savagely snapped from torsos, slimy entrails strewn across the battlefield in front of the besieged castle.

Within minutes, all the intruders had been slain. Blood and gore dripped from the massive maws and enormous claws of the brutal beasts. As Tristan communicated with Garou and the wolves, Issylte dashed into the castle to retrieve her herbal supplies to save Darius.

The precious bag tucked under her arm, she raced back to the wounded knight's side and stanched the bleeding with a poultice of yarrow. Darius pulled himself up a bit with his good arm, reclining against the oak tree whose thick canopy sheltered him from the strong breeze and midday sun. Issylte searched her supplies for calendula soap to cleanse the wound. "Those three knights crept up behind you on your right side. But you didn't hear them coming." His concerned face searched hers as she washed the wound and applied healing herbs. "You're deaf in your right ear, aren't you?" he asked softly.

I would have been killed if not for him. My cursed deaf ear would have cost me my life!

"Yes, I am deaf in my right ear. A serious childhood illness." She met his gentle brown gaze as she cleansed the wound. "I am grateful to you for saving my life, Darius. I would have been killed today. Thank you. From the bottom of my heart."

He lifted her hand and kissed it gently, then motioned his head to indicate his wounded arm. "And thank you, Issylte. For saving mine."

She spotted Tristan, conferring with the wolves near the edge of the forest. His brilliant eyes met hers for a privately shared moment before returning to Lancelot and Judoc, who were examining the coat of arms of the slain enemy.

"These knights bear the boar's head of the dwarf Frocin," Lancelot announced gravely. She looked up from Darius' injury and locked eyes with the White Knight. "He has traced you here, Issylte. Perhaps when you used your magic to heal the injured wolf. We must go to Landuc. At once." Lancelot looked over at Tristan, then returned his stern gaze to her. "The Red Knight's castle is much more heavily fortified than *la Joyeuse Garde*. We can protect you better in the sacred forest of Brocéliande. Within the heart of the Tribe." His face full of concern, he glanced at Darius, then back at Issylte. "Can he ride?"

"He'll need someone to help him stay in the saddle and hold the reins. I'll ride with him." Issylte smiled at her injured patient, then observed Tristan's wary expression. "I'm half the weight of any of the men, so it will be an easier load for the horse. So long as Darius is conscious, he can grip the horn and remain upright." She looked at the deep gash in Darius' arm. "But we'll need to proceed cautiously, so his wound does not reopen."

Lancelot agreed, then gave orders to his men to burn the corpses and bloodied remains of the enemy knights, to honorably bury their own fallen. A few of Lancelot's knights would need medical attention, but none were as severely injured as Darius. Issylte directed the wounded men into the castle where she would treat them.

She asked Judoc and Gaël to help Darius into the *château* where she would stitch up the wound and bandage it properly with healing herbs and raw honey. As they helped the injured knight into *la Joyeuse Garde*, Issylte trotted to the edge of the dense forest where Tristan and Garou were conferring with several other enormous gray wolves.

"I have thanked Garou and his pack for defending us," Tristan said as she joined them. "The soldiers who attacked us were mercenary knights of the dwarf Frocin. Now that he is allied with the Black Widow Queen, Frocin has undoubtedly traced you here. Hunting you. *For her.*" Fierce blue eyes held her gaze. A tingling numbness crept up her arms, as if her stepmother's icy touch now clutched her shaking hands. "I agree with Lancelot that we cannot remain here. We must travel to Landuc, in the Forest of Brocéliande. Not only is the Red Knight's castle more heavily fortified than *la Joyeuse Garde,* but we'll also be near *Le Vallon de la Chambre aux Loups.* The Valley of the Chamber of Wolves. The heart of Garou's domain." Tristan communicated wordlessly with the leader of the wolves. "He promises to defend us. There are hundreds of wolves throughout the sacred forest. And Garou leads them all."

Issylte's magic hummed in the presence of such powerful *otherworldly* allies. She thought of Ondine, the injured wolf she'd healed. Garou's mate. Linked somehow to the turquoise haired sea creature she'd seen in the *sighting.* She looked at Tristan. "Ask him about his mate. Has she recovered?"

Tristan *spoke* with the alpha wolf, then grinned as he replied, "Not only has she fully recovered, but she has also borne him a litter of five wolf pups. Three males and two females. Now that mating season has passed and the pups are old enough, they'll return to *le Vallon de la Chambre aux Loups.* Perhaps our paths will cross theirs again someday." He thanked the wolves again, as did Issylte, and the pack disappeared back into the dense forest. Tristan helped her gather her herbal supplies, her new bow and quiver of arrows, and escorted her into the castle to care for Darius and the injured men.

"Judoc and Gaël, you will remain here, with sixty knights to defend *la Joyeuse Garde,*" Lancelot commanded as they prepared for departure. Issylte had just stitched and bandaged Darius' arm with healing herbs and raw honey. Although he'd lost a considerable amount of blood, he was both conscious and coherent. She was now treating the minor injuries of Lancelot's other soldiers as the White Knight gave orders to his men.

He informed Tristan, "We'll bring four dozen with us to Landuc, to train with the Tribe and Esclados' knights. We'll defend the castle—and Issylte—from Frocin and his legion of dwarves." He flashed her his brilliant boyish grin. She smiled gratefully in return as she finished tending the wounded and began packing up her supplies. A cold chill shivered up her spine.

Once again, I must flee the wicked queen.
But soon, I'll be able to fight back.
With Tristan, Lancelot, and the Tribe at my side.

"We'll train rigorously until the remaining leaders of the Tribe join us in June." Lancelot turned to Tristan. "We'll coordinate and strategize. Decide our best plan of attack."

The next morning, their provisions loaded, the fallen soldiers honorably buried in tribute, the *château* secured by five dozen knights, Lancelot led Tristan, Issylte, Darius, and approximately fifty soldiers east through the dense woods of Bretagne to Castle Landuc.

To the sanctity and safety of the sacred Forest of Brocéliande.

And the legendary Tribe of Dana.

Chapter 8

La Fée des Ombres

The porous walls sweltered with moisture, the dank, fecund scent of the ancient forest permeating the hidden recesses of the dark limestone cave. A knight lit a torch in the embedded wall sconce as two others laid the unconscious victim upon the enormous flat stone, binding his wrists and ankles with ropes, securing them to the thick wooden stakes hammered into the earthen floor. She would be coming soon, for it was the vernal equinox. His Mistress would be hungry. And Frocin, her faithful servant, never failed.

The baron was stirring, groaning as his senses returned, struggling against his restraints. Frocin regarded him with a beady black stare, his yellowed teeth gleaming in the firelight. The victim's eyes widened in fright as he realized his plight. There would be no escape. Frocin snickered in wicked glee.

With a jerk of his head, the hideous dwarf dismissed his three loyal knights, who scrambled to escape the sinister shadows of the ominous cave. The victim writhed and grappled on the stone slab, his wrists and ankles bloody and raw. *My Mistress will smell the blood. She will be most pleased with this one, for he is strong as an ox. He will fight valiantly to the very end.*

Frocin's bones reverberated with the tremors of her

approach. His skin tingled, the electrified air within the cave sparking with energy, lifting his wiry black hair in a dark cloud around his misshapen head. Soon, the sinuous wisps and twisting tendrils of *la Fée des Ombres*—the Shadow Fairy—emerged from the rotting bowels of the cave, descending in a hovering gloom over the doomed victim.

Noxious black swirls slithered up the restrained baron's nose, into his open mouth and down his rasping throat. He gasped and choked, thrashing in vain as he tried to dispel the smothering shadows that seeped into his eyes and ears. Moaning in pain and fear, he fought with every ounce of strength against the intangible darkness that suffocated him slowly.

Every evil pore in Frocin's wizened body awakened to the anguish. Hopping with glee, he licked his cracked lips in anticipatory delight with his long, blackened tongue.

"Use the knife, Frocin. Slice open his skin, that I may absorb his rich red blood as it flows out upon the altar. But slowly. His shrieks of agony will nourish me as much as his ebbing life force."

The sacrificial blade lay at the base of the stone altar. Frocin lifted the weapon, its iron crossguard rusted with dried blood, the cutting edge of each side sharpened to the finely tapered point.

And, as he had done for every solstice and equinox for nearly ten years, Frocin sacrificed a living victim to sate his most insatiable mistress.

La Fée des Ombres, whose dark power intensified each time.

Several hours later, when the victim had at last expired, Malfleur purred in satisfaction like a gloriously glutted cave cat, hovering contentedly above the stone altar where she'd absorbed every last drop of sacrificial blood. Frocin dragged the baron's desiccated body deep into the cave, leaving it to decompose among the others, returning to the gleaming stone slab for his reward. His body stirred painfully in anticipation. Because Malfleur sated him unlike any human female he'd ever had.

Even the nubile daughters that the poor, desperate farmers had blindly entrusted to him, unable to feed another mouth and naively believing that the dwarf would find suitable husbands for the fee they paid him, considerably less expensive than a dowry. Frocin had enjoyed their delicious young bodies before selling them for bags of silver to wealthy lords eager to purchase a slave to satisfy their unbridled lust.

And thus, little by little, Frocin had accumulated enormous wealth. Because of his mistress. Malfleur.

He'd first met *la Fée des Ombres* ten years ago, when he'd been hunting in the nearby Forest of Morois. One of the rabbits he'd snared had still been alive, squealing in terror and pain. As he'd lifted the pitiful creature caught in the trap, Frocin had felt an inexplicable pull from the rocky cliff nearby. His prey in hand, he'd advanced toward the forested ledge and discovered the mouth to an unknown hidden cave. Pulsations had swept over him, inexplicably drawing him inside.

As he'd entered the cavern, barely visible in the dim morning light, a female voice had called to him, beckoning him to follow the sinuous path into the darkest recess of the cave. Intrigued, he'd ventured forth, cautiously creeping down the dank corridor until he'd come to an inner chamber, where barely perceptible shadows had floated like wisps of smoke over an enormous, flat stone slab.

Tightly clutched within his gnarled hand, the dying rabbit had been writhing and shrieking in agony, caught in the metal snare, its blood dripping steadily onto the loamy cavern floor.

"Kill the rabbit with your dagger. Upon the sacrificial altar." Malfleur's velvety voice had been seductive. Sultry. Sinister.

Frocin had trembled in her murky presence. Transfixed and terrified. Enthralled and thrilled. Ensnared like the writhing rabbit in his mangled, misshapen fist.

So, he'd sacrificed the pathetic creature. Slowly. And watched in rapture as *la Fée des Ombres* had hovered over the body, exalting in the squeals of terror and torture, absorbing the flow of blood, strengthening her shadowy essence with his morbid gift of life.

Frocin's malevolent mistress had rewarded him with the *otherworldly* power of clairvoyance. Enabling him to see the poor families struggling with an extra mouth to feed. A beautiful, pouty mouth perfect for satisfying lusty lords.

He'd been able to see the wealthy, aggrieved nobles seeking vengeance. Those needing a swift, silent assassin's blade to eliminate an adversary. Frocin had profited from his exceptional gift, becoming affluent enough to amass an army of ruthless mercenary knights. Wealthy enough to purchase the magnificent Fortress of Morois. A huge stone castle nestled deep in the enchanted woods.

Near his insatiable mistress. *La Fée des Ombres.* Malfleur.

He'd begun by sacrificing small animals. Rabbits, birds, lambs. Then, as Malfleur had gained in strength and power, he'd progressed to larger animals. Deer, wolves, bears. Harder to trap, but Frocin had discovered poisoned darts which he could shoot from a mouthpiece into his prey. He'd coat the sharp, pointed tips with Valerian root, an herbal drug which would render the victims unconscious. So that his knights could drag the bodies into the shadowy cave and secure them to the altar, tying them to the stakes he'd had them drive into the earthen cave floor.

The victims would wake up terrified. Struggle to break free. And die in exquisite agony. To sate his most insatiable mistress. Who always rewarded him most handsomely.

For the past two years, Frocin had doubly profited from his clairvoyance, simultaneously feeding his voracious mistress while satisfying his wealthy, paying customers. Eliminating his clients' troublesome enemies. And sacrificing them to the greedy *Fée des Ombres.*

And now, he stood trembling before the sacrificial altar where the Shadow Fairy would give him the exquisite *otherworldly* reward that satisfied his wizened, hideous body unlike anything in the mortal realm.

Frocin dropped his filthy breeches and lay upon his twisted back on top of the sacrificial stone. And shivered with preternatural delight as the wispy shadows slithered sensually over him. And descended deliciously upon his painfully engorged flesh.

Later, when he was finally able to stand on weakened, wobbly legs, his sated loins glowing with the vestiges of unearthly pleasure, Malfleur's seductive voice whispered in his pointed, puckered ears.

"I have sensed a sinister power aligned with you, Frocin. A malevolent presence in the distant Hazelwood Forest, far across the Celtic Sea. Tell me, my most loyal servant, what dark aura calls to me?"

Frocin stood humbly before Malfleur, his gnarled hands bent in supplication. "The wizard Voldurk, my mistress. A former Archdruid who studied with the famed Merlin. In the enchanted Forest of Brocéliande." The dwarf wiped his sweaty brow and tried to calm his quaking limbs. "I have formed an alliance with him. And with the Black Widow Queen he serves. Queen Morag of Ireland—the betrothed of our very own King Marke of Cornwall." Frocin's beady eyes searched the dark shadows, terrified that he might have displeased his malevolent mistress. He knew all too well what evil she was capable of. He'd witnessed it countless times in this very cave.

Frocin's raspy voice hissed like a distressed snake. "Queen Morag and Lord Voldurk are sailing here from the Hazelwood Forest, accompanied by their royal entourage and palace guards. They shall be my guests in the Fortress of Morois. Until the betrothal is formalized later this summer." Frocin's stomach lurched as Malfleur wrapped sinuous shadows around his putrid body.

Caressing him. Coaxing him. Choking him.

Her sultry, sinister voice slithered down his twisted spine.

"In ten years, you have never failed me, Frocin. Every equinox and solstice, you have nourished me. Satisfied me. Strengthened me." Waves of sensuous pleasure rippled through Frocin's loins.

"This summer solstice, you will bring me the wizard

Lord Voldurk. I wish to offer him extraordinary power. For a service that requires his dark magic to perform. Do not fail me, Frocin. Bring me a human sacrifice. One as delicious as tonight's tasty baron. And deliver this wizard Voldurk. I will reward you most handsomely, my loyal dwarf."

Frocin quivered in ecstasy as sensuous shadows sluiced over him. He collapsed onto the slab, his seed spewing forth, spilling into his soiled breeches. When he could at last speak, he croaked like a horny toad.

"At your command, my mistress. It shall be done. I, Frocin, never fail."

La Fée des Ombres floated off ephemerally into the darkness.

Into the deep, dank recesses of the hidden cave.

The ominous nether land of the magnificent, malevolent Malfleur.

Chapter 9

Le Miroir Aux Fées

Tristan, Lancelot, and Issylte arrived at Castle
Landuc with an injured Darius and four dozen knights
from *la Joyeuse Garde*. Lancelot had sent a messenger
ahead to inform Esclados and Laudine of the attack by
Frocin's men on his *château* and the need to seek
protection in a more heavily fortified castle. He'd also
conveyed that they would be transporting a seriously
wounded knight, so that the Lord and Lady of the
Fountain would have time to prepare a room for Darius.

At the riders' approach, the watchtower guards
lowered the drawbridge so that the travelers could cross
the moat and enter the castle bailey. Lancelot's men
handed their horses to the stable grooms and followed
Agrane, the First Knight of Landuc, to the soldiers' lodge
so they could settle into their new quarters. Kirus and
Dagur helped Lancelot and Tristan bring Darius into the
room that had been prepared for his convalescence. They
removed his boots and eased him into the bed. Then, with
a nod from Issylte, they left with Esclados and headed
for their respective rooms. Laudine was waiting for
Issylte by a table under the window, where she'd
arranged various herbal remedies for Darius' care.

Laudine hugged her in welcome, then gestured to
the tabletop. "I've placed several herbs here for you to

use, should you need them for Darius. I also have my *verrière*—a greenhouse with walls of glass where I cultivate herbs year-round. If you need anything, just let me know."

Issylte squeezed Laudine's hands in gratitude. "Thank you. For everything." She smiled affectionately at the Priestess of Dana, then lit a beeswax candle and burned some sage to purify the air in the room. She and Laudine cleansed Darius' wound with calendula soap and herbs, then added a yarrow poultice and raw honey, bandaging his arm with fresh strips of linen. The long ride had taken its toll on him; he drank some of the sacred water of the Fountain of Barenton, then drifted off easily to restorative sleep.

Once Darius was settled, Laudine led Issylte to the kitchen nook where members of the Tribe were gathered around two rectangular tables, drinking tea, ale, and mead. Adjacent to the servants' area, the cozy alcove was much smaller than the enormous banquet hall on the opposite side of the kitchen, where meals were served for the entire castle.

Afternoon light from a large window in the stone wall shone upon the tables nestled under wooden ceiling beams made of sturdy golden oak. The savory aroma of freshly baked bread and oatcakes, the sweet smell of honey and berries, and the tangy scent of dried herbs greeted Issylte as she entered the welcoming room. Tristan's deep blue eyes met hers as he stood and offered her the chair next to his. She flashed him a grateful smile and sat down beside him as Laudine offered her a soothing cup of chamomile tea. *Tatie's tisane,* Issylte thought lovingly as she sipped the delicious herbal brew.

"The rest of the Tribe will be arriving at the summer

solstice to report on their readiness for battle," Esclados said, washing a mouthful of oatcake with a hearty gulp of ale. "In the meantime, we'll continue training each day, alternating the guards so they're always well rested and alert, should Frocin try to attack again. With our outer and inner walls, moat, and watchtowers all around the perimeter, we're well protected here at Landuc. And now that you have brought four dozen additional knights, Lancelot, we have more than enough soldiers to repel any aggression. And defend Issylte from the wicked queen." Esclados' white teeth gleamed in the sunlight, sparkling against his deep, dark skin. She returned his warm smile, her spirit shining with gratitude.

Nolwenn, seated beside Kirus, spoke next. "We priestesses also train every day, Issylte. You are welcome to join us. Lysara is an excellent archer; she can help you continue the training you recently began at *la Joyeuse Garde* with Tristan." Nolwenn glanced at the Blue Knight, then added hastily, "In addition to your continued training with him, of course." She grinned conspiratorially at Tristan, then smiled at Kirus, who wrapped his arm possessively around her, pulling her close against his chest.

The petite Lysara, nestled snugly under Solzic's burly blond shoulder, sat up to speak to Issylte. "This is Bahja, our newest priestess," she said brightly, indicating a beautiful woman with dark brown skin and long, sleek black hair. "She came to us three months ago, when she escaped a slave ship that had docked in Le Havre, at the mouth of the Seine River leading to Paris. Bahja is from Morocco, like Idris, a warrior you'll meet in June, when he arrives from Aquitaine, a region in the south of France near Spain."

Issylte and Bahja smiled at each other in greeting as Lysara added, "Bahja is highly skilled with knives, which is how she escaped. She slit her captor's throat, dressed in his clothes, and stole his silver, which she used to buy a horse. She'd heard of the Priestesses of Dana from the herbal healers in Morocco, so she rode here seeking shelter. Dressed as a man, she stopped at *le Mont-Saint-Michel* along the way, posing as a pilgrim seeking a bed and a meal. Since her arrival, we've been teaching her to become a healer. And she's been honing our skill with knives. You'll learn quite a bit from Bahja." Lysara grinned from ear to ear as she met the amber eyes of the dark-skinned beauty. A chorus of verdant magic sung in Issylte's hopeful heart.

****

Over the next few weeks, Issylte tended to Darius, whose wound was healing well, then trained rigorously with Tristan, who continued developing her self-defense techniques, skill with the sword, and accuracy with the bow and arrow. Their training sessions always left her quivering with desire from being held in his arms.

At long last, she was ready.

And anxious to show him.

If they could ever find time alone together.

After their morning practice, Tristan always left to train with Lancelot, Kirus, and the Tribe. Issylte sparred frequently with Nolwenn, who was exceptionally talented with the sword. The amethyst-eyed priestess admired the craftsmanship and beauty of *Emeraldfire* as Issylte demonstrated the maneuvers Tristan had taught her. And added a few of her own through Nolwenn's expertise.

She trained with Lysara as well, whose skill as an

archer helped Issylte acquire finesse with the bow and quiver of arrows that Tristan had gifted her. With Bahja, who taught all of the priestesses—including Laudine—how to wield or hurl knives for self-defense, Issylte dramatically improved her handling of *Émeraude,* the dagger Tristan had given her last year when she'd first arrived at *la Joyeuse Garde.*

And, as spring bloomed in the forest of Brocéliande, so did Issylte's strength and skill as a warrior.

And her intense, undeniable attraction to the handsome Blue Knight of Cornwall.

****

She'd ridden with Tristan several times to *le Miroir aux Fées,* hoping to discover what lay hidden in its shimmery depths. To no avail. But she'd spotted quite a few wild plums growing near the shore of the lake. So today, while Tristan and Lancelot sparred nearby, Issylte picked the sweet fruit that she and Laudine would use to prepare a few *tartes aux mirabelles* for the Tribe.

As Issylte harvested the plums, placing them in her woven basket, she felt a magnetic pulse from the mirrored lake.

Awakening her magic.

Calling to her.

Beckoning.

Inexplicably compelled, she knelt by the water's edge, hoping a *sighting* might reveal what lay hidden in *le Miroir aux Fées.*

The sacred object she was meant to protect. Which made her magic sing.

On trembling knees, she leaned over and gazed into the dark blue depths of the mirrored lake.

The *otherworldly* stillness heightened her senses as

she slowed her breathing and emptied her thoughts to focus on the sacred element of water. As she crouched, waiting for the familiar darkness to surround her, she instead felt an ominous premonition. The forest was warning her of imminent danger.

At that moment, she spotted on the surface of the lake the gnarled, wizened skin and black, ratty hair of the dwarf she had glimpsed in the *sighting* with Gwennol. Before Issylte could react, he was upon her, a dagger at her throat, his other arm around her waist, pinning her from behind.

"You're *mine* now," he drooled, slowly licking her neck and the left side of her face with his blackened tongue. His putrid breath poisoned the air as he panted in her good ear. "You taste *delicious,*" he moaned, sighing with pleasure as he rubbed himself against her backside. Issylte shuddered at the hardness that poked at her. The dwarf tore open her bodice, roughly groping, cupping, and squeezing her breasts with his calloused, deformed hand. A thin trickle of blood flowed down Issylte's neck from the steely tip of his sharp blade.

"Before I deliver you to Voldurk, I think I'll have a taste of what's between your pretty legs." He reached down to feel under her skirts, probing her tender skin with dry, crusty fingers as he thrust himself against her. Issylte realized with horror that he was lifting her dress to expose her bare bottom.

"We dwarves are mocked for being *small,*" he sneered, pressing his hardness against her soft skin, "yet our spears are *enormous.*" As he pulled her skirts up over her exposed hips, he crooned, "And my spear wants to pierce your lovely flesh. It has been a long time since it has sampled feminine softness."

Panic struck Issylte as the dwarf was positioning himself to mount her. In her crouched position, she was on all fours, making herself especially vulnerable to his attack.

Think. Remember the defensive moves Tristan taught you. You must break free from his hold!

As the dwarf moved his arm to fiddle with the opening of his pants and extricate himself, Issylte seized the moment of the subtle loosening of his grip and shift in his attention.

She quickly smashed his face with the back of her head, leaning away from the dagger, as she simultaneously pushed it away from her neck with such force that it was flung into the lake. With her other arm, she jabbed him in the ribs, concentrating all her strength into her elbow, as Tristan had taught her.

The dwarf was thrown backward into a sitting position on the ground, his legs hindered by his lowered pants. Issylte sprang to her feet, using the momentum to deliver a semicircular kick, swinging her boot with all her strength as she landed a savage, sickening thud directly into his left temple.

Swiftly, she unsheathed *Émeraude* from its strap at her ankle, and while the dwarf lay on the ground, momentarily stunned and immobile, she slashed his throat without hesitation, leaving him gurgling and choking on his own blood, which pooled and seeped into the black earth near the water's edge.

Tristan and Lancelot burst through the woods into the clearing. Issylte's bodice was torn, her breasts exposed, her neck bleeding, her hair disheveled. She was gasping for breath, clutching the blood-soaked dagger, swaying uneasily beside the mutilated corpse of the dwarf. Tristan ran to her, but she swiveled aside abruptly, dropped her knife, and collapsed to her knees. Overwhelmed with what had nearly transpired, and the fact that she had for the first time killed a living being, Issylte vomited beside a large rock, heaving and sobbing with terror, rage, and shock.

When she had finally finished retching, she wiped her mouth with the bottom of her ruined dress, then covered herself as best she could with what was left of the tattered bodice. Tristan approached her slowly, then gently wrapped his arms around her. Issylte buried her face in his chest, weeping wretchedly and soaking his tunic. Her entire body was shaking uncontrollably. Tristan cocooned her in his strong embrace.

"He was going to rape me," she choked, quavering in his arms. "He had me pinned, with a dagger at my throat. He tore my dress, groped my body…"

Tristan stroked her hair soothingly her as he whispered, "Shhh… It's over now. He's dead. He cannot harm you." He rocked her in his arms to calm her tremors. Gently lifting her chin to meet his gaze, he said, his deep voice strong and clear, "You did well in defending yourself. I am very proud of you, Issylte." He kissed her forehead, then cradled her in his arms.

Lancelot examined the corpse of the dwarf.

"That was Malvon," the White Knight informed them. "One of Frocin's band." Lancelot peered into the trees, inspecting the woods all around them. "But he was alone. This was not an attack on Landuc." He stared pensively at the glassy surface of *le Miroir aux Fées*. "Laudine said the dwarves have been seen searching the Forest of Brocéliande." He looked pointedly at Tristan. "Hunting for something." His concerned gaze focused on

Issylte. "Attacking the priestesses."

Her heart was still pounding furiously, her legs shaking uncontrollably. "The dwarf said he was going to deliver me to Voldurk." She shivered violently, shuddering at the memory of the vile tongue, groping hands, and hardened body against hers. The yellow snakelike eyes of the wizard, watching her, a python poised to strike.

"Let's return to the castle," Lancelot suggested, his gentle voice soothing. "You've had a terrible shock, and we need to inform the others. Issylte…" he said, his vibrant blue eyes full of relief and compassion, "you did well today. You defended not only yourself, but the sacred forest and the Mirrored Lake. The Tribe will be very pleased. Like the Goddess Herself."

Tristan helped her into the saddle atop *Minuit*, then wrapped his cloak around her. Mounting *Aiglon,* he and Lancelot, atop his white destrier *Gringolet*, escorted her back through the woods to the castle of Landuc.

Once they were safely inside the *château,* Laudine tenderly bathed Issylte, washing away all traces of the vile dwarf Malvon with the sacred waters of the Fountain of Barenton, her *églantine* scented soap, and comforting voice. The Lady of the Spring brushed Issylte's hair, plaiting two small sections along her face with golden thread and guelder rose blossoms, one of the many plants she cultivated in her lush *verrière.*

Satisfied with her handiwork, Laudine led Issylte to the alcove near the kitchen where Tristan and Lancelot sat at the table with several members of the Tribe. Seating Issylte beside Tristan, Laudine returned with a cup of *tisane,* just as Maiwenn had done so many times in the Hazelwood Forest. The chamomile tea warmed

Issylte's body as her spirit basked again in the memory of her beloved *Tatie*. She felt safe now, surrounded by friends who cared for and protected her. *Thank the Goddess Tristan taught me how to defend myself.* Indeed, the self-defense techniques she'd practiced so many times with him had saved her life today.

Laudine sat down across from Issylte at the table, between Esclados and Nolwenn. The amethyst gaze of the raven-haired priestess flooded Issylte with a healing aura of calm and peace.

"Issylte has defended the sacred waters of the Goddess Dana in protecting *le Miroir aux Fées* from the dwarf Malvon." Laudine spoke reverently to the members of the Tribe, some of whom were seated at the table, with others gathered around them, leaning against the walls of the sheltered alcove. Esclados' wife faced Issylte, her expression eager. Issylte's pulse quickened, seeking Tristan's fierce blue gaze. The soothing waters of Cornwall washed her in waves of calm.

"The Priestesses of the Tribe of Dana are the guardians of Her sacred waters," Laudine said in a voice hushed with reverence, her shining eyes glinting in the golden light of the setting sun. "We are charged with defending and protecting Her most precious resource."

Laudine took Issylte's trembling hand and gazed knowingly at her. "I am the Lady of the Fountain, the guardian of the sacred spring of Barenton." Laudine indicated Lysara, seated beside Solzic. "Lysara defends *la Cascade du Serein*, the Waterfall of the Fairies, near *le Lac Diane*, the sacred waters for which the fairy Viviane was named the Lady of the Lake." The Lady of the Fountain smiled at the amethyst-eyed priestess seated beside Kirus, the leader of the Tribe. "And Nolwenn protects *la Fontaine de Notre-Dame,* a sacred spring in the Forest of Brocéliande."

The three Priestesses of Dana seated in the alcove smiled knowingly at Issylte, their luminous eyes welcoming and enchanting. Bahja, on the other side of Solzic, remained silent, rapt with attention, her amber gaze gilded in the warm sunlight.

"Since you defended the sacred lake from the vile Malvon," Laudine announced proudly to Issylte, "I propose that you become *la Dame du Miroir aux Fées.* The Lady of the Mirrored Lake." She reached across the table and squeezed Issylte's damp hand. "Priestess of the Tribe of Dana."

The wings of a white dove fluttered in Issylte's heart as magic soared in her veins.

Her breath hitched at the prospect of joining the Tribe. Becoming a Priestess of the Goddess Dana. She looked at Tristan, his proud gaze the brilliant turquoise of the ocean shimmering above his glorious grin.

Welcomed by the sisterhood of the women whose smiles beckoned. Surrounded by the warriors who would take up arms and fight with her against the evil queen. Fortified by Tristan's strength at her side. Issylte indicated her assent and exhaled with reverence, "I would be honored to join the Tribe."

Praise and encouragement circled the table as the members of the Tribe prepared to welcome a new priestess.

"Tonight, you will rest and recuperate from today's ordeal. Tomorrow morning, after breaking your fast, Nolwenn will inscribe our mark inside your right wrist." Laudine extended her arm, showing Issylte the Celtic trio of spirals representing the three sacred elements of the

Goddess. Issylte met Nolwenn's amethyst gaze. The black-haired priestess took Issylte's hand and squeezed it warmly as she flashed an encouraging smile.

The Lady of the Fountain whispered to Issylte, a hint of excitement in her hushed voice, "As my husband did for Tristan, I plan to bestow a special Druidic gift upon *you* tomorrow night at the initiation ceremony." Issylte gaped at Laudine in astonishment. "Part of Issylte's gift will be added to the ink for her tattoo," Laudine informed Nolwenn. "I'll show you in a few moments, after the Tribe has retired for the evening."

Nolwenn smiled enigmatically at Issylte, whose pulse was racing with anticipation of tomorrow's ceremony.

I will become a Priestess and member of the Tribe of Dana.

The Lady of the Mirrored Lake.

Then, with a pointed look at Tristan, Laudine announced—her voice aglow and her face alight with promise—"And you, Tristan, will perform the *conclusion* of the ceremony."

He grinned from ear to ear as Issylte smiled inquisitively back at him, perplexed and curious. *What will he do to conclude the ceremony? From the look on his face, it must be something special. I can't wait!*

The next morning, Nolwenn led Issylte away from the table where the members of the Tribe were breaking their fast. As she followed the tattoo artist away from the dining alcove, she—the Emerald Princess of Ireland—flashed a bright smile, filled with excitement and anticipation, at the alluring Blue Knight of Cornwall. *Soon, I will belong to the Tribe like you, Tristan.* His handsome face beamed back at her with pride and delight.

Nolwenn's room was bright, airy, and clean. The tangy fragrance of fresh herbs welcomed Issylte, and a gentle spring breeze fluttered the white gauzy drapes which framed the opened windows. The priestess helped Issylte remove her outer gown, then laid her down upon a long table resembling a bed, draped in the same white cloth as the windows.

On the small table next to the bed, Issylte spotted a container of green liquid, another of black liquid, two long needles, and several vials of herbal tinctures or oils. A fragrant candle burned on a separate table near the wall, alongside a pitcher, basin, and cup. The clean aroma of sage wafted in the morning wind.

Over the next few hours, as Nolwenn inscribed the mark of a Priestess of Dana upon her wrist, Issylte listened to the same wonders of the Forest of *Brocéliande* that had enchanted Tristan. When the artist was at last finished, satisfied with her work, she carefully anointed some essential oils, enhanced with cleansing herbs, onto Issylte's tender wrist. "This will help alleviate the sting and enable your skin to heal more quickly. It also helps set the ink, so the image remains clear." Tenderly, she massaged the oil into Issylte's wrist and arm.

Then, as Issylte donned her gown, Nolwenn cleaned her tools, stopped up the vials of tinctures, and stored everything back in place. Facing Issylte, she smiled and said warmly, "Let's eat a small meal before joining the others at the clearing. They'll be waiting for you at the sacred well of Barenton. I'll escort you there after we eat. Come, let's go to the kitchen."

The late May twilight was descending by the time

the two women finished their *potage* and bread. A groom had saddled *Minuit* and a horse for Nolwenn; he was waiting for the women in front of the *château.*

On horseback, Nolwenn led Issylte to the heart of the forest of Brocéliande, where the members of the Tribe were seated around a campfire before the sacred Fountain of Barenton. After the two women dismounted, Kirus took their horses away as Laudine emerged from the trees to welcome Issylte. Nolwenn joined the other members of the Tribe seated around the campfire. Issylte spotted many smiling faces. Kirus, Dagur, Lancelot, and Darius. Lysara, Solzic, and Bahja.

Tristan's intense gaze blazed into hers. She stood transfixed, her legs quivering, her hands shaking. Wings of a white dove fluttered in her heart.

Laudine announced the purpose for the gathering in the forest. "Welcome, members of the Tribe of Dana. Tonight, we shall induct a new priestess." Smiling warmly at Issylte, the Lady of the Fountain took her hand, ushering the inductee to her side. Issylte stood before the group, in front of the stoned wall which enclosed the well of the sacred spring. The same well glimpsed in the vision when she'd first gazed into Tristan's eyes.

"The Princess Issylte, daughter of the late King Donnchadh of Ireland and heir to his throne," Laudine continued, "successfully defended the sacred lake, *le Miroir aux Fées*, from the evil dwarf Malvon." Comments of praise rippled through the Tribe. "As a reward for her valor in defending the sacred waters of the Goddess, Issylte of Ireland will be inducted into our Tribe. And become a Priestess of Dana."

Laudine's lyrical voice resounded through the

forest. "Issylte, daughter of King Donnchadh of Ireland, Priestess and Healer of Avalon, do you solemnly swear to defend and protect the sacred waters of *Le Miroir aux Fées*...as a holy Priestess of the Tribe of Dana...and Lady of the Mirrored Lake?"

Her voice strong and clear despite her trembling limbs and quaking body, Issylte replied firmly: "I do so solemnly swear."

"Drink from the waters of *le Miroir aux Fées* that you so valiantly defended. May the sacred Mirrored Lake infuse within you the divine protection of the Goddess as you become a Priestess of the Tribe of Dana."

Issylte accepted the proffered cup from Laudine and drank deeply from the silver chalice.

"And, in recompense for your bravery in defending the sacred *Miroir aux Fées,* I shall bestow upon you the Druidic gift...of *Rose Elder.*"

The Lady of the Fountain then led Issylte to kneel before the sacred well.

At that moment, an archdruid emerged from the trees of the sacred forest, barefoot and clad in a holy white robe. Bowing before the Tribe, then to Laudine, he placed a parcel, wrapped in white cloth, on the flat stone surface beside the well of the spring.

The Druid unwrapped his treasure with great reverence, revealing plants and herbs, pink and white blossoms from delicate flowers, and a handful of tiny red berries. Using a mortar and pestle, he ground the flowers and the berries, adding a few drops from the challis of the sacred waters of *le Miroir aux Fées* that Laudine had served Issylte.

Withdrawing a golden sickle from inside his white

robe, the archdruid meticulously scraped the plants that had been wrapped in his parcel. Adding the contents and a pinch of herbs to the mixture of ground blossoms and berries, he then blended the potion, muttering an incantation under his breath, pouring his creation into the liquid of the silver chalice.

When the concoction was blended to his satisfaction, the archdruid approached Issylte, who was still kneeling before the sacred spring. He extended the goblet to her, his voice resounding over the whole Tribe. "Issylte of Ireland, imbibe the magic of *Rose Elder:* a blend of the sacred elder tree and the divine essence of the guelder rose flower." As Issylte drank the potion, the Celtic priest continued his incantation.

"The Elder tree is highly venerated among Druids, for its essence defends against darkness. It undoes evil magic and protects when walking between worlds. The power of *Rose Elder* peaks during the vernal equinox— the period which marks the flow of death and rebirth between the worlds. During the winter solstice, when darkness threatens to overwhelm light, the protective spirit of *Rose Elder* will ward against evil and defend that which is good and pure."

Standing before the princess who remained kneeling before him, her head bowed in reverence, the Druid touched Issylte's head as he bestowed upon her Laudine's magic gift of *Rose Elder*. "I have blended a sacred flower—the guelder rose—with the essence of the elder tree in creating this gift of Druidic magic for you." Odin lifted her chin. His eyes, crinkled with wisdom, gazed into hers.

"The guelder rose represents the three faces of the Goddess Herself. Its pink and white blossoms, delicate and pure, represent the face of the Maiden. The red berries are the ripe, fertile fruit of the mother. And the black dye, obtained from the stalk of the flower, represents the wisdom of the Crone. It lies in the ink of the tattoo which marks you as a Priestess of the Goddess."

Taking her hand, he rotated her wrist to reveal the trio of curved arms—the Celtic trinity—swirled in a protective embrace of the three sacred elements of the Goddess Dana. The archdruid traced the black dye of the guelder rose flower that Nolwenn had used in creating Issylte's beautiful tattoo. "The guelder rose will warn you of incoming danger and defend you against attack. Any evil spell cast upon you will be blocked. The elemental power of the sacred Elder tree, combined with the natural essence of the guelder rose, shall envelop you with the divine protection of the Goddess."

He raised Issylte to her feet as Laudine approached the two of them. Bowing at the waist, a gesture of respect which the Lady of the Fountain and Issylte humbly returned, the Druid strode back to the flat stone beside the well to wash the chalice and replace it on the branch of the sacred tree, then retrieved his sickle and white cloth parcel. As Laudine led Issylte to face the members of the Tribe seated around the fire, the white robed priest silently retreated into the woods.

"Let us welcome our newest member: Issylte, *La Dame du Miroir aux Fées.* The Lady of the Mirrored Lake. Priestess of the Tribe of Dana."

Smiling faces beamed at her as the members of the Tribe applauded and cheered.

The voices subdued as Laudine raised her hands. "When a warrior is inducted, a priestess—representing the embodiment of the Goddess—welcomes him into Her Tribe." Smiling at Issylte, the newly welcomed priestess, Laudine cast her grin toward Tristan. His hungry eyes devoured Issylte, his feral face ravenous and fierce.

"When a new priestess is inducted, a warrior is selected *to worship the Goddess* within her." Laudine beckoned Tristan, who rose to his feet, all the while staring expectantly at Issylte, his intense eyes aflame. Issylte's legs trembled under her gown. Laudine, her auburn hair glowing in the firelight, announced, "Tristan will complete the final step in your induction into our Tribe."

Holding her gaze with his mesmerizing blue eyes, Tristan strode confidently up to Issylte. The warrior who would welcome her into the Tribe of Dana. Issylte's mouth went dry, her legs quivering at his approach. Power emanated from him, a magnetic aura that beckoned with promise. And made her magic sing.

Taking Issylte by the hand, he led her away from the campfire, through the woods, to the shore of *le Miroir aux Fées.* A shroud of mist enclosed a grassy area near the lake upon which was spread a large white cloth. A small fire crackled nearby, encircled by smooth gray stones. A short distance from the fire, but still within the veil of mist, lay a large flat stone upon which stood two silver goblets and a small vial. All around the perimeter of the enclosed area lay a protective grid of crystals, thrumming with enchantment, glittering in the moonlight, sparkling with starlight.

Leading Issylte inside the circle of mist, Tristan lifted the two goblets, handed one to her, and toasted, "Let us drink to Dana, the Goddess of the Earth." His eyes smoldered like the flames of the nearby fire. "The Goddess whom I will now worship through you, Issylte. Completing your induction into Her Tribe."

The wine was rich, heady, and earthy, spreading a glow of warmth throughout her entire body. Tristan stood before her, powerful and majestic, his strong jaw covered with dark stubble, his mouth parted with the hint of a smile, his eyes radiating welcome and desire.

"I have longed to do this *for months*, Issylte—ever since I first saw you in Avalon." He drank deeply from the wine, stepping so close to her that his breath touched her face. "When I opened my eyes, I saw your face. The green gaze of a goddess, aglow with golden light."

He took the goblet from her hand, strode over to the flat stone, and placed both chalices on the surface. Pivoting toward her, he removed his tunic, allowing her to drink in the sight of his muscular torso, gloriously covered with thick, dark hair which extended down his taught stomach. Issylte's breath caught in her throat.

Tristan laid his chemise on the surface of the stone, then returned to her. He gently removed her deep green velvet gown and placed it on top of the stone next to his tunic. Taking her by the hand, he led Issylte to the edge of the white cloth, extended on the ground before them.

He took the small vial from the top of the flat stone, opened it, and poured a couple drops of oil onto his fingers. Gently, softly, he massaged the tincture into the sensitive area on her inner wrist, where the green and black tattoo marked her as a priestess of Dana.

"This will soothe your skin and help it heal," he whispered into the shell of her left ear, brushing his lips against the side of her face. He replaced the stopper on the vial, put the small flask back on the stone, then returned to stand before her. Issylte's entire body tingled with anticipation.

The fire warmed the air inside the enchanted mist, keeping the evening chill at bay. The dark lake glistened in the moonlight, the steep embankments of the forested ledges surrounding them in a protective embrace. An aura of magic, breathless with discovery.

Tristan, the powerful warrior of Dana, then removed the thin white dress which she wore under her gown, placing it with the discarded clothing on the stone. Returning to stand in front of her, he worshipped her nude body with unabashed yearning in his fierce, enflamed eyes.

"You truly are a goddess, Issylte. A tantalizing, golden green goddess." He lowered his lips to hers in an achingly gentle kiss, then sought her cheeks, her face. Her neck, her shoulders. Ripples of pleasure flowed through her.

He wrapped his arms around her, drawing her against his chest, her bare breasts tingling at the touch of hair and muscle as a muffled whimper escaped her lips.

Tristan grinned slyly as he lowered his lips to her breasts, fully aware of her body's response to his warm, skilled mouth.

"Mmmm," he hummed, suckling first one, then the other, as his hands supported her back. "I have dreamt of doing this to you, Issylte. I have longed to worship your beautiful body…" His words were cut off as he returned to caressing her nipples with his lips and tongue.

Her legs, quivering with desire, could no longer support her weight, and Tristan lowered her gently to lie upon the white cloth. Kneeling at her feet, his hands spread her thighs wide so he could worship every inch of her with his intense blue eyes, burning with adoration and longing.

Issylte's abdomen twitched with anticipation, a hollow ache building deep inside, as she trembled under his gaze.

His eyes met hers, and in the breadth of a moment, a kaleidoscope of images unfurled. A white palace on a cliff, overlooking the sea. A stone cottage in a forest, with the Tribe gathered in a circle. A tattoo, similar to hers, but with subtle differences. A ring, with two round gemstones—an emerald and a blue topaz—swirled together in a band of gold.

In the deep blue pools of Tristan's eyes, Issylte saw a ship sailing from *Bretagne*. A white dove—*it is me, somehow*—flying frantically, desperately clutching something in its beak. A flock of black birds—*sea ravens*—flying with her, the little dove, through the clouds over the open sea. And again, as she had glimpsed in the earlier *sighting* in his deep blue gaze, Issylte beheld the luminous star of the sacred spring in the hidden sea cave. *La Grotte de l'Étoile.*

Tristan lowered his lips to her breasts again, the pleasure of his mouth redirecting the focus of her attention back to her body. Leaving a trail of kisses down her abdomen, he finally tasted her depths as his tongue and lips elicited a guttural moan. He slipped two fingers inside her, lapping with his tongue while thrusting with his hand until she screamed, the pleasure so intense it was nearly unbearable.

"Tristan, please…" she gasped, raising his head with her hands so that he would look at her. "Please. I want you inside of me. *Please.*"

With a feral grin, he rose to his knees, savoring the

taste of her, every pore tingling, his senses heightened preternaturally. His body throbbed with desire, but his ache for her surpassed the physical realm. His *spirit* longed for her; his *mind* sought hers. His entire *being* pulsed with yearning for the very essence of her.

Rising to his feet, he removed his boots, then his breeches, to stand magnificently naked before her, as he had done a year ago in the bathing pool of Avalon. Issylte quickly rose to her knees, whispering "I want to taste you, too," and took him in her mouth. She slipped her tongue between the two halves of the sensitive opening of its tip, tormenting him with desire.

He withdrew himself from her mouth, emblazed with desire, and laid her back down, his breath ragged. Rising to his knees, he slid his hands under her hips, tilted her pelvis up, and thrust deeply inside her with a primal groan.

Issylte wrapped her legs around his back, her arms around his shoulders, pulling him deeper and deeper inside. She lifted her hips to meet his thrusts. He could feel her body tightening, her muscles taut with tension. Like his own. Aching for release.

On the verge of ecstasy, Tristan felt inexplicably compelled to mark her—to claim her as *his*. With the tip of two canine teeth, he pierced a small section of skin at the base of her neck. To his delightful surprise, he felt a nip of pleasure and pain as Issylte marked the same spot on his own.

The salty, luscious taste of her lingered on his tongue, mingling now with the coppery tang of her blood in his mouth. Suddenly—in an instant—images and sensations burst forth. The evergreen fragrance of a forest. *Églantine* flowers and guelder rose blossoms.

Issylte's luminous green gaze exuding a golden, healing light. A stone cottage in a forest, with members of the Tribe sitting in a circle. A ring with blue and green gemstones. A tattoo, different from his, yet similar in Celtic design. A flock of sea ravens flying with a white dove over the vast ocean. And divine light—in the shape of a star—emanating from a fountain, bubbling beneath the waters of a sheltered, hidden sea cave.

The taste of Tristan's seed on her tongue, mingled with the metallic flavor of his blood, awakened every cell in Issylte's body. *"When mates share physical love… and become one…the mating bond is finalized and becomes unbreakable."* Viviane's words flooded her memory.

"When mates join together, becoming one…it is celestial. The physical pleasure and spiritual bliss fill you with unimaginable energy, love, and joy. That, dear princess, is the essence of life…a precious gift from the Goddess…to be treasured above all else."

The waves of pleasure washed over her. Issylte clutched Tristan tightly as he thrust deeply into her, his body shuddering with release. Her rhythmic contractions clamped on him, extracting every drop of his seed, drawing his essence up into hers.

She kissed his neck and shoulders, tracing her tongue around the area where she had claimed him with her mark. Her arms clasped his back, her legs gripped his hips as if she were merging not only her body—but her spirit and soul as well—with his.

Tristan couldn't move, couldn't speak, couldn't breathe. He'd never experienced such an *otherworldly* climax. Not even in the memorable induction ceremony into the Tribe with Nolwenn.

This time, he'd sown his very soul with his seed.

Into Issylte.

His golden green goddess.

He worshipped her—with body, heart, and spirit. He was *joined* with her, two halves of a whole. Lancelot's description of *l'amour fou* came into his mind.

"When you find such a woman, Tristan, the love she gives you fills every empty hollow in your soul. She completes you; she invigorates you; she thrills you. And, when you consummate such a love, the exquisite blend of the spiritual and physical realm will satisfy you more than the finest wine or the greatest victory in battle. The love she gives you with her body will transport you to the stars, and you will never experience a greater joy."

Lancelot was right indeed. Tristan's spirit soared.

Not wanting to crush her with his weight, he slowly eased himself down to lie next to Issylte on the white sheet. Drawing her close with one arm, he bent the other under his head as a cushion.

The stars winked in the dark sky; the waning moon cast a soft glow over them. The fire snapped softly, emitting a comforting warmth like a cocoon. The tang of the lake and the pine scent of the forest enveloped them in Nature's embrace.

He touched the mark he had left on her neck. "I *bit* you. I can't explain why, but I had the undeniable need to mark you—to claim you as *mine*." He kissed the spot on her neck, the taste of her blood sparking his own, making his entire body sing. "When we return to the castle, we'll have Nolwenn ink these marks—to make them *permanent*." He nuzzled her neck, then her breasts, making her moan softly. "I cannot believe how beautiful these are," he said, lavishing attention on them with his soft lips. "Nor can I believe that I have finally—after yearning for you to the point of physical pain—made you *mine* at last."

A tear fell softly down her face as she gazed at him. "You are *my mate*, Tristan." He lay on his back, an arm curled behind his head, while she played with the dark brown hair on his chest. "Viviane told me in Avalon that you and I were *mates,* but I was unsure. Until now." Rising onto her elbow, she kissed his chest, his neck, his lips. "When we made love, I saw images flash in your eyes." She traced her finger along the stubble of his cheek. She kissed his chin, his cheek, his lips.

Her warm lips kindled the flames of fire in his loins. His body stirred in response.

"I saw a ring, a tattoo, a flock of sea ravens…a white castle…" Her fingers roamed across his chest—his body that she had claimed and *marked* as hers. A sea raven soared in his soul.

He sat up enough to wrap his arms behind her neck, pulling her onto his chest, cradling her and kissing her hair. "I saw the same images. And a stone cottage, with the Tribe sitting in a circle." He inhaled her scent, savoring the taste of her on his tongue, wanting her again. *You insatiable bastard.*

She raised her head to look at him. "I saw that, too. And the waters in the cave of *la Grotte de l'Étoile.* On Avalon."

He pulled her on top of him so that he could caress her bottom with light, delicate strokes. She hummed, the reverberations of her voice resonating through his hardened body. Strumming him like a harp, tightening his tension, intensifying his desire.

"I saw the same cave," he said, kissing the side of

her neck, licking the spot where he'd *marked* her. The taste of her blood called to his spirit. "A place I've never been before. I saw a star—a pattern of light—under the water. A fountain, bubbling from a sacred spring. Inside a sea cave."

Issylte twirled the hair on his chest, making little peaks, which she rubbed out with the palm of her hand. Burying her face in the thick hair, she seemed to inhale his scent, as if obeying a primal urge that demanded satisfaction. His body stirred beneath hers, probing and prodding. Pulsing with power. "When I felt the physical pain of the Morholt's blade slice across your stomach in my *sighting*—when I remained unconscious for three days—Viviane told me that only happens between *mates*. And that you were *undoubtedly* mine."

Grinning mischievously, she sat up suddenly, straddled him, and rubbed her tender flesh against him, driving him mad with desire. She leaned down to claim his lips, her hair cascading on either side of him, as she kissed his face, neck, and chest with increasing fervor.

Finally, when he had reached the point of agony, she enveloped him with her warm, lush embrace, sliding down upon his throbbing body, welcoming him home.

When the light of dawn broke over the lake, she lay entwined in his arms, his body curled behind hers protectively. The warrior defending his Dana.

At long last, I have made love with the golden green goddess that my body and spirit have yearned for. I have sown my seed and soul inside her, made my mark upon her elegant neck. I have slept with her, cradled in my loving arms. My heart. My Muse. My mate.

As she awakened, Tristan's body stirred, seeking and probing the entrance between her legs. And, with the sunlight dappling through the sacred trees, he—the valiant warrior of the Tribe of Dana—worshipped his green golden goddess once again.

Their bodies sated—at least for now—they lay together, a tangle of limbs, reluctant to leave their enchanted realm. Tristan propped himself onto his elbow to unabashedly appreciate her nudity, worshipping her beauty with admiring eyes. He kissed her softly.

"I love you, Issylte. With every breadth of my soul. With every beat of my heart. I am *yours*. Now, and forever." His heart soared in the love light shining in her eyes.

"And I love you, Tristan. You are my warrior. My friend. My teacher. The only one who ever *believed* in me. Who promised to *fight* for me. *Beside* me."

Rising onto her knees, she took both of his hands in hers and kissed them. Tears glistening, she whispered, "You gave me weapons. Trained me *to fight*. To defend myself. And *that…*" she choked, gazing at him, "is not only the greatest gift I have ever received. It also saved my life."

She kissed his hands again. "You are helping me *to grow*, Tristan. To *believe in myself*. To face the wicked queen who denies me my birthright. Who killed so many of those I loved. Whose evil threatens us all." Lying down at his side, she laid her head over his pounding heart. He softly stroked her long blonde hair. "You have made me strong, whole, and complete, Tristan. I am totally, utterly, undeniably *yours*."

He held her for a few moments. His wild rose. Then, rising to his feet, Tristan took her hands and pulled her to stand before him. He wrapped his arms around her waist, gazing intently into the deep green eyes of his

Muse.

"*Toi et moi.* So it shall be. You and I are entwined. *Eternally.*"

He kissed her deeply, savoring the last few moments alone together in this sacred, *otherworldly* realm. Reluctantly, he let her go. It was time to return.

They donned their clothes. Tristan doused the fire and retrieved the white cloth, which he shook out and folded over his arm. Issylte collected the gemstones from the protective crystal grid, the two goblets and small vial. Arm in arm, the priestess and the warrior—now eternally joined by their *mating marks* and the finalization of the unbreakable *mating bond*—walked back together to rejoin their fellow members of the Tribe of the Dana.

Eternally entwined.

Chapter 9

Les Fées Dorées

In the clearing of the sacred forest, near the Fountain of Barenton, several members of the Tribe were rousing in their bedrolls, having lingered behind to offer protection to Tristan and Issylte during her induction ceremony. As the couple now emerged from their enchanted shelter on the banks of *le Miroir aux Fées,* Issylte spotted Lancelot, who was extinguishing the campfire and caring for the horses.

When the White Knight saw them approach, his eyes darted to the *mating mark* on the lower left side of each of their necks. He flashed them both a sly grin as he strode over to greet them.

Lancelot leaned down to kiss Issylte's cheeks with *la bise française*, as Maiwenn and Viviane had always done. "You reek of Tristan!" he chortled, a mischievous glint in his eye. He then greeted Tristan with a hearty slap on the shoulder and firm handshake. "It seems you have claimed each other as *mates*," he observed, gesturing to the marks on their necks. "It's about time!" He laughed freely, wrapping an arm around each of their shoulders as they headed toward the campsite clearing near the sacred well.

Kirus, Dagur, and several other members of the Tribe had saddled the horses and were waiting near the fountain. "Everything is ready, Lancelot. Shall we ride to Landuc?"

The White Knight glanced at Tristan, who nodded in agreement. Tristan helped Issylte onto *Minuit*, then mounted *Aiglon* as Lancelot sat astride his white charger *Gringolet*. Kirus, Dagur, Darius, and the others climbed into their saddles and the group headed off together into the Forest of Brocéliande.

They rode back to the Castle of Landuc, where Esclados and Laudine, who had gone home the previous evening after the ceremony, greeted them jovially.

"Welcome back, Priestess of Dana!" Laudine exclaimed, kissing Issylte's cheek as the grooms took the horses to the stables. "Come in, everyone. We have fruit and porridge, meat, and cheese. There's freshly baked bread and plenty of mead to break your fast. Everything is ready for you in the dining area. Enjoy."

Issylte sat next to Tristan, who pulled her close to his side. Lancelot sat down opposite Nolwenn and Kirus—who were sharing an intensely romantic look and satisfied smile. Lysara snuggled with Solzic; he kissed her softly and held her small hand. Eyeing the *mating mark* on Issylte's neck, the petite priestess indicated her approval with a subtle smile, a glint sparking in her dark, twinkling eyes.

As she sampled the crusty bread and sipped the sweet honey mead, Issylte noticed that Kjetil the Viking had arrived from Normandy. He was seated with two other members of the Tribe—Hakon and Erwann—who had just been introduced to her. Issylte observed with a smile that Erwann seemed smitten with Bahja; he couldn't take his eyes off the Moroccan beauty. And Bahja basked in the attention from the burly, bearded

Erwann, smiling coyly at him from the corner of her pleased eye.

Issylte glanced at Tristan, who was watching her eat. His deep blue gaze locked on her tongue as she licked the honey from her lips. A shiver of pleasure rippled through her as he raised his eyes to meet hers. Through the *mating bond* that now joined them, she poured her essence into him and felt his surge in return. Verdant magic flourished in her veins.

The food was delicious, and everyone ate heartily.

Laudine placed a steaming teapot on the table and poured a cup of *tisane* for each priestess, then one for herself. She sat down beside Esclados, across from Issylte. The Lady of the Fountain addressed the members of the Tribe, who listened intently while feasting on the generous buffet.

"Two more dwarves have been seen prowling through our sacred forest," she announced gravely, exchanging wary glances with Kirus, Dagur, and Lancelot. "Bozigan was spotted near *la Cascade du Serein*. And Malgric was seen near *l'Étang des Fées*." She sipped her tea, eyeing the intrigued members of the Tribe. "They are desperate to find something hidden in our sacred waters." Laudine's intense eyes held her gaze. "You, Issylte—blessed by the Goddess with the gift of *sight*—foresaw that a dwarf would seek a valuable object hidden in *le Miroir aux Fées*."

Issylte gulped as she nodded, relieved to feel Tristan's hand reach for hers under the table.

"You also felt compelled to protect the sacred waters. And prevent the dwarf from obtaining the hidden object."

"Yes," Issylte whispered, glancing around the table

to the other members of the Tribe, enthralled by Laudine's words. All eyes were upon her. Issylte's pulse quickened, her palm damp in Tristan's strong grasp.

"There *is* a way for you to discover what hidden object they seek." Laudine sipped her tisane, observing Issylte over the rim of her mug. "You may seek the knowledge and wisdom of the *Gallizenae*."

Issylte's magic flared, her heart thumping wildly. She looked at Tristan, whose keen regard conveyed interest tempered with caution. "What is the *Gallizenae?*" Issylte asked, her mouth suddenly dry. "I have never heard that word before."

Laudine replied, "A group of nine *otherworldly* priestesses who live on the *Île de Sein*. An island off the western coast of *Bretagne*." The Lady of the Fountain took another sip of her *tisane*. "No man may go to the *Île de Sein*. Many sailors who have tried were lured to their deaths, their ships crashing against the treacherous rocks which shelter the island. Drowning in the turbulent seas." Laudine's amber eyes glowed in the morning light.

"The *Gallizenae*," the Lady of the Fountain continued, "are *Mélusines*—mermaids who can shape shift. They control the tides and the seas, invoking horrendous storms to capsize invading ships which threaten their shores." Laudine stared intently at Issylte. "It is rumored that the *Mélusines* are the legendary *Dragons de Mer*. The Sea Dragon warriors who destroy any ship which enters their sacred realm."

Gasps gusted across the table. Tristan squeezed her trembling hand.

"But a *woman* such as a Priestess of Dana may go there," Laudine continued, her fiery gaze glowing with challenge. "Seeking knowledge from the Gallizenae. To protect the Celtic realm. And defend the three sacred elements of the Goddess."

Issylte's breath hitched as realization dawned upon her. "I must go there to discover what lies hidden in *le Miroir aux Fées*." She spun eagerly to Tristan, her heart filled with wonder, excitement, courage.

And fear.

"Yes, Issylte." Laudine reached across the table to squeeze her other hand. "They will tell you what secret lies hidden in the Mirrored Lake. And why the dwarves are desperate to obtain it. It must be an object of tremendous power."

"How can Issylte travel to the *Île de Sein*? If no man may enter, I cannot go with her. To protect her." Tristan's voice was tremulous, his brows furrowed.

"That is correct, Tristan. No man may enter. And only a priestess seeking specific knowledge may consult the *Gallizenae*. Issylte must go alone, through the sacred portal. *La Porte du Dedans.* The Portal from Within. It lies at the bottom of *le Miroir aux Fées*. The Mirrored Lake."

Concern and worry were etched into his face. Tristan looked at Issylte, grasped her hands, and kissed them, as if terrified at the thought of losing her. His intense blue eyes washed her in the waves of the ocean, the deep notes of his voice singing to her soul. "You must go. You're the Lady of the Mirrored Lake, sworn to defend its sacred waters. Your courage, strength, and skill—enhanced by the magic of *Rose Elder*—will guide you. I pray the Goddess keeps you safe, until you return to me. I love you, Issylte. I believe in you. You will succeed. I know it."

She wrapped her arms around his neck and pulled

his face to hers. She devoured his lips, pouring her soul into his in front of the whole Tribe. They'd all seen the *mating marks* on their necks. Everyone knew she and Tristan had claimed each other. Marked each other. Mated for life.

She swam in the depths of Tristan's eyes. Her sea raven warrior. Her *mate*.

He believes in me. He's trained me for this. Given me a sword, dagger, bow and arrow. The confidence to use them. The skill to wield them. By the Goddess, I love him!

Issylte swirled breathlessly toward Laudine, her heart bright with challenge. "I'll do it. But how do I enter the portal—*La Porte du Dedans*?"

Laudine gestured to Lysara, whose dark brown eyes sparkled with mystery. "You must ask permission from *les Fées Dorées*," she whispered, her voice the rustle of a soft summer breeze. Lysara sipped her *tisane*, set down her mug, then glanced around the table, grinning at the Tribe. The sacred moonstone necklace that Viviane had created—and Lancelot had retrieved from the dwarf Gorik—glimmered against her light brown skin. The long tresses of her dark hair framed her pretty face with soft, cascading waves.

The petite brunette explained to Issylte, "They can be summoned at *l'Étang des Fées*—the Fairy Pond. It lies at the base of *la Cascade du Serein*—the Waterfall of the Fairies—whose sacred waters I defend and protect. It is not far from *le Miroir aux Fées*." With a laugh like the peal of a little bell, she chirped, "The whole area is enchanted by fairies!" Her face aglow with excitement, Lysara announced, "We'll go this evening. The Fées Dorées can only be summoned by moonlight."

Issylte's verdant magic thrummed as she held Lysara's brilliant gaze. *Tonight, we'll summon the fairies. And ask permission for me to walk between worlds!*

The Tribe dispersed, with some going to train, others to clean their weapons, hunt for game, or fish in the lake. It was agreed that after *le souper*—a light supper—Tristan and Issylte would follow Lysara and Solzic, accompanied by several armed guards, to *la Cascade du Serein.* The Waterfall of the Fairies. The sacred waters of the petite priestess Lysara.

While they waited for nightfall, Tristan and Issylte went with Nolwenn to tattoo the *mating marks* on their necks. The priestess had not only enthusiastically agreed to make the marks permanent but had also promised to transform each one into a beautiful dark green droplet, outlined in black.

"I have chosen the droplet shape to represent the sacred water that unites you," Nolwenn explained, working her magic on Tristan's mark with needles, inks, and oils. The aroma of clean sage purified the air in the white, pristine room as Issylte watched the priestess perform her artistry. "For Tristan, the sacred water is *la Fontaine de Barenton* which he defended, enabling him to become a member of the Tribe of Dana. The droplet also represents the waters of Lyonesse, his heritage. And the ocean of the Blue Knight of Cornwall." Nolwenn flashed Tristan a beautiful smile as she carefully executed her work.

Once Tristan's tattoo was complete, Issylte took his place upon the table draped in white.

"For you," Nolwenn said softly to Issylte, "the droplet shape represents the healing waters of Avalon and *le Miroir aux Fées*, the sacred lake you defended to become a Priestess of Dana." Glorious amethyst eyes sparkled like the brilliant, faceted gem in her silver necklace as the talented priestess meticulously marked Issylte's neck with herbal mixtures of green and black ink.

"Green represents the sacred forest of *Brocéliande* where you both were initiated into the Tribe of Dana," she explained as she skillfully inked Issylte's *mating mark*. "Where your *mating bond* was finalized. Where you claimed each other with these marks that I am now making permanent." The beautiful priestess smiled warmly at Issylte, whose magic thrummed in her presence. "The deep green also symbolizes Issylte's heritage, as the Emerald Princess of Ireland. And her verdant magic as a forest fairy."

Outlining the green droplet with black ink, Nolwenn explained its significance as well. "The black dye is made from guelder rose blossoms. Issylte's gift of Druidic magic. By etching it into your skin, the essence of the sacred flower is the divine protection of the Goddess who encircles your love."

It had taken all afternoon to complete the artwork, but Tristan and Issylte were beyond pleased with the results. They each now bore a *mating mark* that displayed not only the claim they had made on each other and the bond which united them, but also the Goddess they each served and the forces of nature which protected their lives.

And their love.

Eternally entwined.

****

The Tribe reassembled for the evening meal—a fish

135

stew with herbs and vegetables, accompanied by fresh bread and crisp white wine. The natural effervescence of the sacred water from the Fountain of Barenton accompanied every meal and flowed freely tonight into the goblets upon the dining table. Soon, it was time for Lysara and Solzic to lead Lancelot, Tristan, and Issylte to *la Cascade du Serein*. Six other warriors from the Tribe would accompany them for additional defense, an added precaution deemed necessary, since so many dwarves had been active in the sacred forest. And Frocin had recently attacked *la Joyeuse Garde* in his relentless pursuit of Issylte.

The group rode through the dense trees, illuminated by the torches several guards carried, enhanced by the glow of moonlight and incandescent starlight which twinkled in the black sky. As Lysara had promised, *l' Étang des Fées* was close to the Mirrored Lake, at the base of the Waterfall of the Fairies. Tristan, Issylte, Lancelot, Lysara, and Solzic dismounted, but the six additional warriors remained on horseback, vigilantly scanning the forest for potential danger.

L' Étang des Fées was a clear, freshwater pool at the bottom of a cascading waterfall, whose source was a fountain at the base of a huge beech tree, affectionately called *le Vieux*—the Old One.

Standing now before the Fairy Pool, Issylte looked up to view the thick, gnarled roots of *le Vieux* and admire the breathtaking beauty of *la Cascade du Serein*.

A series of rocks descended like steps from the base of the enormous beech tree perched high on top of a forested ledge. The waterfall cascaded in bubbling, gurgling ripples down over the stones, from the roots of the massive tree to a roar of splashing and frothing in the deep pool of *l' Étang des Fées.*

The four members of the Tribe of Dana stood before the Fairy Pool at the base of the waterfall. From the depths of the pond, a huge rock protruded above the surface of the ebullient water. Pointing to the large stone, Lysara announced, "That is *le Rocher des Fées*—the Rock of the Fairies. Pouring three drops of water from the pond onto the rock will summon *les Fées Dorées.*"

Issylte walked around the pool to approach from the opposite direction, where the stone curved upward and out toward the embankment. Dipping her hand into the cold water, she poured three drops of the liquid onto *le Rocher des Fées*, then returned to her original place beside Tristan at the base of the waterfall.

Three golden fairies soon appeared from an opening among the thick roots at the base of *le Vieux* where the fountain originated. Small, ethereal, and luminescent, their delicate golden wings fluttering like ephemeral butterflies, the *Fées Dorées* floated down the steps of the waterfall upon its cascading waves.

Their glowing torsos were bare; golden tresses of cascading curls flowed past their waists, mingling with ripples of golden, gossamer fabric that floated from their hips. Their skin appeared illuminated from within, as if lit by fireflies, the outlines of their bodies hazy and dreamlike, in constant subtle movement like the flames of a candle. Tiny golden coronets adorned with petite diamonds graced their foreheads and sparkled in the moonlight.

The first fairy, in a musical voice that trilled like the tinkling of a tiny bell, asked Issylte kindly, "Priestess of Dana, why have you summoned us?"

Issylte, unsure how to address such *otherworldly*

creatures, curtsied before the golden fairies, then replied humbly, "I wish to request permission to enter *la Porte du Dedans.*"

The three fairies conferred among themselves, their lyrical voices mingling like the chimes of tubular bells. Finally, the second fairy addressed Issylte. "Why do you wish to enter the portal, dear Lady of the Mirrored Lake?"

Issylte glanced at Tristan—who returned her gaze with encouragement—then to Lysara, who smiled hopefully. "I wish to travel to the *Île de Sein,* so that I may seek knowledge from the *Gallizenae.* I hope to learn what sacred object lies hidden within *le Miroir aux Fées,* the sacred waters I have sworn to protect."

Once again, the *Fées Dorées* conferred in hushed, musical voices, then the third fairy spoke.

"Your permission has been granted. You may traverse the sacred portal to the island of the *Gallizenae.* In addition, each of us will bestow upon you a gift of magic—representing the three sacred elements of the Goddess—to aid in your quest."

Issylte smiled graciously at each of the golden fairies, her heart aflutter with anticipation, her magic soaring in her veins.

The first fairy twinkled, "My gift shall represent the sacred element of the *forest.*" She floated across the water, waving her golden hand over Issylte's head.

"Three sacred trees: *le chêne, le hêtre,* and *le frêne*—the oak, the beech, and the ash—will cloak you from danger. Should you ever be pursued or threatened, hiding in one of these sacred trees will make you invisible to your enemies."

The second fairy floated over Issylte, casting her

enchanted gift as she spoke. "My gift is derived from the sacred element of *water*. I bestow upon you *la Voix de l'Eau*—the Voice of Water. You may communicate through any body of water, from the tiniest rivulet to the greatest ocean, to speak to your *mate*. When you touch a source of water that flows from you to him, you may cast your voice—which he alone will be able to hear."

The third fairy hovered in front of Issylte, her tiny golden wings shimmery as spun silk. "My gift represents *stone*, the third sacred element of the Goddess. You shall now be able to walk between worlds, through stone portals such as *la Porte du Dedans*. Be aware that although some portals do lead to darkness, you possess the Druidic magic of *Rose Elder*, which deflects evil and protects you from harm. May these three gifts from *les Fées Dorées* help you in your quest, Priestess of Dana, *la Dame du Miroir aux Fées*."

As quickly as they had appeared, the three tiny golden fairies floated back up *la Cascade du Serein* to disappear into the fountain within the twisted roots of the ancient, giant beech tree, *le Vieux*.

Lysara grasped Issylte's hands with unabashed enthusiasm. "Three gifts from *les Fées Dorées*! Now you can go through the portal, and their magic will protect you. Oh, Issylte, this is incredible. I am so glad we summoned them tonight!"

Tristan hugged her excitedly, lifting her off the ground to spin in a circle as he laughed in relief and joy. "I feel much better about your voyage, knowing that their gifts will protect you. I, too, am very glad we summoned *les Fées Dorées*."

Solzic added his congratulations and words of encouragement, then suggested, "Let's return to the castle. Everyone will want to hear what has happened."

Back in the castle of Landuc, the members of the Tribe of Dana were thrilled to hear of the gifts from *les Fées Dorées* and delighted that Issylte had obtained permission to traverse the portal of *la Porte du Dedans* at the bottom of the Mirrored Lake. There was concern for her safety, given the risks of walking between worlds and traveling to the *Île de Sein,* but the general atmosphere was enthusiastic, supportive, and optimistic. Issylte had received the Druidic magic of *Rose Elder* and now was blessed with gifts from *les Fées Dorées*. She would be well protected when walking between worlds.

As the Tribe said goodnight, retiring to their chambers, Issylte proudly led Tristan by the hand to share her bed. Everyone knew they were *mates*; there was no need for pretense. And she longed for him to the very depths of her soul.

Aware that this night might be their last together, the Emerald Princess and the Blue Knight of Cornwall made love passionately, desperately, and repeatedly in the soft glow of moonlight streaming through the gossamer drapes.

In the morning, they shared a last intimate farewell before joining the Tribe to break their fast. Laudine and Lysara were packing provisions for her, wrapping each item in the woven flax fiber of sailcloth used for ships.

"This fabric will protect your clothing and supplies as you swim to the bottom of the lake." Laudine placed each small parcel, wrapped in sailcloth, into a larger cloth, which she then placed inside a harnessed pack which Tristan would strap to Issylte's back. "I don't know what the *Île de Sein* has to offer, but I have enclosed some food, fresh water, healing herbs, protective crystals, needle and thread, cloth, and flint. I pray the Goddess will watch over you, guiding you safely to the *Gallizenae*. And back to us." Laudine pulled Issylte into her arms, hugging her tightly and kissing her cheeks.

Lysara, Nolwenn, and Bahja embraced her, too, as did Darius, Esclados, Kirus, Dagur, and Solzic. Lancelot held her firmly in his arms, reluctant to let her go. He finally kissed the top of her head and murmured, "*Que la Déesse te protège.* May the Goddess protect you." He released her to Tristan, who wrapped one arm around her, pulling her to his side as he slung the pack of supplies over his other shoulder. Silently, he led Issylte to the saddled horses awaiting them at the castle gate. He strapped her bag onto *Minuit*'s back, then helped her up into the saddle. Astride *Aiglon*, he led her—his *mate*—through the enchanted forest to the sacred Mirrored Lake.

When they dismounted at the bank of *le Miroir aux Fées,* Tristan's lips sought hers as he held her body against his. "Come back to me," he whispered into her good ear, kissing it, too.

"I will, Tristan. I promise." Her throat constricted and her heart hammered in her chest. She prayed she could keep that promise.

Brushing his lips softly with her own, Issylte touched his face and swam in the deep pools of his intense blue eyes. She held his fierce gaze, stroking the dark stubble on his strong jaw, absorbing his essence into hers through their *mating bond*.

She retrieved the pack of supplies from her horse, which Tristan strapped to her back. As she walked to the loamy shore, her magic surged with increasing intensity the closer she came to the water's edge.

And, with one last desperate look at her *mate,* filled with all the love in her heart, she dove into the sacred lake.

Le Miroir aux Fées.

The Mirror of the Fairies.

Chapter 11

La Fée du Coeur

Dense oaks framed the grassy glen, resplendent in fragrant blooms of sea pinks, bluebells, and buttercups. Fluffy clouds floated in the brilliant blue sky like enormous primrose blossoms in the soft summer breeze. The salty spray of the ocean wafted east into the thick Forest of Morois as Frocin, crouched among the bilberry shrubs, aimed his poisoned dart at the unsuspecting fairy Aimée.

La Fée Rouge. The Red Fairy who protected the red-blooded creatures of the forest.

Affectionately called *La Fée du Coeur.* The Heart Fairy. For her boundless love of the animals she defended.

His mistress Malfleur wanted her.

And Frocin, her faithful servant, never failed.

Earlier this morning, the summer solstice had begun with the traditional sacrifice to his malevolent mistress. As he had done every summer solstice for the past ten years, Frocin had delivered the unfortunate victim to *la Porte des Ombres,* where his loyal mercenary knights had stretched the unconscious, robust lord onto the stone slab, securing his bound limbs to the thick wooden stakes hammered into the earthen cave floor.

His mistress had been delighted with the fierce,

futile struggle of the strapping victim. The shrieks of agony. The stench of fear. The slow suffocation and surrender. The ruby red blood.

A voracious Malfleur had savored every last drop of the sacrifice that strengthened her sinister shadows. Readying her for the service that Lord Voldurk would perform. A service that somehow required *la Fée Rouge.* The fairy Frocin was now hunting.

He would deliver this prey to his mistress. And she would reward him handsomely, as promised. As she'd done this morning. Like always. Pleasure almost painful rippled through his wizened body.

Clearing his lusty thoughts, he returned his focus to his prey.

He'd been hunting *la Fée du Coeur* all afternoon. Waiting for the perfect moment.

And now, at long last, he'd found it.

She was alone. Picking wild strawberries in this sheltered glen. No trees obstructed his view. Nothing stood in the way.

The perfect opportunity to strike. Quickly. Lethally.

His crinkled cheeks billowed as he inhaled and puffed, blowing the poisoned dart forcefully and unerringly into Aimée's fragile neck. Adrenaline raced through Frocin's vile body.

The thrill of the kill.

La Fée du Coeur crumpled in a helpless heap, her long red hair gloriously unfurled among the vibrant wild poppies. At his signal, Frocin's three mercenary knights rushed to the victim, binding her wrists and ankles, carrying the unconscious fairy to the awaiting horses.

And on to *la Porte des Ombres.* Where Malfleur awaited. With Lord Voldurk.

As Frocin and his armed guards rode through the dense Forest of Morois with the priceless prize, the dwarf reflected upon the wizard's recent arrival in Cornwall with the Irish Queen. The king's betrothed. And Frocin's royal guest for the past month.

King Marke had been delighted that Frocin was hosting Queen Morag and her entourage in the Fortress of Morois until the upcoming royal wedding. The king had appointed his champion Lord Indulf to the honorary position of personal guard for his betrothed, commanding that the knight reside in Frocin's fortress with her, serving as her royal protector.

Accompanied by two dozen palace guards from the Castle of Tintagel, Indulf had joined Frocin and his mercenary knights in welcoming the queen and her court at the Cornish seaport. Frocin, as host of the king's intended bride, had escorted her safely to his Fortress of Morois, where Queen Morag's attendants, palace guards, and personal protector would reside until the Yuletide season, when the royal wedding would take place in the Castle of Tintagel. In a double wedding, Sir Indulf would also marry his betrothed—Lady Elowenn—in a second ceremony, after which he and his new bride would report to Ireland. To serve as the new Earl of Dubh Linn for the Irish Queen.

In preparation for hosting the monarch, Frocin's servants had lavishly decorated his fortress, preparing an entire wing for the king's betrothed. Queen Morag had been pampered with a luxurious bedroom and antechamber, with several rooms for her attendants and ladies. Aware of the illicit liaison between the seductive queen and her enigmatic Royal Advisor, Frocin had bequeathed the room for Lord Voldurk that connected to the queen's chambers via a secret passageway hidden in a paneled wall. Both Lord Voldurk and the queen had been most satisfied with the clandestine arrangement.

The dwarf had also noticed the unbridled lust in the hawklike stare of Sir Indulf as the brazen knight held the regal gaze of the exquisite queen. And Frocin had seen the equally unabashed passion in the black obsidian eyes of the king's betrothed. So, much to Indulf's delight, Frocin had also provisioned a room for him adjacent to Queen Morag's royal bedchambers. As her personal guard, he had explained affably, Indulf needed to serve at the queen's side.

And between her royal legs.

Frocin snickered in wicked delight.

In late May, King Marke had hosted a sumptuous reception feast and elegant ball to welcome his future queen and officially announce their betrothal. Since then, the king had been visiting frequently, obviously besotted with his bewitching bride.

Just as King Donnchadh of Ireland had been nine years ago.

Perhaps the Black Widow Queen will poison King Marke, too. Frocin snickered again.

They were almost at the entrance to the cave. *My mistress will be most pleased. And reward me again.* Frocin's body throbbed at the thought.

This morning, dutifully obeying Malfleur's orders, Frocin had brought Lord Voldurk to *la Porte des Ombres* to meet his mistress. On the summer solstice. Just as the Shadow Witch had commanded.

The sacrificial victim had been splayed on the slab. Still unconscious.

Malfleur had ordered Frocin to wait outside the cave

while she conferred with Lord Voldurk. Irritated at first, Frocin had quickly become agitated and anxious. Afraid that his mistress had planned to replace him as her loyal servant.

With the powerful Lord Voldurk.

Yet, when the wizard had exited the cave, he'd muttered to Frocin, his voice the unearthly hiss of a predatory snake, "Your mistress will see you now. The victim is awake." Frocin had shuddered in Voldurk's hypnotic stare. In the golden, glowing gaze of a python, ready to strike. "I shall return at dusk to meet you here. Malfleur has a service for me to perform." The gilded eyes of a dragon had transfixed him with terror. "And another for you."

Frocin cast aside his disturbing reverie as the riders now approached *la Porte des Ombres.* Where his mistress awaited. Impatiently.

The entrance to the cave was barely discernible in the gloaming twilight. Thick trees ensconced the rocky ledge as the riders dismounted. One knight tethered the horses, then lit a torch and handed it to Frocin as the other two guards lowered the still unconscious fairy from the saddle. Frocin led his three loyal knights—carrying *la Fée du Coeur* —into the bowels of the fetid cave.

Down the long, curving corridor to the dank inner chamber.

Where the golden eyes of a snake lurked in the darkness.

Surrounded by the swirling, sinister shadows of Frocin's mistress.

Malfleur. *La Fée des Ombres.*

Frocin had disposed of the desiccated body of the solstice sacrifice this morning, dumping it in the darkest shadows of the cave with the other rotting corpses and skeletal remains of previous victims. His knights now secured *la Fée du Coeur* on the stone slab before the golden-eyed wizard and the diabolical fairy, skulking in the shadows.

"Have your men guard the cave entrance and await further orders, Frocin. We will need them later." Malfleur's shadows slithered up his spine.

The three knights exited the dank cave, leaving Frocin alone with Voldurk, his mistress, and the unconscious prey. *La Fée du Coeur.*

"I have taught Lord Voldurk an extraordinary enchantment, which he will perform for me now," Malfleur croaked, her voice like creaking branches in an icy storm. "Frocin, my faithful servant, you will sit on the stone and observe in silence. I have another task for you to accomplish when the wizard has finished."

He crept over to perch on the empty stone under a wall sconce where the flames of a torch illuminated the gloomy cavern. Aimée, still asleep, lay perfectly still on the sacrificial slab, the waves of her long red hair cascading like the flowing blood of Malfleur's numerous victims.

"Have you prepared the gemstone?" *la Fée des Ombres* demanded menacingly as Voldurk approached the prone victim.

"Yes, Malfleur. Exactly as you commanded." Voldurk withdrew from the pocket of his black robe a large ruby, which he displayed to the twirling tendrils hovering near the stone slab. The gem was the size of a flat walnut, sparkling in the wizard's outstretched palm, shaped in the form of a heart that glowed and pulsed in the shining torchlight.

"Excellent," Malheur hissed. "Let us proceed. Quickly, while she remains unconscious. Unlike human victims, a fairy may use magic to resist, should she awaken."

As Frocin observed in silent rapture, Lord Voldurk held the glowing ruby in one hand as he swept his other downturned palm over the length of the victim's restrained body.

Malfleur's twirling shadows seeped up into Aimée's nose, causing the fairy's mouth to open as she gasped for air. Enabling even thicker, more noxious tendrils to flow down the victim's pale white throat. Choking her. Suffocating her.

While shadows permeated the fairy's fragile face, Voldurk's hand hovered over the victim's breast. The wizard's fist opened and closed rhythmically in a pumping squeeze, mimicking the pulsations of a beating heart. The ebb and flow of lifeblood in the victim's body.

Frocin watched the dark shadows of his mistress emerge from Aimée's mouth, coaxing and extracting glowing red tendrils that curled and twisted, flowing into the glowing ruby in Lord Voldurk's outstretched palm. As the crimson twirls entered the gleaming red gem, the blood red glow pulsated in the wizard's palm with each squeeze of his fist. As if he were pumping the blood from the fairy's body, forcing it into the heart-shaped ruby in his manipulative hand.

After several minutes, Malfleur's shadows receded from *La Fée du Coeur*, hovering in the darkness near the stone slab. The glowing red tendrils no longer flowed from the victim's mouth, and Lord Voldurk ceased the rhythmic pulsation of his squeezing fist. The scarlet glow of the ruby in his flattened palm dulled and darkened, as if the brilliant flames of a life had been extinguished.

Or imprisoned.

"Well done, Lord Voldurk. Give the ruby to Frocin," Malfleur purred contentedly. As the wizard placed the precious gem in Frocin's trembling hand, he examined the faceted jewel. Encased in an intricately carved golden bezel adorned with roses, the heart shaped ruby was attached to a delicate chain in an exquisitely stunning, breathtaking necklace.

"You will safeguard this priceless treasure, Frocin. In ten long years of loyal service, you have never failed. Do not fail me now as I entrust you with the most crucial task of all."

Malfleur's shadows floated over to where he was seated against the cavern wall. "Notice how the ruby is dormant, Frocin. There is no glow. No pulsation. *La Fée du Coeur's* magic essence has been captured inside that ruby, and Lord Voldurk has enchanted it. You, my faithful servant, will wear this necklace. Guard it with your life. Aimée must never come in contact with it, for if she does, her magic essence will be reunited with her body. What's worse, she will obtain the very power that Lord Voldurk embedded in the stone to perform this enchantment. That must never happen, Frocin. Aimée must never be reunited with her magic. Your life depends on it. You must not fail."

Frocin glanced at the pale body of *la Fée Rouge*, her luxurious locks cascading in scarlet ripples over the stone slab. Her pearlescent white skin, creamy as milk. The magic of the lovely *Fée du Coeur* was now trapped in an enchanted ruby. Which he held gingerly in his gnarled, misshapen hand.

His mistress spoke again, the vehemence of her

voice reverberating in his bones.

"You will wear this necklace, Frocin. It will enable you to find what I seek. Because the ruby will pulsate and glow. When you are in the presence of a woman who carries a son descended from a king. The essential element I need for the final spell."

Swirling shadows slithered over Frocin's twisted body. Sluicing him with delicious waves of sensual pleasure. "When the ruby glows and pulsates, Frocin, you must capture the pregnant woman. Place the necklace around her throat. The magic essence of *la Fée du Coeur* that Lord Voldurk has embedded and enchanted in this ruby will render the woman compliant. Malleable. Easily controlled. You will keep her for me, Frocin. In your tower. Feed her lavishly. Pamper her. I want the child born robust and healthy. When the woman's labor pains come, have the very best midwife deliver her son and provide care for the new mother and child. At the equinox or solstice, kill the midwife, and bring the new mother and her infant son to me. In this cave. For the final sacrifice."

La Fée des Ombres floated like wisps of smoke in the dimly lit cave. Swirling seductively along his deformed body. Taunting him. Tempting him. Torturing him.

"Your guards outside the cave will place *la Fée Rouge* in the enchanted alcove I have prepared for her. My magic shall preserve and protect her body until you bring me the new mother and child. You'll sacrifice the young mother first—to nourish me with her agonizing screams and rich red blood. And the final sacrifice—the royal blood of the infant son descended from a king— will enable me, at long last, to regain physical form. To enter the voluptuous body of *la Fée Rouge*. My vessel. So that I may leave this infernal cave where I have been reduced to shadows and imprisoned for an eternity. I shall enjoy once again the pleasures of the flesh denied to me for far too long."

La Fée des Ombres slunk into shadows near the wizard. "Frocin, you will wait there against the wall while I reward Lord Voldurk for his exceptional performance. For capturing the magic essence of *la Fée du Coeur* within the enchanted ruby. And then Frocin, my most loyal servant, I shall reward you as well."

Frocin's heart raced. Would his mistress reward Voldurk the same way she always rewarded him? And he, Frocin, would witness it all?

His questions were answered as the shadows of his mistress swirled around the wizard's face. The smoky tendrils curled up into Voldurk's nose, just as they had done with Aimée. Yet, the wizard did not sputter and choke. On the contrary. He opened his mouth and inhaled the slithering shadows deep into his lungs. His golden eyes began to glow more brightly, steadily increasing in luminosity. As if lightning now flowed in his venomous veins.

After several minutes, Malfleur's shadows withdrew and retreated. But the golden glow of the wizard's reptilian gaze did not diminish. Voldurk's tongue darted in and out of his mouth, like a predatory snake sensing its prey. A devilish grin spread across the wizard's darkly handsome face, his sharp teeth gleaming in the torchlight.

"My power is greatly enhanced," Voldurk growled in pleasure. "Fury sizzles in my veins." He squeezed his fists in the same pumping action he'd just done to entrap the essence of *la Fée du Coeur.* "Thank you, Malfleur," he hissed contentedly to the Shadow Fairy. "Should you ever need me, I am at your service. Send Frocin, and I will come at once." Smoothing his long black cape, Lord Voldurk bid *adieu* to *la Fée des Ombres* and her faithful dwarf. "And now, I wish you both goodnight. Farewell."

Malfleur's tenebrous shadows wafted in the dim light before the wizard. "Thank you, Lord Voldurk. I shall need you again. And yes, I'll send Frocin. Farewell and goodnight, dark wizard. Until we meet again."

Voldurk bowed before *la Fée des Ombres,* inclined his head to Frocin, and slithered down the dark twisting corridor to exit the foul, fetid cave.

"Frocin," his mistress commanded, her voice penetrating his very core. "Clasp the enchanted ruby around your neck and conceal it under your tunic." He complied, the heart shaped gem hanging perfectly over his wildly thumping heart. "And now, my loyal servant, I shall give you a most generous reward."

Frocin lowered his filthy breeches and reclined on the flat stone where he now sat, since the fairy's body still occupied the sacrificial slab. And, as she had done repeatedly over the last ten years, his mistress rewarded him with nearly unbearable, *otherworldly* ecstasy.

Later, when he was finally able to stand, Frocin hitched his breeches and commanded his men to place the body of *la Fée Rouge* in the enchanted alcove that Malfleur had prepared. His knights laid the fairy's fragile body on her back, and Frocin arranged her long red hair to cascade over her shoulders, down her soft pink gossamer gown, and along her slender, delicate arms. A protective barrier of black shadows formed, encircling and concealing the immobile fairy in the dark, sheltered alcove of the sinister cave. Bowing to his malevolent mistress, Frocin removed the torch from the wall sconce and led his loyal mercenary knights out of the gloomy cavern.

The cave of the wicked fairy.

La Fée des Ombres.

Malfleur.

Chapter 12

The Abduction

Frocin, with his gift of clairvoyance, had glimpsed the frequent romantic interludes between Prince Kaherdin of Armorique and the voluptuous Lady Gargeolaine. Instinct told him she might very well be the woman he sought in his quest for Malfleur.

So, the Leader of the Dwarves informed Lord Voldurk of his intent to sail to *Bretagne* to investigate, with explicit instructions for performing the essential sacrifice to Malfleur in *la Porte des Ombres* for the autumnal equinox during his absence. Voldurk accepted the responsibility, cognizant of the need to satisfy and strengthen the insatiable Shadow Fairy they both served.

Malfleur. *La Fée des Ombres.*

Frocin, a wealthy shipping lord, sailed to the northern coast of France and requested a royal audience with King Hoël and Prince Kaherdin, purportedly to discuss the use of seaports in Armorique for the importation of his merchandise. As a royal guest in the sumptuous *Château Rose*, Frocin met the fiancée of the Prince of Armorique, the lovely Lady Gargeolaine. And, to his wicked delight, the heart shaped ruby did indeed pulsate under his tunic when he kissed the delicate white hand of the auburn-haired beauty.

And now Frocin, with twenty of his mercenary

knights—mounted and fully armed—were hidden among the trees along the road to Trégastel, a short distance from *le Château Rose* in Armorqiue.

Waiting to abduct the Lady Gargeolaine.

Who carried the son descended from a king.

The carriage they awaited, containing the curvaceous redhead and her doddering chaperone, had left the village and was now en route, expected to pass by within minutes. His highly capable, loyal men were armed and ready. They had their orders: dispatch the royal guards, silence the crone, and capture the russet-haired beauty.

I'll place the necklace around Gargeolaine's neck and keep her in my Tower of Frégart while we prepare to sail for Cornwall. Once we arrive in Britain, the beauty who carries the heir to the throne of Armorique shall remain prisoner in my Fortress of Morois until her son is born. Then, I'll bring them both to Malfleur for the sacrifice. And be handsomely rewarded in return. As always.

His engorged body throbbed with anticipated pleasure.

When the royal carriage at last appeared on the road from Trégastel, Frocin's mercenary knights made quick work of killing the half dozen armed guards, the coachman, and the old woman. The redhead had put up quite a struggle, but was now subdued and docile, the enchanted ruby gleaming around her creamy throat. His men had hoisted Gargeolaine into the saddle of the awaiting horse and were now leading her back to his tower in the dense forest of Frégart. The abduction had gone perfectly. Now they need only prepare for the return voyage to Cornwall. Frocin could not wait to inform his mistress when he next saw her—for the winter solstice sacrifice—that he had once again performed his faithful duty.

He, Frocin, never failed.

****

At the *château* of Landuc, in the Forest of Brocéliande, the Tribe had resumed its regular routine of training, hunting, preparing for battle, and stocking supplies for winter. Issylte had been gone for four weeks now, and although Tristan trained harder than ever, trying to keep his mind occupied with something other than concern for her, his *mate* was constantly in his thoughts. He had no idea how long she would be gone, nor what she would encounter on the *Île de Sein*. He forced himself to remain optimistic, to believe in Issylte's strength and intelligence, and to trust that the *Rose Elder*—as well as the gifts from *les Fées Dorées* — would protect her from harm.

That evening, as the Tribe was finishing supper, one of the guards from the barbican defense towers burst into the dining area to inform Esclados that several riders were fast approaching, bearing the standard of Prince Kaherdin of Armorique. The Red Knight, along with several members of the Tribe, including Tristan and Lancelot, rushed to the entrance gate as the knights dismounted, handing their lathered horses to the castle grooms.

"They've taken Gargeolaine!" Kaherdin sputtered, gripping Lancelot's forearm as he gasped for breath.

"Come in, Kaherdin. Tell us what has happened." Esclados led the men into the reception room near the front entrance of the castle. Laudine and her servants placed pitchers of water and goblets for the prince and the dozen knights who had ridden with him to Landuc. Kaherdin, clad in full Elven armor like his knights, removed his headpiece to speak more clearly and recover his breath. He gratefully gulped from the goblet of spring water that Laudine served him, concern shadowing her bright amber eyes.

"It was the dwarf Frocin," Kaherdin spat. "He and his armed men attacked Gargeolaine's carriage. They killed her guards and chaperone. They've abducted her, Esclados. They've taken my Gargeolaine! We must save her. We must ride at once!"

Kirus approached, his disfigured face glowering with rage. "The dwarves have been attacking our priestesses. Now they've abducted one of our women. This is intolerable. We must retaliate immediately. Free Gargeolaine. And kill this bloody dwarf." Kirus, donning his mail armor, locked his fierce gaze on Esclados. The Red Knight bowed his head in solemn agreement.

Lancelot approached Kaherdin, who was pacing restlessly, raking his fingers through his long dark hair. "Do you know where they've taken her?"

"Frocin has a tower in the Forest of Frégart," Kirus announced, adjusting his armor. "My *eyes*—I have spies everywhere in these woods—have reported recent activity there. Supplies delivered, armored knights arriving. Frocin himself has been spotted, overseeing preparations of some kind. That is undoubtedly where he has taken her," Kirus reported gravely, strapping on his sword.

"Lancelot…Gargeolaine is with child. The future heir to the kingdom of Armorique. We must save her…and my babe which she carries. By the Goddess, we must free her!"

"We will, Kaherdin," Tristan promised, placing a reassuring hand upon the prince's shoulder. "We'll leave at once."

"How many men does Frocin have?" Dagur stepped forward, already clad in full armor, buckling his sword and donning his helmet.

"My spies estimate two dozen," Kirus announced, his deep voice grave. "We surround the tower. Take out the archers and the sentries. When they change guards, we storm the front entrance. Engage any knights we encounter. Dispatch Frocin quickly. Any reinforcements will be eliminated before they reach the fortress." Kirus, as leader of the Tribe, barked out orders as the warriors donned armor and weapons. Kaherdin and his knights were given fresh horses, which they quickly mounted, readying for battle.

Within minutes, the Tribe of Dana was thundering through the forest with knights from Armorique and Landuc, headed northeast to the Tower of Frégart. The late summer sky was streaked with the last vestiges of pink and violet hues as twilight descended upon the warriors conferring under the thick oaks on a forested ledge near the entrance to Frocin's domain.

The stone tower in the clearing before them stood forty feet tall, a lone cylindrical structure with a pointed, wooden roof above a row of arrow slit windows, whose interiors—illuminated by torches—outlined the bodies within. The only entrance was the main gate to the enclosed stone curtain wall, which was flanked by two armed guards, with others patrolling on horseback within the fortress grounds.

The Tribe had divided, with Dagur, Solzic, Hakon,

and Kjetil each leading eight men to circle the tower, and Kirus remaining with Tristan, Lancelot, Esclados, and Kaherdin to launch the attack from the front. Night had fallen, and light shining from a window at the top of the tower indicated where the dwarf was most likely keeping Gargeolaine. A full moon shone brightly over the fortress grounds.

"I count four archers and eight guards," Kirus reported to the warriors on horseback beside him, hidden in the dense woods in front of the fortress. "We wait until the changing of the guard. When the front door opens, we attack." Kirus spoke quietly; heads bobbed in the moonlight. Tristan's heart pounded under his chain mail armor, his entire body a tightly coiled spring.

They waited in the darkness at the edge of the forest until two armed guards exited the walled gate of the tower. The Tribe swiftly eliminated them and infiltrated the fortress grounds. Quickly and furtively, the patrolling guards were silenced. Kirus' men charged the front gate, and the clashing of iron summoned the knights from within.

Arrows rained down upon the attackers and four knights from Landuc fell instantly. Hakon, Solzic, and two of their men deftly eliminated the archers, then engaged in battle at the base of the tower. A dozen knights emerged onto the grounds of the fortress, swords swinging and shields up.

The Tribe of Dana had the advantage of superior numbers, weapons, and strength, bolstered by the element of surprise. The dwarf Frocin's defending soldiers were quickly eliminated. The Tribe of Dana had taken possession of the Fortress of Trégart.

Kaherdin raced upstairs to free Gargeolaine.

Kjetil and Tristan discovered Frocin hiding under the stairwell at the rear of the tower, where the two warriors of Dana now had the vile dwarf cornered. Frocin's blackened tongue lolled as his breath rasped heavily, his wrinkled face contorted, fury gleaming in his beady eyes, yellowed fangs bared in rage.

As quick as a snake, Frocin lashed out with a dagger, deeply slicing Tristan's left leg. The dwarf lunged again, and Tristan blocked the blow with his shield, knocking the blade from his assailant's grip.

Kjetil, with a fierce slash of his Viking sword, severed Frocin's head, which rolled in a trail of blood and gore, grotesquely separated from the disfigured body. Black blood oozed from the severed neck and pooled thickly on the gray stone floor. Tristan's mouth was dry as a bone, his muscles quivering, the slice in his leg sizzling with painful fire.

Leaning down to help Tristan to his feet, Kjetil chortled, "Saved your bloody ass, didn't I, Tristan? Me, a fuckin' Viking!"

Grinning ear to ear despite his agony, Tristan hobbled to a stand, tightly gripping Kjetil's tree trunk arm. "Indeed, you did. You saved my sorry ass. And I thank you...you fuckin' Viking." Tristan wiped grime and blood from his face with his free hand and shot Kjetil a grateful grin.

Kjetil guffawed with a hearty laugh, slapping Tristan soundly on the back. Tristan winced from the affectionate blow which caused his weakened leg to buckle, lowering himself carefully to sit upon a stair. He tore a section of the chemise under his armor to create a makeshift bandage, pressing it firmly against the wound. As he stanched the flow of blood from his leg, Esclados approached, his white teeth gleaming in a satisfied grin. The Tribe of Dana had prevailed.

Noting Tristan's injury, the Red Knight said reassuringly, "Laudine will stitch that up for you. Cleanse it with some of her herbs. You'll be fine in no time." Tristan relaxed slightly at Esclados' encouraging grin.

Dagur entered from the front gate, where the Tribe had secured the tower. "All clear. We've taken the fortress." He removed his helmet and gauntlets, wiping a hand across his sweaty, bloody brow. "And Gargeolaine is safe."

Kaherdin, his arm wrapped protectively around his unresponsive fiancée, emerged from the room where he'd remained at her side. He led her carefully down the stairs, skirting around Tristan, to join the warriors who had successfully rescued her. "Thank the Goddess you are safe, my love," he whispered again, kissing her blank face, hugging her tightly, stroking her long, thick hair. She seemed oblivious to his ministrations and all that was transpiring around her.

Tristan remarked the empty stare of the normally vibrant, passionate redhead. *She's in shock. Once she's safely back at Landuc, she'll be herself again.*

"Come, let's return to Landuc. Laudine can assess you and be sure that both you and the babe are safe." Esclados spoke gently to Gargeolaine, gesturing for Kaherdin to bring her outside to the awaiting horses.

Solzic brought forth Kaherdin's horse and helped the prince seat Gargeolaine in the saddle. Kaherdin then sat behind her, wrapping his arms securely around his bride to be. The warriors on foot mounted their horses, with Kjetil giving Tristan a boost into the saddle to avoid further injury to his wounded leg. Bringing their four fallen warriors with them, the Tribe rode back through the moonlit forest to the *Château de Landuc,* the auburn-haired beauty safe in their midst.

Once the Tribe had returned to the castle with an unresponsive but otherwise unharmed Gargeolaine, Laudine brewed a calming *tisane* to soothe her as the men prepared the fallen knights for an honorable burial in the morning. Stable grooms took care of the horses, and the warriors of the Tribe cleaned their weapons and armor with the help of squires and pages in preparation for sleep. Laudine cleansed Tristan's wound with calendula soap, stitched up his injured leg, applying an antiseptic healing ointment of yarrow and honey, bandaging it securely. "We'll keep this clean, and the ointment will prevent it from festering." Laudine's smile was as soothing as her healing herbs, but Tristan desperately missed Issylte's loving touch.

Now that Tristan's injury had been properly treated, the Priestess of Dana directed her nurturing attention back to the pregnant Gargeolaine. "Thank the Goddess you are safe, my dear. And the babe is fine as well. Your prince summoned us quickly, and the Tribe of Dana rescued you. Now, you must rest, my dear." She flashed a knowing smile to Kaherdin. "I've prepared a room for the two of you." The Prince of Armorique responded with a grateful bow of his head.

Nolwenn, who had greeted her love Kirus, grateful that the Tribe had returned safely and that the injuries—including Tristan's—had not been life threatening, had been silently observing Gargeolaine's blank stare from the quiet kitchen alcove. She approached Kaherdin's betrothed, who was slumped in the chair, mindlessly sipping the *tisane* that Laudine had placed in her hand. A glowing ruby hung around Gargeolaine's throat. Nolwenn lifted the gem to examine it in the candlelight that burned on the table in the nook where they were seated.

"This ruby…" Nolwenn muttered, the warning tone in her voice capturing everyone's attention, "…is *enchanted with evil.*" Her brilliant amethyst gaze locked on Laudine. "I sense a darkness within. And something else…that I cannot name." Nolwenn unclasped and cautiously removed the necklace from Gargeolaine's throat, placing the jewel in a carved wooden box. "I'll keep it stored in this covered container until Issylte returns. Perhaps she can identify what lies within the ruby."

With the necklace removed, Gargeolaine swooned, her head rolling as if she would faint. Kaherdin rushed to kneel beside her chair, taking her hand, which he kissed fervently. "I am here, my love. You are safe."

Gargeolaine opened wide her exquisite amber eyes, observing her surroundings in confusion and fright. "Where am I?" she asked Kaherdin, her voice quavering with panic.

"You're in the castle of Landuc, home of Lord Esclados and Lady Laudine," he responded comfortingly, stroking her shaking hand. "You remember, love? We met them at Lancelot's castle, *la Joyeuse Garde*, last summer."

Gargeolaine's frightened gaze scanned the room, taking in the smiling faces all around her. Kaherdin said gently, "The Tribe of Dana—and the knights from Landuc and Armorique—rescued you. Do you remember what happened?"

Seeming to return to her senses, Gargeolaine nodded as a visible, violent shudder rippled through her. "We were attacked. The carriage was surrounded. They killed the royal guards. And Aliénor!" She sobbed into her hands, her entire body shaking at the memory of the bloody ambush. "I remember the dwarf. He was hideous! His men captured me. Pinned my arms behind me. And the dwarf…he put something on me. A necklace."

Nolwenn removed the cover from the box which held the ruby, displaying it to Gargeolaine without allowing her to touch it. "This one," she replied, showing her the glittering jewel. "The ruby is enchanted with an evil spell which must have overpowered you somehow. I'll keep it covered in this box until Issylte returns. Perhaps she can tell us what it is. In the meantime, we are grateful that you are yourself once again. And that you and the babe are both safe." Nolwenn kissed Gargeolaine's tear-stained cheek as Kaherdin rose to his feet.

"Thank the Goddess you've been returned to us. And thank the Tribe of Dana for the valiant rescue." The Prince of Armorique addressed Tristan and Kjetil, who were sitting at the table in the alcove with Lancelot, unwinding from the brutal battle with a hearty mug of ale. "Tristan—you and Kjetil killed the dwarf that abducted my Gargeolaine. You must come—with Lancelot—to *le Château Rose.* To meet my father, King Hoël. I know he will want to show his appreciation for the valiant warriors who saved his son's betrothed." Kaherdin flashed a brilliant smile at Gargeolaine, love light glowing in his luminous eyes. "And the future heir of Armorique." He beamed at his beautiful bride to be, who returned his adoring smile, her face alight with love.

Kjetil, Tristan, and Lancelot exchanged quick glances. The Viking grinned from ear to ear. "I, for one, want to meet the King of Armorique. Be a royal guest and all. I accept!"

Tristan considered the invitation. There was no knowing how long Issylte would be gone, and they were counting on Armorique as an ally in the upcoming challenge against Queen Morag. It would be an important gesture of friendship in formalizing their alliance with King Hoël if he accompanied Kaherdin, Lancelot, and Kjetil to *le Château Rose*. Although he most definitely did not look forward to spending time with Princess Blanchine, it would be ill-advised to refuse a royal invitation.

"I would be honored to meet your father the king. But…" he added cautiously, "I do wish to come back to Landuc soon, to await Issylte's return."

It was agreed. Tristan, Kjetil, and Lancelot would accompany Kaherdin, Gargeolaine, and their palace guards for a celebratory *séjour* at King Hoël's castle. The battle-weary soldiers followed Sir Agrane, First Knight of Landuc, to the knights' lodge. The Tribe of Dana retired to their respective rooms, and the Prince of Armorique and his betrothed were escorted by servants to their royal guest chambers.

And in the morning, after a delicious buffet, the royal guests of Prince Kaherdin rode off to the majestic pink granite castle of *le Château Rose*.

To meet King Hoël of Armorique.

Chapter 13

The Gallizenae

Issylte dove through the cold water of the lake to the bottom of *le Miroir aux Fées.* She swam through the entrance to the stone portal—*la Porte du Dedans,* emerging above the surface of the water inside a deep stone cave with large, scattered rocks strewn along the embankments.

Pulling herself from the lake, she stood on the ground within the cave, took off her soaked gown, wrung out the excess water, and draped it over one of the large boulders. She then removed a towel and quickly dried off, selecting a dress and cloak from her pack, which thankfully had been kept dry by the sailcloth that Laudine had wrapped everything in.

She donned her dry robe and cloak, grateful for the warmth, as she was shivering from the chill of the Mirrored Lake. Inspecting her surroundings, she noticed a tunnel leading deeper into the cave from the portal where she now stood. Deciding to leave her soaked dress behind and bring only her pack of supplies, Issylte ventured farther into the depths of *la Porte du Dedans.*

Although the cave was dark, the brilliant water was a luminous green, glowing from a source of light that seemed to brighten as she followed the path away from the portal farther into the tunnel. The water flowed beside her from the opposite direction, fed from a source deep within the cave and emptying into *le Miroir aux Fées* behind her.

A wide path along the water's edge permitted her passage, leading at last to a vast, open cavern where a magnificent waterfall flowed along one side of the cave, emptying into the water which fed into the lake. The earthen path curved around the wall of the tunnel, opening onto a sunlit exit at the mouth of an astonishing sea cave.

Issylte emerged from the grotto to the tangy scent of salt air, the squawk of seagulls, and the roar of ocean waves pounding onto the craggy shore, spraying white froth high into the brilliant blue sky. She was on an island, with huge stone cliffs sheltering the sea cave behind her, and a rocky beach in front of her. Twisting around to get a panoramic view, she spotted dense woods in the distance atop the forested ledge from which she had just emerged. The nearly blinding summer sun shone through scattered fluffy clouds in a glorious sky. And, not far from where she now stood on the rocky shore, Issylte spotted another sea cave.

Beckoning her.

Taking care not to twist her ankle on the large rocks which covered the beach, she entered the second cave, whose wide mouth allowed lots of natural light, revealing a brilliant turquoise interior. Sea water flowed along one side of the cave into a deep ocean pool of a vibrant aqua hue. The intense jade color reflected off the lustrous white limestone walls like a gleaming jewel. Verdant magic thrumming in her veins, Issylte basked in the exquisite natural beauty of the secret cave as she stood on a patch of sand amid several large rocks on the cave floor.

"This is *la Grotte des Sirènes.* The Mermaid Cave. Why have you come to the *Île de Sein,* Priestess of Dana?" A lovely female with long blonde hair arose from the water to recline upon one of the large stones protruding from the ocean pool inside the cave. Her eyes were a deep teal green, like the scales on the lower half of her body, which formed a long tail that divided into two softly flowing fins fluttering in the water below the rock. Her torso was bare; her alabaster skin glowed like a rare pearl.

Startled, Issylte spun toward the lilting voice. The lovely sea creature was flanked by two other *sirènes* emerging from the pool to stretch upon adjacent stones. One mermaid had long waves of black hair, lavender scales, and light purple eyes, the other with cascading curls of red hair and a seafoam green tail.

"*Bonjour, Mesdemoiselles.* I am Issylte, the Lady of the Mirrored Lake, and I have come to seek knowledge from the nine Priestesses of the *Gallizenae.*"

At these words, six other mermaids swam into the center of the cave, lingering in the water near Issylte, their arms draped across the rocks, tail fins floating in the brilliant aqua pool. Each had long, wavy hair and scales of different colors, from light aquamarine blue to deep amethyst purple. They, too, drew themselves up out of the water with strong arms to recline upon the rocks beside their mermaid sisters, tailfins floating in the ocean pool. Nine sea creatures now faced Issylte, standing on the rocky shore of the hidden sea cave.

"We are the *Gallizenae*, the priestesses and sentinels of the *Île de Sein*. What knowledge do you seek, Lady of the Mirrored Lake?" the dark-haired mermaid with lavender scales asked in a liquid, lyrical voice.

"I wish to discover what sacred object lies hidden in *le Miroir aux Fées* and why the dwarves seek it. For they have been searching the Forest of Brocéliande and attacking the Priestesses of Dana."

The mermaid with long red hair and light green scales responded in a soft, ethereal voice. "They seek the *orb*, crafted by *Morgane la Fée*, for the wizard Voldurk. It contains tremendous power, which he is anxious to obtain."

Unsure if she would be permitted more questions, Issylte dared to ask, "What power does the orb contain? And why does Voldurk seek it?"

A mermaid with lilac-colored hair and deep purple scales responded in a voice that rippled and flowed like the glimmering waters beneath her. "*Morgane la Fée* imbued the orb with powerful spells of enchantment. Much like she did in crafting the sacred scabbard for King Arthur Pendragon. The orb has inordinate power. A protective talisman which renders the bearer invincible in battle."

A silver-haired mermaid with sapphire blue scales spoke next. "If Voldurk obtains the orb, he will be impervious to the deadly eye of the cyclops who guards the dragon portal. Protected by the priceless orb, the wizard could slay the fearsome *Mordrac*. The only means of his defeat."

The blonde mermaid spoke gravely to Issylte. "*Mordrac* is the last remaining dragon in the entire Celtic realm, and the only source of *dragonfire,* an element necessary to defeat the dark wizard. The sole means to slay Voldurk is with an Elven sword, forged in *dragonfire.* Crafted from the molten ore hidden within

La Grotte de l' Étoile—the Cave of the Fallen Star. On the island of Avalon." The green gaze of the *Gallizenae* priestess sparkled like the deep waves of the jade ocean in the sacred sea cave. "This unparalleled weapon, crafted on Avalon, forged in *dragonfire*—like the legendary Excalibur of King Arthur Pendragon—is the only means to defeat Voldurk. And the dark mistress he now serves."

As if her stepmother's icy hands had reached across the Narrow Sea, a chilling numbness crept up Issylte's arms. *The dark mistress he serves. The Black Widow Queen!*

At that moment, three more sea creatures swam into the cave, emerging from the ocean pool in front of Issylte, pulling themselves up onto an empty rock protruding from the cavern floor. Issylte inhaled sharply as a *sirène* settled onto the stone before her, displaying the familiar turquoise hair and deep green scales she'd glimpsed in the *sighting* when caring for the injured wolf. Issylte's heart thumped wildly as her magic soared to life.

"You are the healer Églantine," the mermaid trilled, her melodic voice liquid like a golden harp. "You saved me from a poisoned arrow which had pierced my left flank." The deep green gaze of the mermaid locked onto Issylte. "While I was in wolf form."

As Issylte stood, mouth agape, trying to comprehend the mermaid's words, two smaller *sirènes*, each with turquoise hair and deep green scales, pulled themselves onto the same rock before Issylte.

"You are Ondine?" Issylte asked incredulously of the larger mermaid.

"I am," the *sirène* replied, smiling warmly at the

shocked Issylte. Wrapping an arm around each of the smaller mermaids at her sides, Ondine said, her voice filled with pride, "and these are my daughters. My mate *Garou* has our sons with him. In *la Tribu des Loups*. The Wolf Tribe."

At Issylte's look of astonishment, Ondine laughed gaily and explained. "We *Mélusines* cannot bear young in our mermaid form. So, during mating season, we shift into mammals. Half of us mate with the shape shifting men of *la Tribu des Loups*—the Wolf Tribe. The remaining *Mélusines* mate with the shifters of *le Clan des Ours*—the Bear Clan. The mammal form we take is determined by our father. If sired by a wolf, we shift into lupine form to mate, with others assuming the bear form of their ursine fathers." Ondine stroked the long turquoise hair of her two daughters, who smiled shyly at their mother's side. "We give birth in mammal form, protected by our mates who remain at our side until the pups or cubs are weaned. Mothers then bring the female offspring back here to the *Île de Sein* and nearby islands, where the young retain mermaid form until puberty. At the age of fifteen, young mermaids shift into mammal form for the first time. They travel with their mothers to the forests, to meet the young members of the Wolf Tribe or Bear Clan, selecting the male they will mate with for the first time at eighteen. Fathers raise the male offspring within their Tribe or Clan. Like the females, the young males do not shift until they reach puberty. They remain in human form, like their fathers, shifting into bears or wolves to mate with us. The *Mélusines*."

Ondine smiled at Issylte. "Garou and I usually mate in *Brocéliande*, near his home in *le Vallon de la Chambre aux Loups*. But this year, we were inexplicably drawn to the forest near *la Joyeuse Garde*."

The *Mélusine's* deep green eyes locked with hers. "I believe the Goddess brought us there so that I would meet you, Lady of the Mirrored Lake. She has entwined our fates. You, Healer of Avalon, saved my life. And I will help you in your quest. For you see, we *Mélusines* do not only shape shift into wolves or bears to mate. We also shift into *les Dragons de Mer*. Sea Dragon Warriors. *To fight*."

Issylte forced a swallow, her breath catching in her throat. The wings of a white dove fluttered in her breast.

"Priestess of Dana, one of the three *Fées Dorées* gifted you with *la Voix de l' Eau*. The Voice of Water. Enabling you to speak to your mate across any body of water that connects you. So that he—and only he—will hear your voice. I shall expand upon that gift, Lady of the Mirrored Lake. If you should ever need *les Dragons de Mer*, you may summon us through any ocean. Cast your voice into the sea, and I will come to your aid."

Ondine slipped the lower half of her body down into the water, her daughters close behind. With a look of profound gratitude, the *Mélusine* smiled at Issylte and whispered, "*Au revoir, mon amie*. Goodbye, my friend. Until we meet again." She then disappeared into the ocean, her teal tailfin flowing in the waves, her two small daughters swimming at her side.

Issylte watched them go, then faced the nine *Gallizenae* sentinels who remained on the large rocks before her. A chorus of magic sang in her hopeful heart.

The *Gallizenae* had revealed the treasured object hidden in *le Miroir aux Fées*. The priceless orb which the wizard sought. Issylte now suspected why the Priestesses of Dana were being attacked. They were the guardians of the sacred waters of the Goddess. And the orb was hidden in the Mirrored Lake. Did Voldurk know that?

Issylte spoke to the blonde *Gallizenae* mermaid, her voice eloquent and reverent. "The dwarves have been searching the sacred Forest of *Brocéliande.* Attacking the Priestesses of Dana, guardians of the sacred waters of the Goddess. Does the wizard Voldurk know where the orb is hidden?"

"No," replied the blonde *sirène.* "But Frocin traced it to a body of water within the Forest of *Brocéliande.* Voldurk's power is born of dark magic, so he cannot enter the sacred realm of the Goddess. Yet, the dwarves—*otherworldly* inhabitants and native denizens of the woods—may search the forest for him. And if they capture the priestess who guards the sacred water where the orb is hidden, Voldurk can force her to retrieve it for him."

Issylte shuddered to think that she, as the Lady of the Mirrored Lake, would be the very priestess Voldurk sought. A shiver ran up her spine at the thought of his yellow, reptilian eyes. And her stepmother's icy, numbing hands.

The blonde *Gallizenae* priestess—who seemed to be the leader—spoke encouragingly to Issylte. "Although the dark wizard seeks the orb to destroy the last remaining dragon, a warrior of the Tribe of Dana may wield its power as well. Not to kill *Mordrac*—an *otherworldly* creature sacred to the Goddess Dana—but to obtain the *dragonfire* necessary to forge the sword which will defeat Lord Voldurk."

Issylte's magic soared in her veins, her pulse pounding in her throat.

"Your *mate,* Lady of the Mirrored Lake, has been

prophesied to defeat the dark wizard with a weapon of unparalleled power. A sword, forged in *dragonfire*—by the Avalonian Elf, the descendent of Gofannon. Blacksmith of the Gods."

Her knees weak and trembling as comprehension dawned, Issylte whispered, "Ronan."

Ronan is the only one who can forge the sword for Tristan. A vise clamped around her pounding heart.

"Yes. And you, *La Dame du Miroir aux Fées*, must retrieve the orb for your *mate* from the depths of the Mirrored Lake. You must convince the Elf—whose heart you have broken—to forge the sword for the Blue Knight of Cornwall. That Tristan may defeat the dark wizard Voldurk. And the malevolent mistress he now serves. Malfleur. *La Fée des Ombres*. The evil Shadow Fairy."

The mermaid's *otherworldly* eyes shone with compassion. And conviction.

The silver-haired *Gallizenae* priestess spoke, her voice conveying urgency and need. "We will teach you what must be done to forge the sword *Azeldraig*—which will exceed even the legendary weapon Excalibur. And we will teach you how to cast your spirit as the little white dove which lies within your breast. For your *mate* needs you, Lady of the Mirrored Lake. The dark wizard and the Black Widow Queen hover over him, and you must hurry. Listen carefully, and the *Gallizenae* will grant you the knowledge you seek."

Chapter 14

The Seduction

The dwarf Bothor stood nervously in the lush antechamber of Queen Morag in the Fortress of Morois, former residence of the late dwarf Frocin. Exquisite in her gown of rich red velvet, sumptuous as the elegant drapes of the large windows behind her gilded throne, the beautiful queen regarded him with eyes black as obsidian, dark as the enraged wizard who spat at him from her regal side.

"Frocin *failed*—as did Malvon," Voldurk hissed, his voice seething with venom. "The victim escaped. Did you at least retrieve the ruby necklace?"

"No, my lord. We scoured the entire Tower of Frégart. There was no trace of it."

"I am surrounded by incompetent, impotent idiots! Why do *you* now stand before me, Bothor? Am I to believe that *you* will not fail as well?" Voldurk sneered, his face contorted with fury.

"My lord, while it is true that others before me have failed," Bothor replied evenly, struggling to keep his voice steady and confident, "I *will not*." Staring at the sinister wizard before him, the new Leader of the Dwarves mustered the courage to prove his worth.

"I am here to provide information which I believe you will deem *invaluable*. And to present a proposal which will provide you—and Her Majesty the Queen—the perfect solution to obtain that which you both seek. I request permission to speak."

Voldurk fixed his serpentine stare on Bothor, intrigue apparent in his golden gaze. He glanced at the beautiful brunette queen at his side. Her black, regal eyes conveyed conspiratorial interest as she ducked her chin imperceptibly, indicating her approval.

"Proceed, Bothor. You have piqued our curiosity. Explain how you will succeed when even the infallible Frocin has failed."

Bothor pushed his long, black hair away from his feral face and straightened his shoulders, pulling himself up to his full height. Taller than most dwarves, he could be taken for a man of short stature, and although he was not handsome, his was not the disfigured, misshapen visage of many of his brethren. In a deep voice resonating with conviction, he unfolded the details of his ingenious plan.

******

Morag purred contentedly, stretched across her plush bed scented with the same lavender she'd always preferred in her royal chambers of Castle Connaught in Ireland. As Voldurk teased a pink nipple with his skilled serpentine tongue, she luxuriated in the afterglow of their amorous embrace. The golden dragon whose flames blazed deliciously in her enflamed loins.

"We'll inform the king that you wish to travel to France to purchase fabric for your wedding gown and jewels for the royal ceremony," Voldurk exhaled, lavishing attention on her voluptuous breasts. He raised his face to look up at her, a devilish grin spread across his wickedly handsome face. "Sir Indulf, as your royal guard, will accompany us with two dozen knights. While we meet with Bothor to implement his proposed plan, Indulf and his men can scrutinize the shores of Armorique. Strategize for the renewed assaults and Viking slave raids which will target the coast of France."

He returned to his oral adoration of her curvaceous body, perhaps to soften the impact of his next words. "My queen," he cooed, his lips coaxing her nipples into aching peaks, "I have a confession to make. A necessary indiscretion you must forgive." He replaced his tongue with skilled fingers, his golden gaze hypnotic as his eyes danced with hers.

"Last summer, after the failed invasion of Cornwall, I rekindled an old flame in Bretagne." Morag's attention was quickly diverted from sensual pleasure as she scrutinized his face warily.

"I seduced *Morgane la Fée*," he continued, massaging her nipple with a smooth, flat palm. "The fairy who had been infatuated with me as a young Druid." His fingers traced a trail down her stomach to the soft curls between her legs. Morag moaned softly under his magic touch, the pleasure too intense to ignore.

"I convinced Morgane that I loved her," he whispered, his tantalizing touch distracting. "So that she would craft a talisman for me. An orb of inordinate power. For she, *La Fée Blanche des Rochers*, was skilled beyond measure with knowledge of the sacred stones."

Morag gazed into his glowing dragon eyes, hovering now above her flustered face. "Did she create the talisman? The orb?" She gasped as his fingers caressed the delicate nub between her thighs.

"She did indeed. But Morgane—like your elusive stepdaughter Issylte—has the gift of *sight*. Within the depths of the orb, she glimpsed my love affair with you. Blinded with jealous rage, she enchanted it. And hid it in the sacred forest of Brocéliande. To keep it from me."

Voldurk stroked and probed her tender flesh as she writhed under his insistent hand. "The orb lies hidden in *le Miroir aux Fées*. The sacred waters that your stepdaughter, a Priestess of Dana, is sworn to protect. My queen—the Princess Issylte is now the Lady of the Mirrored Lake." Morag widened her eyes in wonder. "And she will obtain the orb for me."

Her breath hitched, equally stimulated by his seductive words as his skilled touch.

"Bothor's plan is perfect," Voldurk hummed, increasing the intensity of her pleasure with his long fingers. "I will be able to obtain the priceless talisman. And you, my queen, shall avenge the Morholt with the death of the Blue Knight of Cornwall. And rid yourself of the Emerald Princess who poses the only threat to your Irish crown."

Her legs quivering, her body trembling, her heart pounding, the Black Widow Queen succumbed to sizzling pleasure as her golden dragon mounted her. And filled her darkest depths with liquid flames.

****

Tristan, Lancelot, and Kjetil, escorted by Prince Kaherdin, arrived at *le Château Rose* to a warm welcome by King Hoël and his daughter, Princess Blanchine. Both monarchs—delighted that the Tribe of Dana had rescued Kaherdin's betrothed and shocked to hear of the enchanted ruby necklace—had arranged a celebratory feast in their honor, attended by many lords and ladies of the court. A royal wedding was planned for the upcoming Yuletide season so that Gargeolaine's babe, due in February, would be born in wedlock, eliminating any question as to the legitimacy of the future heir of Armorique.

Blanchine, though pleased for her brother that his love had been returned safely to his side, was nevertheless unhappy that she had been selected to serve as a temporary replacement for the unfortunate Aliénor, the chaperone killed during the abduction.

Having sent his royal condolences and a hefty sum to ease the bereaved family's grief, her father the king had decided that Blanchine would remain at her future sister-in-law's side, for the wedding would take place in a few short weeks. There was no need to employ a new governess, especially since Gargeolaine was living at the castle—and residing in the room next to her own. Blanchine was now subject to the relentlessly cheerful, incessant chatter of her brother's fiancée every day. And the endless cries of ecstasy every night.

It was unbearable, especially when what Blanchine wanted most of all was to be alone with Tristan. The irresistible Blue Knight of Cornwall.

He was so incredibly handsome; she couldn't take her eyes off him. She'd informed her father that she'd met a most attractive suitor at Sir Lancelot's castle, and that she hoped he might arrange a royal wedding for her with the Prince of Lyonesse.

She'd explained that Tristan had been banished from Tintagel due to treachery, which could be exposed if her father were willing to sail to Cornwall—or send a messenger on his behalf—to speak to King Marke. To her dismay, her father had not only deemed it unwise to create a confrontation with Tristan's uncle, but until the banishment were revoked and the nephew's status as heir to the throne restored, he had no intention whatsoever of pursuing such a marriage for his precious royal daughter. Blanchine, *la Demoiselle aux Mains Blanches*, would have to take matters into her own *white hands*.

She would have to find a way to seduce Tristan.

Blanchine was now seated beside Gargeolaine in the reception room of *le Château Rose*, where several cloth merchants and jewelers were dazzling the royal ladies with their sumptuous wares, eager to earn a handsome profit with the upcoming royal marriage. Her brother, father, and honored guests—including the dashing Blue Knight of Cornwall—were off hunting, leaving the ladies of the court with their personal guards to decide on the feminine fripperies involved in planning a wedding.

As Gargeolaine and a few lovely courtiers ogled the finest laces and silks for their royal wedding attire, Blanchine noticed a dark-haired man staring at her most intently. Upon catching her attention, the mysterious merchant gathered a few of the jewels he had brought to display and approached her surreptitiously while the other ladies chatted exuberantly nearby.

"Your Majesty, may I show you my exquisite jewels? I am certain you will be most pleased with their exceptional quality." The strange man extended a black velvet case which contained a glittering necklace and earrings that were indeed enticing.

As she examined the alluring array, the enigmatic jeweler spoke quietly into her ear. "Forgive my boldness, your Majesty, but I wonder if you might be interested in a trinket which would capture the heart of the one you most desire?"

Blanchine regarded the odd merchant with

skepticism—but unbridled curiosity. "Perhaps," she replied cautiously.

****

"I can offer you the means to control the heart of anyone you wish, Your Royal Highness." Bothor smiled enigmatically at the princess whose attention he now held in the palm of his hand. Precisely as he'd hoped.

"How is this possible? Do you sell such a talisman?" Blanchine gasped, seemingly breathless with anticipation.

"No, Your Majesty, I do not." He was thrilled to see her face fall in disappointment. She had taken the bait. Now, to reel her in... "However, I *do* know someone who possesses such power. A wizard, capable of crafting such an enchantment. Would you be interested, Princess Blanchine? In obtaining a powerful spell to capture the heart of the one you love, binding him to you...and to you alone?"

"Yes," she whispered tremulously. "I am very interested."

Bothor glanced around, eyeing the merchants he'd engaged to help with this subterfuge. Everything was proceeding smoothly; the ladies of the court were ordering fabric and jewels precisely as anticipated.

With a sly grin, he uttered furtively, "Come tomorrow at two o'clock to *la Belle Bijouterie* in the village of Trébourden. Say that you wish to see a necklace that I mentioned today, which I keep locked inside my shop. Bring some of the ladies of the court as a distraction, and I shall take you into the back room to meet the wizard. He will tell you what he needs to cast the spell. You will not be disappointed, Your Majesty. I, Bothor, give you my word." His pulse thrummed with adrenaline as the Princess of Armorique eagerly agreed.

****

The next day, Blanchine, along with three ladies of the court, traveled by coach with two dozen royal guards to the village of Trébourden to see a diamond necklace at *la Belle Bijouterie*. Kaherdin had insisted that Gargeolaine remain in the castle and had tried to dissuade his stubborn sister from going, but she'd insisted on seeing the exquisite jewel. Her father, having spoiled his precious princess her entire life, had relented, doubling the number of royal guards escorting Blanchine into town as an added precaution.

And now, while her three companions were kept occupied by his assistants, the dwarf Bothor led Blanchine behind a black velvet curtain, through a wooden door, and into a back room where a tall, dark-haired man with astonishing golden eyes sat next to a strikingly beautiful woman with hair as black as jet. Both were dressed entirely in black, and Blanchine noticed a royal coronet made of silver and adorned with diamonds glittering upon the forehead of the intriguing female. *A queen! Could this be the intended bride of King Marke of Cornwall?*

"Your Royal Highness, may I present the Princess Blanchine of Armorique?" Bothor effused, bowing reverently to the monarch in black. Then, to Blanchine, he said gallantly, "Your Majesty, allow me to introduce Her Royal Highness, Queen Morag of Ireland. Betrothed to King Marke of Cornwall." The dwarf then gestured to the man in black. "And her Royal Advisor, Lord Voldurk."

Blanchine curtsied regally before the elegant queen. "A pleasure to meet you, Your Highness. I am honored by your presence and grateful for this audience." She addressed the dark wizard. "*Enchantée*, Lord Voldurk," as he rose to dutifully kiss her royal hand.

"Please, Princess Blanchine, be seated. We are delighted that you have joined us." Queen Morag smiled graciously as Blanchine made herself comfortable in the velvet wing chair facing them. "Lord Bothor, see that we are not disturbed."

"Yes, Your Majesty. I shall await just outside the door." The dwarf retreated from the room, leaving Blanchine with the queen, whose smile evoked a cat who had just trapped a mouse, and the wizard with the gleaming eyes of a snake. Blanchine had the sudden, urgent impulse to flee. *The wizard can bind Tristan to me. It will be worth it. No matter the cost.* Swallowing her trepidation, she smoothed her skirts and addressed the man in black.

"Lord Voldurk," she began, suppressing the tremor in her voice with considerable effort, "the jeweler Bothor has informed me that you are capable of crafting an enchantment which would bind the heart of the man I love to me and only me. Is this correct, sir?"

The wizard grinned expansively, his sharp white teeth gleaming against his darkly handsome face. "It is indeed correct, Your Highness. I need only three items from the man whose heart you wish to control in order to cast such a spell."

After a brief pause, his mesmerizing serpentine eyes engaged hers. Blanchine's breath hitched when Lord Voldurk suggested coyly, "It is Tristan of Lyonesse whom you wish to enchant. Is that not so, dear princess?"

Blanchine cast a glance at the queen, whose black eyes pierced her to the quick. Inhaling deeply, summoning courage, Blanchine stammered, "Yes, Sir Tristan of Lyonesse. I love him, but…"

"He is in love with the Princess Issylte of Ireland, the woman whom you believed to be the Lady Opale of Camelot." Queen Morag's icy voice chilled like a blast of winter frost. "The false name was a ruse for her protection. *To hide her from me.*"

Blanchine gulped, suppressing the urge to run to the door and escape the malevolent presence of the sinister queen.

"But fear not, dear princess, for Lord Voldurk and I have found the perfect solution."

Queen Morag stood and walked regally to the display case, where lovely jewels glittered in the candlelight of the darkened room. Blanchine, transfixed with breathless anticipation, watched the foreboding figure with gnawing trepidation. "If Prince Tristan were to marry the Princess Issylte, their children would be heirs to the thrones of Ireland, Lyonesse, and Cornwall. A most unwelcome threat to my power as queen of those three kingdoms."

She swirled abruptly to Blanchine. "But if I were to convince my betrothed to restore his nephew as the Prince of Lyonesse—perhaps even have him crowned king—then Sir Tristan would be worthy of you, dear princess. And a royal marriage to *King* Tristan would make you his *queen*, Princess Blanchine."

Morag stroked the smooth edge of the wooden display case with her long, slender fingers. "Princess Issylte could return to Ireland, for I would recognize her as my late husband King Donnchadh's daughter and rightful heir. Thrilled to regain her father's throne, she would be more than content to become the Emerald

Queen of Ireland. And, thus separated from Tristan—who would be bound to *you* through Voldurk's spell—Issylte would pose virtually no threat to your royal marriage to the Prince of Lyonesse."

Morag dazzled Blanchine with a generous, ingenuine smile. "And I, married to Tristan's uncle, would become Queen of Cornwall." Gleaming black eyes danced in wicked delight. "Issylte of Ireland. Blanchine of Lyonesse. Morag of Cornwall. A trio of satisfied, powerful queens." The malevolent monarch held Blanchine in her hypnotic stare. "As you see, dear Blanchine...*everyone wins.*"

With the satisfied smirk of a feline who'd snared a mouse, the seductive queen purred, "We do need your help, however. In order to cast such an enchantment, you must obtain three things from Sir Tristan." Queen Morag bowed her head to the wizard. "Please explain, dear Voldurk," she crooned, returning to her regal seat at his side.

"You must mark him as yours," the wizard began, leaning forward to entice Blanchine with mesmerizing golden eyes. He placed a small vial on the wooden table before her. "You will scratch his neck to *claim* him, drawing blood. Which you will collect and place in this container."

Voldurk then set another vial on the table—somewhat larger, with a black stopper in its mouth. "This flask contains a powder which you must pour into the wound—the *claim* you have made on his neck. It contains a drug which will bind the spell with his blood."

Blanchine glanced nervously from the wizard to the queen. Both exuded power which thrilled and terrified her. Her hands were drenched, her mouth parched, her heart pounded with adrenaline. She returned her gaze to the intoxicating Lord Voldurk. Desperate to hear more.

"I will need the sample of blood, a lock of his hair, and the key ingredient. His *essence*." The wizard chuckled softly, casting her a dark, diabolical stare.

"His *essence*?" Blanchine asked, perplexed. She looked at the queen, who was smiling patiently, waiting for her to comprehend.

"His *seed*, dear Blanchine. The *essence* of his love. It is crucial for the spell to be effective."

Blanchine's heart fluttered in her throat. "But…how do I obtain his seed?"

The wizard rose to his feet, strode to an armoire against the wall, and removed a long, blonde wig and dark green robe. "You will don this disguise." Voldurk held them out for her to see, allowing Blanchine to touch the soft hair and gown. "You'll enter his room—he'll be drugged, of course, his senses dimmed. You'll say that you are Issylte, returned from her voyage. We shall drug him with a powerful aphrodisiac—so that he will be in a most *amorously aroused* state." Voldurk grinned devilishly, his face a lascivious sneer. "Once you obtain his seed, put it in this container," he instructed, placing a large, stoppered vial on the table, "and bring the three samples to me. I shall be waiting at the edge of the forest tomorrow night, by the servants' entrance to *le Château Rose*. In the morning, when you awaken, the heart of Tristan of Lyonesse will be *yours*."

Voldurk and the queen grinned wickedly at each other. Blanchine wiped her hands nervously on her dress, her eyes lowered in embarrassment.

"What is it, Blanchine? Are you unwilling to assist Lord Voldurk?" The queen leaned forward menacingly, her slender hands pressed firmly, flat against the table.

Blanchine raised her gaze meekly to the queen and stammered, "No, I am most willing. But...*how* do I obtain his seed? I do not understand."

The wizard and the queen exchanged quick, surprised glances. Morag then replied, "Why, by pleasuring him with *your mouth*, of course."

Bewildered, Blanchine confessed, "But I do not know how to pleasure a man with my mouth. I have never *been* with a man before."

Queen Morag grinned ferally at the dark wizard at her side. "Lord Voldurk, would you allow me to demonstrate for Princess Blanchine?"

The wizard, a seductive smile reaching his gleaming golden eyes whispered, "Of course, my queen. It would be...my *pleasure*."

"Indeed, it will," the queen cooed in a sultry feline voice.

"Now, dear Blanchine, watch. And *learn.*"

****

The evening meal had been delicious, and now, in the conservatory of *le Château Rose,* Blanchine was delighted to see that Kaherdin and Gargeolaine had finally decided to retire so that they could do more than just devour each other with their eyes. Soon, Lancelot followed their example, leaving Tristan and Kjetil to finish their game of chess.

Her heart pounding wildly, the princess poured three goblets of wine, adding the contents of the aphrodisiac into Tristan's as she served the two men at the table and sat down to join them. "This is an exceptional vintage. It is one of my favorites."

As the Blue Knight of Cornwall and the Viking

lifted their goblets to hers, Blanchine proposed a toast. "To Kaherdin and Gargeolaine. May the Goddess bless their union. And to the brave warriors of the Tribe of Dana, whose valor and prowess safely delivered my brother's betrothed to rejoin us here at *le Château Rose*."

She watched with bated breath as Tristan finished his wine. *The drug needs about a half hour to take effect, Voldurk said. I shall watch them play chess until the symptoms begin to show.*

Tristan seemed to have difficulty concentrating. He appeared woozy, as if he had consumed too much wine. He rose unsteadily, grasping the back of his chair. "I am feeling extremely tired, my friend," he said to Kjetil. "Perhaps we can finish our game tomorrow. I'll bid both you and Princess Blanchine goodnight. *Bonne nuit*." He bowed gallantly on wobbly legs.

Kjetil stood and stretched his long arms above his head. "I could use a good night's sleep myself. We train tomorrow, then return to Landuc the following day. I'll see you in the morning, Tristan. Goodnight, Princess Blanchine." The tall blond Viking kissed her hand, then followed Tristan down the hall and upstairs to their respective guest quarters.

Blanchine scurried to her own room and quickly donned the blonde wig, pulling the green gown over her own blue one. *I can simply remove the outer one and still be dressed underneath to meet Voldurk. That way, I'll be able to leave Tristan's room more quickly.*

Verifying that she had the necessary items in the bag which she now gripped tightly, Blanchine peeked out her door into the darkness. No one stirred and all was silent in the castle.

She slipped quietly into the corridor, illuminated

softly by the moonbeam shining through the window at the end of the hall, tiptoeing quickly and stealthily to Tristan's room. Without a sound, she entered his chamber, closing the door behind her.

The interior was shadowy, lit by dying embers in the fireplace and by the moonlight glowing through the twin windows on the far wall which faced the sea. Tristan lay in his bed, his tunic tossed in a chair and his sheathed sword leaning against it.

Blanchine quietly removed the vials and placed them on the table next to his bed, keeping the sack in which she would store the samples from Tristan at her feet. Leaning over the bed, she let the long blonde hair from the wig touch the side of his face as she whispered, "Tristan… It's me, Issylte. I have returned to you, my love."

He raised his head and moved toward her, his eyes glazed and unfocused. "Issylte… I have missed you so…" Wrapping an arm behind her head, he pulled Blanchine down to him and kissed her passionately. "By the Goddess, I yearn for you…"

Pulling the blanket away from Tristan, she could see that the aphrodisiac was working well indeed, from the outline of his body straining at the top of his breeches. He attempted to pull her down next to him. "I feel woozy, my love. Come lie down beside me."

Blanchine gently pushed him back down on the bed. Kissing him softly, she whispered, "Shhh, let me take care of you, Tristan. I have longed for you, too." Despite his initial protests, he quickly succumbed to moans of pleasure once Blanchine unfastened his pants and lightly caressed the tip of him with her tongue. As Queen Morag had shown her, Blanchine took him into her mouth, grasping him tightly with a hand beneath her lips as she plunged down with persistent, rhythmic strokes. She could feel his leg muscles tightening, his abdomen clutching, and soon, his body shuddered, erupting in waves of pleasure as he emptied every drop of his precious essence into her eager mouth.

He rolled over onto his side, humming contentedly, while Blanchine opened the large vial, carefully deposited the contents from her mouth inside, then replaced the stopper. "I can't keep my eyes open..." Tristan whispered.

"Just sleep, my love," Blanchine cooed into his ear, tucking the blankets over his shoulder. *Once he experiences physical release, the drug will make him sleep. He will not awaken until morning, when he will be yours.* The princess shivered deliciously at the promise of Voldurk's words as Tristan began to snore softly beside her.

If there is a mark on his neck, you must scratch it out and claim him with your own fingernails. Once his blood flows, collect a few drops, then pour the dark powder into the wound. It will bind the spell to his blood.

Blanchine spotted a green teardrop shaped tattoo on Tristan's neck. *Issylte's mark, which I will scratch out— to claim him as mine.* Although she hated the idea of gouging Tristan, she knew that his blood was essential for the enchantment. And her own mark would override the false one—for Tristan was *hers*, not Issylte's.

The first scratch did nothing but make Tristan stir in his sleep. The second attempt left red marks but did not puncture the skin. Determined to bind the man she loved to her through Voldurk's spell, Blanchine dug her fingernails sharply into the green mark on his neck, drawing blood at last.

She collected several droplets into the small vial, then replaced the stopper. Carefully pouring the black powder into the wound and massaging it into his blood, she replaced the stopper on that vial as well.

Using the small knife the wizard had given her, Blanchine cut a lock of Tristan's hair. She put it into the small pouch, which she placed on top of the table beside the vials.

Removing the blonde wig and the green gown, she folded and placed them, along with the knife, into the sack at her feet. Blanchine retrieved the two empty vials—which had contained the aphrodisiac and the black powder—and placed them into the sack as well.

Finally, she gathered the three samples from Tristan's body—his blood, his essence, and his hair—and put them into a small bag, taking care to not spill the contents. She placed it into the sack which she grasped tightly, preparing to leave.

After examining the room to be certain she had left no trace behind, Blanchine peered into the dark corridor and, seeing no one, slipped through the hall, down the stairs, and out the servants' entrance off the kitchen. Scanning the forest, she spotted the dark outline of a man who emerged from the trees onto the moonlit castle grounds.

Glancing around nervously to be sure she had not been followed, her heart racing with adrenaline, Blanchine ran breathlessly to Voldurk, who watched her with golden, predatory eyes.

"Did all go as planned?" he asked warily.

"Yes. I have everything in this bag," she gasped, her limbs trembling with excitement.

"The wig, the gown, and the knife?"

"Yes, and the empty vials for the aphrodisiac and the black powder." She opened the sack to show Voldurk the contents. "And here are the three samples from Tristan's body." Blanchine indicated the small bag within the larger sack.

"Excellent. Well done, Princess. I shall return to the Tower of Frégart and cast the spell tonight. In the morning, Tristan of Lyonesse will be yours, Blanchine. All yours."

She handed the sack to Voldurk, beaming with excitement. *Tristan will be mine! Queen Morag will convince King Marke to restore Tristan's birthright and crown him King of Lyonesse. Father will approve of the royal marriage, and I shall be Tristan's queen. We shall live in le Château d' Or, his father's majestic castle, on the distant shore of Lyonesse. It all begins tomorrow. I cannot wait!*

Her heart filled with love for Tristan, her mind racing at the possibilities for the future she envisioned with him, Blanchine was startled by a sharp prick in her neck. Spinning her head quickly, she saw Voldurk's pointed teeth bared in a feral grin, his snake-like eyes gleaming with malice, as darkness overtook her, and she collapsed in the grass.

****

Armed guards stormed into Tristan's room as morning sunlight flooded his chamber. His head pounding, his tongue swollen and thick, his stomach roiling, he couldn't comprehend what was happening. Grabbing the chamber pot beside the bed, he heaved the contents of his stomach as the room whirled around sickeningly.

"Tristan of Lyonesse, you are under arrest for the murder of Princess Blanchine of Armorique." The guards seized him, yanking him out of bed and chaining his arms behind him as Kaherdin burst into the room.

"You fucking bastard!" Kaherdin bellowed, landing his fist squarely in Tristan's jaw, pounding his face and torso while the guards held him fast. "We shelter you in our castle. Our bloody *guest of honor*," he shouted as blood poured from Tristan's nose and mouth. "And you fucking *murder my sister*! I'll kill you myself!" Kaherdin unleashed his fury, pummeling Tristan's stomach, causing him to vomit profusely over the prince's royal boots.

"Take him to the dungeon! Twenty lashes!" King Hoël boomed, having just entered the room to stand beside Kaherdin. The king's grief-stricken face mirrored his son's.

"I swear, I did not touch Blanchine!" Tristan shouted desperately as the guards hauled him to his feet.

"You killed her, you bastard! She has blood under her fingernails. And you! You have this jagged scratch and dried blood on your fucking neck!" Scraping his finger along the mark Blanchine had made the night before, Kaherdin vehemently spat in Tristan's face. "They even found your hair in her fist, you fucking liar. You *killed* her. You'll be executed for her murder. And I will chop your bloody head off myself!"

The guards dragged Tristan to the moldy, murky dungeon in the bowels of the castle. They chained his arms to the stone wall and flogged him with a leather whip which split open his skin, rendering his back into a bloody, meaty mess. The effects of the drug still clouding his thoughts and sickening his body, Tristan succumbed to the excruciating pain as he slipped mercifully into unconsciousness. When he came to several hours later, he sat slumped on the hard stone floor of the prison, his head lolling forward, wondering who on the Goddess' green earth had killed Blanchine.

A guard bringing bread and water was the only human Tristan saw for several days. Then, unexpectedly, several armed guards rushed into his cell, yanked him to his feet, and dragged him out of the castle, forcing him into a carriage which was then locked and chained. Flanked by several guards on horseback, Tristan was transported to a ship, where his captors relinquished the prisoner into the hands of a slender, black-haired queen and a tall, mysterious man with golden eyes, both of whom were dressed in black and surrounded by heavily armed knights.

"You are my prisoner now, Tristan of Lyonesse. On behalf of my betrothed, King Marke of Cornwall, I am transporting you to the castle of Tintagel. Where you shall be executed for treason against your king. And the murder of Princess Blanchine of Armorique."

To the knights at her side, the Black Widow Queen commanded, her steely voice lethal as a sharpened blade: "Take him below deck, into the belly of the ship. Keep him under close guard until we reach the shores of Cornwall."

For ten interminable days, Tristan languished in pain and misery as Queen Morag and Lord Voldurk sailed across the Narrow Sea to remand the banished knight to his uncle's kingdom.

To the dank, dark dungeon of Tintagel.

Where he would be executed.

By the merciless, ruthless, and relentless Black

Widow Queen.

Chapter 15

Le Cheveu d' Or

Issylte wrapped her cape tightly around her shoulders and pulled her hood up over her damp hair, for the early October wind chilled her to the bone. The frigid water of *le Miroir aux Fées* had nearly paralyzed her limbs when she left the island of the *Gallizenae* and traveled through *la Porte du Dedans*. She now rubbed her arms briskly and trotted through the woods toward *le Château de Landuc* to warm up as best she could, eager to return to the Tribe and share her newfound knowledge.

On horseback, the trek would only take minutes, but on foot, it had taken over an hour to finally reach the castle gate, which she now approached in the afternoon setting sun. The sentries spotted her from the barbican defense towers and called for the gate to be opened so that she could enter. Issylte crossed the wooden drawbridge over the moat into the castle bailey where members of the Tribe of Dana rushed to welcome her home.

Laudine, Esclados, Lancelot, and others rushed to greet her, anxious to hear news of her trip to *l' Île de Sein* and the Priestesses of the *Gallizenae*. The Lady of the Fountain took her cloak, wrapped a warm blanket around her, and settled Issylte in front of a roaring fire with a cup of mulled wine. The warm, spicy taste made her think of Ronan, which also reminded her that she now needed to travel to Avalon to ask him to forge the exceptional sword for Tristan. She shuddered to think of facing him—and of asking him for such an extraordinary favor. *He just has to say yes. I must find a way to convince him.*

After she'd warmed up and eaten a light meal, Issylte looked at the expectant faces of the friends who were seated around her at the table in the cozy alcove of the kitchen. Kirus had his arm wrapped around Nolwenn; Lysara rested her head on Solzic's shoulder; Lancelot sat beside Issylte, his presence comforting and reassuring. Laudine hovered over them all like a mother hen. Issylte's heart overflowed with gratitude for this Tribe. Her family. Whose help she now needed to rescue Tristan.

Kjetil and Lancelot had told her of the ordeal at *le Château Rose* where Blanchine had been murdered and Tristan imprisoned for the crime. He'd been arrested and taken by ship to Cornwall, where he now languished in the dungeon of Tintagel, facing execution.

Issylte informed the Tribe of Dana that she'd learned from the *Gallizenae* that Voldurk and the queen had duped Blanchine and killed her, making it appear as if Tristan had committed the murder.

"We must rescue him," Issylte urged the Tribe, whose concerned faces were rapt with attention. "The *Gallizenae* taught me how to cast my spirit as a white dove." She locked eyes with Lancelot, her heart racing with adrenaline. His brilliant blue gaze blazed with intensity. "I must fly into his prison cell and undo Voldurk's evil spell with *le cheveu d'or*. A lock of my golden hair, soaked in the verdant magic which flows in my blood."

Whispers circulated around the table as Issylte continued breathlessly. "The *Gallizenae* explained that I, as the white dove, must peck at Tristan's neck, enabling his blood to flow from our *mating mark*—the site of the wizard's dark spell. I must hold *le cheveu d'or* against the wound, so that my blood—rich in the Druidic magic of *Rose Elder*—can block and undo Voldurk's evil enchantment. And rekindle the unbreakable *mating bond* between Tristan and me."

Issylte spoke to Esclados, the Red Knight who had bestowed Tristan with the Druidic magic that was now crucial to her plan. "Tristan has the gift of *l'herbe d'or*, which permits him to communicate with birds. I'll be able to speak to him as the white dove. Inform him of our plan to help him escape. I'll bring medicine on the ship to treat him on the return voyage here to Landuc." She gripped Lancelot's forearm, imploring him with desperate eyes. "We must sail for Cornwall immediately. Before they execute him!" She struggled to regain her composure, swallowing her agonizing fear, then raised her gaze to search his distraught face. "Once we reach Tintagel, you and two or three members of the Tribe must row ashore to meet Gorvenal and convince him to free Tristan. He knows you; he'll listen to you. When he learns that Voldurk and the queen killed Blanchine—and that Tristan is innocent—then Gorvenal, as the First Knight of Tintagel, can obtain the keys to unlock Tristan's chains."

Lancelot rubbed his chin briskly, battle strategy forming in his fierce scowl. "I know Gorvenal from the Tournament of Champions. He was Tristan's mentor. Like a brother to him. He'll recognize me—I'll be able to approach him. Talk to him. Convince him of Tristan's innocence. We'll free Tristan, then bring him into the woods, where Solzic and Dagur will be waiting." The White Knight looked to his fellow Tribe members, who ducked their chins affirmatively, their faces feral and determined. "We'll bring both Tristan and Gorvenal with us to the small boat and row out to the waiting ship. Once we're all on board, we'll sail back here to Landuc."

Heads nodded as the Tribe agreed with the dangerous undertaking. "Gorvenal will be a powerful ally in the future when we sail to Cornwall to save Tristan's uncle," Lancelot continued, embellishing the escape plan. "The knights of Tintagel will be loyal to him and want to defend King Marke and the castle. Especially once they learn that Queen Morag—the Black Widow—*is poisoning their king.*"

"Laudine and I will remain here with Kirus, the members of the Tribe, and our knights—to defend Landuc," Esclados, the *châtelain,* informed Lancelot. "Solzic, Dagur, and Lysara will sail with you to Cornwall, with two dozen knights to defend your ship, in the event you are attacked." To the Tribe of Dana, the Red Knight ordered, "Help Lancelot, Dagur, and Solzic prepare to sail for Tintagel in the morning. Pack sufficient provisions for the weeklong voyage and the return trip."

Kirus, Solzic, and Dagur rose to their feet and dispersed with the remaining members of the Tribe to prepare the ship, clean weapons, and pack supplies.

Laudine spoke to Issylte, her somber expression filled with concern. "In the *verrière* I have the herbs you'll need for Tristan's medicine and the poultice for his wounds. The queen and wizard have most likely ordered him to be beaten and flogged in prison. Come, I'll help you concoct the tinctures and ointments to bring on the ship." Issylte rose, preparing to head to the greenhouse, beckoning Lancelot to approach. She needed to speak to him before he left to prepare for the journey.

The White Knight approached Issylte, standing beside Laudine. Meeting Lancelot's intense blue gaze, she whispered, "If we're successful in freeing Tristan, we must return here and prepare to defeat the dark wizard." She glanced at Laudine, then raised her face to her trusted friend. "The *Gallizenae* told me what can destroy the wizard Voldurk," she exhaled in hushed expectation. "A sword, similar to Excalibur. Forged in *dragonfire*, on the island of Avalon." She locked eyes with the White Knight, her heart in her throat. "By the descendent of Gofannon. The Blacksmith of the Gods."

Recognition dawned in Lancelot's brilliant blue gaze. "*Ronan.*"

Issylte lowered her head, fingering the lace on the sleeve of her dress.

Lancelot's voice was barely audible. "You must ask the Elf—whose heart you broke—to forge the sword. For the man who took you from him." He searched her face, compassion and empathy glowing in his glorious blue eyes.

She gazed up at him, a tremulous quiver in her lips. "I must find a way to convince him. That sword is the only way to defeat Voldurk."

Lancelot squeezed her hands, his boyish grin illuminating his handsome face. "I will go with you to Avalon. Ronan trained me; we know each other very well. Perhaps, between you and me, we can convince him to help us."

Issylte smiled with relief, gratitude, and hope. She glanced at Laudine, her solid presence a comforting support. "I have also learned what is hidden in *le Miroir aux Fées*. And why the dwarves have been prowling through the sacred forest, attacking our priestesses."

She described how the *Gallizenae* had informed her about the precious orb that *Morgane la Fée* had crafted for Voldurk. How it lay hidden in the Mirrored Lake, inaccessible to the dark wizard—who was relying on the dwarves to discover its location. And capture a priestess. "If the dwarves abduct a priestess of Dana, Voldurk can force her to yield the sacred power of the waters she protects. And if the orb lies within those waters, he can torture or enchant her to retrieve it for him. If the wizard obtains the orb…" she added, her voice quavering, "he will be invincible."

Issylte swallowed the massive lump in her throat, summoning the courage to face her fear. "And if Voldurk discovers that the orb is hidden in *Le Miroir aux Fées*, then he will wish to abduct *me*. The Lady of the Mirrored Lake." Her eyes darted nervously between Lancelot and Laudine. "When we sail to Tintagel, and I cast my spirit to fly into the castle dungeon to save Tristan, Voldurk must not capture the little white dove. For if he does, my spirit cannot return to my body."

The Lady of the Fountain looked gravely at Issylte, then at Lancelot. "He will not capture your spirit dove, Issylte. You will fly swiftly and surely, guided by the Goddess. We must believe that. We must have faith."

****

The voyage had been difficult, for the seas were rough. Issylte spent most days on the deck—despite the frigid salt spray which chapped her face—to avoid the inevitable sea sickness which always plagued her in the cabin. Lysara and Solzic were huddled together on deck as well, snuggling under a blanket in which they had wrapped themselves. The kisses they shared made Issylte desperate with longing for Tristan. Soon, the ship would be close enough to shore for her to cast her spirit. Adrenaline made her limbs tremble and her stomach roil. Although she had practiced casting her spirit a few times on the *Île de Sein,* she had never done it when necessary, and never under such dire circumstances. She prayed the Goddess would guide her flight.

The castle of Tintagel loomed in the distance, perched high on a curved cliff, boldly braving the turbulent sea. The larger ship on which they now sailed would remain here, well offshore and hidden by the curved, forested cliff which sheltered the castle but also shielded them from view. Lancelot, Solzic, and Dagur would row ashore with three knights, providing additional manpower if necessary while still not exceeding the capacity of the smaller vessel. Leaving enough room for Tristan and Gorvenal to join them when they rowed back to the larger ship.

Having prepared at Landuc the herbal remedies she would need to treat Tristan, Issylte now had everything stored in her cabin, ready to use when they had him safely aboard ship. She clutched the precious *cheveu d'or*—a strand of her golden hair—painstakingly soaked and coated with her own blood. Rich in the Druidic magic of Rose Elder.

The little spirit dove would carry *le cheveu d'or* tightly in her beak as she flew to Tintagel. To save Tristan. Her *mate*. And free him from Voldurk's evil spell.

Leaving her body lying peacefully in the bed of her cabin, Issylte cast her spirit into the small white bird, clasping *le cheveu d'or* in her beak. Taking flight from the deck of the ship, she soared over the ocean toward the castle of Tintagel. *This is the vision I saw in Tristan's eyes when I felt as if I were a bird, flying over the open sea, desperate to reach him. And now here I am, frantic to save him. Please, dear Goddess, help me succeed.* Her heart hammering in her fragile breast, she fluttered her wings furiously.

And flew to Tristan.

Lancelot had told her that the dungeon was situated on the southwest corner of the castle, facing the sea. A single window, low on the exterior wall—but well above a prisoner's head inside the bowels of the cell—would permit her entry, for the iron grid would allow a small bird to fit through its thick bars.

As she approached the castle, she noticed *un hêtre*—one of the three trees which would keep her hidden from her enemies, thanks to the forest gift from *les Fées Dorées*.

After I break Voldurk's spell, I will remain hidden in that beech tree to watch Lancelot and Gorvenal free Tristan. Then I will fly back to the ship to rejoin my body, Goddess willing.

The little white dove perched carefully on the ledge of the castle window to peer down into the dungeon.

Tristan sat hunched on the floor, his arms bound in chains. His head was lolled forward, with stringy, filthy hair in his face. A dingy gray shirt clung to his back with dried, blackened blood. His breeches were tattered and torn, his feet bare and scraped raw. His ankles and wrists were bloodied and bruised from the weight of the iron chains that bound him. Issylte's heart broke to see him in such abject misery.

Clutching *le cheveu d'or* in her beak, the white dove fluttered her wings, lowering herself down into Tristan's cell, landing on the floor before him. His normally vibrant blue eyes were dulled a dim, milky white due to the enchantment. Tristan did not seem to notice her presence or respond to the little dove who observed him with keen eyes. She carefully placed *le cheveu d'or* in his lap as she hopped onto his hunched stomach.

The *mating mark* was barely perceptible behind a hideously crusted scab that oozed a noxious black liquid. She pecked at it, wiping her beak on his shirt, until she finally broke the skin. The wisdom gleaned from the *Gallizenae* replayed in her mind.

Allow his blood to flow freely for a few moments, to wash out the toxins that Voldurk placed in the wound. Then, hold le cheveu d'or against the wound so that the magic of the Rose Elder in your own blood will block the evil enchantment in his, undoing the wizard's dark spell, and reawakening the mating bond that binds your spirit to Tristan's.

Remembering the instructions given by the *Mélusine* priestesses, Issylte's spirit dove retrieved *le cheveu d'or* with her beak and placed it against the flow of blood coming from the *mating mark* on the left side of Tristan's neck. She held it there for a long time, allowing her blood to cleanse his, reversing the evil enchantment, rekindling the *mating bond* between them.

After a while, Tristan's milky white gaze burned a brilliant blue once again, and he seemed to become aware of the small white bird perched on his stomach, observing him with intelligence and comprehension. Her heart aflutter, she hopped down onto the stone floor and *spoke* to him wordlessly. "Tristan, it's me. The *Gallizenae* taught me how to cast my spirit as this little dove. And how to break Voldurk's enchantment on you."

She fluttered her fragile wings before him. "Lancelot, Dagur, and Solzic are waiting in the woods just outside the castle to the southwest. Gorvenal will help them free you. They'll bring you to the small boat hidden in the woods. And row out to the ship we have anchored just around the bend in the cliff to the west. I'll wait in the giant beech tree outside your window until I see that you are safely with them. Then, I will fly back to the ship. And we'll all sail home to Landuc. Together."

Issylte's white dove hopped excitedly on the dungeon floor. "I have medicine on the ship to treat you during the return voyage. I must leave now and be extra cautious. No harm must come to this little bird. Or my spirit will not be able to return to my body."

She tilted her avian head to say goodbye, then flew up to the window's ledge where she perched and looked down at him one last time. "Come back to me, Tristan. I cannot bear for us to be apart. I love you." Flapping her fragile white wings, Issylte's spirit dove flew out of the dungeon window to the safety of the giant beech tree.

****

Lancelot, Solzic, and Dagur had rowed ashore with three knights, hidden with the small boat in the woods at the edge of the cliff. Leaving the warriors to guard the vessel, Solzic and Dagur had come to the castle grounds with Lancelot, where the three now crouched in the grass among the trees. The bodies of two Tintagel guards who had been patrolling the area now lay hidden behind them as Lancelot donned the armor of one of the slain knights. The second set of armor he retained for use if necessary. But first, he had to speak to Gorvenal.

Lancelot remembered—from the time he'd spent here for the Tournament of Champions—that the knights of Tintagel trained vigorously with Gorvenal until late afternoon. The men then returned to their quarters, changed out of their practice armor, and headed to the banquet hall for the evening meal.

He spotted Gorvenal walking toward the west entrance of the castle. Clad in the armor of a knight of Tintagel, Lancelot quickly approached Tristan's former mentor and hailed him. "Gorvenal! A word please, my lord!"

Gorvenal walked over to Lancelot, who spoke quickly, his voice lowered. "Gorvenal, it's me, Lancelot. I've come to request your help." Gorvenal eyed Lancelot suspiciously, but listened, nonetheless. "Tristan has been wrongly accused. He's innocent of all charges. The wizard Voldurk conspired with Queen Morag to kill Princess Blanchine. To make it appear as if Tristan were guilty. The Queen plans to marry King Marke and poison him. As she did her first husband, King Donnchadh of Ireland." At this, Gorvenal looked squarely at Lancelot, his countenance unreadable. "I'm here to free Tristan. We plan to launch an assault and challenge Queen Morag and the evil wizard. We must save King Marke before it's too late. I need your help, Gorvenal."

Lancelot continued, his urgent expression fixed on the First Knight of Tintagel. "We must go to the prison cell and overcome the guard. Free Tristan and bring him with us. There's a ship waiting just around the bend to the west. Please come with us. You'll be invaluable in planning how to take Tintagel and free King Marke. Will you join us, Gorvenal? We need you. *Tristan* needs you."

Gorvenal seemed to consider Lancelot's words, peering into his eyes as if searching his soul. He must have glimpsed the truth he sought there, for he finally acquiesced, muttering under his breath, "Come quickly. There's one guard. We'll lock him inside the cell. Swap his armor for Tristan's filthy rags. A good blow to the skull should put him out for a few hours, buying us enough time to get to the ship and out to sea. Let's hurry, before we're spotted."

Lancelot followed Gorvenal into the castle and down to the dungeon. They made quick work of incapacitating the guard, rendering him unconscious. Tristan grinned with obvious relief as his best friend and former mentor entered the prison cell to help him escape. They quickly exchanged clothes with the guard, then walked out of the castle, all three of them dressed as knights of Tintagel. They headed quickly toward the woods, joining the waiting members of the Tribe and the hidden rowboat.

****

Issylte, as the little white dove, had watched from a branch in the beech tree as Lancelot approached Gorvenal, who then accompanied the White Knight into the castle. A few minutes later, she spotted three men clad in the armor of the knights of Tintagel striding swiftly toward the woods. *They've done it! They have freed Tristan! Now I must fly safely back to my body on the ship.*

Taking flight, heading west to the seaworthy vessel, the little dove glimpsed a large predatory bird swoop into the air from a nearby oak at the same moment she soared from the beech tree. Flapping her wings frantically, trying her best to outrun the hawk, Issylte realized that as a small bird, she had no means of protection from such a powerful assailant. The hawk was gaining momentum with each flap of his tremendous wingspan. He would soon overtake her.

She swooped, dived, and circled, but the hawk was right on her tail, ready to clutch her in its sharp, extended talons. Her tiny heart nearly burst with fright.

Just as the hawk was about to strike, a falcon tore through the sky and seized the predator's neck with its sharp beak, ripping and shredding tendons and feathers as he carried his prize away from the white dove. A few moments later, a flock of black birds—Cornish *chough,* the sea ravens—formed a protective semicircle around her, escorting her little spirit dove safely back to the ship. *I saw this in Tristan's eyes…I remember the sensation of being a white dove, flying over the open ocean, surrounded by sea ravens. He used his magic—l'herbe d'or—to summon these birds to save me. He must have summoned the falcon, too. To take out the hawk. By the Goddess, I love him!*

The ship came into view as she, the little white dove, flew amidst the sea ravens. She landed on the deck, and the flock of Cornish *chough* flew off toward the open ocean. She then fluttered below to her cabin, where her body was reclined on the bed, as if sleeping.

As the little white bird, she hopped onto the chest of her prone self, and her spirit slid gently back into her human body. Her eyelids fluttered, and she opened them to find Lysara sitting beside her in the cabin. "Welcome back, Issylte." The priestess hugged her close, then asked, her voice almost desperate, "Were you able to save Tristan?"

Issylte, overjoyed to be reunited with her body, still shaking from being hunted by the enormous hawk, told Lysara what had transpired in the dungeon cell. Soon, the voices of the knights on deck alerted them that Lancelot's small ship was approaching.

Dagur and Solzic, with Tristan, Gorvenal, and the three knights from Landuc who'd accompanied them, quickly rowed out to join the larger ship. Now, as they docked the smaller boat to the side of the seaworthy vessel, Tristan climbed aboard first, followed by Gorvenal, then the others.

Issylte ran to him, and he wrapped weak arms around her, staggering on unsteady legs. Kissing his haggard face, she reunited blissfully with her *mate* as the ship headed west to the open ocean and back to Bretagne.

Once the members of the Tribe had welcomed Tristan, expressing their relief that he was back among them, Issylte led him below deck into her cabin to inspect his wounds. She helped him remove the armor and chemise underneath, drawing a sharp intake of breath when she saw the extent of his injuries.

Striated scars and scabs in various stages of healing marred his entire back, some fresh and still oozing with blood while others, which had crusted over, were angry red, inflamed, and exuding pus.

"Lie down on your stomach, Tristan. I'll cleanse the wounds and apply a soothing poultice which will draw out any toxins and help your skin heal." Slowly, tenderly, and gently, Issylte washed and dried his back, then applied yarrow and honey with the healing herbs she'd brought from Landuc.

When the ointment was properly applied, Issylte covered Tristan's back with clean bandages, then washed and combed his hair. She fetched a new bucket of clean water, in which she dipped a sponge, and with the fresh calendula soap that she'd made in Landuc, Issylte tenderly and lovingly washed his entire body.

Gently, she massaged his feet and legs, adding the healing ointment to the wounds around his ankles. She caressed his hands, arms, and chest, applying a soothing blend of essential oils, honey, and herbs to his bloodied wrists.

"My ring is gone," he said softly, showing her his bare hand. "They must have taken it from me while I was under the wizard's spell." He rubbed the left index finger where he'd always worn it since the day in Tintagel when his uncle had named him the Blue Knight of Cornwall. "I always looked into the eye of the sea raven for courage before battle. I feel empty without it."

His forlorn gaze melted her heart. She knew how much that ring had meant to him. A powerful link between Tristan and his king. The uncle who had raised him like a father. The last remaining member of his family.

"Perhaps, when we free your uncle, we'll get it back." Issylte kissed the empty finger, then massaged his hands some more, hoping to infuse courage and hope with her loving hands.

When she finished washing every inch of him, bandaging his wounds, Issylte helped Tristan into soft, clean clothing. She seated him carefully at the small table in her cabin, and helped him eat a light meal of bread, meat, cheese, and wine. When he finished, she led him to her bed, kissed him softly and tucked her blankets all around him. He was asleep almost instantly, and she sat at the table for a long time, loving him with grateful, relieved eyes.

A while later, she went up on deck to tell the others that he was doing well, that she had applied the herbal remedies, had fed him, and that he was now asleep. She hugged Lancelot, Dagur, Solzic, and Lysara, thanked Gorvenal and the knights who had helped rescue Tristan, then went below to return to her cabin. After eating some of the bread and cheese, she crawled into bed with Tristan, curling up in front of him so that she would not disturb the bandages on his back, and slept soundly in his arms.

In the morning, she was delighted to feel the familiar hardness of him against her backside. Lifting her dress out of the way, she welcomed him back into her body with passion and joy. When they at last emerged from the cabin to join the others who were breaking their fast in the galley kitchen, contentment shone on the faces of the Tribe as they smiled warmly to greet the reunited lovers.

Later in the day, after Issylte changed Tristan's bandages, they enjoyed an exceptionally exuberant reunion, then climbed back up onto the deck of the ship to join Lancelot, Gorvenal, Dagur, Solzic, and Lysara, who were leaning against the taffrail in the mild, late autumn sun.

The strong winds billowed the sail on their ship, spraying whitecapped waves into the salty air, carrying them swiftly across the Narrow Sea to the Breton coast. If this favorable weather continued, they would reach the shore of *la Bretagne* in about a week, a few days earlier than anticipated.

"Ah, there you are! I wondered when you would finally have enough of each other to rejoin the rest of us!" Lancelot chuckled heartily, while Solzic pulled Lysara against him, wrapping his arms around her, making room for Tristan and Issylte.

Gorvenal and Dagur grinned from ear to ear as the lovers joined them against the taffrail. Tristan shot Issylte an impish grin, then pulled her close while he kissed the side of her neck and the tender *mating mark* which he'd just renewed in the cabin. She had first pecked his as the little white dove and had just now bitten it in passion, reclaiming him as her *mate*. "*We'll have Nolwenn restore the droplet shaped tattoos when we return to Landuc. They'll be even larger and more beautiful than before,*" he'd said in their cabin. He buried his nose into her neck, holding her tightly against him. He must have realized that Lancelot was speaking to him, for he tore his lips away from her, coming up for air.

"Issylte traveled to the *Île de Sein* and the *Gallizenae,*" Lancelot began, cautiously searching Tristan's face. "She discovered the means to defeat the dark wizard Voldurk."

Tristan looked at Issylte, his eyebrows raised in curiosity.

"Once you recover your strength a bit more," she told him, "we must sail to Avalon. The only way to defeat Voldurk is with a sword like King Arthur's Excalibur. Forged in *dragonfire,* on the island of Avalon. By the descendent of Gofannon. The Blacksmith of the Gods."

Tristan shot Lancelot an incredulous look. "*Ronan,*" he exhaled, as Lancelot ducked his chin in acknowledgment, his downcast expression conveying the dauntless task ahead.

Issylte raised her voice to address them all. "There is more," she ventured, gathering the courage to speak. Her eyes met Tristan's, flooding him with all the love, fear, hope, and courage that surged in her heart.

"I also discovered what the dwarves have been seeking in the sacred forest, and why Voldurk is desperate to obtain it." Suppressing the dreadful memory of the dwarf Malvon who had nearly raped and abducted her at the Mirrored Lake, she gulped, summoning the strength to continue.

"The wizard seeks an enchanted orb. Created by *Morgane la Fée*. Hidden in the Mirrored Lake." Taking Tristan's hand in hers, she said to her *mate,* "I will retrieve it for you, Tristan. For you must obtain the *dragonfire* that Ronan will need to forge the sword. *Azeldraig.*" He gazed at her, his glorious blue eyes widened in wonder. "The *Galizenae* explained the significance of the name. *Az* represents the azure of the Blue Knight of Cornwall—you, the warrior prophesied to wield the *otherworldly* sword. *El* is for the Elf Ronan, the descendant of Gofannon who will forge the weapon on the island of Avalon. And *draig* symbolizes the dragon Mordrac, whose fire will fuel the forge for the blade to be crafted. *Azeldraig,* a weapon of unparalleled excellence. And the only means to destroy the evil wizard Voldurk."

Tristan stared at the horizon. "Did the *Gallizenae* explain how I am to use the orb in order to obtain the *dragonfire?*"

"Yes," she replied, tugging his hand to draw his attention back to her. "There is a dragon portal inside a cave, on an island off the coast of Armorique near *le Château Rose*. It is guarded by *Béliagog*, a Cyclops whose bolts of lightning will kill anyone who attempts to enter." Issylte raised her face to his. "But the orb will reflect the flash of lightning back onto *Béliagog*, temporarily blinding him. It will also amplify its own power by absorbing the energy from his thunderbolts. You'll be able to slip by the cyclops and enter the dragon cave. The orb will make you impervious to the dragon Mordrac, enabling you to capture a plume of his fire when you trespass into the portal."

Issylte glanced at Lancelot, then the Tribe, before returning her gaze to Tristan. "We'll need a cauldron made from black obsidian—the molten ore inside *la Grotte de l' Étoile*. It's the only substance which can transport *dragonfire*." She looked up into the eyes of her *mate*, awash in their intense blue depths. "We'll bring the cauldron and the orb to the dragon portal during the winter solstice. Voldurk will be in Britain—in Cornwall, performing a human sacrifice to the dark power he serves. We'll be able to obtain the *dragonfire*, avoid the wizard, and return quickly to Avalon. Where Ronan—if he agrees—will forge *Azeldraig*."

Lancelot had been quiet and pensive while Issylte spoke. He now tore his gaze away from the sea to face her. "Ronan is delivering an order of weapons and armor to *le Château Rose* for the winter solstice. If we could convince him, perhaps we could sail with him. Hidden in his ship. There are no dwarves on Avalon—no spies to report to Voldurk of our trip to the dragon portal. If Ronan agrees to forge *Azeldraig*, he might allow us to sail to Armorique with him for the winter solstice. We can retrieve the *dragonfire*, then sail back to Avalon in the Elven ship, hidden from Voldurk's spies."

Issylte enthusiastically agreed. "The *Gallizenae* also said that Voldurk performs a sacrifice during each equinox. That is when we must trap him in *la Porte des Ombres*—the Shadow Portal near the Forest of Morois in Cornwall. It is where he performs human sacrifices, and where he will be for the spring equinox. Renewing his dark power."

Lancelot agreed solemnly. "That gives us three months, if all goes according to plan. From the winter solstice, when we obtain the *dragonfire* and Ronan forges the sword. Until the spring equinox—when we face the wizard." He looked at Solzic and Dagur, his voice grave. "Three months to prepare our army for the siege of Tintagel." His intense gaze fixed on Tristan. "Three months to coordinate with our allies to save your uncle." Deep blue eyes locked on Issylte. "Three months until we challenge the wicked queen."

The white dove in Issylte's heart soared over the open ocean with the sea raven in Tristan's gaze. She squeezed his hand.

Otherworldly mates. Eternally entwined.

Chapter 16

Le Clan des Ours

It was wonderful to be back at *le Château de Landuc,* reunited with the Tribe. Everyone was now settled in the cozy kitchen alcove, sipping Laudine's chamomile *tisane* or the hearty ale that Esclados was generously serving. A crackling fire snapped in the hearth along the wall near the kitchen, the afternoon setting sun casting a golden glow from the high window down onto the cheerful nook.

Warmly welcomed by the Tribe—immensely grateful for his invaluable aid in liberating Tristan— Gorvenal joined the others who listened, enthralled by tales of Issylte's trip to the *Île de Sein,* how she'd cast her spirit as a white dove, and the daring rescue of Tristan from the desolate dungeon of Tintagel. Issylte shared her newly gleaned knowledge about the hidden orb, the *dragonfire*, and the forging of the Elven sword on Avalon to defeat the evil wizard. All eyes and ears were focused on her now as she revealed the unexpected encounter with Ondine, which she had shared privately with Tristan in the cabin of the ship sailing back from Cornwall.

"Do you remember when I treated the injured wolf near Lancelot's castle?" she asked the Tribe, seated around her in the cozy alcove. "Garou's mate, Ondine?"

Heads nodded as they exchanged curious glances. Lancelot's deep blue eyes glistened in the firelight as he listened intently.

"When I touched the wounded wolf's fur," Issylte explained, "I had a *sighting*. A vision of a lovely turquoise-haired mermaid with deep green scales." She smiled at Tristan, his eyes dancing with hers. "On the island of the *Gallizenae*, I saw that same mermaid. *Ondine*." She glanced at Darius. His handsome face regarded her with wonder. "*A shapeshifter*."

Laudine and Nolwenn gasped in surprise. Looks of confused delight greeted her from the Tribe.

"Ondine recognized me as Églantine, the forest fairy who had healed her in wolf form," Issylte explained. "In the sea cave on the island of the *Gallizenae*, I also met her two young daughters. And learned that Ondine is a *Mélusine*. A member of *les Dragons de Mer*." She grinned at the astonished faces gathered around her. "Sea dragon warriors who shape shift into mammals. And mate with the wolves of Garou's *Tribu des Loups*. Or the men of *le Clan des Ours*. The Bear Clan members who dwell in caves."

She smiled expansively at the enthralled Tribe. Issylte spoke to Lysara, cuddled next to the bearded blond giant Solzic. "Ondine enhanced my gift of *la Voix de l'Eau* from *les Fées Dorées*." Lysara's eyes widened in wonder, her mouth agape in awe.

Issylte glanced at Lancelot, then Darius—whose arm had fully healed and who was grinning at her—then at Kirus, seated beside an obviously enthralled Nolwenn. "I can now cast my voice into the ocean and summon *les Dragons de Mer* when needed." Issylte's attention darted between the three warriors. "They'll be formidable allies when we attack the wicked queen and her Viking armada."

Lancelot and Kirus smiled in stunned satisfaction as they absorbed the enormous significance of Sea Dragon allies against the fearsome *drakaar* warships. Gorvenal and Tristan shared a conspiratorial grin as well.

While the men were considering their good fortune in obtaining such valuable allies, Nolwenn rose from Kirus' side and disappeared into the castle, returning a few moments later with a carved wooden box. She placed it on the table before Issylte, her amethyst eyes aglow. Issylte looked up at her friend and whispered, "What's this?" Verdant magic quickened in her veins.

Nolwenn opened the box before her, removing a black velvet pouch. "Gargeolaine was abducted by Frocin's band of mercenary knights. She was wearing this necklace when the Tribe found her imprisoned in the dwarf's fortress. They brought her safely here, but she was not herself. She was empty. Enchanted. Entranced." Nolwenn took the necklace out of the pouch and laid it on the table before Issylte. The ruby gleamed in the golden sunlight. "I sensed an evil within this gem but couldn't identify it. When we took it off Gargeolaine, she became herself again. Vibrant, lively, vivacious. This necklace exudes evil. But there's something else inside. I just don't know what." Nolwenn pointed to the wooden container on the table. "I've kept it in this box until you returned. Hoping that your gift of *sight* might reveal the enchantment. Whatever it is, it was used to control Gargeolaine. To make her docile. Easy to manipulate."

A dark aura emanated from the heart shaped gem on the table. Issylte's Druidic gift of Rose Elder flared in warning. Glancing at Nolwenn, Laudine, and finally

Tristan, Issylte mustered the courage to reach for the ruby. Wings of the white dove fluttered wildly in her heart.

She lifted the necklace off the table, holding the ruby flat in her palm, gazing into its fiery depths. Her verdant magic flowed into the blood red gem, probing its essence, searching with the gift of *sight*.

A vision unfolded in its crimson glow, revealing a lovely female with long waves of vibrant red hair, splayed upon a stone slab in the dark recesses of a hidden cave. As Issylte's magic probed the heart of the ruby, she glimpsed the evil wizard Voldurk leaning over the immobile figure who seemed unnaturally still. *She is drugged*, Issylte realized, as she sensed the kindred magic in the victim's blood. *She's a fairy, like me.*

Her *sight* perceived an evil presence lurking in the dark recesses of the gloomy cavern. As Issylte watched in horror, thick curls of smoky shadows wafted up into the fairy's nose and down her throat, while the wizard held the heart shaped ruby flat in his hand. Dark tendrils then exited the victim's mouth, drawing forth a trail of glowing red light, which flowed from the fairy's body into the scarlet gem in the wizard's outstretched palm. His other hand clenched in a tight fist, the wizard squeezed rhythmically, as if he were pumping the life force and magic essence of the red-haired fairy into the pulsating ruby in his flattened hand.

Tristan's face hovered over hers as Issylte regained her senses, her eyelids fluttering as she became conscious. She must have collapsed onto the table in the sheltered alcove, for Tristan, seated in his chair, now cradled her with one arm while caressing her face with his other hand.

"Welcome back, my love," he whispered, kissing her softly. She sat up slowly, woozy and disoriented. Laudine placed a steaming cup of *tisane* in front of her and coaxed, "Drink this. It will restore you."

Issylte sipped the herbal tea, gazing around the table at the concerned, loving faces of the Tribe.

Her family.

A warm glow eased the ominous chill in her frightened bones.

She smiled weakly at Lancelot, Darius, Nolwenn, and Kirus. Cast an affectionate glance at Lysara, Solzic, and Dagur. Looked warmly into the empathetic faces of Laudine, Esclados, Bahja, Erwann, and Kjetil.

By the Goddess, she loved them all.

"I saw the wizard Voldurk in the depths of the ruby," Issylte croaked, her throat parched, her voice quavering. "And a faceless evil. Dark, sinister shadows." She shuddered, shivering uncontrollably. And not from the brisk autumn air.

Laudine wrapped a warm blanket around her shoulders with a comforting hug, then returned to her chair at Esclados' side. Her amber eyes shone with concern as she regarded Issylte, cocooned in the blanket. And Tristan's loving arms.

"They trapped the essence of a fairy inside that ruby," Issylte spluttered, staring intently at the mysterious necklace before her. "I saw thick shadows enter the victim's nose and mouth, overwhelming and smothering her. Then the shadows exited the fairy's mouth, coaxing a red glow from her body into the gleaming ruby. Which pulsated like a beating heart in the palm of the wizard's hand."

Issylte's eyes locked with Tristan's. Her heart

thumped wildly, panic flowing through her veins. "They've trapped her in a dark cave somewhere. The empty shell of her body is lying there. And the essence of her life is *here*." She pointed at the ruby necklace, her hand shaking, her legs quivering. "But where?" She implored the caring faces of the Tribe of Dana. "A dark cave with sinister shadows."

"*La Porte des Ombres.*"

Dagur's deep voice resonated through the sheltered alcove. Heads swiveled toward the burly, dark-haired warrior. Issylte's stomach lurched; she gripped Tristan's hand tightly under the table. "The Cave of Shadows. In the Forest of Morois, near Frocin's fortress."

Dagur's deep brown gaze fixed on Issylte. "The dwarf has been making sacrifices there for years. To the Shadow Fairy Malfleur. *La Fée des Ombres.* The Dark One he serves."

The members of the Tribe exchanged looks of astonishment. Kirus spoke to Dagur, his voice incredulous. "How do you know this?"

Dagur fixed his fierce gaze on the leader of the Tribe. "All members of *le Clan des Ours*—the Bear Clan—avoid that evil cave. We know every grotto in the entire Celtic realm."

Feral eyes locked on Issylte. Her heart fluttered in anticipation. "For that is where we mate with the *Mélusines*. The Sea Dragon Warriors of the *Gallizenae*."

Issylte gasped, her voice a barely audible whisper. "You are a member of *le Clan des Ours*."

Fierce ursine eyes glinted with power. "I am indeed."

Dagur glanced at the members of the Tribe seated around the table, his expression sorrowful, dark, and bitter. "I have not seen any of the Clan since the death of my pregnant mate seven years ago. When mercenary knights slaughtered her as she hibernated in our cave. So that their leader—the dwarf Frocin—would have a magnificent bearskin cloak to keep warm."

Everyone exchanged looks of shock. No one had known of Dagur's tragic past.

"We males of the Clan shift back and forth from human to bear form to defend our pregnant mates while they hibernate in winter. I had gone into town for supplies to bring back to the cave. When I returned and found her mutilated body, I shifted. Tracked them down. Tore them apart with my huge claws and massive jaws."

He lowered his gaze, anguish written across his bearded, crumpled face. "I passed through the cave portal, walked between worlds—which members of the Clan can do while in bear form. I came to Bretagne, far from the bloody Forest of Morois in Cornwall. I attacked a band of marauders who were camped on the outskirts of the Forest of Brocéliande, planning to ambush a passing caravan. I killed one of the rogue knights and stole his armor, shifted back to human form. Came here to Landuc. And joined the Tribe as a *chevalier itinérant*. A knight errant."

Dagur growled in pain, a gravely injured beast. "I haven't seen the Clan since my mate's death. Haven't shifted for seven years—so no one could trace me. I've shunned all contact with my former life. And have mated with no one but Delen, whose death I should have prevented. Guilt and grief have consumed me ever since."

He succumbed, burying his face in his arms folded on the table. Lysara rose from Solzic's side and rushed to Dagur. She wrapped her arms around him, resting her head comfortingly on his shaking shoulders. After a while, he quieted and raised an agonized face to Lysara, a hint of gratitude gleaming in his suffering gaze. He lifted his head to face Issylte, his expression resolute.

"But it's time now. Time for me to atone for the past. Acknowledge my failure in preventing her death. And act, to save another." He reached for Issylte's hand and lifted it to his lips, his anguished eyes shining with renewed hope. "In bear form, I can traverse the sacred stone portals. Go to the troglodyte caves of Anjou and Aquitaine. Reconnect with *le Clan des Ours*. And bring them with me when I go to *la Porte des Ombres.*"

Dagur looked at Tristan, Lancelot, and Kirus. "The Shadow Fairy can only enter the cave during an equinox or solstice—when the forces of light and dark shift between worlds. But she will undoubtedly have guards stationed there to defend the fairy's body. As bears, we'll go to the cave, see how many knights are posted there. Plan our attack. Then return here for you, Issylte." Dagur's thickly bearded face grinned through his grief. "We'll escort you to *la Porte des Ombres.* Take out the guards and protect you while you save the red-haired fairy. Then, once she is free, we'll bring you back safely through the portal. Back to the sanctity of the sacred forest." He focused on Tristan as the two men shared an intense, impassioned regard. "And the loving arms of your warrior *mate.*"

Tristan's deep voice cracked, fierce and desperately protective. "Defend her for me, Dagur."

Dagur bowed his head in brotherhood, then locked eyes with Tristan as he fisted his heart.

"With my life, Tristan."

Brave ursine eyes blazed with power and promise. Tristan ducked his chin, then clutched Issylte tightly to his chest, showering soft kisses in her long, golden hair.

****

The Tribe ate together, the servants of Landuc having prepared a celebratory meal to welcome Tristan home. When everyone finished, it was decided that in the morning, they would accompany Dagur to the stone portal of *Huelgoat*, where he would shift and walk between worlds. He'd travel to the troglodyte caves of Anjou in the Loire Valley, then on to *la Grotte de Lascaux* in the region of Aquitaine in southwestern France, reconnecting with his brothers of *le Clan des Ours*. And return with Issylte's escorts as soon as possible, so that they could free the fairy now.

In early November.

Long before *la Fée des Ombres* and the dark wizard came into the cave for the winter solstice.

And the inevitable, horrible, human sacrifice.

In the morning, they rode from Landuc through the Forest of Brocéliande to the stone cave portal of *Huelgoat* to see Dagur safely off. Tristan, Lancelot, and Darius brought along three additional sets of armor and weapons to place in the cave portal for the Bear Clan members who would need them when they returned. Dagur explained that the Bear Clan were naked when shifting back into human form and would therefore need armor and weapons. Dagur, who planned to disrobe in the cave, would leave his own gear behind to await his return.

After Dagur left, the members of the Tribe returned to Landuc and resumed their daily routine of training in preparation for the siege of Tintagel. Each day, Issylte changed the bandages on Tristan's back, which was healing well, but would be forever riddled with hideous scars.

Badges of honor he'd proudly bear as evidence of his triumph over evil.

****

A week after his departure, Dagur returned with three enormous warriors, one of whom was well known by the Tribe who greeted him with hearty hugs and lively laughter. A massively built man with skin as black as midnight and teeth as white as moonlight grinned broadly when introduced to Issylte.

"This is Idris." Dagur beamed as the Bear Clan warrior kissed her hand in greeting. Dagur shot him a sly grin. "A warrior of the Tribe of Dana who is also a member of *le Clan des Ours.* Like me." Dagur's heavily bearded face crinkled in a craggy smile as he spoke to Idris. "I have been hiding here for years. Since Delen was slaughtered. It is good to see you again, *mon frère.*" The burly Idris, who was every bit as massive as Dagur and considerably taller as well, crushed his fellow Clan member in a fierce bear hug as the two friends reunited at long last. Issylte's heart flooded with joy.

"And may I present Gralon and Nazur," Dagur said cheerfully as two more bulky, bearded warriors kissed her slender hand.

The giant members of the Bear Clan ate a hearty meal of meat, cheese, bread, and ale with the knights of Landuc and the Tribe of Dana in the glorious Great Hall of Landuc.

"We counted two guards at the entrance to the cave, and two more patrolling the nearby woods," Dagur said between mouthfuls. "Once we enter *la Porte des*

Ombres, we'll take out the four guards, then defend Issylte inside the cave as she revives the red-haired fairy."

Lancelot looked inquisitively at Issylte. "Do you know how to save her?"

Issylte swallowed a bite of cheese, washing it down with a gulp of ale. "When I cast my spirit as the white dove, I was able to rejoin my body when the bird landed on my chest. I'll place the ruby over the fairy's heart and see if physical contact works for her as well. If not, we'll return immediately through the cave portal and come up with a different plan to rescue her. None of us can transport others through the portal, so we would need to sail to Cornwall to retrieve her body. And bring her back here until we find a solution."

Lancelot shared concerned glances with the leaders of the Tribe, then replied, "We'll ride with you to the cave of *Huelgoat.* And wait there for your return."

Tristan shot a look at Dagur. "If you encounter any problem, bring Issylte back immediately. Take no chances."

Dagur ducked his chin solemnly. "You have my word."

When they finished eating, Tristan helped Issylte strap her bag of herbal remedies and the carved wooden box with the enchanted ruby onto *Minuit*'s back. Esclados provided three horses for Idris, Gralon, and Nazur to ride as a dozen members of the Tribe readied for the trek to the cave of *Huelgoat.*

"We'll be waiting at the entrance to the cave. May the Goddess bless you all," Lancelot said as Issylte kissed Tristan goodbye.

The deep blue waters of her *mate's* gaze washed

over her in waves of calm.

"Come back to me, my love." He kissed her softly, watching intently as she entered the cave with the warriors of *le Clan des Ours.*

Inside the cave of *Huelgoat*, Issylte turned her back so that the men could disrobe, store their armor, and shift into ursine form. When a cold nose nuzzled her hand, she twisted around to face a huge brown bear with Dagur's twinkling eyes. She cast her gaze to the three other enormous beasts, all of which were nearly double the size of ordinary bears. They bobbed their massive heads, then led Issylte down the darkened path into the hidden depths of the cave portal.

When they emerged into *la Porte des Ombres*, the foul stench of death was overwhelming. Issylte covered her nose with the sleeve of her gown, stumbling behind the bears, arriving into an open chamber within the dank cavern where the reek of rotting flesh permeated the putrid air. Along one wall of the cave was a pile of human bones and decaying corpses which Issylte realized were the remains of the victims of human sacrifice to the evil *Fée des Ombres.* A violent shudder shivered up her spine as she plodded on toward the outer chamber.

Issylte drew a sharp intake of breath when she spotted the long tresses of vibrant red hair cascading down a stone slab in a corner of the inner room. Dark, smoky shadows undulated in waves, forming a protective barrier around the fairy's immobile body.

As Issylte stood transfixed, staring at her kindred sister, shrieks of agony and bellowing roars from the forest outside the cave shattered the silence, then stilled. Spotting Dagur—who had returned to her side—from the corner of her eye, Issylte summoned her gift of *Rose Elder* to banish evil as she crossed the shadowy barrier and entered the enchanted prison chamber.

The fairy's face was pale as death, yet her skin felt warm to the touch. Her pulse was faint but steady; her chest rising and falling in shallow, rhythmic breaths. *Thank the Goddess she is alive. Dear Dana, guide me now, that I may save her.*

Issylte lowered the bag of supplies from her shoulder to the cavern floor, opening it to find the carved wooden box inside. She retrieved the black velvet pouch from inside the container and removed the ruby necklace. The glittering gem glowed in her hand as Issylte's verdant magic sparked to life.

She placed the heart of the ruby over the fairy's own heart, bringing the gem in contact with the deathly pale skin. Casting the flow of her own magic into its fiery red depths, Issylte watched in wonder as the ruby began to glow more intensely, pulsating rhythmically with the beat of the fairy's heart. To her delight, the shadows surrounding the fairy dissipated, like wisps of smoke evaporating into the air.

Lovely green eyes fluttered awake and beheld her in a frightened gaze.

Issylte's voice was gentle and soothing. "It's all right. I have come to save you. You were trapped here by the dark wizard Voldurk and the wicked fairy Malfleur. I have reversed the evil spell and freed you. Come, let me help you up so that you can leave this foul cave. They have kept you imprisoned here for a long time."

The fairy sat up, squeezing her fists, rotating her ankles, rolling her head around on her shoulders. She stretched her arms and extended her legs, then, clutching Issylte's arm, rose unsteadily to her dainty feet. She spotted the ruby in Issylte's hand and recoiled in horror.

"What is that?" she gasped, her fragile voice ephemeral as a summer breeze.

"This is the enchanted gem where they trapped your magic essence," Issylte replied, holding the ruby flat in her palm. "I have the gift of *sight*," Issylte continued, her voice calm and reassuring. "I saw you trapped inside. Thick, dark shadows entered your nose and mouth, coaxing the red glow of life from your body into this ruby where they trapped your spirit."

Issylte gestured to Dagur, sitting a few feet away, watching them with intelligent, human eyes.

"This is Dagur, a member of *le Clan des Ours* who knew of this evil cave where dark shadows lurked. He and three members of his Clan saw you trapped here and brought me back to save you. My name is Issylte. I'm a healer from Avalon and a Priestess of the Tribe of Dana. I'm also called *La Dame du Miroir aux Fées*. The Lady of the Mirrored Lake. Please tell me…what is your name?"

"I am Aimée, *la Fée Rouge.* Also known as *la Fée du Coeur*—the Heart Fairy, for my love of the forest animals that I protect. I'm eternally grateful to you, Lady of the Mirrored Lake," Aimée whispered with a reverent bow of her head. Then, to Dagur, she said, "And to you, Dagur, and *le Clan des Ours. Merci—du fond du coeur.* Thank you, from the bottom of my heart."

Aimée picked up the ruby from the stone slab and held it flat in her pale hand. With a flick of her fingers, wisps of black shadow emerged from the gem and dissolved into the dank, foul air. *La Fée du Coeur* then laid the ruby back down upon the stone slab where she'd been imprisoned, lifted a large stone from the cavern floor, and heaved it down upon the heart shaped gem, crushing it into shattered fragments. Then, with another flick of her long white fingers, flames erupted upon the stone slab, reducing the remains of the ruby into harmless ash.

With a satisfied smile, Aimée said to Issylte, "I wish to thank you for risking your own life to save mine. As a token of my gratitude, I'll bestow upon you a gift of magic. *La Voix du Coeur.* The Voice of the Heart." Aimée's delicate fingers fluttered over Issylte's heart.

Verdant magic thrummed as vibrant energy surged into her veins.

"If you ever need me, place your hand over your heart and call my name. I shall hear the voice of your heart. *La Voix du Coeur.* And somehow, someway, I will find the means to reach you."

Aimée kissed Issylte's forehead, then took both of her hands, giving them a friendly squeeze. She walked over to Dagur, who grunted with pleasure while she scratched his head as if he were a giant dog. *La Fée du Coeur* fondly stroked the fur of the other three massive bears who had been guarding the cave entrance and had approached the affectionate fairy whose boundless love for animals exuded from her generous heart.

Waving goodbye, Aimée said brightly, "I live nearby, in the primrose and poppy glen of the Forest of Morois. Remember, Lady of the Mirrored Lake—if you ever need me, call with your heart. *La Voix du Coeur. Au revoir, mon amie.*"

And, with a heartwarming smile, *la Fée Rouge* disappeared into the thick Forest of Morois.

Idris, Nazur, and Gralon gave a nod of their enormous furry heads, then led the way back into the inner chamber. Issylte followed them past the stench of decay, down the long winding corridor, back into the portal between worlds.

A few moments later, Issylte and her ursine escorts traversed the portal, arriving inside the cave of *Huelgoat*, where the sets of armor awaited the warriors of *le Clan des Ours*. She faced away once again while the Clan shifted into human form and donned their gear, then followed them out of the cave into the sacred Forest of Brocéliande.

And into the loving, protective arms of her smiling, relieved *mate*.

Chapter 17

Les Noces

Tristan was waiting with Lancelot and the members of the Tribe as they welcomed Issylte and her Bear Clan escorts at the cave portal entrance of *Huelgoat*. They rode together back to the castle of Landuc and gathered around the wooden table in the cozy alcove. As they shared mulled wine and oat cakes dipped in honey, they listened as Issylte explained how she'd reunited the fairy Aimée with the magic essence trapped in the enchanted ruby. How she'd received the gift of *la Voix du Coeur*, enabling her to summon the fairy when needed. Dagur and Idris described the rotting stench of the foul cave and the evidence of human sacrifices in *la Porte des Ombres*.

The cave portal where—Goddess willing—Tristan would defeat the wizard Voldurk during the vernal equinox.

Nazur, Idris, and Gralon said goodbye, returning to their troglodyte cave dwellings and the pregnant mates waiting for them. Now huddled together before a crackling fire, enjoying the rich flavors of cinnamon, cloves, honey, and red wine, the Tribe finalized plans to sail to Avalon in three weeks.

Waiting until early December would allow Tristan more time to recover from his injuries yet still be soon enough for Issylte to retrieve the orb and go to Avalon through *la Porte du Dedans*—the cave portal at the bottom of the Mirrored Lake. Since Tristan, Lancelot, and the others could not walk between worlds, they would sail to Avalon and arrive several days after Issylte. This would give her time to speak with Ronan before his voyage to *le Château Rose*—to deliver the weapons and armor to King Hoël and Prince Kaherdin for the winter solstice. Goddess willing, Ronan would agree to forge the sword *Azeldraig*. And allow the Tribe to sail with him to Armorique.

To obtain the *dragonfire* of the beast Mordrac. Verdant magic thrummed in her veins.

Now that night had fallen and the Tribe had finished celebrating their safe return and retired to their respective chambers, Issylte sat at her vanity, brushing her hair and looking into the mirror at the reflection of Tristan lying in bed, waiting for her.

He seems especially pensive and quiet. Lost in thought. He's worried about sailing to Avalon. Speaking to Ronan. Obtaining the dragonfire. Especially when he's not even fully recovered from his imprisonment. I'll distract him from his worries.

Dropping her gown to the floor, Issylte stood nude at the foot of the large bed, which was centered between two enormous windows where the luminous glow of moonlight shone through the sheer white drapes. In the hearth across the spacious room, embers glowed, warming the chamber and casting a dreamy, golden haze. Lust glowed in Tristan's eyes as he watched her climb onto the bed beside him.

Showering his face, neck, and chest with kisses, claiming his lips and further arousing his passion, she straddled him, taking him into her body as she brought them both to a shared climax that left each trembling and quivering with pleasure.

As Issylte lay down at his side, their bodies and spirits now sated, Tristan pulled her against his chest, his face conveying an inner turmoil. Issylte's pulse quickened.

"I love you," he whispered, kissing her softly. "We are entwined, body and soul, in every realm. Except one." Rising onto one elbow to support himself as he turned to face her, he caressed one of her breasts with his free hand. "We are *mates*, eternally bound in the spiritual realm. We're lovers, friends, sparring partners. Even political allies. But I want *more,* Issylte. I want us to be bound to each other in *every* realm."

He sat up, pulled back the blankets, and got out of bed. He walked around to her side and knelt before her on one knee. Taking her left hand into both of his, he brought it to his lips and kissed it softly. "Issylte, I want us to be joined in the *human* realm as well. I want you to become my *wife*. To share my life. To bear my children."

His fierce gaze blazed with intensity and yearning. "Issylte…will you marry me?"

She leaned toward him, her eyes brimming with tears. "Yes! A thousand times yes! I love you with every breadth of my soul, Tristan. I want very much to become your wife." She rose from the bed and pulled him to his feet. He swept her into his arms, kissed her exuberantly, then laid her back down on the bed and made love to her again.

Pleasurably entwined together, he whispered, "We'll ask Esclados and Laudine to arrange the wedding so that we're married before we sail to Avalon." He nuzzled her breast, tracing idle circles around her nipple with his finger. "I want us to be married in the heart of the sacred forest. Joined together by the Goddess. Surrounded by members of our Tribe. Our family." She agreed earnestly, tears of joy spilling down her face. "We'll have Nolwenn repair my *mating mark*. She can work her magic and make it even more beautiful than before."

They drifted off to sleep in each other's arms, snuggled under the blankets. Imagining the Celtic wedding that would unite them in the world of mortals just as they were bound together as *mates* in the realm of the Goddess.

Eternally entwined.

****

Laudine and Esclados were thrilled to plan the wedding—*les noces*—which would be held in the upcoming week. The Red Knight sent for a goldsmith to come to Landuc and discuss with the young couple what type of wedding rings they wanted him to craft. When the jeweler learned of their sacred gemstones and the vows that Tristan had written, he decided to create a crossover ring for Issylte, a style which in French was called "*toi et moi*"—you and me—to symbolize the bride and groom.

The goldsmith explained that he would diagonally join two round gemstones—a sparkling emerald and a brilliant blue topaz—in an infinity swirl of gold, evoking the Celtic tattoos of the Tribe of Dana.

For Tristan's ring, the jeweler would engrave three infinity swirls onto a gold band, symbolizing their eternal union. At the center of each of the three swirls, he would join an emerald and a blue topaz, the sacred stones of the bride and groom.

"The emeralds represent Issylte, the Emerald Princess of Ireland, but also her sacred element of the forest. The blue topaz stones symbolize Tristan, the Blue Knight of Cornwall, and his sacred element of water. And, since emeralds and blue topaz gems are stones, all three of the sacred elements of the Goddess will be bound together in your wedding bands—just as She has bound the two of you as eternal *mates*."

The goldsmith needed three days to create the rings, which he would deliver to the castle when completed. The wedding would take place on the first of December.

Laudine had the servants of Landuc prepare a wedding feast for the eve of the ceremony. She and Lysara decorated the entire *château* with pine boughs, holly, elder berries, and garlands of evergreen. The fresh fragrances of pine, hellebore, and guelder rose blossoms filled the festive air throughout the cheery castle.

"Your wedding will be the first time in twenty years that a warrior and priestess of Dana have been married in this sacred forest." Lysara's brown eyes twinkled with glee. "The first wedding since Esclados le Ros and his bride Laudine were married in front of *la Fontane de Notre-Dame*—the Fountain of Our Lady, the Goddess Dana." Casting a glance at Solzic, who was eating a snack at the alcove table with Lancelot, Tristan, Kirus, and Dagur, she whispered to Issylte, "I hope Solzic asks me to marry him, too." Then, hiding a sly smile with her hand, Lysara added, "I am certain he will, once he learns that I am with child."

Issylte opened her mouth in surprised delight. She squeezed Lysara's hands. The pretty face of the petite brunette lit up in a glorious smile. "I plan to tell him the night of your wedding."

The two women shared a warm embrace as Issylte whispered, "Congratulations, Lysara. You will be a wonderful mother. Solzic is a lucky man indeed."

That evening at dinner, Laudine and Esclados explained that a wedding between a priestess and a warrior of the Tribe of Dana involved a ceremony called the *Triple Trinity,* in which three sets of three sacred items would unite the couple in Celtic matrimony.

"The first trinity includes three symbols of your marriage. The rings, the vows, and the wedding tattoos—which Nolwenn will ink upon your upper left thighs," Laudine informed them as the Tribe gorged on fresh fish from *le Miroir aux Fées,* listening intently to their beloved Lady of the Fountain. Issylte glanced at Tristan, who grinned at her over his wine goblet. Her heart raced at the thought of finally becoming his *wife*. She beamed back at him as Laudine continued.

"The second trinity represents the three sacred elements of the Goddess Dana," she said reverently, her amber eyes twinkling in the candlelight. "You'll exchange vows in the Forest of Brocéliande, upon the altar of the stone temple of the Goddess, before the spring of *la Fontaine de Notre-Dame*." The white dove in Issylte's heart fluttered with joy as Tristan lifted her hand to his warm lips, his eyes dancing with hers.

"The third and final trinity involves the joining of your bodies," Laudine murmured, flashing a seductive smile at her dashing Red Knight husband, whose dark gaze blazed with desire at his voluptuous wife. "The archdruid Odin—the same priest who inducted each of you into our Tribe—will perform the ceremony." Laudine smiled warmly at the two of them, perhaps remembering her own ceremony with fond memories.

"He'll slice the tips of your wedding ring fingers, blending your blood. Your wedding vows will be sealed with a kiss, and your marriage consummated during three glorious days in the enchanted cottage. In the heart of our sacred forest."

Issylte basked in the lovelight shining in Tristan's eyes. Surrounded by the familiar faces of the Tribe of Dana. The warm family who would witness and welcome their Celtic wedding. A symphony of verdant magic sang in her veins.

****

Two days before the wedding, Tristan and Issylte were with Nolwenn in her *atelier*. She'd just completed the reparation of Tristan's *mating mark* and, as she enhanced Issylte's tattoo to match, the amethyst-eyed priestess explained what she had so artistically done.

"I enlarged the droplet shape to cover the damaged skin and scar tissue caused by the dark wizard's spell. Now, Tristan's *mating mark* is the beautiful deep green of the herbs and plants of our sacred forest that I used to create the ink. And the black outline—made from the guelder rose blossoms that Laudine grows in her *verrière*—is the essence of Issylte's Druidic magic of *Rose Elder*."

Issylte admired the bold, beautiful *mating mark* on Tristan's neck. All the ugliness from Voldurk's spell had been replaced by the magnificent dark green droplet. It was perfect. As Nolwenn finished dabbing the healing essential oils onto her tattoo, Issylte smiled at her husband to be, who was beaming at her from a chair beside the table where the artist worked.

A few hours later, when Nolwenn had finished, Tristan and Issylte each bore their wedding tattoos on

239

their inner thighs—the three loops of a Celtic knot, with a *toi et moi* infinity swirl between each, all encircled by an eternity band. *This is the tattoo I saw in his eyes— similar to the Tribe's, but unique. Now we have a mating mark and a wedding tattoo—bound together in both realms. Otherworldly and human. Eternally entwined.*

The *Château de Landuc* was joyfully preparing not just for Tristan and Issylte's wedding, but for the upcoming Yuletide season, when Esclados and Laudine's three sons—Gaultier, Bastien and Cardin— would be returning home from their training as squires for King Guillemin at *le Château de Beaufort* in western Bretagne. Although the three sons would not arrive in time for the wedding, Tristan and Issylte hoped to meet them before the departure for Avalon.

The wedding feast, celebrated on the eve of the ceremony, was lavish, with fresh trout from le *Miroir aux Fées*, stuffed pheasant, roast venison, late harvest vegetables, assorted cheeses, delicate pastries, and plenty of fine French wine. Lancelot toasted them, as did Kirus, Darius, Kjetil, and Gorvenal. Several members offered them gifts: warm woolen blankets, hand woven baskets, soaps, bottles of wine, and a lovely needlepoint, embroidered by Lysara, depicting their names and wedding date, amidst a trio of images of their wedding tattoos. The embroidery was encased in a frame made of polished elder wood—the tree of Issylte's Druidic magic—carved by Solzic into the shape of a scrolled, swirled shield. A truly exceptional wedding gift. *Someday, it will hang in the home I share with Tristan. Wherever that may be. It doesn't matter, so long as we are together.*

"Oh, Lysara and Solzic—it is exquisite! We shall

treasure it always." Issylte thanked them genuinely, giving her friends a warm hug as they huddled in front of the fire in the hearth, surrounded by the Tribe, the wedding gifts, and the festive decorations. In the morning, they would break fast together, then the Tribe would lead Tristan and Issylte into the forest where the Archdruid Odin—who had given the couple the gifts of *l'herbe d'or* and *Rose Elder*—would perform the Celtic ceremony.

That night, in the moonlight cascading through the double windows into their bedroom chambers, Tristan whispered to Issylte, "This is the last time we make love as *lovers*. Tomorrow, we make love as *husband and wife*."

****

The mild December sun shone through fluffy white clouds as Laudine, Nolwenn, Lysara, and Bahja brushed Issylte's waist length hair and placed the garland they had woven upon her head. As she sat before the mirrored vanity, watching her four closest friends adorn her hair with flowers in preparation for her wedding, nostalgic memories of her father's castle and the plaits that her attendants Roisin and Aislynn had woven in her hair as the Emerald Princess for his royal marriage flashed through Issylte's mind.

Now, instead of a crown of emeralds and diamonds, her coronet held fragile white guelder rose blossoms— lovingly cultivated in Laudine's *verrière*—which peeked out of a garland of ivy, holly, and strands of evergreen. Issylte's wedding gown was made of dark green velvet, embellished at the gathered bodice with embroidered green lace, enhanced by long, flowing sleeves of emerald silk.

Tristan wore a cornflower blue velvet tunic over black breeches. His chestnut brown hair fell in waves to his chin, and a soft stubble covered his square jawline. His cobalt blue eyes blazed as he beheld her. She was an emerald fairy, clad in shades of deepest green, ready to ride *Minuit* into the sacred forest with Tristan where the wedding—*les noces*—would take place.

The Tribe was already gathered at the Temple of Dana, assembled before the sacred spring of *la Fontaine de Notre-Dame.* The Archdruid Odin stood at the altar, facing the members of the Tribe, who were standing behind the area designated for the bride and groom.

Tristan and Issylte, who had followed Esclados and Laudine, Nolwenn and Kirus, Solzic and Lysara to the clearing, dismounted from their horses and took their places, kneeling at the altar of the temple of the Goddess. Odin began the ceremony.

"Members of the Tribe of Dana, we gather here at the sacred temple of the Goddess to witness the Celtic wedding of Sir Tristan of Lyonesse, the Blue Knight of Cornwall, and the Princess Issylte, the Lady of the Mirrored Lake."

He opened a small box, revealing two magnificent rings, and extended it before Tristan.

"Take Issylte's wedding ring, place it upon her finger, and declare your vows."

Tristan placed the emerald and blue topaz ring upon Issylte's finger. The two gems—*toi et moi*—sparkled in the morning sunlight, joined together in an infinity swirl of white gold. Tristan reverently uttered his vows—a simple poem he'd composed for her, his Muse, when they had finalized their *mating bond* during her induction into the Tribe of Dana.

"*Toi et moi.*
So it shall be.
You and I are entwined.
Eternally."

Odin instructed Issylte to place the ring upon Tristan's finger and declare her vows to him.

"*Toi et moi.*
So it shall be.
You and I are entwined.
Eternally."

The archdruid then placed the small jewelry box on a flat stone near the altar where Tristan and Issylte knelt before him.

"The Triple Trinity of this ceremony is nearly complete. You have shared three symbols of your union—the wedding rings, tattoos, and vows. We are gathered here in the heart of the three sacred elements of the Goddess: the Forest of Brocéliande, the waters of *la Fontaine de Notre-Dame,* and the stone altar of the Temple of Dana. And now, for the final trinity—the three ways your bodies will join as one. The blending of your blood. A kiss to seal your vows. And the consummation of your marriage in the sacred forest."

With his golden sickle, the Druid carefully sliced the tip of their wedding ring fingers, drawing blood, joining them together. The little white dove soared with the sea raven in her joyful heart.

"I bind you in sacred marriage through the blending of your blood. Now, seal your wedding vows with a kiss." Tristan and Issylte leaned toward each other, still kneeling on the altar, and shared a romantic kiss. Appreciative remarks whispered through the Tribe.

"In the presence of the divine Goddess, in the heart of Her three sacred elements, with the Tribe of Dana as witnesses, I solemnly swear that you are husband and wife, bound together by the Triple Trinity of this Celtic ceremony." The long white sleeves of Odin's robes wafted in the winter breeze as he waved his wizened hands over the newly wedded couple. The Archdruid lowered his arms and smiled sagely at Tristan and Issylte, his wise voice weathered by the wisdom of ages.

"Lord Esclados and Lady Laudine will lead you to the enchanted cottage, where you will spend three divine days together to consummate your marriage. Go now, as husband and wife. And celebrate your sacred union." Odin bowed reverently before them, cleansed his sickle in the sacred water of the fountain, and disappeared into the enchanted Forest of Brocéliande.

The jubilant Tribe huddled around the newlyweds, congratulating and hugging them, expressions of joy all around. Laudine and Esclados led the procession, with the Tribe following Tristan and Issylte, as they walked a short distance into the forest. They came to a clearing where a stone cottage with a thatched roof—much like Maiwenn's in the Hazelwood Forest—beckoned the newly married couple. *This is the stone cottage I saw in Tristan's eyes when our mating bond was finalized,* Issylte mused with delight.

"We spent our three days together in this cottage, twenty years ago," Laudine whispered to Issylte, as she held her hands and kissed her cheek. "It belongs to us now, as part of the domain of Landuc. We preserve it for special occasions. Celtic weddings—such as yours."

"Congratulations, Tristan. You have a most beautiful bride. Enjoy these three days of marital bliss. With the Tribe's blessing." Esclados shook Tristan's hand, clasped his shoulder amicably, then kissed Issylte's cheek. "The domain is well stocked with provisions and protected with a triple layer of enchantment. You will be guarded by warriors of the Tribe who remain nearby but out of sight, hidden in the forest. Each morning and evening, freshly prepared food will be brought and left on your doorstep. In three days, an escort will come to lead you back to the castle of Landuc," Esclados exclaimed warmly as Laudine beamed at the newlyweds, tears of joy glimmering in her expressive amber eyes.

Kirus and Nolwenn, Solzic and Lysara, Lancelot, Darius, Gorvenal, and the others all wished the couple well before departing. As the last members of the Tribe left the clearing, Tristan lifted his bride in his arms and carried her—laughing with glee—across the threshold into the enchanted cottage.

For three days, they made love frequently, eating occasionally when they were hungry, drinking the delicious wine, savoring every moment together. They entwined in amorous ardor before the roaring fire in the hearth, on the kitchen table, in the hot springs behind the cottage, and of course, in the sumptuous bed that took up most of the sleeping chambers. They couldn't get enough of each other, their lust and love insatiable. With each joining of their bodies, their souls mingled more deeply, the ecstasy of the physical realm transporting their spirits to the stars and further strengthening their *mating bond*.

Kirus, Dagur, Lancelot, and Solzic came for them

on the third day after the wedding, bringing *Minuit* and *Aiglon* for the ride home to Landuc. Although it was difficult to leave the enchanted cottage, Tristan and Issylte looked forward to fighting side by side as husband and wife, confronting the evil which threatened the Celtic realm.

Together, forever.

Eternally entwined.

Chapter 18

Return to Avalon

The Tribe was busy assembling provisions for the four-day voyage to Avalon. Everyone was hopeful that Ronan would agree to forge the sword *Azeldraig*. Even if he refused, at the very least, they would obtain the molten ore needed from *la Grotte de l' Étoile*. And pray that an alternate Elven blacksmith could be persuaded in his stead.

Solzic, Dagur, Darius, Gorvenal, Tristan, and Lancelot would ride to the coast, load the supplies onto their vessel, and sail across the Narrow Sea with two dozen knights, leaving sufficient warriors behind to defend *le Château de Landuc* in their absence.

Issylte would retrieve the orb from the depths of *le Miroir aux Fées* and—using the gift of *les Fées Dorées* to walk between worlds—go directly from *La Porte du Dedans* at the bottom of the Mirrored Lake to the portal within *la Grotte de l' Étoile* on Avalon. That way, there was no risk of encountering either Lord Voldurk or any of his diabolical dwarves, for the wizard could not enter the Goddess' sacred realm, and the dwarves did not have the power to walk between worlds. Both Issylte and the priceless orb would be safe.

Traversing the portal directly also meant that Issylte would arrive in Avalon several days before the Tribe, giving her time to reunite with Viviane and with the other priestesses, visit Gwennol and her former patients.

And ask Ronan to forge the sword.

Issylte was now in her chamber with Lysara, who was helping her pack a few things to bring in her sack. "Did you tell Solzic about the babe?"

"No, I decided to wait," Lysara whispered. "I want him to focus entirely on this quest. Sail to Avalon. Travel to the island near Armorqiue. Help Tristan obtain the *dragonfire*. I don't want him to be preoccupied or distracted in any way. So that everything goes well—and he returns safely to me. I'll tell him then."

Issylte hugged her friend, then headed downstairs to join the group waiting near the front of the *château*. Several members of the Tribe, including Tristan and Lancelot, would accompany her to *le Miroir aux Fées*. Once she was safely inside *la Porte du Dedans*, the men would ride to the coast, where the ship awaited them. They would sail to Avalon and join Issylte there in four or five days.

The lake would be ice cold, Issylte knew, but once she emerged from the frigid water into the cave portal, she would quickly disrobe and don one of the several warm gowns she'd placed in her sack, wrapping everything in sailcloth to keep it all dry. She'd packed a cape, woolen scarf, leather gloves—and a special pouch in which to store the sacred orb, whose location she'd discovered through the nine *Gallizenae* priestesses on the *Île de Sein*.

Tristan's eyes searched hers as she kissed him goodbye on the bank of the Mirrored Lake. The others waited on horseback in the nearby trees, affording them a bit of privacy. The cold winter air stung her cheeks, the fresh tang of the lake and the pine scent of the forest filling her lungs as she looked up into his brilliant blue gaze.

"We'll be together soon in Avalon," she reassured him. "I'll miss you terribly, my *husband*." She thrilled to say the word, smiling at her wedding ring as she withdrew her arms from around his neck. With a wave to the riders on horseback, she cast one last loving look at Tristan, and dove into the glassy, icy lake.

She swam quickly to the bottom, her skin burning from the freezing cold. The orb was hidden in a small carved wooden box, concealed from view behind a trio of large rocks on the north side of the entrance to the portal. Retrieving the box quickly, for her lungs were nearly bursting from the effort and her body was numb from the chill, Issylte cradled the orb in one hand as she swam to the water's edge. She lay the treasure box on the loamy bank on the cave floor and emerged from the depths of the Mirrored Lake.

She shed her soaked gown, her body shaking with cold, dried off with a towel she'd packed, and dressed in warm clothing. She wrung out and wrapped her wet gown in the sailcloth, then retrieved the treasure box and carried it to sit upon a large, dry stone and examine her discovery. Opening the container carefully, Issylte marveled at the exquisite beauty of the luminous oval orb which sparkled like a fallen star and fit perfectly into the palm of her hand.

Its surface was faceted like a flawless diamond, illuminated from within, radiating a stellar brilliance which exuded tremendous power. Issylte's verdant magic sparked in response.

Morgane la Fée crafted this orb from the sacred

crystal of la Grotte de l' Étoile. The same crystals I used to save Tristan in Avalon when he was wounded by the Morholt's poisoned sword. The same molten, astral ore that Ronan—if he agrees—will use to forge the sword Azeldraig. No wonder I saw the sacred spring with the light of a star—la Grotte de l' Étoile—reflected in Tristan's eyes. It's entwined with our destiny.

Issylte replaced the orb within the small wooden box, securing it inside the sack she had brought, and stored it safely within the garments inside her pack. Retrieving her sailcloth-wrapped wet gown, she ventured deeper into the dark cavern, following the long, sinuous path through *la Porte du Dedans,* emerging into the hidden sea cave portal on the island of Avalon.

Amid the deafening roar of the sacred fountain amplified by the walls of the limestone cave, the brilliant crystals glimmered beneath the pure spring water of *la Grotte de l' Étoile.* Issylte's breath hitched at the sight of the star shaped pattern of five jet sprays bubbling from the turquoise depths over the luminous crystals she and Lancelot had obtained for her to save Tristan. The same astral ore that Ronan would use to forge Azeldraig. And the same raw crystal that *Morgane la Fée* had used to craft the celestial orb.

Which, Goddess willing, Tristan would use to defeat the dark wizard Voldurk.

Emerging from *la Grotte de l' Étoile* onto the beach, she followed the trail leading from the sandy shore up to the top of the forested cliff. She continued walking through the dense woods, following the path to the snow-dusted clearing where—upon the elevated plateau near *le Lac Diane*—the gleaming white limestone walls of *Le Centre* glistened in the afternoon sun. As Issylte walked up the cobblestone path to the familiar entrance, she saw Cléo and Nyda running to greet her.

"Lilée! You have returned! How wonderful to see you again!" Cléo cried, hugging Issylte and kissing her cheeks. Tears of bliss streamed down Issylte's face.

"Come, let's find Viviane. She'll want to welcome you back!" Nyda exclaimed jubilantly, taking Issylte's hand and leading her toward the Lady of the Lake's quarters in *Le Centre*.

Viviane was overjoyed to see Issylte, and after a brief reunion, the High Priestess of Avalon led her former acolyte to the Women's and Children's Centers so that she could visit her previous patients. Issylte was thrilled to see Mara and her son Gwilherm, who was now a healthy and robust toddler. She was especially glad to see Gwennol, under whose direction the Women's Center was obviously thriving.

When Issylte revealed her true identity as the Princess of Ireland and her desire to challenge the evil Queen Morag to reclaim her throne, Gwennol shared a surprising bit of information.

"You know that I was a servant at the *Château de Tintagel*, where I worked in the kitchen. I'm very familiar with the layout of the castle. There's a stream fed from a lake behind the *château* which flows right under the foundation of Tintagel, emptying into the ocean in front of the fortress. A small brook also flows from a fountain in the heart of the forest directly into *la Chambre de la Reine*—the Queen's royal chambers. Perhaps you can gain entry there and attack her unaware."

Gwennol chortled. "Wouldn't it be ironic if I—the old, worthless woman that the Vikings left behind when they attacked Cornwall—knew the very secret that would lead to their downfall?"

Issylte hugged her friend warmly, thanking her enormously for the valuable information that she tucked away to share with Tristan and Lancelot once they arrived. Then, bidding her former patients and the residents of the Centers a fond farewell, Issylte returned to speak privately and more at length with Viviane.

She told the High Priestess all that had transpired since she'd left Avalon. The months spent at *la Joyeuse Garde* training with Tristan, meeting Garou of *La Tribu des Loups.* The ordeal with the dwarf Malvon by the Mirrored Lake, the induction into the Tribe of Dana. The Druidic magic of *Rose Elder*.

She told of the gifts from *les Fées Dorées*, the trip to the *Île de Sein* and the knowledge gleaned from the *Gallizenae,* the encounter with Ondine of *les Dragons de Mer,* and how Tristan, wrongly imprisoned for the murder of Princess Blanchine of Armorique, had been the victim of evil enchantment by the wizard Voldurk.

She shared with Viviane how she'd cast her spirit as a white dove to save him, the abduction of Gargeolaine, the rescue of Aimée, *la Fée du Coeur*, with the help of *le Clan des Ours*. The beautiful triple trinity of their Celtic Wedding in the sacred Forest of Brocéliande.

And how she'd now returned to Avalon for the purpose of asking Ronan to forge the sword *Azeldraig,* just as Gofannon—Viviane's former lover—had crafted Excalibur years ago.

"I must find a way to convince him, Viviane. The *Gallizenae* explained that it's the only means to defeat the wizard Voldurk. I was hoping you'd allow me to borrow a horse so that I might ride out to Ronan's cottage and speak to him."

"Of course, you may borrow the horse. And I will speak to Ronan as well." The Lady of the Lake sat at the table in her room, across from Issylte, who was sipping the *tisane* that Viviane had prepared for the two of them. The setting winter sun cast golden rays of light through the large windows that overlooked the effervescent spray of the fountain in the courtyard of *Le Centre.*

"Just as his father Gofannon did for me when he crafted Excalibur," Viviane explained, staring into the ebullient waters of *la Fontaine de Jouvence,* "so Ronan must imbue this extraordinary weapon with all of his knowledge as a blacksmith descended from the gods. All of his exceptional skill as an Avalonian Elf. And all of his love for you, the woman for whom he forges the sword." Viviane locked her limpid eyes on Issylte. "For that is the magical essence of the sword. The very soul of the Elf who crafts it. *For the woman he loves.*"

The Lady of the Lake gazed out the window, smiling as she reminisced about the past. "Gofannon came here to Avalon after his wife died, shortly after I'd founded *Le Centre.* He and I became lovers and remained so until his death, just a few years ago." Viviane directed her attention back to Issylte. "I asked him to forge a sword of unparalleled power for King Arthur. So that I could find a way for my son Lancelot to become a Knight of the Round Table." With a nostalgic smile, Viviane whispered, "Gofannon put all the love that he felt for me into that sword. And now, Ronan must do the same—as he forges this weapon for you."

Squeezing Issylte's hand affectionately, the High Priestess added, "Perhaps it will help him find closure for the guilt and grief which have consumed him since you left. Although he could not be the warrior you asked him to be, leading your army to Ireland so that you could challenge Queen Morag and reclaim your kingdom, Ronan—and *only* Ronan—can forge the sword which is the key to your victory."

"You once said that Ronan would play a very important role in my destiny," Issylte whispered, staring pensively at the sacred waters of the fountain which tied Ronan—and all the Elves—to Avalon. "You were right, Viviane. You knew that Tristan was my *mate*. And that Ronan would be essential to my fate, which the Goddess had finally revealed. I pray now that I can find the words to convince him to forge this sword. For *my mate* to wield. To defeat the evil wizard and stop the Black Widow Queen."

****

Issylte rode through the familiar woods to the village of Briac, where she greeted several of the local shopkeepers along the way to Ronan's cottage. Newly fallen snow lightly dusted the evergreen trees, the crisp, fragrant scent of pine and fresh salt air filling her lungs as her horse dashed through the dense forest.

When she spotted his silvery-blond hair in the field tending to his horses, a wave of emotions flooded her. Tenderness for the Elf she had so passionately loved. Nervousness about what she now needed to ask of him. Apprehension of his inevitable anger. And fear that he might very well refuse her request.

At the sound of her approach, he lifted his head and glowered at her. *Things do not bode well for this visit. Dear Goddess Dana, please help me find the right words.*

She dismounted from her borrowed horse, tethered

it, then walked over toward Ronan who now strode over to meet her.

"Hello, Ronan." She smiled. "You look well."

"Issylte," he greeted her tersely with a duck of his chin. His deep green eyes raked over her, fixing on the *mating mark* upon her neck, the wedding ring upon her finger. "I heard that you had returned to Avalon." His intense gaze scrutinized her face, and Issylte awkwardly averted her eyes and looked out toward the horses. Following her lead, Ronan suggested, "Would you like to say hello to Marron, Maëva…and Noisette?"

She swallowed a lump in her throat at the thought of seeing the foal which would have been hers. "Yes, I'd love to. Thank you, Ronan."

He escorted her out onto the field where clumps of grass protruded among patches of snow. Ronan handed her two apples. "The horses will be more eager to greet you with these," he chuckled softly. At his whistle, Marron trotted over, with Noisette following cautiously behind. The filly was every bit as magnificent as her mother, with a rich chestnut coat and glorious black mane.

"Hello, Marron, here's a lovely apple for you," Issylte crooned as the mare took the fruit from her hand. She stroked the horse's shoulder lovingly as she eyed the beautiful filly who lingered near her mother. "Here's an apple for you too, pretty Noisette." Issylte extended her hand and waited patiently for the young horse to come forward and take it from her outstretched palm. When Noisette did at last eat the fruit, Issylte stroked her shoulder, mane, and forelock.

"She's nearly two years old." Ronan stood on the other side of the filly, petting Noisette, leaning around to speak to Issylte. "She has her mother's rich brown color and black mane. She's a beauty, isn't she?" His bitter smile conveyed the message behind the words. *She could have been* yours. *Look at what you gave up.*

Maëva and Noz also came over to say hello and receive an apple. After a fond reunion with the horses, Ronan offered, "Would you like to come inside for a goblet of mulled wine? It is chilly today."

"That would be lovely. Thank you." Memories of sipping mulled wine before the roaring fire gripped her heavy heart. *How I loved him,* she thought, following the silvery-blond head and once-beloved broad shoulders as they headed toward the stone cottage.

He led her inside his cozy home, so familiar and yet so foreign now. Issylte gazed at the oak table and two chairs in the kitchen, remembering the meals they'd shared together. The *tarte aux mirabelles* and fresh seafood delicacies she'd made for him here. The love they'd shared in this snug kitchen.

She spotted the settee in front of the hearth where a crackling fire emitted warmth and golden light. Glanced at the closed door to the bedroom where they had shared so much passion. Once, she'd been most welcome here. But now, Issylte felt like an intruder, trespassing into his private domain. A shiver crept up her spine.

"Please, sit," he said courteously, as he poured some mulled wine into two mugs, handing her one and gesturing to the settee before the fire. Issylte noticed his decorations for the upcoming Yuletide season as she lowered herself onto the deep green cushions of the welcoming sofa.

Evergreen garlands adorned the mantelpiece above the fireplace, and a lovely wreath with holly and berries decorated the front door. The cluster of mistletoe hanging above the entrance reminded Issylte of how she'd once made the amber talisman for Ronan to wear around his neck, and he'd given her the lovely deep green, fur-lined cloak. And matching gloves. *Neither one of us wears our gift this year*, she reflected with a bittersweet smile.

Ronan, seemingly satisfied that his guest was now seated comfortably and had a mug of mulled wine to warm herself before the fire, sat down in a chair to the left of the settee and sipped his own brew. After a moment, he said, "I wondered why you had returned to Avalon. It appears that I am about to find out." His gaze conveyed curiosity, apprehension, and thinly veiled contempt as he stared at Issylte, waiting for her to explain the reason for her visit.

"When I left Avalon," she began, "I stayed with Lancelot and Tristan at *la Joyeuse Garde*, then traveled to *le Château de Landuc*, where I became a priestess of the Tribe of Dana." She showed Ronan the tattoo on her inner right wrist. He stared at the wedding ring on her left hand as she pulled back her sleeve.

"While living at the castle, I learned that there had been many dwarves hunting for something in the sacred Forest of Brocéliande. They had even attempted to abduct the priestesses of Dana." She met his intense eyes, shuddering at the horrid memory of the dwarf Malvon near *le Miroir aux Fées.* "I myself was attacked and nearly abducted, just as Laudine—the hostess of Landuc and Lady of the Fountain—had been victimized the year before."

She took another sip of mulled wine to calm her nerves. "Shortly after that ordeal, I ventured to the *Île de*

Sein, to seek knowledge from the nine *Mélusine* priestesses of the *Gallizenae*. They told me what the dwarves were seeking in the sacred forest…and why."

Issylte removed the small bag within the sack that she had placed at her feet. She withdrew the wooden box which held the orb and handed it to Ronan. He looked at her warily as he took the box and opened it to reveal the luminous, exquisite orb glistening in the firelight.

"*That* is what the dwarves are seeking," Issylte explained, meeting Ronan's incredulous look. "The fairy Morgane crafted it for her former lover Voldurk—the dark wizard who helped Queen Morag poison my father. The same wizard who killed Princess Blanchine of Armorique. And who now controls King Marke of Cornwall with evil enchantments."

Ronan held the orb in his long, calloused fingers, examining its glittering facets in the firelight. "This orb exudes tremendous power. Radiates a brilliance…like a star." Raising his deep green gaze to Issylte, he asked, "What is this made of?"

"The ore from the fallen star. The sacred crystal from *la Grotte de l' Étoile*." Ronan's astonished look locked upon her. "Voldurk seeks it, for this orb offers the only means to destroy him. If the wizard obtains it, he'll be invincible."

Ronan placed the orb back into the wooden jewelry box, which he stored inside the small sack and returned to Issylte. "Why have you brought this to me? I do not understand."

Issylte put the small sack carefully back into her bag, then took a deep breath and exhaled, gathering her courage. "I have come to ask for your help, Ronan. The wizard must be defeated before he and Queen Morag poison King Marke of Cornwall. Before they unleash untold evil upon the entire Celtic realm. You are the only one who can help me."

"Please explain." Ronan eyed her cautiously as he drank his mulled wine.

"There is a dragon portal off the coast of Armorique, near *le Château Rose,* where the cyclops *Béliagog* guards the beast Mordrac. This orb is the key to obtain its *dragonfire.*"

Pushing herself to the edge of her seat as well as her nerves, she dared voice her request.

"Ronan, I am here to ask if you will forge the sword *Azeldraig.* The weapon which will surpass even the legendary Excalibur. To slay the wizard Voldurk. And stop the evil queen."

Ronan rose abruptly to his feet and strode away from her. Shaking his head in disbelief, he faced her, angry and sullen. "Forge a sword...for you? You have no right to ask me this!"

He paced back and forth at the edge of the kitchen, raking his fingers through his hair. Flashing his furious green gaze at her, he bellowed, "You *left me*, Issylte. I wanted to *marry* you, and you *left* me. For *another man.*" He strode up to her, leaned down into her face, and spat, "And now, you are asking me to forge a sword. For *him.*" He stood up and shook his head, a wild stallion livid with fury. "No, I cannot. I *will* not."

Rage blazed across his rugged face. "You left me *broken*, Issylte. *Alone*. You threw away *everything* I offered. My love. My horses. *My life.*" Ronan sneered, his voice breaking with scorn and grief. "You chose *him*—not me. And now, you have no right to come here and ask me this." He retrieved her cloak from the hook

259

near the front door and handed it to her. "I want you to leave."

Issylte rose from the settee, fighting back tears, and donned her wrap. She picked up her bag, her head bowed in defeat, and quietly walked to the front door. As she prepared to depart, she turned to him and said gently, "I am truly sorry that a future for the two of us was impossible, Ronan. You couldn't leave Avalon, and I couldn't stay. I hope you can forgive me. And I hope that somehow—you might reconsider."

She beseeched the scowling face that she had once loved so desperately.

"Even if you cannot forge this sword for *me*, Ronan, perhaps you might be willing to forge it for the kingdoms which would otherwise fall prey to Queen Morag and the evil wizard. For the thousands of innocent victims who—if not killed outright in the attacks which will undoubtedly resume—would suffer interminably as slaves to their Viking conquerors. Please, Ronan. Do it to stop the evil which threatens us all. Only you can forge the sword to slay Voldurk. I hope you'll reconsider my request. If, by chance, you should change your mind, I'm staying at *Le Centre* with Viviane. Thank you, Ronan. I wish you the very best. Always." She smiled softly. "Farewell."

Issylte quietly closed the door behind her, mounted her waiting horse, and rode off through the snow-covered forest.

****

A few moments later, a young priestess with long, light brown hair emerged quietly from Ronan's bedroom. She saw him sitting in his favorite chair, his head in his hands, overcome with emotion. She quietly walked up behind him, leaned forward to wrap her arms around him, and placed her head comfortingly against his bulky shoulders.

"You were eavesdropping." He leaned his head against one of the arms in which she had enveloped him.

"Yes." She kissed his cheek and nuzzled his ear with her nose.

"I refused her request."

"I know." Nimue released his shoulders, sat down at his feet, and rested her head upon her arms, folded across the tops of her bent knees. She cast a loving gaze at him, remaining silent, waiting for him to speak.

"She wants me to forge the sword *Azeldraig*. A magnificent weapon, like Excalibur." He scowled at the fire, his jaw clenched. "For *him*." Ronan glared at the stone hearth, his eyes blazing like the flames before him. "I cannot. I will not. I refuse to craft a sword for the man who took her from me. I *despise* him. I want to *kill him*."

Nimue was an exceptional healer, having come to Avalon shortly after Issylte's departure. She'd met Ronan—heartbroken, grief-stricken, filled with rage and guilt—and, with infinite patience and tenderness, had become first his friend, then his confidante, and recently, his lover. She knew he needed to process all the conflicting emotions that were smothering him. She also knew that Issylte's request could very well be exactly what Ronan needed to heal his broken heart. She just had to help him see it.

"Why did Issylte say that only you could craft the sword she needs?"

"Because I learned from my father how such a weapon must be forged. When I helped him craft the sword Excalibur for King Arthur."

"And how must it be forged, Ronan?"

"It must be crafted from the ore of the fallen star, hidden within the sacred cave of *la Grotte de l' Étoile*. A weapon of this caliber must be forged in *dragonfire,* here on the island of Avalon, by a descendant of the god Lugh—my ancestor."

Ronan poured a mug of mulled wine and offered it to Nimue. He took a large swallow from his own goblet, his eyes blazing into hers. He returned his intense gaze to the flames of the fire, as if imagining himself at his forge. "The Elf who crafts such a sword must love the woman for whom he forges it. He must apply all his knowledge as a blacksmith, his skill as a craftsman, his *otherworldly* magic as an Elf." Ronan's fierce eyes danced in the firelight. "But he must also imbue all the love in his heart—the very essence of his soul—into the molten ore of the fallen star. And forge the sword in the flames of *dragonfire.*"

His deep green gaze locked with hers. "My father Gofannon forged Excalibur for Viviane. She'd been his lover for several years after my mother's death." He stared into the flickering flames, lost in the past. "He put all of his grief, all of his anguish and guilt, and all of his love for the Lady of the Lake who had healed him—into that sword."

Ronan took another large gulp of mulled wine and looked deeply into Nimue's eyes. *Can he see the love that blazes there, as scorching as the flames in the hearth?* "I watched as my father hammered away his rage and despair, to craft a weapon of unparalleled beauty, power, and strength. Cleansed in fire...reborn... like the phoenix."

Recognition dawned in Ronan's eyes. Nimue could

see it. She smiled knowingly at him, coaxing him to say it, her heart filled with pride and encouragement. And love.

"Do you think I could pound away my grief and guilt over losing Issylte, and forge myself anew, as I craft the sword?" His face, crumpled in pain, reflected a fragile glimmer of hope.

Tears brimmed in Nimue's grateful eyes. "I do." She nodded, rising to her feet, extending her hands to raise him up to stand before her. "You were not able to lead her army and fight at her side," she said softly. "The one thing she asked of you. You, who would have given your life for her, could not leave Avalon and be the warrior she needed. Not only were you unable to accompany her so that she could challenge the queen, but neither could you keep her here on this island with you." Kissing his hands, which were clasped within her own, Nimue looked up into his sorrowful, soulful green eyes. "Issylte must fight for her people and restore Ireland to the peace and prosperity of her father's reign. The guilt and grief of failing her—and losing her—have *consumed* you, Ronan."

Nimue touched the side of his face, gently stroking the dark-blond stubble. "But now, you can do this for her. Although you could not grant her first request—to be her warrior and leave Avalon—this request, Ronan, you *can* do." She poured all the love she felt for him into the look which she hoped would melt his hardened heart.

"You, Ronan—and *only you*—can forge the weapon that will help Issylte become the queen she is meant to be. The Emerald Queen of Ireland."

She locked eyes with him. "And Ronan, if you put all your grief, rage, guilt—and love for Issylte—into this magnificent sword, then you will feel immense pride in doing what is right. Not just for her, but for *yourself.* For the *entire Celtic realm.* You will finally be able to forgive yourself. And maybe, if all the love you have for Issylte can be forged into this weapon," she whispered, stroking his broad chest with slender, elegant fingers, "then maybe there will be room in your heart...*for me.*"

She raised up onto her tiptoes and kissed him softly on the lips. "I'm going back to the Women's Center to help Gwennol now. Reflect upon this, Ronan. Search your soul and tell me in the morning what decision you've reached. Goodnight, my Elf. May the Goddess bless you. Until tomorrow."

****

Long after Nimue had gone, Ronan sat in his favorite chair, staring at the glowing embers in the fire, drinking his mulled wine.

Thinking of his father.

Remembering the past.

Fueling the flames of his Elven forge.

The next morning, he arrived on his horse in front of the Women's Center. Nimue donned her warm cloak and stepped outside to greet him at the door.

"Walk with me," he requested, offering her the crook of his elbow as he led her to the bench near the pond. The winter sun peeked in and out of the clouds as he settled Nimue onto the wooden seat at the edge of the forest. The crisp December chill nipped at his calloused hands.

He sat down and twisted to face her, smiling softly. "You were right. I have been consumed with guilt and grief, angry with myself for being unable to grant the one request Issylte had asked of me." He pushed a strand of light-brown hair away from her hopeful, expectant face and lifted Nimue's chin tenderly. "But you were also right that this is a request I can fulfill. A request which will end my despair and alter the direction of my life's path."

Ronan took Nimue's delicate hands and held them tightly. "I will forge a weapon to surpass all others. The most magnificent sword I've ever crafted. For Issylte. For myself. For the Goddess." Raising one of her hands to his lips, he met Nimue's beautiful blue eyes as he whispered, "And for *you.*"

She threw her arms around his neck and pulled him down to her, kissing him deeply. "I'm so proud of you, Ronan!" She kissed his cheeks, his lips, his face, tears spilling down her cheeks.

He wiped them away tenderly, then stood, raising her with him as he wrapped her in his arms. "I will ride to *Le Centre* now and speak to Issylte. She'll be thrilled to hear I've changed my mind." Leaning down to kiss Nimue, he whispered in her ear, "Come to the cottage later this afternoon. We'll make love in front of the fire…" He nuzzled her neck. "And celebrate our future."

She nodded mutely, too overwhelmed with emotion to speak. Ronan led her back to the Women's Center, where she stood and watched him mount his magnificent black horse and ride up the cobblestone hill.

****

Issylte was blending herbs with Viviane and several priestesses when she glimpsed the sunlight shining on Ronan's golden head through the window as he strode up to the entrance of *Le Centre*. Her heart pumping wildly, her mouth dry with anticipation, she ran outside to greet him, forgetting her cloak in her haste.

"Ronan!" she gasped, afraid to say anything more lest he change his mind.

He smiled genuinely at her, his face conveying the message she was desperate to hear. "I have reconsidered, Issylte. I will forge the sword *Azeldraig*."

She ran to him, wanting to throw her arms around his neck, but did not, for their relationship was very different now, and she was Tristan's wife. "I cannot thank you enough, Ronan. Only you can forge such a sword. Thank you, from the bottom of my heart."

He lowered his head, smiling humbly, then asked, "Have Lancelot and Tristan arrived?"

"Not yet, but I expect them soon. Perhaps later today or tomorrow. It's been four days now, so the ship should dock very soon."

"Excellent. When they do arrive, please come out to my cottage. We'll discuss the details at that time."

"Thank you, Ronan. For everything." She flashed him a grateful smile. He grinned, then mounted his stallion Noz. She watched as the Elf she had once loved with all her heart rode down the hill, across the snowy, grassy field, through the woods. Back to his cottage.

And his forge.

The white dove in her spirit soared in the pale winter sky.

****

The following day, Lancelot and Tristan arrived with the warriors who had sailed from Landuc. Viviane and Issylte greeted them warmly at the dock, flanked by Cléo, Nyda, and several Avalonian Elves who defended *Le Centre*. Issylte had a joyful reunion with Tristan and the members of the Tribe, informing them all that Ronan had agreed to forge the sword *Azeldraig*.

266

Wrapping her arms around Tristan, pressing her body against the hardness which made her weak with desire, Issylte whispered in his ear how she couldn't wait until they were alone together in the quarters that Viviane had made available for them during their stay in Avalon. He whispered gruffly, "Let's go there now." She smiled conspiratorially, as the group dispersed to their various quarters, eager to refresh from the sea voyage.

Mounting the horses provided for them, Lancelot led Gorvenal, Solzic, Darius, Dagur, and their knights to the lodging where they would stay amongst the Elves, training each day until the departure for Armorique. Tristan and Issylte followed Viviane, Cléo, and Nyda to *Le Centre*, where the newlyweds quickly disappeared into their quarters, barely able to resist each other, not emerging until several hours later, when the bells chimed to announce supper in the dining area.

****

The following day, the members of the Tribe of Dana rode with Issylte through the forest to Ronan's cottage. He greeted them cordially and introduced the lovely young priestess at his side to the group. Issylte remarked with gratitude how Nimue looked at Ronan with love light shining in her adoring eyes. *Thank the Goddess he has found love again. I wish him all the happiness that I was unable to give. I am glad that he now has this beautiful Nimue, whose pure heart radiates the love he so richly deserves.*

"Since I am sailing to Armorique, you could voyage with me," Ronan offered to Lancelot and the Tribe, gathered around the settee where Issylte and Nimue were seated before the stone fireplace inside the cottage. Issylte smiled warmly at Nimue, hoping to convey the respect and admiration that filled her heart. The young priestess returned the smile, her expressive blue gaze gleaming, then shifted her attention to Ronan, who was speaking to the Tribe.

"I plan on taking two ships. I'm delivering weapons and armor to King Hoël and Prince Kaherdin at *le Château Rose* for the winter solstice."

Issylte responded eagerly to Ronan, "That's perfect timing, for we must obtain the *dragonfire* without Voldurk's knowledge." She looked at the beloved members of her Tribe and announced somberly, "The *Gallizenae* informed me that the wizard performs *human sacrifices* during the winter solstice in *la Porte des Ombres*. The cave where Dagur and the Clan helped me free Aimée, *la Fée du Coeur.*"

Her heavy words hung in the air. A few moments later, Lancelot announced to the fierce warriors gathered around Ronan's hearth, "Since Voldurk will be occupied in Britain, we can sail to Armorique, hidden in Ronan's Elven ships. Avoid Voldurk's spies. Retrieve the *dragonfire*. And return here to Avalon, where Ronan forges the sword *Azeldraig*. The only means to defeat the dark wizard." Heads bowed in solemn agreement as the Tribe exchanged stark, determined glances.

Issylte's heart raced, her palms growing damp, as she leaned forward to retrieve the bag at her feet. She removed the orb from her belongings, holding it flat in her extended palm for all to see. Its astral brilliance sparkled in the firelight, radiant with celestial power. Whispers of wonder rippled around the hearth.

"Tristan must use this sacred orb to obtain the *dragonfire* that Ronan will need to forge the sword," Issylte explained. "The last remaining dragon—

Mordrac—lives in a cave on an island off the coast of Armorique. He is guarded by the giant *Béliagog*, a cyclops who fires bolts of lightning from his eye onto anyone who trespasses into the dragon portal." She swallowed hard, envisioning Tristan's arduous quest. His impassioned face revealed the same fire she felt blazing in her own heart. "This orb will reflect the lightning from the cyclops' eye, momentarily blinding him, so that Tristan may enter the cave. And capture a plume of fire from the dragon."

She looked at her *mate,* her heart clenching at the thought of losing him. As she beheld his loving gaze, his achingly beautiful smile took her breath away. The white dove in her spirit soared with the sea raven in his sky-blue eyes.

She turned to Lancelot, finding strength and courage reflected on his valiant, virile face. *I am glad you will be with us, my friend. You and Tristan are the finest knights in the Celtic realm. And the warriors of the Tribe are as fierce as the Elves of Avalon. Goddess willing, we will prevail.* She poured all the love she felt for him into her most encouraging smile. He flashed her his disarmingly charming, boyish grin. She took a deep breath, exhaled slowly, and continued.

"The *dragonfire* must be contained in a cauldron of black obsidian," Issylte announced to the rapt faces of her Tribe. "The only substance that can withstand its intense heat. It must then be transported back here to Avalon. Where Ronan will use it to forge the sword." She beheld the handsome, chiseled Elven face that she had so often caressed with loving fingers. She hoped her own face revealed the intense gratitude that filled her heart.

Ronan's impassioned green gaze held hers for a long moment. He then looked away to address Tristan, his deep voice foreboding. "When you're in the portal, after you've obtained the *dragonfire*, there is something else I need you to do before you leave the cave."

Issylte's eyes darted to Tristan, who shot her a quick, inquisitive glance. He refocused his attention on Ronan, who had fetched a large cloth sack from his kitchen, returning to sit with the Tribe in front of his hearth. The massive Elf locked wary eyes with her anxious *mate*.

"Inside the portal, you'll see the huge green dragon scales that Mordrac has shed, scattered across the cave floor. They're enormous—a foot or more in diameter— and poisonous to the touch. While you hold the orb, you'll be able to select three of the largest, placing them in this bag." He handed Tristan the cloth sack. "Bring them—and the cauldron of *dragonfire*—back to my ship. I'll use them to forge the sword when we return to Avalon."

Tristan accepted the bag. He flashed Issylte a brave smile, but she could see the apprehension in his warrior regard. She sent soothing verdant magic through her fingers as she touched his scarred hand. A smile of acknowledgement eased the tension in his fierce, feral face.

Raising her voice to recapture the attention of her Tribe and the knights of Landuc who had accompanied them, Issylte referred again to the luminous gem glowing in her flattened palm. "If Voldurk obtains this priceless orb, he will be impervious to Béliagog's lightning and Mordrac's fire. Enabling him to slay both. Eliminating any chance of forging the sword which can defeat him.

Making himself *invincible*." She implored the rugged faces of her beloved Tribe. "We cannot allow that to happen. We *must* defeat the wizard. And the Black Widow Queen he serves. The combined evil that threatens us all." Tristan squeezed her hand, pride shining in his loving gaze.

Darius, Dagur, and Solzic exchanged solemn glances. Their resolute faces reflected the same conviction and courage that Issylte glimpsed on the faces of the knights of Landuc. Grave expressions reflected the enormity of the task ahead. And the commitment to helping Tristan obtain the *dragonfire*.

Whatever the cost.

Ronan spoke again. "I sail for Armorique next week. Today, we'll ride with several of my Elves to the sacred cave. *La Grotte de l'Étoile*. We'll obtain the black obsidian for the cauldron, and the molten ore I'll need to forge the sword." He faced the men leaning against the walls of the cottage, gathered around the welcoming hearth. The fire snapped and crackled in the pensive silence, the somber faces contemplating the dangerous quest. "I'll craft the cauldron tomorrow, so it will be ready when we sail for Armorique. I'll be grateful for your help in loading the armaments onto my two ships for the delivery to King Hoël."

With a fierce glance at Lancelot and Tristan, the warrior Elf in Ronan emerged.

"When we sail to *le Château Rose,* you'll hide in the belly of one of my ships, among the armor and weapons, protected from view. When we arrive at the castle, my Elves and I will unload the merchandise. Nightfall comes early for the winter solstice, so you'll be able to row to the island of the dragon portal under cover of darkness.

Retrieve the *dragonfire* and the poisonous scales. And return quickly to my ship."

Ronan locked his intense gaze on Tristan. "The castle is still mourning the death of Princess Blanchine. I'll inform King Hoël and Prince Kaherdin that it was Voldurk—not you—who killed her. I'm certain that once they learn the truth, you'll be able to count Armorique as an ally. United with you against the dark wizard and the wicked queen." Ronan stared at Lancelot, Dagur, Gorvenal, Darius, and Solzic, his forest-green eyes ablaze. "When you're safely back on my ship, we'll sail immediately for Avalon. Although it will be dark, the moonglow and starlight will be sufficient for us to navigate. We'll be safely home before the wizard has time to react."

Their plans finalized, the Tribe joined six enormous Avalonian Elves in loading tools onto their horses, preparing to ride with Ronan to *la Grotte de l'Étoile*. With a promise to see them later, Issylte kissed Tristan, and Nimue said goodbye to Ronan. The priestesses then returned to the Women's Center, as Ronan and the Tribe rode off through the forest toward the shore where the sea cave lay hidden at the base of the craggy stone cliff.

****

Inside *la Grotte de l'Étoile*, Ronan showed his Elves where to procure the black obsidian for the cauldron to transport the *dragonfire*. He and the Tribe used shovels and pickaxes to obtain the molten ore from the fallen star that he would smelt in forging the sword *Azeldraig*. Soon, the men and Elves were working collaboratively, mining the precious celestial metal from the sacred cave.

They worked tirelessly all afternoon, finally mining enough of the astral ore just as the rays of the setting sun streaked the sky with brilliant hues of pink, orange, and gold. Grinning as they packed their gear onto the horses, the group rode back to Ronan's cottage and unloaded the tools, black obsidian, and stellar ore for his forge. Ronan informed them all that he would ride up to *Le Centre* as soon as the cauldron was finished, and the Tribe returned home to their various quarters.

A few days later, Ronan rode up to *Le Centre* and spotted Issylte walking with Viviane toward the herbal workshop. She ran to greet him as he dismounted.

"*Bonjour, Issylte,*" he said jovially, bestowing the friendly French greeting, *la bise,* on both of her cheeks. "The cauldron is finished." He grinned broadly, then kissed each of Viviane's cheeks as she joined them.

"That is wonderful! Thank you very much, Ronan." With a warm smile, she said enthusiastically, "Now we can obtain the *dragonfire* for you to forge the sword." Viviane beamed at them both, obviously delighted to hear the good news.

"Tomorrow, we'll load the armor and weapons onto the ships," he announced, indicating the distant shoreline where his Elven crew was preparing the two Avalonian cog ships. "Then the supplies. We'll depart the following day. And arrive at *le Château Rose* on the winter solstice, just as planned." He grinned at Issylte again.

"That is perfect. Thank you so very much, Ronan." Issylte smiled up at him, gratitude shining in her glorious emerald eyes. *By the Goddess, how I loved her. Part of me always will. But finally, by forging this sword, I shall be able to move on.* "I'll head back to the cottage now," he said cheerfully. "I'll see you soon. Good day to you both. *Au revoir, Mesdames.*" With a goodbye kiss on both of their cheeks, Ronan mounted his stallion, waved to Issylte and Viviane, and rode home through the verdant forest.

****

Issylte watched Ronan's silvery-blond head disappear, fond memories of him flooding her heart. Swallowing forcefully, she looked away, finding comfort in Viviane's knowing smile and empathetic face. Hooking elbows with her mentor, Issylte returned to the herbal workshop and the awaiting patients. Soon, Tristan would return from the day's training.

In two days, the Tribe would sail to Armorique with Ronan.

For Tristan to wield the sacred orb against the Cyclops and the beast Mordrac.

And obtain the *dragonfire*.

Chapter 19

The Winter Solstice

Bothor hesitantly followed Lord Voldurk into the ominous cave, his nostrils assailed by the rank odor of death and rotting flesh. The dank limestone walls were smeared with a noxious black slime that caused the dwarf's wizened skin to shrivel and shrink. The two knights carrying the victim laid the baron on a large stone slab, then secured his ankles and wrists with ropes attached to thick wooden stakes driven into the ground. Once they'd restrained the unconscious man, the soldiers quickly retreated, anxious to leave the cavern of death.

"This is where we sacrifice the victim," Voldurk rasped, his voice the rattling hiss of a snake. "Every solstice and equinox. *Without fail.*" Yellow eyes with the vertical slits of a poisonous python transfixed him in terror.

"Malfleur—the mistress we serve—must have a human sacrifice in order to strengthen her power. For years, Frocin performed this service. Today, as his replacement, you—the new Leader of the Dwarves—will sacrifice the victim. And be rewarded handsomely in return. This she promised upon the autumnal equinox, when I informed her of Frocin's death."

The sizzling thrum of a current sparked the air, the ground reverberating with tremors from the dark depths of the cave, as if a monstrous storm were imminent. A surge of power seeped into Bothor's bones, causing his muscles to quiver and twitch uncontrollably. His mouth went dry as a deafening hum filled the chamber, the pressure pulsing and pounding in his pointed ears. Dark, thick shadows emerged from the bowels of the cave, hovering over the unconscious victim, fouling the air with a repulsive, revolting odor.

An intense burning pain suddenly gripped Bothor's entrails, as if a branding iron had seared and twisted his innards. The dwarf fell to his knees in agony as wave after wave of incapacitating nausea rolled over him. He began to vomit profusely, his bowels liquefying, running in hot fiery streams down his bowed legs as he heaved and retched repeatedly. A virulent poison was eviscerating him with toxic, caustic flames.

Voldurk moaned and bellowed beside him, clutching his stomach as he, too, writhed in anguish on the cavern floor. The wizard began twitching as seizures racked his body, then, like Bothor, began projectile vomiting in abject misery.

For long minutes that stretched like interminable days, Bothor and Voldurk languished in physical torture as the murderous voice of Malfleur burrowed into their brains.

"She is *GONE!* Someone infiltrated this cave and *freed her*! You have FAILED!"

Bothor shrieked as a white-hot flame charred his insides, eliciting violent, incessant purging.

"The agony you now endure is *nothing* compared to what will happen if you fail again!"

As quickly as it had arrived, the pain was gone. Bothor lay on his back whimpering, tears of utter relief streaming down his wrinkled cheeks. Voldurk rose to his feet, wiping vomit from the side of his face with the sleeve of his long robe. He brushed himself off and stood shakily before the wretched Shadow Fairy.

La Fée des Ombres. Malfleur.

"Voldurk, you will prepare another gemstone. For the vernal equinox, when I next appear."

The wizard bowed his head humbly. "As you command, Mistress. It shall be done."

Malfleur seethed, her voice the crackle and spit of sizzling flames. "Is this the new Leader of the Dwarves you have brought before me?"

Voldurk gestured for Bothor to approach the sinister shadows rippling above the victim, who had regained consciousness and was now shivering upon the stone slab before them. "It is indeed, Mistress. This is Bothor, whom I have brought today to perform the sacrifice."

Malfleur's voice slithered into the dwarf's ears along winding wisps of smothering shadows. "You, Bothor, shall capture *another fairy* to replace the one who escaped. Bring her to me on the vernal equinox. When Lord Voldurk brings the enchanted gem."

"I shall, mistress," Bothor stammered, his body still shaking from the sudden, incapacitating illness.

"So that you may foresee where to trap her, I shall grant you the same power that I gave Frocin. The gift of *clairvoyance.* You will hunt her, Bothor. Drug her with a poisoned dart." Malfleur floated in tenebrous shadows before him, the stench of death overwhelming. "And deliver her here—unconscious—the evening of the vernal equinox. In the gloaming, when my power peaks during the twilight hour."

Both Voldurk and Bothor uttered their consent, their

heads bowed deferentially.

"Step forward, Bothor. I shall bestow upon you the gift of clairvoyance."

Terrified, his stomach twitching, he approached the sinuous swirls, his fouled, filthy legs wobbly and unsteady. As he stood before the stone slab where the horrified victim lay quivering and whimpering, dark shadows slithered over Bothor's body, coiling in wisps up into his nose. He snorted and choked, opening his mouth to gasp for air, permitting even more suffocating shadows to slink down his scorched throat.

Power suddenly surged through him, his heart pounding wildly, then—as the shadows receded from his body—a pleasant glow flowed through his veins.

Clairvoyant magic. A gift for him to serve her.

"And now…perform the sacrifice, Bothor. I *hunger*."

He retrieved the dagger from the small stone near the sacrificial slab. And, under the watchful, reptilian gaze of Lord Voldurk, Bothor sacrificed the screaming victim to his insatiable, despicable mistress.

Malfleur. *La Fée des Ombres.*

****

Morag positively purred, basking in the afterglow of an especially exquisite tryst with Voldurk. They lay entwined together in the lavender scented bed of her royal chambers in the Fortress of Morois, which the dwarf Bothor had inherited from the late Frocin. As the new Leader of the Dwarves, Bothor had received not only this fine fortress and its band of merciless mercenary knights, but all of Frocin's impressive wealth, including the Tower of Frégart in Bretagne. Where his loyal spies were hunting her stepdaughter Issylte. The

Lady of the Mirrored Lake.

Who would deliver the priceless orb to Voldurk. And then disappear quietly, the lethal thorn in her side removed once and for all.

Voldurk was now tracing tantalizing circles around her left nipple with skilled fingers as she hummed with pleasure. The hidden passage in the wooden paneling between their rooms was delightfully convenient. She spent most mornings with the Royal Advisor who satisfied her body.

And her lust for power.

As he was right now.

"With this ring that I have enchanted," the wizard whispered, showing her a man's wedding band with a large, glittering black diamond, "you will be able to manipulate King Marke." His warm mouth coaxed her nipple into an aching pink peak.

"It will make him docile. Gullible. Amenable to your every suggestion."

He kissed her swanlike neck, then nibbled the delicate lobe of her ear. He grinned wickedly, his white teeth gleaming as he reached for another black velvet jewelry box on the end table beside her plush bed.

"Tell him you had his wedding ring crafted to match yours. *This one*." The wizard opened the *écrin* to display an elegant bridal ring with an enormous black diamond solitaire and matching wedding band, encrusted with a dazzling array of tiny black diamonds.

"With Marke under your control, there will be no need to poison him. At least, *not yet*."

Morag laughed in wicked delight as she admired the beautiful rings, thrilled at being able to control the mighty King of Cornwall.

Who would soon become her lawfully wedded husband in a matter of days.

She gazed into the hypnotic, seductive stare of her golden dragon. Power exuded from his every pore.

"Once you are legally married," he continued, tweaking her nipple teasingly, "you—as the newly crowned Queen of Cornwall—will issue the order to track down your husband's renegade nephew Tristan. The infamous outlaw. The treacherous Blue Knight of Cornwall." He lowered his lips to further entice the tweaked pink peak. "An escaped prisoner who must be apprehended. And brought before *you* to face the charges of treason and murder. You, my beautiful queen, will finally be able to avenge the Morholt, your beloved Black Knight. By executing the traitor, Tristan. Eliminating the only threat to your new crown."

He sucked and licked, his tongue driving her as wild as his seductive words. "And you, the undisputed Queen of Cornwall, will be crowned the Queen of Lyonesse."

Morag's pulse raced, her heart thumping wildly, as she succumbed, engulfed in the scorching flames of her sizzling golden dragon.

****

The castle of Tintagel was lavishly decorated with all the *accoutrements* of a splendid Yuletide royal wedding. Fragrant garlands of pine and fir enlaced with heady hellebore blossoms adorned the walls of the beautiful castle, where boughs of holly and mistletoe graced the mantel over the enormous fireplace in the vast Great Hall. Pine floors gleamed with sweet smelling beeswax, crystal chandeliers glistened, and bouquets of white Christmas roses and hawthorn flowers graced every tabletop throughout the entire castle.

Morning sunlight filtered through the brightly colored ogival stained glass windows of the chapel as the court of Tintagel observed Yuletide mass, followed by the royal wedding of King Marke of Cornwall to Queen Morag of Ireland, officiated by the Bishop of Lostwithiel. His Excellency also performed the second, subsequent wedding, joining Sir Indulf of Hame—the King's Champion and newly appointed Earl of Dubh Linn—to Maid Elowenn, daughter of Lord Treave and Lady Melora of Kennall Vale.

Now gathered in the Great Hall, bathed in glorious golden light as the winter sun set over the savage Atlantic Ocean far below the craggy stone cliff, the royal guests of Tintagel watched as the Bishop of Lostwithiel crowned King Marke's newly wedded wife.

Queen Morag of Ireland.

The new Queen of Cornwall.

Power surged in her regal veins.

A sumptuous feast of several courses ensued in the Banquet Hall, where guests enjoyed a vegetable potage, roast duck and pheasant, wild boar glazed with apple and honey, venison, and stuffed fresh trout. Sweet tarts, pastries, and candied fruits delighted the royal palates, and copious amounts of fine French wine flowed freely at every table. Lively music of fiddles and bagpipes—a tribute to her as the Irish Queen, the king's bride—invited jubilant dancing and a joyous conclusion to the Yuletide wedding festivities. At long last, the newly wedded couples were escorted to their royal bedchambers.

For the consummation of their royal marriages.

King Marke, seated in his elegant antechamber, patiently waited for word from the attendants of his blushing bride that she was ready to receive him in her regal bed. So that he could perform his kingly duty.

Lady Elowenn, dressed by her doting servants in finest white silk and lace, awaited her newly wedded husband, Sir Indulf, in the plush bed of her royal guest chambers.

And, while their spouses patiently waited for the consummation of their royal marriages, Queen Morag and Sir Indulf writhed in ecstasy in her lavender scented bed.

"I wanted a proper goodbye before you sail to Ireland in the morning," Morag whispered, reclining now in his arms, twirling the dense hair on Indulf's broad chest. "I shall miss you terribly, my golden hawk." She buried her nose in the thick blond tufts, then traced her finger over the blue topaz eye of the sea raven ring she'd given him. He'd been at her side when the prisoner—that damned Blue Knight of Cornwall—was chained in the dungeon of Tintagel. Indulf had asked for the ring that King Marke had given his traitorous nephew. The bloody bastard who had slain her beloved Black Knight. Morag had been delighted to award it to him, the king's new champion.

The eye of the sea raven winked in the firelight.

"And I shall miss you, my beloved queen. But know this…" he said, rising onto one elbow to gaze down at her, "…my heart will always be *yours.*" He kissed her softly, then moved his lips along her swanlike neck, down to her voluptuous breasts.

"My men have been fortifying our Viking fleet," he exclaimed proudly, lavishing attention on her right nipple. "We'll be ready to recommence the slave raids in late spring." He raised his head to flash her a savage smile. "We'll pummel the coasts of France—Armorique, Anjou, Aquitaine. Perhaps one day…" he chuckled, his warm mouth suckling her left breast, "… you'll be crowned the Queen of Armorique."

She pulled his face up to hers to bestow a luscious kiss, conveying her gratitude for his love and unerring loyalty. And impressive amorous skill.

He then sat up, kissed her slender hand, and smiled sadly. "As much as I hate to leave, I must. Elowenn and her attendants are expecting me." He rose from the bed and strode over to his clothes, which he'd recklessly strewn across the floor earlier, consumed with passion. "We set sail in the morning, so I must bid you adieu, my queen." He donned his fine tunic, breeches, and sword. He kissed her hand, his dark eagle eyes locked with hers. "Until we meet again." With a gallant bow and a look of longing that pierced her heart, her golden hawk swooped away.

Morag rose from her canopied bed, brushed her long black tresses, then slipped into an exquisite nightgown of finest Belgian lace. She added a drop of lavender scented oil to her cleavage, then called for her attendants to send word to her husband that she was ready for him. As they scampered down the corridor to the king's bedchambers, Morag poured two goblets of wine and sat down at her damask covered table.

When he entered her bedroom, Marke smiled blandly as she escorted him to the chair and seated him at the small table.

"My husband, let us share this exquisite wine," she coaxed, enticing him with a silver goblet. Sitting down across from him, Morag sipped from her chalice and chatted aimlessly about the charming Yuletide decorations, the two lovely wedding ceremonies, the joy of being crowned Queen of Cornwall. Marke agreed enthusiastically, the black diamond of his wedding ring glinting in the light of the sweet-smelling beeswax candle burning on the table before them.

After about twenty minutes—which Morag considered adequate time for a lusty husband to consummate his royal marriage—she said to the king, "My husband, now that you and I have consummated our marriage in joyful wedded bliss, you will return to your chambers, so that your steward may prepare you for bed. Sleep well, my love. I bid you a fond good night." She kissed him chastely on the forehead, then led the king to the door. He smiled sheepishly, then wandered aimlessly out of her room, greeted by his personal attendants, who led him down the hall into his royal bedchambers.

Morag's own attendants helped her prepare for bed, noting the sex-crumpled sheets and obvious evidence of the consummation of the royal marriage. Concealing girlish giggles in the palms of their hands, the two ladies in waiting helped the queen into her plush, lavender scented bed.

Where Morag regaled in her newly acquired power as the undisputed Queen of Cornwall.

Chapter 20

Dragonfire

The pink granite castle stood majestically atop a peninsular cliff on the rocky coastline of Armorique. Issylte admired the magnificent *Château Rose* from her hidden view on Ronan's ship as it approached the northern coast of *Bretagne.* Sea gulls cawed in the clear blue sky, the tang of salty sea spray whipping off the choppy waves as the enormous vessel neared the craggy coast.

The four-day voyage had been uneventful, with cold but clear weather and decent winds, so that the two Avalonian ships transporting the Elven armor and weapons to King Hoël were arriving as scheduled today.

The winter solstice.

The black obsidian cauldron was wrapped in a blanket at her side, the luminous orb secure in its pouch within the sack at her feet. At nightfall, she would hold them in her lap on the boat as she accompanied Tristan, Lancelot, Dagur, Gorvenal, and Solzic—along with several knights from *la Joyeuse Garde*—to the island of the dragon portal. Once ashore, Tristan would take the orb and cauldron with him as he entered *la Porte du Dehors* to face the cyclops Béliagog and the dragon Mordrac. Her entire body thrummed with adrenaline.

The Elves had been unloading the armor and

weapons for several hours when night finally fell. A smaller boat, which could accommodate twelve, was lowered onto the coastal waters from Ronan's cog ship, anchored at the castle dock.

Lancelot dropped the rope ladder along the side of the Elven ship and descended into the small vessel first. Tristan climbed halfway down the rope so that Issylte could hand him first the cauldron, then the orb—which he passed down to Lancelot, balancing himself carefully as he stood in the boat. Once Tristan was settled in the small ship, Issylte climbed down the rope ladder next, followed by the remainder of the warriors traveling with them to the island for additional defense.

The stars and nearly full moon shone brightly in the night sky, glimmering on the ocean waves as they rowed from Ronan's ship toward the island of the dragon portal. In the distance, Issylte perceived dense trees and a craggy cliff which hid the sheltered sea cave.

When they landed on the rocky shore, they quickly disembarked and hid the boat in a copse of nearby woods. Using the moon and starlight to navigate, they followed the curve of the stone cliff until they came upon the entrance to the dragon portal, its dark mouth agape like the maw of a massive beast.

Lancelot dispersed them among the trees to guard Tristan as he prepared to enter the portal. Issylte watched her *mate* withdraw the orb from the velvet pouch, which he clutched tightly in his fist. His sword was strapped to his waist, with a dagger on his other side and another concealed at his ankle. The cauldron in his left hand, the orb in his right, Tristan entered the dragon portal while Issylte held her breath and prayed the Goddess would guide him on his perilous quest.

While she stared at the mouth of the cave as Tristan disappeared into its dark depths, the *Rose Elder* in her blood flared, warning her of impending danger. She motioned to Solzic at her side, indicating with a jerk of her head the direction of the incoming assault. He leapt to his feet, drawing his sword, as Issylte did the same, unsheathing *Emeraldfire* from her hip.

A clash of metal alerted her that a battle had begun when a dwarf and two knights emerged from the woods, swords drawn, to challenge them. Solzic immediately engaged one of the knights while the dwarf and the other warrior moved to entrap Issylte.

His heavy plated armor glistened in the moonlight. He towered over her and outweighed her by at least a hundred pounds. Her heart hammering, her legs trembling, she focused on the skills Tristan had honed into her as she gripped *Emeraldfire* tightly, poised to strike. The knight lifted his visor to laugh at her, dismissing her as a threat because she was a mere woman.

"Well now, isn't that pretty," he snickered, ridiculing her sword with his gauntlet covered hand. "It even has a shiny…"

He never finished his sentence. Issylte thrust her sword into his mouth, impaling him through the back of the throat. He sputtered and choked as blood gushed forth, collapsing in a gruesome heap at her booted feet. As she withdrew Emeraldfire, she spotted four more knights advancing to enclose her in a tight circle.

Tristan had trained her well—she could wield *Emeraldfire* deftly and surely. And thanks to Bahja, she could hurl her dagger with speed and accuracy. Yet Issylte knew that she could not take on four heavily armored knights.

Her only chance for escape was to run.

With a deceptive feint, Issylte surprised and flustered the closest knight by throwing her sword in his face, spinning away, and sprinting into the woods.

"After her! Do not let her escape! I want her taken *alive*!" The dwarf bellowed to his knights, who quickly sheathed their swords and took off after her.

Issylte was breathless, her heart hammering, her legs hurtling her through the trees. The relentless knights would soon overtake her. Scanning the woods frantically, she spotted *un hêtre*—a beech tree—where she could hide from her enemies using the gift from *les Fées Dorées*. She dashed to the tree, leapt up to grasp a branch above her head, grateful for the strength in her upper arms thanks to the months of training with Tristan. Swinging her feet to meet her hands, she pulled herself up to scale the tree, climbing higher and higher into the dense branches to view the atrocities unfolding beneath her.

Perched at this height, she could see in the brilliant light of the full moon that Lancelot and Dagur were engaged with swords against enemy knights on the beach near the cave portal. Gorvenal had slain two and was battling a third, while only four of the six knights from *la Joyeuse Garde* were still fighting, for two of Lancelot's men had fallen.

Solzic had killed the enemy he'd been battling, as well as the dwarf who had ordered the knights to pursue Issylte. He was now facing one of the knights who'd been chasing her—who had doubled back to challenge Solzic. As she watched helplessly, Issylte observed with horror as another dwarf snuck up behind him, notched an arrow, and was now taking aim at her friend's back.

She let loose a scream just as Solzic killed the knight but took the arrow in his left rear shoulder. From her perspective in the tree, Issylte watched Lancelot run forward, decapitate the dwarf with a savage slice of his sword, then rush to Solzic's aid. Scanning the beach, she noted that the dwarves' men had all been slain, and that Lancelot's knights were dragging the enemy corpses deep into the woods. Issylte prayed that the Goddess would guide Tristan, who was still inside the cave.

****

When he entered the dragon portal, a rank odor and musty dampness in the limestone walls permeated the oppressive air. Total darkness enveloped him in a deafening silence. His pulse raced, adrenaline surging into his tensely coiled muscles, his mouth bone dry.

The glittering orb illuminated the eerie portal with a glow of astral light. After a few moments, Tristan's sight adjusted enough for him to venture farther inside, creeping stealthily along the curved path into the gloomy, cavernous depths. The obsidian cauldron grasped tightly in his left hand, the luminous orb in his right, Tristan advanced cautiously along the path, following the dank, mildewed wall of the dark, foreboding cave.

The cyclops Béliagog was slumped on an enormous rock, his bald head bent forward, his gargantuan body blocking further access into the portal. The giant, hearing an intruder, picked up a massive club in his right fist and rose to his full, astonishing height. Although Tristan stood well over six feet tall, he only reached the belly of the angry beast who was now lumbering toward him, grumbling and snapping from slathered jaws, fury seething from his furrowed face.

Béliagog was rippled with enormous muscles across his bulky chest and bulging arms, each of his powerful legs as thick and hairy as a wild boar. Clad in animal hides and furs, the gruesome giant bared his enormous fangs and roared a thunderous growl at Tristan. Talons as long and sharp as daggers protruded from the cyclops' thick paws, and the single eye in his forehead was as black as the obsidian cauldron Tristan clutched in his trembling left hand.

The giant slammed his bludgeon against the stone wall of the cave, sending shock waves which reverberated through the cavern floor right up into Tristan's bones. Béliagog bellowed like a beast, then fixed his eye upon the intruder and blasted a bolt of lightning directly at Issylte's *mate*.

Holding the sacred orb flat against his palm, Tristan deflected the thunderbolt, which burst into brilliant light, refracting like a giant prism, sparkling like the sun and stars. Béliagog howled in pain, dropping his truncheon and raising both of his paws to cover his eye, bending forward to shield himself from the blinding radiance.

Tristan quickly slithered past the incapacitated giant, venturing deeper into the gloom. The salty smell of brine permeated the limestone cave. Dark, morbid, and dank. A deep, rumbling growl that crept up his legs and into his spine alerted Tristan that he had at last encountered Mordrac.

Dark green scales and enormous spikes covered its mammoth reptilian body. Two powerful hind legs and two small forearms, each bearing four enormous claws several inches in length, supported the serpentine beast. The dragon's massive head was a profusion of thorny spikes, with two giant horns extending outward and back behind its fiery golden eyes.

Mordrac's jaws displayed huge, pointed teeth and sharp fangs; its forked tongue flickered like an enormous python sensing its prey. The dragon's long tail was covered with spines, ending in four huge spikes. As the beast advanced on Tristan, it flared two tremendous wings—tipped with sharp claws upon each of the three peaks—and bellowed a monstrous roar that shook the earth beneath him.

Clutching the orb in his right hand, Tristan removed the lid from the cauldron just as Mordrac spewed a plume of fire which engulfed the entire cave. An invisible shield formed around Tristan, protecting him from the inferno, enabling him to capture some of the flames in the cauldron. He quickly replaced the lid and began to retreat slowly.

Large green dragon scales, shaped like gigantic water droplets, were strewn across the muddy earthen floor of the portal. Setting the cauldron of *dragonfire* at his feet, Tristan removed the cloth sack, which he'd tucked into his sword belt. Crouching down carefully, keeping an eye on the enormous beast in front of him, he selected three of the largest deep green scales and quickly slid them into the woolen bag. Slinging the sack over his shoulder, he lifted the cauldron and cautiously backed away from Mordrac, retracing slow steps toward the cave exit. The dragon roared in fury, another volcanic plume of fiery flames erupting from his massive jaws. Tristan held the luminous orb aloft, dispersing the infernal blaze with its protective stellar shield.

He continued his stealthy retreat, deflecting the incessant onslaught of *dragonfire* with the enchanted orb, until he at last passed the curve in the wall and Mordrac was no longer in sight. Tristan quickly spun around and strode past the cyclops, who was still bent forward in crippling pain, covering his eye with his huge paws, moaning in abject agony.

When Tristan emerged from the cave, the sack slung over his shoulder, clutching the cauldron and the magic orb, immense relief flooded through Issylte, who descended quickly from her perch in the beech tree. Once her feet reached the ground, she rushed to Lancelot and Solzic, who was bleeding profusely from the wound.

"Do not remove the arrow. He'll lose too much blood. I must return with him to Landuc where I can carefully extract it, treat him with herbs to stanch the flow of blood, and prevent the wound from festering."

She kissed Solzic's cheek, tears streaming down her face. "I'll heal you, my friend. You'll be fine in no time," she whispered into his ear, praying that her words would prove true. To Lancelot, she exhaled, "I just saw Tristan come out of the cave. Let's join him and hurry back to the boat, so we can row out to Ronan's ship."

Lancelot agreed, then—handing her the sword *Emeraldfire*—teased with an impish grin, "That's the most unusual defensive move I've ever seen with a sword." She blushed with embarrassment, sheathed her blade, then cut a section of her gown with her dagger, *Émeraude*. Placing the cloth over Solzic's wound, she applied pressure to stop the bleeding, taking care to avoid the imbedded arrow.

The remaining four knights approached Lancelot and Issylte, crouched over Solzic. Carefully, they helped the injured warrior to his feet, half carrying him as the group walked back to the beach to join Tristan and the others. Lancelot's hand replaced hers to hold the bandage in place. With a gesture of his head, he indicated that she should join Tristan, who approached from the beach.

Issylte ran to Tristan as Gorvenal, Dagur, and Darius retrieved the bodies of their two fallen knights, placing them, and then Solzic, into the boat. "Thank the Goddess you're all right!" She threw her arms around his neck, smothering his face with grateful kisses as he balanced himself against the loving onslaught. Recovering herself a bit, she withdrew her arms and faced him, her tone becoming serious. "I must go with Solzic back to Landuc," she whispered breathlessly as Tristan replaced the orb carefully into its pouch, tucking it deep inside the pocket of his breeches. He lifted his concerned face to search hers.

"He's seriously injured," she exhaled, quickly scanning her *mate,* gratefully noting the lack of injuries and the fact that he seemed unharmed. "I must save him. Not just because he's our friend and member of the Tribe, but because Lysara carries his child. She and the babe need him *to live.*"

Lancelot raced up to them. "Come, we must leave at once. Solzic is losing too much blood." The three of them dashed to the boat, rocking in the gentle waves at the water's edge. Tristan carefully placed the cauldron in the rowboat, then helped Issylte to her seat. He and Lancelot climbed in, and—under the moonglow and starlight rippling on the dark waters of the Narrow Sea—rowed back to join Ronan and the Elves on the seaworthy vessels.

When their small boat at last approached the two Avalonian ships, Issylte noticed a group—including

Ronan—standing on the beach of the castle grounds, motioning for them to come ashore. Once their small vessel reached land, Kaherdin, Gargeolaine, Ronan, and another dark-haired man rushed forward to greet them.

Lancelot, Tristan, Gorvenal, and Issylte got out of the small boat, while Dagur and Darius remained on board, supporting an unconscious Solzic. The four knights from *la Joyeuse Garde* remained in the vessel as well.

"Tristan, I'm so sorry…" Kaherdin heaved in grief, placing a hesitant hand on Tristan's shoulder. "We understand now that it was the wizard and the wicked queen who killed our Blanchine. *Not you.* We wrongly accused, imprisoned, and *tortured* you. Please forgive us."

The dark-haired man—*that must be King Hoël,* Issylte realized—stood beside Kaherdin, his expression contrite, his demeanor apologetic. "We will ally with you. Against Morag and Voldurk. My army…my fleet…are yours." King Hoël clasped Tristan's shoulder, then bowed his head respectfully to Lancelot and Issylte.

Issylte addressed Kaherdin and a very pregnant Gargeolaine. "Our warrior Solzic is badly hurt. I must return to Landuc to treat his injuries." She cast Ronan an urgent glance, then spoke quietly to Tristan and Lancelot. "You must leave *immediately* and sail for Avalon. Voldurk will hear of the ambush near the dragon portal. He'll know we have the *dragonfire.* And try to intercept it. You must hurry before he can react."

Issylte whirled to Kaherdin, her urgent voice imploring. "Will you please have a dozen of your best knights escort me, the wounded Solzic, and our two fallen knights, back to Landuc? Your men can stay at the castle overnight, then return to you in the morning. That will guarantee us safe passage and help me transport Solzic."

Holding Lancelot's gaze firmly, Issylte promised, "I will see that your men are nobly buried in sacred ground and receive an honorable tribute for their valor." He inclined his head gratefully, his warrior eyes blazing into hers.

Kaherdin quickly agreed to Issylte's request and gave orders to his men to saddle the horses and prepare for the ride to *le Château de Landuc*.

"I'll stay just long enough to be sure that Solzic recovers," Issylte whispered to Tristan as he rushed to her side, trying to dissuade her from leaving. "Then I will travel through the portal in *le Miroir aux Fées* and meet you in Avalon." He was shaking his head, not wanting to release her, but she continued before he could interrupt. "I can't bring anyone through the portal with me. My gift allows me to walk between worlds, but I must travel alone." Kissing his hands, which she had clasped and raised to her lips, she insisted, "You must leave now and sail back to Avalon, so that Ronan can forge the sword. I'll join you in just a few days. As soon as Solzic is out of danger."

Rising onto her tiptoes, she kissed his lips, then turned to Ronan and Lancelot. "Leave at once. Don't delay. Voldurk will move quickly, and we must not allow him to intercept the orb or foil our plans. I'll join you as soon as Solzic is out of danger." Meeting Ronan's deep green gaze she whispered, "Thank you for everything. May the Goddess guide you safely back to Avalon."

With one last desperate kiss, Tristan reluctantly

walked away from her and followed the men who were headed for Ronan's ships. Gargeolaine rushed to join Issylte as Kaherdin and King Hoël supervised the knights who were lifting the bodies of the fallen soldiers and the injured Solzic onto the horses.

"I am so glad that Ronan told Kaherdin and his father the truth! I knew Tristan could not have harmed Blanchine. He is an honorable knight—and a trusted friend." Gargeolaine's rosy cheeks bloomed with the glow of pregnancy. Issylte hugged her, then whispered, "I must leave. Solzic is badly hurt."

The auburn-haired beauty cried, grasping Issylte's hands, "I had hoped you, Tristan, and Lancelot could come to our wedding. We were planning it for Yuletide, but that is impossible now, for we still mourn Blanchine. It has been postponed until the New Year. I do wish you could come."

Issylte kissed her friend's cheeks. "I am so sorry for what happened to poor Blanchine. There is no limit to the evil of Voldurk and the wretched Black Widow Queen." With a warm hug, Issylte whispered, "We can't attend the wedding, for we'll be in Avalon. But you, dear friend, will be a beautiful bride and a wonderful mother. Congratulations to you and Kaherdin. Now, please forgive me, but I must leave. Solzic's life depends on it."

Disengaging herself from Gargeolaine's affectionate embrace, Issylte dashed to the assembled group of knights from *le Château Rose* and mounted the horse they had waiting for her. As they rode off into the forest, she waved one last time to the departing vessels, Prince Kaherdin, the beautiful Gargeolaine, and King Hoël of Armorique.

The horses thundered through the Forest of

Broéliande and soon arrived at Landuc. Issylte and her guards were met by Esclados' knights, who helped unload the bodies of the two fallen soldiers as others rushed Solzic into the castle.

Lysara, upon seeing the severely wounded Solzic, dropped to her knees in grief, burying her sobs in her hands.

Issylte ran to her, touched her shoulder comfortingly, and said, "Help me save him." She then ordered the young priestess to retrieve a needle and thick embroidery floss, several candles, fresh water and soap, bandages, and a very sharp knife. Laudine, eager to help, brought the herbs Issylte requested to prevent festering, ointments and salves to dress the wound, and Valerian root to ease his pain and help him sleep. Nolwenn fetched the gemstones Issylte needed to create a crystal grid, just as she had done to save Tristan in Avalon and Ondine in the woods near Lancelot's castle.

Solzic had been placed on his stomach, upon a table in the room where Nolwenn performed her tattoo artistry. He was breathing rhythmically, but still unconscious, so there was no need to give him herbs to help him sleep.

Issylte pushed Solzic's long, blond hair away from his shoulder. She cut his bloodied tunic and removed it to inspect the wound. It was inflamed and swollen, but the bleeding had stopped. For now. The arrow was deeply embedded in the muscle of his shoulder, but fortunately, had not punctured his lung or any vital organs. She would need to cut into the skin around the arrowhead in order to remove the tip without forcing it deeper into his shoulder. She would then cleanse the wound with soap and herbs, stitch it meticulously, apply the healing ointment, and bandage him thoroughly.

Nolwenn arrived with the sacred stones, with which Issylte created a triple-layered crystal grid to channel the healing energy of the Goddess into Solzic, just as she had done for Tristan when he'd been nearly fatally injured by the Morholt.

Lysara delivered the supplies needed to remove the arrow and stitch the wound, and Laudine brought in the necessary herbs, tinctures, and ointments. Issylte burned some sage to purify the air, then washed her hands and Solzic's back with calendula soap, wiping away the blood from his injured shoulder. She held her knife over the flame of a candle, for she'd learned that fire was essential for purifying the blade. With precision and skill, she deftly cut into the area near the arrowhead, removed it, and ascertained that no part of the weapon remained in the wound. She then applied herbs to prevent festering, and yarrow to stanch the bleeding, which had begun anew. With meticulous, loving stitches, she painstakingly closed the wound, adding antiseptic herbs to prevent infection.

Issylte cleansed his entire back, pleased to see that the bleeding had stopped, and applied the healing ointment and raw honey over the wound and surrounding skin. With Lysara's help, she wrapped bandages around his torso to secure the stiches in place and keep the injury covered. Now he needed to rest.

"The bleeding has stopped, and the wound is clean. He is young, very strong, and healthy. I truly believe he'll recover quickly." Issylte's glowing smile was meant to reassure Lysara as much as the words that the petite priestess was desperate to hear. She, Issylte—the healer from Avalon—had just saved the life of the man her beautiful friend loved with all her heart. Whose child Lysara carried in her fertile womb.

Lysara's body heaved with sobs of relief as she cried in Issylte's arms. "Thank you," she whispered, her luminous brown eyes filled with tears and gratitude. Issylte smiled reassuringly, pulling Lysara into her arms, rocking her as they watched over the injured Solzic, who slept peacefully.

Esclados had seen that Kaherdin's men from Armorique were settled into sleeping cots, and plans had been arranged for the honorable burial of Lancelot's two fallen knights in the morning. Four knights transported Solzic to a bed that had been prepared for him in a nearby room, where Lysara would sleep in a cot next to him, alerting Issylte when he awakened.

The following day, Solzic regained consciousness and did not show any signs of fever. Lysara told him the joyful news of her pregnancy, and the loving couple quietly and privately celebrated their good fortune. Lancelot's knights were buried with honor on sacred ground in the Forest of Brocéliande, and Kaherdin's men returned to *le Château Rose*.

For the next few days, Issylte changed Solzic's bandages, administered herbal treatments, burned purifying sage, spoon fed him nourishing soups, and prayed to the Goddess that his wound would not fester. Finally, a week after the removal of the arrow, she was certain that her patient would recover. Anxious to rejoin Tristan, for separation from him was unbearable, Issylte prepared for departure.

To meet her anxiously awaiting *mate* on the *otherworldly* island of Avalon.

Chapter 21

La Chambre aux Loups

"Malgric and Duldir have been slain, my lord. Their bodies were found, along with six of their knights, near *La Porte du Dehors* on the island off the coast of Armorique. The dragon portal."

He stood before the dark wizard in the *château* of Tintagel in Cornwall. As the new Leader of the Dwarves, Bothor had received the bleak news from his network of spies in Bretagne and was now reporting to Voldurk the loss of two more dwarves, killed by Lancelot and his men, near the portal where Tristan had obtained the *dragonfire.* "The Princess Issylte was spotted riding through the forest back to Landuc, escorted by a dozen knights from *le Château Rose.* It appears that one of the warriors of the Tribe of Dana was injured in the ambush. A likely assumption is that she remains there to treat his injuries, for she is a gifted healer from Avalon."

"Thank you, Lord Bothor. Position your dwarves and their knights at every portal throughout the realm. Princess Issylte will want to rejoin her *mate*, walking between worlds to do so. We must therefore intercept her. She will be caught and brought to me. *Alive.*" The wizard's snakelike eyes smoldered, transfixing Bothor with predatory power.

"Yes, my lord. At once." Bowing, his arm extended

across his stomach, Bothor retreated from the malevolent presence of the dark lord and the wicked queen seated to his right.

****

"Tristan of Lyonesse has obtained the *dragonfire* and is undoubtedly on the island of Avalon, where the Elf will forge the sword." Voldurk fired his molten gaze upon her. "I cannot touch him there. Avalon is protected by the sacred enchantment of the Lady of the Lake."

"Then we abduct his *mate*. Entrap her in the darkness when she walks between worlds. Or have your dwarves seize her when she exits a portal." Morag stroked the wizard's chiseled jawline, clenched in fury. She kissed his long, serpentine neck. "When Tristan learns that you have his *mate,* he'll pay any ransom for her. *Even the orb.*" With a seductive, wicked smile, Morag purred, "He'll bring it to us. Then we'll kill them both. And you, dear Voldurk, will be *invincible.*"

She rose from the table, sauntered seductively to her wizard's side, then settled onto his lap, nestling her voluptuous bottom into his ardent loins. *Power is such a potent aphrodisiac,* she mused, thrilled to feel his response to the rhythmic rolling of her luscious backside. "And I shall be the most powerful queen in all of Europe."

Teasing him with her full lips, she kissed him playfully, tugging at the corners of his mouth, delighted to sense his intense arousal beneath her lush bottom. Voldurk grasped a fistful of her luxuriant hair and yanked back her head, exposing her swanlike neck. He pinned her in his arms as he devoured her mouth, neck and shoulders, his teeth tugging her bodice lower as his lips ravaged her rounded breasts.

With a guttural bark to the armed guards, he ordered them to leave the room and ensure that they were not disturbed. Once they were alone, Voldurk hoisted her off his lap, bent her roughly across the table, and hastily lifted her regal gown. He parted her royal legs with a savage jerk of his knees, lifted her rounded bottom with his powerful hands, and pummeled her with amorous ardor until she screamed in the throes of passion, engulfed in the fiery flames of her molten, golden dragon.

****

At *le Château de Landuc*, Solzic had continued to improve and was now able to walk unassisted, slowly regaining his strength. Issylte hugged him and Lysara as she bid them farewell in front of the castle, where several members of the Tribe sat astride their horses, ready to escort her to the sacred Mirrored Lake.

She mounted her horse *Minuit,* her supplies loaded, and rode off through the forest of *Brocéliande* to *le Miroir aux Fées*. She planned to swim to the bottom of the lake, enter the cave portal in its hidden depths, and exit into *la Grotte de l' Étoile* on the island of Avalon. Issylte was immensely grateful for the gift from *les Fées Dorées,* for the portal at the bottom of the Mirrored Lake, located within the sacred forest, was inaccessible to the dark wizard.

Providing her safe passage as she walked between worlds.

Esclados, Laudine, Kirus, and Nolwenn were among the group who rode with her to *le Miroir aux Fées*. They stopped short at the edge of the lake, where Issylte had entered the portal just a few weeks earlier to travel to Avalon when she'd retrieved the orb.

But now, the lake was frozen solid. She wouldn't be able to swim to *la Porte du Dedans* at the bottom. She'd need to take another portal. The universal Druid portal.

Les Menhirs de Monteneuf.

Accessible to Voldurk.

Panic surged as she envisioned the vertical slits of his poisonous python gaze. Watching and waiting. Hunting her.

Her limbs began to quiver; her mouth went dry. She stared at the ice-covered Mirrored Lake.

"With the lake frozen," she said abjectly, avoiding Laudine's worried look, "I won't be able to access the sacred portal. I must ride to *les Menhirs de Monteneuf,* on the other side of the lake. At the edge of the forest."

Laudine eyed her husband and Nolwenn uneasily. "*Les Menhirs de Monteneuf* is a universal portal, leading to sacred caves—such as *la Grotte de l' Étoile* on Avalon. It's used by Druids who walk between worlds, such as Merlin and the archdruid Odin."

Laudine's gaze fixed Issylte with dread, the unspoken warning blazing in her amber eyes. "Voldurk was once a powerful Druid," she whispered. "Although he can't enter the sacred Forest of Brocéliande, he can enter a portal which connects with *les Menhirs de Monteneuf.* It's a universal portal, connecting with all others throughout the Celtic realm." Laudine's voice was barely audible. "Even the portals of darkness."

Issylte swallowed forcefully, mustering her courage. "I know."

She met the worried looks of Kirus and Esclados, astride their horses beside her. "Voldurk has undoubtedly learned of the attack near the dragon cave. He may very well be monitoring the portals between worlds. But my gift of *Rose Elder* will alert me of danger if he comes near me inside the cave. It will also block any evil spells he may cast. I'll go quickly through the darkness, looking for the light of the star which shines from *la Grotte de l' Étoile*. And pray the Goddess guides me safely to Avalon."

Nolwenn spoke quietly to Issylte. "The dwarves cannot enter the portals, for they do not have the Druidic magic to walk between worlds." Amethyst eyes held her gaze. "But Voldurk can position them at the exits. To entrap you as you emerge." The Tribe shared uneasy glances, then looked back at Issylte. She nodded solemnly in comprehension.

There was no other choice. The cave of *Huelgoat* led north to *la Porte des Ombres* in Cornwall, where Malfleur had trapped Aimée. Or south to the troglodyte caves in western France. But not to Avalon. The passage through the Druid portal was the only choice. A calculated risk she had to take.

Issylte locked eyes with Kirus. His handsome, scarred face was implacable. She saw in his fierce gaze that he, like she, knew there was no other choice. His voice deep and gruff, the Leader of the Tribe barked, "We ride. To *les Menhirs de Monteneuf*!" Kirus pulled his horse's reins and urged his mount onward, leading the group away from *le Miroir aux Fées*.

The others followed suit, riding across the Forest of Brocéliande, to the Druid portal where they dismounted to say goodbye.

Issylte hugged and kissed her friends, then, accepting the pack of supplies that Kirus handed her, courage and love blazing in his warrior eyes, smiled and waved farewell as she entered the dark *otherworldly* portal.

To walk between worlds.

****

The fecund scent of rich black loam and decomposing leaves evoked the depths of a primordial forest. The preternatural aura and eerie stillness were reminiscent of the *sightings* which came upon her while peering into the still waters of a lake. The cave was shadowed and gloomy, but a dim illumination—like the gloam of twilight—enabled Issylte to see the sinuous, curving path which extended before her.

As she walked swiftly through the portal, she observed openings, like stone doorways, veering off the main pathway on either side. *These are exits to different portals throughout the realm. I must find the one with the light of the star. La Grotte de l' Étoile. Please, dear Goddess, guide me.*

Issylte reached out with her gift of *Rose Elder* as she passed by open exits, sensing evil and danger lurking behind some, the safety of the sacred forest beyond others. She hurried through the shadows, passing many portals, with none offering the light of the shining star of *la Grotte de l' Étoile.*

A sudden chill crept up her spine, the hairs on the back of her neck rising as her Druidic magic flared a dire warning of danger. A brilliant flash of blinding white light shot past her, sizzling with power and crackling with flames. *A thunderbolt of lightning. Voldurk is in the portal! But where? With my deaf ear, I can't tell where the sounds come from. Is he behind me? To the left? To the right? Dear Goddess, please help me!*

Another lightning bolt shattered into blinding radiance all around her, deflected from her body into countless rays of brilliant light. Charged energy filled the stillness, her hair electrified as if a powerful storm hovered in the air. A flash of fiery red light blasted the wall of the cave beside her, crumbling into huge boulders which blocked that exit and prevented her escape.

I must find an exit! Now!

Issylte raced through the cave, her stomach quivering, her heart hammering, her breath rasping. Using her gift to seek a safe exit, she despaired as each one she passed exuded evil. More fiery blasts struck the cave walls on either side, an avalanche of crumbling stones rolling across her path.

She jumped and hurdled over falling stones, ducking and dodging, an arm bent protectively across her head. Her heart thundering in her chest, she plodded on, climbing over rocks, her legs burning with exertion, her sword hindering her efforts, desperately searching for a safe portal exit.

Finally, one up ahead beckoned. Not daring to look behind, Issylte dove through the opening to her right, emerging at the base of a wooded cliff nestled within a dense, verdant forest.

Frantically scanning the woods, her heart thumping furiously, she searched for one of the three sacred trees which would protect her. A massive oak stretched its broad arms out to welcome her, its branches abundant in leaves where she could hide. Issylte sprinted to the tree, jumping up to catch a low-lying branch and swinging one leg up to hook onto it. With difficulty, for *Emeraldfire* was strapped to her hip, she pulled herself up, grateful once again for Tristan's strength training and the power that surged in her upper body. She climbed higher and higher until she was safely ensconced in the foliage, her breath heaving in ragged gasps.

Her limbs twitching, her body shaking, Issylte watched the wizard emerge from the portal and scan the forest. Hunting her. The air around him shimmered with visible power as Voldurk raised his long, thin hands, probing the woods with preternatural senses. His reptilian eyes scanned the forest, searching for her, his tongue darting from his mouth like a predatory snake.

From her perch in the tree, Issylte observed the wizard wordlessly summon a dwarf with a command of his hands. The gnarled, deformed little creature arrived on horseback soon thereafter, accompanied by a dozen heavily armed, mounted knights. The dwarf dismounted and rushed to Voldurk, whose fury seethed as he barked orders and gestured to the forest.

The dwarf nodded vigorously, bowed to his lord, and returned to his horse. Climbing back into the saddle, the wizened creature spoke to his men, then galloped off into the woods, followed by his band of knights.

Hunting her.

The wizard swept the forest again with his hands, as if to feel for her presence. Issylte shivered in the tree, her knees knocking against the branches. She prayed he could not see or hear the rustling of the leaves.

Or the hammering of her heart.

Voldurk scanned the forest one last time, his tongue darting in and out, his nostrils flaring to trace her scent. He then slunk to the portal and slithered back into the rocky cave.

A poisonous predatory snake.

Issylte waited a long time, expecting the dwarf and his men to double back and search the forest where she remained hidden in the giant oak. After what seemed like hours, she descended and ventured farther into the woods, dashing away from the cave, expecting Voldurk to lunge out at any moment from the darkness.

Extending her gift of Rose Elder outward to scan the forest, Issylte was relieved to sense no sign of immediate danger. Yet, she had no idea where to go and didn't even know where she was. Patches of snow covered the forest floor; the darkening sky overcast and gray, as if more threatened to fall. She needed to find shelter. Quickly, for the dwarf and his knights were prowling the forest. Hunting her.

On the ground just up ahead, a cluster of red berries against the white snow caught her attention and drew her near. Bending down to examine them, she was delighted to discover that they were elderberries—the fruit of her sacred Elder tree.

The source of her Druidic magic.

Perhaps the forest fairies are guiding me with elderberries, since églantines do not bloom in the winter.

Scanning the snow-covered ground around her, she spotted another cluster of elderberries deeper in the forest, to her right. As she approached, Issylte glimpsed a third pile of red berries. Then a fourth.

The woodland creatures are guiding me. Just as they did in the Hazelwood Forest. When they led me to Tatie's cottage.

Following the enchanted trail of elderberries, Issylte ventured deeper and deeper into the thick woods. The familiar fragrance of pine and the rich earthy scent of loam and fresh snow reassured the verdant magic flowing in her veins. Far off to her left, the forested cliff where she'd emerged from the cave portal curved above the wooded ground where she now walked. The stone cliff was a deep purple hue, thick brush dusted with clumps of snow carpeting the base of the trees along the ledge above her. The scent of the forest and the tang of decaying leaves comforted her. The Earth Goddess mother nurturing her forest fairy daughter.

Another cluster of elderberries pulled her along the enchanted trail.

Thirst forced Issylte to rest for a moment as she withdrew the flask of water from her pack. Not wanting to linger, for fear of the dwarf returning, she quickly repacked, following the beckoning call of the woodland creatures and the sacred elderberries.

Ahead in the distance, Issylte spotted a clearing within the forest, where a pile of elderberries lay atop a huge, flattened stone. When she arrived at the clearing, the air thrummed with enchantment, yet her *Rose Elder* gift did not alert her of any danger. On the contrary, her own verdant magic sang in response, urging her forward, propelling her toward the large rock.

And the enticing, enchanting elderberries.

A forested cliff of purple rose thirty feet above her head in the near distance behind the large flat rock where she now stood. At the top of the ledge, two giant stones captured her attention. They were connected, yet cloven apart—two halves of a broken heart. As she admired the majestic beauty of the magnificent stones, a woman appeared, standing to the left of the rock formation at the top of the cliff above Issylte's head.

Long, thick waves of glossy black hair cascaded to the woman's slim waist. A black cloak, lined in ermine, parted below the clasp at her neck, revealing a gown of deepest purple, enhanced by the same violet hues of the natural stones which surrounded her. A lyrical voice evoking the mellow notes of a harp floated through the wintry air. "Priestess of Dana, Lady of the Mirrored Lake, you have entered my domain. *Le Val Sans Retour.*"

Le Val Sans Retour! The Vale of No Return, the enchanted valley of Morgane la Fée. Rumored to be an evil sorceress. A malingering presence in this haunted valley. And yet—she founded the Center of Healing with Viviane on the island of Avalon. And my gift does not warn me of evil...

"Please forgive the intrusion, my lady," Issylte apologized to the mysterious stranger who watched from above. "I was traversing the portal, trying to reach Avalon, when I was attacked and pursued by the wizard Voldurk." Wiping her damp palms along the sides of her dress, Issylte summoned her courage. "I was forced to exit the cave portal at the base of this cliff. A dwarf and his dozen knights are hunting me as we speak. If they trap me, I will be delivered to Voldurk, who will torture and kill me. I apologize for trespassing into your domain. I mean no harm."

Issylte gestured to the large pile of elderberries on top of the rock where she now stood. "I've been following a trail of elderberries that the woodland creatures left for me. Leading me here. To you, it would seem, *Morgane la Fée.*"

Morgane floated down a winding path leading from the top of the cliff to the snow-covered clearing where Issylte stood at its base. The dark-haired fairy strode up to her, raking silvery blue eyes over the face and body of her intruder as Issylte assessed the enchantress in return.

Morgane's features were exquisite, from her high cheekbones and delicate nose, to her pearlescent, porcelain skin, luminous as moonstone. The fairy's eyes were palest blue, like a wintry sky, in striking contrast to her magnificently thick, dark locks. At her throat was a necklace of sparkling amethysts in the same deep purple as the velvet of the gown which clung to her ample bodice, skimmed over her slender waist, and flared out gracefully to the ground beneath her. The sleeves of her dress floated like wings in the winter wind under the thick, ermine-lined cloak as Morgane reached out to grasp Issylte's trembling hands.

"Come with me to my castle. It lies within this enchanted realm, where neither dwarf nor wizard may enter. I will share with you my sacred knowledge, which will protect you and help your *mate*—the warrior of the Tribe of Dana. The one prophesied *to* slay the evil wizard Voldurk. Come, Lady of the Mirrored Lake. I have much to teach you."

Issylte smiled uncertainly at the beautiful, mysterious enchantress. *She knows all about me. Even that Tristan is my mate. Her magic is powerful indeed.*

The intriguing fairy, still holding Issylte's two hands, released one, leading her with the other. They walked back up the narrow, winding path to the top of the forested cliff, where the enormous rocks faced each other, two halves of a fractured whole.

Indicating the stones before them, Morgane smirked, "This is *le Rocher des Faux Amants*—the Rock of the False Lovers—which I created when the wizard Voldurk betrayed me." A wicked gleam danced in the fairy's ice blue gaze. "A heart, cloven in two. Just like mine was—when he broke it."

Morgane gestured to the clearing below them, then swept her arm out to the forest beyond. "I have enchanted this entire valley. At first, I cast a spell to entrap faithless knights—which your friend Lancelot of the Lake broke, freeing them. Now, the enchantment protects the extent of my domain, so that no evil may enter this sacred realm. You will be safe here with me, Lady of the Mirrored Lake. Come, let me show you my castle, *le Château Lumineux.* This way."

Issylte followed the raven-haired fairy through the dense woods atop the precipice which overlooked *le Val Sans Retour* below them. The atmosphere thrummed with magic, the ancient, gnarled trees blocking nearly all sunlight, enshrouding the forest in marvel and mystery.

They arrived at a clearing, where a small castle—its turrets touching the clouds, its white limestone walls gleaming in the sun which had just emerged, as if the Goddess were shining divine light down upon them—sat perched upon a plateau of the same deep purple rock which was abundant in the valley. Thick, dense woods encircled the perimeter of the castle grounds, encasing the luminous *château* like a creamy pearl within its purple oyster shell.

A single white tower stood beside *le Château Lumineux*, connected to the main building by a second story walkway, covered in the same mauve stone as the peaked roof and rock foundation beneath the castle. Behind the structure, Issylte spotted two swans swimming upon a magnificent lake, reminding the princess of Lancelot's castle, *la Joyeuse Garde.*

And Vivane's revelation that she and Tristan were *mates*.

Swans mate for life.

Issylte followed Morgane up the stone walkway to the carved wooden entrance doors of the castle, which were opened by servants who greeted their mistress and quickly obeyed the orders given to prepare a light meal for *la châtelaine* and her honored guest.

An expansive hallway led from the front entrance to the back of the *château*, where a wall of windows extended from floor to ceiling, offering a panoramic view of the lake and surrounding forest. Two enormous rooms sat on either side of the main corridor; a central staircase led to the second floor.

Morgane invited Issylte to follow her upstairs to the guest room which awaited.

On the second level of the *château*, there were four bedrooms, with two on each side of the central hall. The castle faced south, and the slanted rays of the winter sun shone in through the window atop the landing of the stairwell. Morgane led Issylte into the large chamber at the front of her domicile, on the southeast corner which connected the tower to the main building.

"This is my bedroom. And that tower," the fairy explained, indicating the cylindrical building which abutted the *château*, "is where I observe the stars, prepare herbal mixtures, store my sacred stones. And perform enchantments." A corner of Morgane's mouth raised slightly in a mysterious, enigmatic smile. "That is where I will share my sacred knowledge with you, Priestess of Dana. But first, let me show you to your chambers."

Taking Issylte by the hand, Morgane led her down the hall to the rear of the castle, into the spacious room where a balcony extended from windowed doors to overlook the lake. The walls and floor were of the same white limestone as the entire castle, gleaming in the firelight from the hearth on the eastern wall. The decorations were simple, with a bed, table, chair, and small armoire. On top of the wooden table, Issylte sensed a powerful aura emanating from a raw emerald stone as large as her hand, its deep green essence beckoning her with the mystery of a verdant, enchanted forest.

Morgane observed with delight the apparently intended effect of the gemstone on her guest. "Emerald is your sacred stone. This enchanted gem has been waiting for you for a long time."

Stunned, Issylte spun her head to regard her hostess. "You knew I would come here?"

"Of course. I simply did not know *when*." Smiling coyly, Morgane remarked, "Like you, Lady of the Mirrored Lake, I have the gift of *sight.*" Floating up to the table, the fairy picked up the huge emerald and placed it in Issylte's dampened palms. Her magic roared in response.

"This stone is enchanted with spells of protection. For you, Issylte." Morgane's *otherworldly* gaze bore into hers, wintry blue eyes dancing in the firelight. "The Goddess sent you to Maiwenn, the fairy who sheltered you in the enchanted Hazelwood Forest. Who helped you discover your own latent verdant magic. Who sent you to Avalon, to become a gifted healer. Where fate entwined you with your *mate.*"

The large emerald thrummed in Issylte's trembling hand, the pulse of its power pumping into her veins.

"And now, the Goddess has led you here. To me. So that I may give you this sacred gem." Morgane lovingly touched the enormous emerald, then gazed into the depths of Issylte's soul. "Because you, dear Issylte, Lady of the Mirrored Lake, are destined to inherit Maiwenn's legacy. And become *La Fée Émeraude des Forêts Enchantées*. The Emerald Fairy of the Enchanted

Forests."

Issylte's breath hitched as her power intensified, the verdant magic of the enchanted emerald flowing freely into her forest fairy body.

Embracing her.

Embellishing her.

Empowering her.

"*La Fée Émeraude*," Morgane whispered, her *otherworldly* voice humming with magic. "The Emerald Fairy. Destined to protect the sacred forests of the Celtic realm."

Morgane floated her fingers over Issylte, an *effleurage* of virid magic caressing her body as verdant power surged into her veins. "The Hazelwood Forest of Ireland," Morgane murmured, as if in incantation, her fairy fingers fluttering over Issylte. "The Forest of Morois in Cornwall." Morgane's slender digits drifted over Issylte's head. Her heart pounded wildly as the verdant magic of the forest flourished and bloomed within her. "And the sacred Forest of Brocéliande in Bretagne. The heart of the Goddess Dana."

Morgane lowered her hands, an ethereal smile glowing on her pearlescent, moonstone face.

Issylte closed her eyes, her forest fairy body bathed in virid magic. The enchanted essence of the emerald in her hands flowed into her. Pumping through her forest fairy heart.

"We'll craft a protective talisman from this enchanted emerald," Morgane exhaled, her voice the whisper of a winter wind. "It will defend you against Voldurk. The dark power he serves. And the wicked Black Widow Queen."

Issylte was awestruck by the sizzling power flowing

through her veins. And the magnificent gem in her hand.

An enchanted emerald.

Her sacred stone.

Its verdant magic waiting just for her.

"I will share with you a secret—a way to ensure that Voldurk never lays a hand on you. I have much to teach you, Lady of the Mirrored Lake. Come, let me show you my tower."

Issylte laid the large emerald gently back onto the table, then followed Morgane down the hallway toward the front of the *château*. Slanted rays of the setting sun shone through the window as the raven-haired fairy led her guest through the wooden door and into her own chambers.

The white limestone of the *châtelaine's* bedroom glistened in the sunlight, streaming in through the large windows of the southern exposure. Lush potted plants flanked the wall of glass, the windows extending from ceiling to floor. On each surface—the fireplace mantel, the tabletop, the nightstands on either side of the bed—stood enormous raw amethyst stones, weaving a web of magic throughout the enchanted air.

A wooden door on the left wall opened onto the covered walkway which connected Morgane's bedroom to the two-story tower beside the *château*. Motioning for her guest to follow, the fairy exited her chambers, crossed the small bridge which adjoined the two buildings, and opened the wooden door leading into her dual-level workshop.

Inside the tower, a spiral staircase led up to the observation deck on the roof and extended in the opposite direction, down to the ground level below the area where the two fairies now stood.

On the lower level, Issylte noted the purple stone floor, wooden tables which held various flasks and dishes, and drying herbs suspended from hooks on the walls. *Like Tatie's cottage, in the Hazelwood Forest, where we used to prepare herbal remedies so long ago.*

She followed Morgane into the workshop on this second story level, where wooden shelves—filled with hundreds of gemstones in all shapes, sizes, and colors— lined the entire wall space on either side of the entrance to the room. A small stained-glass window above a workshop table cast rays of radiant color from the sunlight which entered from the front of the castle. Stairs leading down to the lower level stood at the opposite end of the wooden floor.

"This is where I will teach you how to craft a sacred scabbard, similar to the one I created for King Arthur Pendragon of Camelot." Morgane's wintry blue eyes sparkled with magic. "I will show you how to weave powerful spells of enchantment into gemstones as you craft the sacred scabbard for your *mate*. And, just as Arthur's sheath protects him in battle—so that he never loses a drop of blood—so shall the sacred scabbard you craft for Tristan of Lyonesse defend him from his enemies."

The wings of the little white dove fluttered wildly in Issylte's heart.

Morgane walked across the floor to one of the walls where countless gemstones were stored inside small wooden compartments. Some were enclosed within pouches, others were encased in glass, and many stood alone. Scanning the contents of the cache in front of her, the enchantress withdrew a purple velvet pouch from a tiny compartment and led her guest to a small table nestled under the sunlit window.

As Issylte watched in wonder, Morgane carefully poured the contents of the pouch onto the table, spilling forth several large, luminous gems that sparkled brilliantly in the setting sun.

"*La pierre de l'étoile.* The stone of the fallen star." The black-haired beauty placed some of the dazzling gems in Issylte's hands. "Just as the molten ore of the earth cools into the black rock which forms the flawless diamond, *so la pierre de l' étoile* is formed from the celestial ore of a fallen star."

Issylte looked at Morgane in astonishment. "These are the same sacred crystals I used to heal Tristan in Avalon," she whispered, her pulse racing in her throat. "The same gemstone you used to craft the sacred orb. The one you hid within *le Miroir aux Fées.*" Issylte's legs weakened at the knees.

An enigmatic grin lit up the fairy's lovely face. "It is indeed. The same orb that you fetched for your *mate.* To obtain the *dragonfire.*"

Issylte's breath hitched. "You knew that I had retrieved the orb?"

"Of course. That's why I hid it in *le Miroir aux Fées.* The Goddess revealed to me that you would be the one to find it. The Lady of the Mirrored Lake. Whose *mate*, the Blue Knight of Cornwall, would vanquish the evil wizard that threatens our realm. Warrior and Priestess of the Tribe of Dana, whose destinies She had entwined. For that very purpose."

Issylte, astonished, returned her gaze to the dazzling gems in her hand. Illuminated from within, the radiant image of a star glowed in their depths. The light of the sacred spring within *la Grotte de l' Étoile.* The starlight she had seen in Tristan's eyes. And in the crystals she'd used to save him.

"These are remnants from the sacred orb I crafted," Morgane explained as Issylte marveled at the sparkling gems. "A powerful talisman of protection for the man who seduced me. With *lies*." Morgane traced her fingers over the stellar stones scattered across the tabletop. "I embedded the very essence of my power—the ancient magic I'd learned from my mentor, the archdruid Merlin—into this *pierre de l' étoile*." Fixing Issylte with eyes that glowed with infinite wisdom, Morgane smiled softly and declared, "We shall use these to craft the sacred scabbard for your *mate*."

The peal of a small bell jingled from the lower level. "Our supper is ready. Come, let's eat—and I shall tell you more of what I plan to teach you, dear Lady of the Mirrored Lake."

****

Over the next several weeks in the enchanted castle of *le Château Lumineux*, Morgane taught Issylte how to craft the sacred scabbard which would encase the legendary *Azeldraig*, the sword Tristan would wield to destroy the evil wizard.

To create the enchanted sheath for Tristan's Elven sword, Issylte selected the same two gems as the sacred stones in their *toi et moi* wedding rings. Emeralds—her sacred stone—crafted from the large, raw gem that Morgane had kept in Issylte's guest chambers. Blue topaz—the sacred gem of her *mate*, symbolizing the waters of Cornwall and Lyonesse. And the Fountain of Barenton which he had defended to become a warrior of the Tribe of Dana.

To complete a Celtic trinity of sacred stones, Issylte

319

added a third gem.

The precious *pierre de l' étoile*—the starstone of the enchanted orb.

The very gem which would defeat the wizard Voldurk.

With her new skill in wielding the ancient knowledge of the archdruid Merlin, her own verdant power—infinitely enhanced by the magic gift of Morgane la Fée and the essence of the enchanted emerald—Issylte cast protective spells into the trinity of gems for Tristan's sacred scabbard.

She channeled the energy of the earth and stars, imbuing each stone with the divine protection of the Goddess Dana that she embodied. She infused into the trinity of sacred stones all the love in her heart and spirit for her *mate*. All her skills as a healer—a gifted *guérisseuse* of Avalon. Her innate verdant magic as a forest fairy, trained by Maiwenn in the beloved Hazelwood Forest.

And her newly enhanced virid power as the Emerald Fairy of the Enchanted Forests, gifted by *la Fée Blanche des Rochers Sacrés*. Morgane la Fée. The White Fairy of the Sacred Stones.

When the sheath was complete, Morgane praised Issylte's exceptional skill. "This sacred scabbard surpasses even my own handiwork, Priestess of Dana. For you love the warrior for whom it was crafted with all your heart and soul. You've instilled your very *essence* into its creation. It is truly magnificent."

The brunette fairy laid the enchanted scabbard upon the table in the second story *atelier* of the tower where she and Issylte were working. Looking up at her, Morgane said quietly, her pale blue eyes twinkling, "And now, I will share my secret. We shall craft a talisman so that Voldurk may never touch you."

Together, the two fairies cut a huge pear-shaped gem from the enormous, enchanted emerald, along with several smaller teardrop shaped stones. Encasing everything in precious silver, they added faceted gems from the remnants of the sacred orb into a talisman of inordinate power.

"This necklace," Morgane explained, as she clasped the jewel around Issylte's slender neck, "contains your sacred emeralds, imbued with the verdant magic of the forest. The stones of *pierre de l'étoile* channel the celestial energy of the stars and the divine power of the Goddess into a protective talisman which repels evil."

Admiration glistening in her wintry blue gaze, Morgane smiled with satisfaction at their *otherworldly* creation. "My secret, dear Lady of the Mirrored Lake, is this. If Voldurk should ever lay a hand upon you, while you wear this talisman of protection, the celestial energy of *pierre de l'étoile* from the enchanted orb will burn him with *starfire*—a blaze hotter than the fiercest flame on earth."

Morgane touched the deep green jewels which gleamed brilliantly among the surrounding starstones. "And the emeralds from this enchanted gem—your sacred stone—are imbued with the protection of the forest of Brocéliande, where you and the Blue Knight of Cornwall became warrior and priestess of the Goddess Dana. Where you finalized your *mating bond* and were joined in the triple trinity of marriage. Where you inherited the legacy of Maiwenn. And became *la Fée Émeraude des Forêts Enchantées*."

The White Fairy of the Sacred Stones placed the

large emerald at the base of Issylte's throat, the smaller stones dangling along the silver chain creating a dazzling display of deepest green and sparkling starlight.

Morgane kissed Issylte's forehead. "Wear this talisman, Lady of the Mirrored Lake. And Voldurk cannot touch you."

****

Now seated at the table in the dining area which looked out upon the shimmery lake, a winter wind rippling across its glassy surface, the two fairies discussed how Issylte could return to Avalon.

"Your talisman will protect you from Voldurk's touch, and your Druidic gift of *Rose Elder* will block his evil spells. But he may try to harm you in unforeseen ways—with a poisoned dart, blade, or arrow. It's best that you avoid the universal portal where he undoubtedly still lurks, waiting to ensnare you as his prey. Snake that he is."

Morgane sipped a *tisane,* evoking Issylte's memories of the kitchen table where she and her beloved *Tatie* had first discussed a voyage to Avalon over a cup of herbal tea. Her heart glowed with nostalgic love as she smiled and sipped the chamomile brew.

"But there is another portal," the raven-haired fairy continued, her ethereal voice wary. "Although it's located within the sacred Forest of Brocéliande—where Voldurk may not enter—the portal lies beyond the realm of my enchanted domain." Morgane's pale blue gaze was disquieting. "Which means that the dwarf and his knights will be guarding the entrance to the portal. Waiting for you."

Issylte shuddered. How could she return to Avalon? She couldn't go back to the cave portal where she'd emerged into the forest, for Voldurk would surely be lurking there. Nor could she face a dwarf with an army of at least a dozen knights. How could she possibly reach Tristan?

"*Les Fées Dorées* bestowed three sacred gifts upon you," Morgane said pensively. "What powers did you receive?"

Issylte smiled at the memory of the golden fairies floating down the waterfall—*la Cascade du Serein*, the sacred waters that Lysara defended as a priestess of Dana. "The gift from the forest fairy allows me to hide from my enemies in sacred trees. The water fairy's gift—*la Voix de l'Eau*—grants me the means to communicate with my *mate* by touching any body of water that connects us. He alone may hear my voice, transported by the sacred waters. And the gift of stone from the third fairy allows me to walk between worlds, through stone portals and caves. Such as *les Menhirs de Monteneuf*, which brought me here to you."

Morgane mulled over Issylte's words, contemplative and pensive. "And the archdruid Odin bestowed the gift of *l'herbe d'or* upon your mate."

"Yes…but how did you know that?"

The fairy smiled enigmatically. "Odin and I are… close," she smirked.

Morgane stared reflectively at the cool waters of the lake behind *le Château Lumineux*. "My lake, *le Lac Trémelin*, empties into the Narrow Sea, which surrounds the island of Avalon. If you touch the water of the lake, you can use *la Voix de l'Eau* to communicate with Tristan." Morgane's wintry blue eyes glistened like the shimmering waters before them. "Ask him to use his Druidic gift of *l'herbe d'or*. To summon the wolves of *le*

Vallon de la Chambre aux Loups. The Valley of the Chamber of Wolves."

Issylte's pulse quickened, the white winged dove taking flight in her heart. *Garou's tribe! La Tribu des Loups. This is his domain!*

"I once healed a wounded wolf." Issylte exhaled, her voice breathless with excitement. "The mate of Garou, leader of *la Tribu des Loups*—the Wolf Tribe. This is his domain. He promised to help us, if we ever needed him." Issylte's mouth went dry as she locked her gaze onto Morgane. "Tristan can summon the wolves of *la Tribu des Loups*."

Eyeing Issylte over the rim of her *tisane*, the dark-haired fairy grinned ferally. "That will eliminate our problem with the dwarf. And his pesky knights." Morgane chuckled darkly, reaching across the table to grasp Issylte's hand, giving her a reassuring squeeze. "The cave portal of *la Chambre aux Loups* connects directly with *la Porte du Dedans.* The portal at the bottom of the Mirrored Lake."

Issylte gasped as comprehension dawned. "If I enter the portal here at *la Chambre aux Loups,* I can cross through the sacred portal, inaccessible to Voldurk. And emerge directly into *la Grotte de l' Étoile* on Avalon!"

Setting down her cup of tisane, Issylte rushed to Morgane's side, thrilled at having found a safe means of rejoining Tristan. Morgane rose to her feet and wrapped her arms around Issylte.

Hugging the beautiful fairy who had become her mentor and friend, Issylte kissed Morgane's cheek. "Thank you so very much. I am forever grateful."

The *châtelaine* beamed, pushing a strand of golden hair from Issylte's face. "Come. Let us go to my lake, where you may call upon your gift from *les Fées Dorées*. And use *la Voix de l'Eau* to speak to your *mate.*"

****

Tristan, Lancelot, and the Tribe had arrived in Avalon with Ronan, who had begun forging *Azeldraig*. Each day, for the past eight weeks, the warriors had been training with the Avalonian Elves, with Ronan frequently joining them between various stages of completion of the *otherworldly* sword.

Consumed with worry about Issylte, having had no word from her despite her expected arrival weeks ago, Tristan welcomed the rigorous training and subsequent physical exhaustion as he honed his body back into peak condition. He, along with Lancelot, fellow members of the Tribe, and the knights who had traveled with them, had been residing among the Elves until Issylte returned. Having just finished his morning meal, he was now headed for the lodge they shared near the eastern shore of the island to begin the day's training.

"Tristan, I have found a way to speak to you, using my gift of water from les Fées Dorées."

Issylte's melodic words floated to him from the sea. Heart pounding, flooded with relief to hear her beautiful voice, he raced down the path from the forested ledge where the Elves resided to the sandy shoreline at the water's edge. White-capped waves lapped gently at his feet.

"I must cross a different portal, for le Miroir aux Fées is frozen." The ethereal voice of his *mate* drifted across the waves, as if transported in a dream. *"The cave I must enter is guarded by a dwarf and his knights, waiting to entrap me. Tristan, you must summon the wolves from le Vallon de la Chambre aux Loups.*

325

Garou's domain. Command them to eliminate the danger. So that I may to return to you, my love. Use your Druidic magic. Summon the wolves."

Adrenaline surging through his body at the thought of her threatened by the dwarf and his knights, Tristan focused on the forest of Brocéliande, drawing upon his gift of *l'herbe d'or,* envisioning Garou's lupine face. His Druidic gift traveled through the sacred forest, deep into the woods of *la Chambre aux Loups,* summoning the Wolf Tribe. Wordlessly, Tristan conveyed the order to attack and kill the dwarf and his men, leaving no survivors. Transmitting the image of his beautiful blonde wife, he commanded the wolves to protect her—his *mate* —so that she could safely enter the portal and return to him.

Garou's voice reached him from the depths of the Forest of Brocéliande. "Just as you saved my mate, Warrior of Dana, I shall now save yours."

****

From their hidden perch atop the forested ledge overlooking the valley, Issylte watched with *Morgane la Fée* as dozens of enormous gray wolves furtively encircled the unsuspecting dwarf and his knights who were relaxing near a campfire, eating a meal, totally unprepared for the lupine assault. As the men scrambled to their feet, rushing for their weapons, *la Tribu des Loups* attacked with fatal precision.

Some wolves launched themselves at the scurrying knights, knocking them to the ground, sharp fangs tearing open the throats of their screaming victims. Others chomped at the legs of the men attempting to flee, the wolves banding together to fell the warriors, savagely ripping bloody limbs from flailing bodies and disemboweling their writhing prey.

Dangling from the bloodied maw of a massive wolf who shook the limp body like a slab of meat, the dying dwarf shrieked in agony, his piercing screams echoing through the verdant Valley of the Chamber of Wolves.

Finally, when all was quiet, Issylte stood, shaking violently with the brutality of what she'd just witnessed. She brushed herself off and strapped *Emeraldfire* to her waist with trembling hands. Ensuring that *Émeraude* was sheathed upon one calf and Cian's dagger strapped to the other, her enchanted emerald talisman secured around her neck, and Tristan's sacred scabbard safely ensconced in her pack, Issylte hoisted her leather bag to her shoulder and prepared to leave the domain of *Morgane la Fée*.

Hugging her friend one last time, Issylte kissed each of the fairy's cheeks with *la bise* of farewell, then followed the winding trail from the wooded ledge at the top of the cliff down to the gruesome carnage scattered across the forest floor.

Her gaze glued to the dark mouth of the cave entrance, avoiding the sickening stench of bloody bodies and disemboweled entrails, Issylte staggered into the cave portal of *la Chambre aux Loups.*

To walk between worlds toward *la Grotte de l' Étoile.* Back to her anxiously awaiting mate.

Chapter 22

La Grotte de l' Étoile

Issylte emerged from the portal of *la Chambre aux Loups* into the cave of *la Grotte de l' Étoile,* on the island of Avalon, to find Tristan standing before her. Amid the roar of the effervescent fountain and the turquoise splendor of the luminous cave, his sparkling eyes shone with relief, basking her in lovelight, bathing her in waves of calming blue. Horrified by the violent assault she'd just witnessed, her limbs shaking, she was still in shock, her emotions raw and vulnerable. The sight of Tristan took her breath away.

He was truly the most handsome man she'd ever seen. His chiseled jawline was covered with dark stubble, the chestnut waves of his rich, glossy hair brushing the collar of his blue tunic. Her legs trembled as the earthy scent of him—pine, leather, fresh sweat, and spice—assaulted her senses.

Beckoning her.

Intense eyes devoured her, his gaze raking over her body, lingering on her breasts and hips, which tingled in anticipation. He stared at the curves of her rounded form, outlined by the deep green gown which clung to her, his face longing with a primal need.

Her husband. Her *mate.* She couldn't move, couldn't take her eyes off him. She just stood there, quavering with emotion. The bag she was carrying slipped quietly from her grasp onto the cavern floor. She was vaguely aware of the crackle and warmth of a fire, a woolen blanket near Tristan's feet.

In a flash, he was upon her, ensnaring her in his arms, devouring her.

"By the Goddess, I've missed you." He groaned, kissing her face, lips, and shoulders. He removed her cloak, unstrapped *Emeraldfire* from her waist, dropping the belted sword beside them. He unbuckled the daggers from her ankles and removed her boots, his hands sliding up her trembling legs, sending thrills of pleasure with his skillful touch.

He unclasped her talisman and placed it gently upon the corner of the blanket. Then, supporting her with one arm, he pushed her head back, baring her neck for his eager lips.

Tristan licked and nipped at the *mating mark*, sending quivers of delight which ran down her spine and settled deep in her pelvis, creating a painful, throbbing ache.

"The Elves told me that the *mating mark* is a sensitive erogenous zone." He whispered into her left ear as he sucked and lapped at her neck. She emitted a guttural moan, shaking in his arms. He pulled her hips tightly against his, pushing against her softness with the hard outline of his body.

Her insides were like liquid fire, pulsing with rhythm and desire, as longing overwhelmed her senses. Tristan yanked the shoulders of her gown down to reveal her bare breasts, which he ravished with his warm mouth and skilled tongue.

Paralyzed, she couldn't speak, couldn't think about

329

anything but the desperate need for *him.* To wash away the horror she'd witnessed. To fill the unbearable, hollow ache between her weakened legs.

He removed her gown and the chemise underneath, marveling at her exquisite nakedness as he ran his hands up and down her body, sending tingles everywhere he touched. He unstrapped his sword and dagger, then threw off his boots, breeches, and tunic. She inhaled sharply at the sight of the dark hair covering his chest, the magnificent ripples of hardened muscle over his torso, his sculpted arms, and thick, powerful legs.

And when she looked below his navel, the sight of his arousal made her swoon with *want.*

He lowered her down onto the blanket, kissing her lips and neck, swirling his tongue and scraping his teeth over the *mating mark.* He devoured her breasts, sucking mercilessly until she gasped with pleasure and writhed underneath him.

His lips worshipped her, grazing over her abdomen until his tongue was between her legs, savoring her taste, tormenting her with nearly unbearable pleasure. Rising onto his knees, he positioned himself between her legs, parting her thighs savagely with his own. He slid his hands under her hips and tilted them up toward him. His face dark and possessive, he cast her one last feral look as he plunged inside her, thrusting to the hilt when she wrapped her legs around his waist and pulled him in even deeper with the tight grip of her thighs.

Their lovemaking had always been intense, but this coupling was primal, fierce, and *raw*—unlike anything Issylte had ever experienced. She lost herself in him.

Her body contracted rhythmically with each of his thrusts, pulsing with his every movement, drawing the very essence of him into the very essence of her. He groaned with fury and need; she moaned with yearning and ache.

When the tension finally peaked, shattering them both, Tristan thrust deeply into her and shuddered, filling her depths with his copious seed. Their two bodies convulsed, gripped tightly together, waves of pleasure washing over them as the roar of the sacred spring reverberated in their divine release.

Neither of them could move. Her legs were still wrapped tightly around his waist, her hips tilted up to meet his. He nuzzled her neck and chin. "That was *intense*," he whispered in her ear, grazing her *mating mark* with his lips.

Tristan eased himself down beside her on the blanket, pulling her close and pushing the long strands of blonde hair back from her face. He kissed her shoulder and breasts. Tingles of pleasure rippled through her. Verdant magic sung in her veins.

"I waited here for you…made this fire so we would be warm." His eyes glinted in the firelight as he rose onto one elbow, hovering over her. In a raspy breath, he exhaled gruffly, "I wanted to *reclaim* you…before sharing you with the others. I simply *had* to have you. I couldn't wait any longer." His tongue and lips swirled and sucked at the *mating mark*. He chuckled softly at the effect it had on her. Raising his ocean blue gaze into her forest fairy eyes, he whispered, "I love you."

"*Toi et moi*. So it shall be. You and I are entwined. Eternally." Issylte whispered their wedding vows as she buried her nose into the hair of his chest just above her face, inhaling his scent deep into her lungs. She grinned at the thought of what he had just done to her. By the

Goddess, she wanted him again.

The necklace, forgotten in their passion, twinkled on the blanket nearby and drew Tristan's attention. The deep green stones sparkled, and the clear, luminous gems—interspersed among the darker ones—glinted in the firelight. The magnificent emerald hung in the center, its large teardrop shape reminiscent of the droplet form of their *mating mark*.

"This is *beautiful*," he exclaimed, extending his arm across her to reach for it.

"It is a protective talisman," she whispered, as he sat up to examine the glittering jewels in his callused hands. She lifted herself up to sit cross-legged on the blanket beside him. Tristan clasped the talisman behind her neck, carefully placing the large emerald droplet at the base of her throat. It thrummed and glowed, enchanted with tangible power.

"*Morgane la Fée* crafted this for me. From an enormous raw emerald she kept in a guest bedroom of her castle. She knew that one day, I would come to her." Tristan raised his gaze from the necklace to marvel at her, his eyes wide with wonder.

Issylte shared the astral brilliance of the radiant droplets along the sides of her pendant. "This is *la pierre de l'étoile*. Remnants from the priceless orb which Morgane created—and hid in *le Miroir aux Fées*. Knowing that I would be the one to retrieve it one day. For *you*."

Tristan gazed at the luminous gems sparkling at her throat. "They thrum with power." He touched the glittering stones reverently. "Just as the orb did in my hand. When I was in the dragon portal."

"*La pierre de l'étoile*—the stone from the fallen star.

Taken from this sacred cave. The same crystals I used to heal you—when you came to Avalon, poisoned by the Morholt's blade."

His eyes held hers, awed by the entwined fate which had enjoined them as *mates.* And had brought them here, to *la Grotte de l' Étoile.*

The Cave of the Fallen Star.

"Morgane had foreseen everything in a *sighting.*" Issylte whispered, stroking the dark hair on Tristan's chest, swimming in the deep pools of his intense blue eyes. "She knew that you were my *mate.* That we were members of the Tribe of Dana, gifted with Druidic magic. And that our destiny had been interwoven with her own."

The emerald talisman sparkled at her throat, dazzling in brilliance. Thrumming with power.

"Morgane enhanced my magic with the enchanted essence of this sacred stone," she whispered, lifting the large pendant with reverent fingers. "She bestowed upon me the title of *La Fée Émeraude des Forêts Enchantées.*" She smiled at him, his rapt gaze gleaming in the firelight. "The Emerald Fairy of Enchanted Forests—a sacred Celtic trinity. The Hazelwood Forest of Ireland. The Forest of Morois in Cornwall. And the Forest of Brocéliande in Bretagne."

She rose onto her knees and straddled him with her thighs, leaning down to kiss his lips softly. Her long blonde hair cascaded down, encasing him in a soft, golden waterfall.

"The emeralds and the *pierre de l'étoile* have been imbued with protective power." Issylte whispered, kissing Tristan softly. "If Voldurk tries to touch me, the verdant magic of the forest and the celestial power of the orb will burn him. With *emerald starfire.*"

He grinned broadly, kissed the large teardrop stone, then placed it back between her soft breasts. His gaze held hers. He was intoxicating, irresistible. Slowly, seductively, she removed the necklace and carefully laid it on the blanket, lowering herself down to recline beside him. She could read the urgent need in his eyes.

His lips sought hers, gently at first, then more insistently as desire enflamed him. His tongue lapped the mating mark, then the peaks of her breasts, eliciting guttural moans of pleasure from the back of her throat. He flipped her onto her stomach, lifted her rounded hips and drove them both over the edge as he poured every ounce of himself into her once again.

They lay entwined together, wrapped in each other's limbs, gazing at the fire. She told him of Solzic's recovery, meeting the three strapping sons of Esclados and Laudine during the Yuletide celebration at Landuc. She shared her harrowing escape from Voldurk in the portal of *les Menhirs de Monteneuf,* the enchanting *séjour* with Morgane in *le Château Lumineux,* and the horror of witnessing the bloody, brutal wolf attack.

After a while, savoring the delicious warmth in his arms, Issylte whispered, "I have something to show you." Disentangling herself from his embrace, she plodded softly across the cave.

She felt his admiring gaze on her naked body. She knew he loved the way her long blonde hair unfurled to her small waist, the rounded curves of her hips. Her long lean legs, toned and firm. She smiled softly at him, the love in his eyes filling her spirit as his seed flowed within her body.

She retrieved the scabbard and returned to his side.

Sitting down on the blanket, drawing close to him for warmth, she offered this man she loved to the very depths of her soul the treasure she had imbued with her Emerald Fairy essence.

"I crafted this scabbard for you. For your sword, *Azeldraig.*" He looked at her in wonder as he accepted the priceless gift, his eyes glistening with awe. And love. "Morgane taught me the technique she used when she created King Arthur's sheath for Excalibur." He stroked the rich brown leather and dazzling gems, running appreciative fingers over her intricate work. "These emeralds—my sacred stone—are from the same raw gem that created my talisman," she explained, caressing the deep green jewels ensconced in the leather. She rested her head against his shoulder, kissing the arm which he'd wrapped around her. Every pore in her body tingled in his presence. And the magic of the sacred stones hummed in his calloused, warrior hands.

"Blue topaz is your sacred stone…as the Blue Knight of Cornwall and heir to Lyonesse. And these," she whispered, indicating the brilliant, radiant gems on the leather sheath, "are from the same *pierre de l' étoile* that created the magic orb. The same gems as in my talisman." She touched the necklace on the blanket, caressing the glittering jewels with reverent fingertips. "The same sacred crystals I used to save you."

He examined the enchanted jewels, then raised appreciative eyes as brilliant as the blue topaz gems in the sacred scabbard.

"All of these stones have been enchanted to protect you," she whispered, "just as King Arthur's scabbard prevents him from losing blood in battle." The emeralds in the scabbard and talisman blazed with virid flame.

"Morgane was one of Merlin's pupils. *La Fée Blanche des Rochers Sacrés*. One of the trio of fairies that included both Maiwenn and Viviane." He raised a curious eyebrow, his lips curling upward in an intrigued grin. "Morgane possesses unsurpassed skill with sacred stones. That's why Voldurk had her craft the orb for him. And she shared that sacred knowledge with me. So that I could craft this scabbard for you."

Issylte shivered a bit from the chill, despite the warmth of the fire. Tristan laid the scabbard down, then unfolded a banket which lay nearby. He wrapped it around her shoulders, pulling her into his arms, nestling her on his chest. She breathed in his scent, humming with contentment. Verdant magic stirred in her soul.

Reveling in Tristan's broad shoulders, muscled arms, and rippled torso, she lowered her head to kiss the dark hair on his chest, her heart bursting with love for this man who had believed in her. Who had trained her to fight. Who had forged the sword *Emeraldfire* for her. And who had promised to lead her army as she reclaimed her right to the throne of Ireland.

Her warrior. Her husband. Her *mate*.

"Morgane said that because I love you, the power I cast into these stones will surpass even the protection of King Arthur's sacred scabbard." Issylte placed the sheath in Tristan's palms, closed them with her own, then lowered her lips to kiss his hands. Sealing her magic with a kiss. "This scabbard will defend you with the divine essence of the stars, the sacred elements of the Goddess, and the infinite power of the love of your *mate*." She raised her eyes, brimming with tears, to meet his. "I love you, Tristan. I am totally, completely, and utterly *yours*."

She raised herself up onto her knees, letting the wrap

fall from her shoulders, leaning forward to kiss him as he lowered himself down onto the blanket, pulling her toward him.

Issylte crawled over him, her hair draping his shoulders as she placed her legs astride his body once again. She nuzzled his neck, licking and nibbling at the *mating mark,* smiling softly as she felt that it aroused him the same way it did her.

She kissed his neck, shoulders, and chest, rubbing the soft, tender flesh between her legs against his hardness. He moaned, grabbed her hips, and pulled her down upon himself. She gasped as he thrust upward, lifting her hips up and down to match his rhythm, pulsing into her until they shattered together in shared ecstasy.

She lay down beside him and laughed softly. "I never want to leave this cave. Let's just stay here…and make love."

"Mmmm…" he hummed. "I like that idea." He kissed the top of her head, pulled the blanket over them, and drew her into his arms so that his body cradled hers from behind. Like two spoons nestled together.

In the safety of his embrace, her body sated at last, Issylte felt the fiery liquid from Tristan's loins spread up through her. Into her.

Idly, she thought of how they needed to get dressed, leave this sacred tryst, and greet the other members of the Tribe. To plan, discuss, and strategize.

She knew that soon, they would sail to Cornwall with the Tribe, bringing an army of knights, horses, and men-at-arms in the large cog ships that sailed from Bretagne.

Once they arrived on the shores of Britain, she and Tristan would ride with the Tribe to *la Porte des*

Ombres—the portal where Voldurk made sacrifices to his dark power—just before the vernal equinox. With the dozen *pierre de l'étoile* gemstones that she had reserved, Issylte would cast the ancient spells Morgane had taught her, creating a crystal grid barrier that would enchant the portal and trap Voldurk inside when he entered the cave.

Issylte remembered the kaleidoscope of images she'd seen within the depths of Tristan's eyes when their *mating bond* was finalized in the Forest of Brocéliande. She remembered wondering why she'd glimpsed the luminous star shining within the sacred spring of *la Grotte de l' Étoile* in his eyes when Ronan had been the one to introduce her to this sacred cave. But now she knew.

La Grotte de l' Étoile. The sacred cave where they'd obtained the black obsidian to transport the *dragonfire.* Where Ronan had mined the ore from the fallen star to forge *Azeldraig,* the only weapon with the power to slay the evil wizard.

La Grotte de l' Étoile. The sacred cave where *Morgane la Fée* had found the divine gemstone to craft the sacred orb, the talisman around her neck, and the scabbard which would protect Tristan.

Issylte thought of the recent *sighting* she'd had while gazing into the waters of *le Lac Trémelin* behind Morgane's *Château Lumineux.* The image of a chubby toddler, an adorable little boy with sparkling blue eyes and golden-blond hair. She understood now.

Just as Merlin had used magic and *glamour* to bring Uther Pendragon and Queen Igraine together so that they would conceive Arthur, destined to become the High King of Britain, the Goddess had orchestrated this sacred tryst in *la Grotte de l'Étoile.* The Cave of the Fallen Star.

So that Issylte would conceive Tristan's son.

She'd exhausted her supply of contraceptive herbs at the beginning of the eight weeks she'd spent with Morgane at *le Château Lumineux*. She'd had her monthly flow two weeks ago and had planned on asking Cléo for more of the herbs when she arrived at *Le Centre*.

Yet, with the shock of the wolves' attack, the sight of Tristan, the way his scent assailed her senses, the way her body craved his…she knew. Their fates had been entwined once again.

The Goddess had brought Tristan to Camelot. So that he would meet Lancelot and learn Elven swordsmanship, defeating the Scourge of the Celtic Sea. And, when wounded by the Black Knight's poisoned blade, the White Knight would bring Tristan to Avalon.

To meet Issylte, the healer trained in Ireland, where the Morholt had obtained the poison for his deadly sword. The *guérisseuse* of Avalon, loved by the Elf Ronan, descendent of Gofannon—who would forge the legendary sword *Azeldraig*.

Priestess of Dana. Tristan's *mate*. And now, his wife.

The Goddess had brought them together. For Tristan to lead her army. For Issylte to fetch the precious orb, meet *Morgane la Fée*, and craft the sacred scabbard for her warrior.

For the two of them to slay the dark wizard and wicked queen, eliminating the evil which threatened the entire Celtic realm.

And the Goddess had brought them here today, to *la Grotte de l' Étoile*.

So that she and Tristan would conceive the son who was now implanting in her womb.

A king destined to rule over Ireland, Lyonesse, and Cornwall. A trinity of Celtic kingdoms. In a divine realm of peace.

Issylte kissed the hair on the arm which held her in Tristan's embrace. Soon, they would sail for Cornwall. Goddess willing, they would slay Voldurk and lay siege to the castle of Tintagel. They would save King Marke and imprison the evil queen who threatened their future.

If they were victorious, she hoped Tristan's uncle would restore his right to the throne of Lyonesse and renew his status as the heir to the crown of Cornwall. Yet, even if King Marke did not, the Tribe would use the conquered castle of Tintagel as a stronghold where they could launch the attack on Ireland. And eradicate all traces of the evil Black Widow Queen.

With their allies from Anjou, Aquitaine, and Armorique, she and Tristan would attack Dubh Linn, where they'd challenge Indulf, the traitorous knight who had tried to kill Tristan. Who now, as the Earl of Dubh Linn, ruled over the Viking slave center established by the Morholt.

Goddess willing, they'd reclaim her father's castle of Connaught, and Issylte would be crowned the Emerald Queen. Then, and only then, would she tell Tristan that she carried his child. Not before. Not when he needed to focus his strength and will on defeating Voldurk and liberating Tintagel. And leading her army.

Her warrior. Her champion. Her *mate*.

The fire was dying, the sun was setting, and the late winter chill was beginning to permeate the cave. As much as she hated to leave this idyll, Issylte knew that they needed to get back to *Le Centre* and join the others.

Snuggled in his arms, wrapped in the blankets, she

rolled toward Tristan, raising a knee up onto his waist as she nuzzled the *mating mark* on his neck. He stirred, having dozed off, growling softly as he pulled her hips towards his. "If you keep doing that, we'll never leave this cave." His blue topaz eyes twinkled wickedly.

She smiled, kissed the hair on his chest, and said softly, "We need to go."

He nodded, perhaps thinking of the horses which he must have tethered to trees on the forested ledge near the cave. There would have been plenty of warm sunlight and patches of grass for them to graze, but now, with the sun setting, they would feel the chill.

Rising to his feet, Tristan helped Issylte stand, then wrapped his arms around her waist. He kissed her lips softly. "I'm glad we had this time alone together." Cupping the curve of her bottom, he pulled her body against his and whispered in her ear, "I needed that."

He helped her dress, pulling first the soft white chemise and then the dark green gown over her head, smoothing it with hands that glided over her curves. He fastened the talisman around her neck, placing the large emerald at the base of her throat.

"By the Goddess, you are beautiful." He pulled her to his chest. "And *mine*. All mine." The side of his mouth curled upward in a feral grin as he nuzzled the *mating mark,* then helped her feet slip inside the leather boots. He clasped the fur-lined cloak at her neck, smiling at the glittering talisman. He watched as she strapped *Emeraldfire* back upon her waist, *Émeraude* to one ankle, and Cian's dagger to the other. She smiled at him, sending all the verdant love in her emerald fairy heart through the *mating bond* which connected their entwined souls.

Tristan quickly donned his breeches, tunic, boots, and weapons. As Issylte wrapped the scabbard in a blanket, then placed it—along with the other blankets she had folded—into her bag of supplies, he donned his heavy cloak. Tristan kicked sand from the floor of the cave onto the fire to extinguish the dying embers, then hoisted Issylte's pack over his shoulder.

With one last, lingering glance at the sacred site of their romantic tryst, she and her *mate* left *la Grotte de l' Étoile.*

Followed the narrow path which led from the sandy beach to the top of the forested cliff where the horses awaited them.

And, side by side, rode back to *Le Centre* of Avalon.

Chapter 23

Azeldraig

The smiling faces of the priestesses of Avalon, the members of the Tribe of Dana, and several former patients welcomed Issylte back to *Le Centre* as she entered the packed dining room with Tristan.

A reunion had been planned, for Tristan had told Lancelot and the others that Issylte would be returning to Avalon today. He'd explained that she had communicated with him across the waters of the Narrow Sea, using her gift of *la Voix de l'Eau*, informing him that she would be coming through the portal of *la Grotte de l' Étoile.*

Tristan had confided that he wanted to be there to greet her alone, which had elicited hearty laughs, bawdy remarks, and slaps on the back from the lusty warriors of the Tribe. They knew how starved their fellow knight was for his beautiful wife and were more than willing to grant his request for privacy.

Lancelot had spoken to his mother Viviane, and she, along with the priestesses of Avalon and the kitchen staff of *Le Centre,* had organized the gathering to celebrate both Issylte's safe return and her recent marriage to Tristan, whom she'd met upon this Island of Healing.

Now, as she reunited with Viviane, Cléo, Nyda, Gwennol, and the other priestesses of Avalon, tears of joy streaked Issylte's face. Lancelot nearly broke her back with his exuberant hug. Dagur, Darius, and the Tribe were all greatly relieved and immensely pleased to hear of Solzic's recovery and the heartfelt reunion of Esclados and Laudine's three chivalrous sons for the Yuletide celebration at *le Château de Landuc.*

A tall blond warrior emerged from the group to greet Issylte. Kjetil—the Viking who had slain the dwarf Frocin and saved Tristan's life when they freed Gargeolaine from the Tower of Morois—crushed her in his bulky arms.

"Welcome back, Princess!" Kjetil chortled, his blond beard bristling against her face as he planted a brusque kiss upon her soft cheek. "We all missed you, but this one here," he smirked, grinning wickedly at Tristan, "drove us all crazy. He was wantin' you so bad, his balls were burstin'. Weren't they now, Tristan?" Kjetil guffawed, slapping her husband on the back, as raucous laughter rippled through warriors of the Tribe.

The delicious aromas of roasted meat, fresh fruit, sweet pastries, and beeswax candles filled the air of the celebratory feast. They all sat together in the spacious dining hall of *Le Centre*, listening with rapt attention as Kjetil shared how he'd married his betrothed in a lovely ceremony in the picturesque village of Lisieux, Normandy. He told everyone how he and his new bride Cosette had been privileged guests at *le Château Rose* for the royal wedding of Prince Kaherdin of Armorique to the lovely Lady Gargeolaine.

"Kaherdin couldn't come with us here to Avalon," Kjetil explained, wiping ale from his bearded grin with the sleeve of his tunic. "Gargeolaine just gave birth to their son in early February, and he refused to leave her side. But…" the burly Viking grinned, his white teeth gleaming amidst his thick blond beard, "the prince sent two ships from Armorique to sail with us to Cornwall. Four dozen armored knights—in support of Tristan's quest to save his uncle."

Kirus, who had sailed with Kjetil and had arrived in Avalon with Nolwenn, Bahja, and Erwann, grinned at her, his handsome, scarred face a sight for sore eyes. Nolwenn, tucked under his arm, smiled at Issylte, her amethyst gaze glowing. "Lysara and Solzic send their love. He is nearly fully recovered. And she will give birth in June. In time for the summer solstice." The wings of a white dove fluttered in Issylte's full heart as she thought of the tiny babe now implanting in her womb. *Our children will be very close in age. Perhaps they, like us, will be close friends.* She flashed Tristan a loving smile as Kjetil spoke again.

"Prince Kaherdin also promises two hundred additional knights for the voyage to Ireland," he said exuberantly, his deep voice bellowing through the dining hall. "Donning the Avalonian armor and wielding the Elven swords that Ronan forged—and delivered to *le Château Rose* for the winter solstice."

Issylte glanced at Ronan, his silvery-blond hair shining in the candlelight. His deep green eyes met hers as they shared a look of friendship and recognition. The lovely Nimue sat at his side, her gentle face filled with obvious adoration for her enormous Elf. Issylte smiled warmly at Ronan's new love.

Several other Elves had joined the priestesses of Avalon and the Tribe of Dana to celebrate Issylte's safe return and to congratulate the newlyweds for their recent marriage. Everyone had gorged on fresh fish, seafood, roast venison, assorted cheeses, pastries, cider, wine, and ale. Now that the feasting was over, servants were clearing away platters of food and refilling goblets as Ronan rose from his seat to address the assembled group.

"We are all most pleased that you have safely returned to Avalon, Princess Issylte." The deep, rich baritone of Ronan's voice carried across the throng gathered in the dining hall. "May I offer my congratulations on your wedding with a toast?"

Lifting his goblet of wine, prompting the rest of the celebrants to do the same, Ronan proposed, "To Tristan and Issylte, members of the Tribe of Dana who have become *mates,* as well as husband and wife. Congratulations on your wedding, and best wishes for a happy and prosperous future together."

"To Tristan and Issylte!" Hearty cheers rippled through the crowd as the Elves, priestesses of Avalon, members of the Tribe of Dana, and knights from *la Joyeuse Garde* and Landuc all congratulated the newlyweds and toasted their future.

As she took a sip of wine—just one, thinking of the tiny babe in her womb—Issylte observed Ronan over the rim of her chalice. He spoke privately to Nimue at his side, her shiny hair gleaming in the candlelight, her pretty eyes filled with love for the warrior she obviously adored.

I am glad he has found her. Ronan is so deserving of love. And Nimue will want to remain here in Avalon with him, something I could not do. She will make him happy. Thank the Goddess for bringing her into his life.

Ronan's forest-green gaze met Issylte's. For a moment, she remembered how much she had loved him, the intense passion they'd shared. But now, that fire had mellowed into the warm embers of friendship which glowed as she held his intense gaze. He smiled at her, ducking his chin in a gesture of acknowledgment. He then stood, raising his voice to address the group once again.

"I would like to make a second proposal," Ronan boomed, grinning at the crowd. "As you know, I have been commissioned to forge a weapon of unparalleled excellence." Hie cast his fierce gaze around the crowded room. All eyes were locked on the silvery-blond giant. "A sword to surpass even King Arthur's legendary blade, Excalibur." A few in the rapt audience gasped as the crowd listened intently, enthralled with Ronan's oratory. "The most magnificent weapon I have ever crafted. Into which I have poured all of my skill. My power. My *essence.*"

Ronan locked his fierce gaze onto Tristan, grinning savagely at Issylte's *mate.*

"The sword *Azeldraig.* Forged in *dragonfire.* On the *otherworldly* island of Avalon. By the descendant of Gofannon, Blacksmith of the Gods."

Murmurs rustled through the crowd, then hushed as Ronan spoke again, the notes of his baritone voice deep and rich. "I propose that we meet here again—in three days. When I shall present the most exceptional blade I have ever forged. The sword *Azeldraig.* To Tristan of Lyonesse, the Blue Knight of Cornwall."

Cheers erupted from the assembled group. It was agreed that a second celebration would take place three nights' hence. Ronan, who had helped his father forge the sword Excalibur, would bequeath an even more formidable weapon to Tristan, who had been healed upon this very island of Avalon.

As the welcoming celebration ended, the Tribe agreed to train together in the morning with the Elves and the knights who had sailed to Avalon. It was also agreed that Lancelot, Tristan, and Ronan would meet with the Tribe after the evening meal tomorrow night to discuss strategy. Viviane, Issylte, Nolwenn, Bahja, and Gwennol would join them as the group planned the entrapment of Voldurk in *la Porte des Ombres* and the subsequent siege of *le Château de Tintagel.*

Everyone said goodnight and congratulated the newlyweds, who were now alone at last in the guest quarters that Viviane had prepared for them during their stay at *Le Centre.*

Issylte sat at her vanity, brushing her hair as Tristan undressed for bed. She watched him in the mirror, taking in the bulk of his taut muscles, the dark hair on his chest that she so loved to touch, the scars he bore from various battles, the badges of his courage.

She rose to her feet, removed her gown, and knelt before him. She bathed him with lovelight as she held his gaze and spoke wordlessly.

She tenderly kissed the long, jagged scar across his stomach, remembering the stitches she had meticulously sewn when he'd been nearly mortally wounded by the Morholt. She kissed his torso, his stomach, his legs, delighting in his ardent response to her caresses.

She took him into her mouth, tantalizing him with her skilled tongue and lips, licking and sucking as he groaned with pleasure. Lovingly, painstakingly, and thoroughly, she worshipped every inch of his magnificent body, like a deity whom she adored with the divine offering of her mouth.

****

In the morning, after breaking their fast, she and Tristan completed her usual training routine, after which he joined the Tribe to train with the Elves. Nolwenn and Bahja, delighted to have time alone with Kirus and Erwann, disappeared with their lovers into the respective guest quarters that Viviane had arranged for them. Issylte accompanied Cléo, Viviane, and Nyda to the Women's Center to visit some of her former patients and reunite with Gwennol. She now sat with her friend on the same bench at the edge of the forest where they had often chatted before. Where Issylte had *sighted* the evil dwarf Frocin with the dark wizard and the Black Widow Queen.

"I was a servant at the castle of Tintagel for quite some time," Gwennol began. "I've already told you about *le ruisseau*—the strong stream that flows from Lake Tintagel in the forest directly under the foundation of the *château*. Tonight, at the meeting, I'll share that information with the warriors who will sail with you to Cornwall. I have an idea—which I think will be most valuable in planning how to infiltrate the castle."

Gwennol grinned from ear to ear. "And the Vikings left me behind—because I was old and worthless." She chuckled heartily, her wrinkled face alit with mischief. "Little did they know."

****

After supper that evening, while still gathered in the dining hall, the Tribe finalized the plan to trap Voldurk in *la Porte des Ombres*.

They'd sail from Avalon to Cornwall next week, landing on the southeastern coast of Britain, where they'd unload supplies, knights, and weapons. Since Lancelot, Tristan, and Gorvenal might be recognized at the port, it was agreed that Kirus would pose as a shipping merchant, with Dagur and several knights from *la Joyeuse Garde* and Landuc posing as his crew. The rest of the Tribe, clad in chain mail, would be hidden among the merchandise to be unloaded from the ships and hoisted furtively onto wagons at the dock. Once the men and supplies had reached the safety of the dense Forest of Morois, the Tribe would emerge from the hidden cargo and disperse through the thick woods to establish hidden encampments near the cave portal.

Issylte would enchant *la Porte des Ombres* with the gemstone remnants from the sacred orb, and the knights would wait and watch for Voldurk to enter the cave. Once the wizard was trapped inside, unable to traverse the enchanted portal, Tristan would follow. The sacred orb and scabbard would protect him from Voldurk's dark powers, and—Goddess willing—the warrior of Dana would slay the evil wizard with the sacred sword, *Azeldraig.*

Issylte had planned on entering the portal with Tristan, but he was resolute in his refusal.

"You are well trained with the sword, my love. Your gift of *Rose Elder* blocks the wizard's evil spells, and Morgane's enchanted talisman protects you from his touch. Yet, there is still the chance that he might hurl a dagger at you, or shoot a poisoned dart, or the Goddess knows what other diabolical weapon he might possess." Tristan's impassioned gaze blazed with intensity. "If you are in the portal with me, I will not be able to take my eyes off you, wanting to defend you from him. That is a distraction we cannot risk. I alone must face him, for I alone will be shielded by the sacred orb and scabbard. And I alone will wield the Elven sword which will kill him."

She lowered her head, for he spoke the truth. If she were in the portal with him, Tristan's focus would be on protecting her, rather than on slaying the wizard. He was right. He had to enter *la Porte des Ombres.*

Alone.

Kirus spoke, his scarred face solemn, his tone foreboding. "It won't work." All eyes flashed to the leader of the Tribe of Dana. "The wizard won't travel alone. He'll have dwarves and knights as his personal guards. He'll most likely have a sacrificial victim with him as well. Tristan won't be able to follow him in. Think about it."

Experience in battle and expertise in weaponry shone in Kirus' intelligent, dark eyes. "Voldurk enters the cave, and Tristan tries to follow. The guards intercept him, and we engage. The wizard hears the clash of metal, realizes there's an attack, and slithers from the cave. He takes out a few of us with his dark magic. And slips through our hands."

The seasoned warrior proposed a different tactic. "Tristan needs to be inside the cave. Before Voldurk arrives. *Waiting for him.*"

Lancelot and Tristan exchanged a fierce glance as they considered Kirus' plan.

Kirus met the rapt looks of the Tribe seated around him. "Voldurk enters the portal. We're lurking in the forest, surrounding the cave. We distract a few of the guards with noises coming from the woods. They check out the disturbance; we eliminate them. The knights who remain at the entrance to the cave, we take out quickly and quietly." Heads nodded in agreement. "When the entrance is clear, Issylte enchants it—blocks it with the same crystals she used inside. The wizard won't be able to cross the inner portal...or exit the cave." Kirus met and held Issylte's gaze with a mesmerizing stare. "Voldurk will not emerge *alive*."

Issylte exhaled sharply, locking eyes with his. She would create a crystal grid barrier using gems of *la pierre de l'étoile* to enchant the exit with sacred astral power. If Voldurk tried to leave, he would be consumed in the flames of *starfire*.

Remembering the dark shadows within the enchanted ruby where Aimée, *la Fée du Coeur,* had been trapped, Issylte announced, *"*Morgane also told me that the sacred crystals from *la Grotte de l' Étoile* will repel the *dark power* that Voldurk serves." All eyes turned to her. Lancelot raised an eyebrow, his curiosity piqued, as she whispered, "The wizard performs human sacrifices to *La Fée des Ombres*. The Shadow Fairy."

She glanced around the table at the intrigued faces of her beloved Tribe.

Lancelot. Kirus. Dagur. Darius. Gorvenal. The warriors who would fight at her side with Tristan. She inhaled deeply, then blew out a ragged breath. "Malfleur. A malevolent fairy once known as *La Fée des Fleurs.* The Flower Fairy. Destined to protect the Celtic realm with the curative power of flowers. But, like Voldurk— once as revered a Druid as Merlin—Malfleur was seduced by dark forces, abusing her innate power to harm and kill, rather than heal. She was reduced to shadows by the Goddess Dana, who imprisoned her in *la Porte des Ombres*. Where she has been trapped for an eternity. A shadow of her former self."

Issylte faced the burly, bearded Dagur. The Clan member who helped her free Aimée. "Malfleur wishes to inhabit a body once again. That's why Aimée was trapped in the cave. Malfleur and Voldurk had drained all of her magic essence, trapping it in that enchanted ruby. Aimée's body was the empty vessel for Malfleur to invade." She shivered convulsively at the thought, grateful they had been able to free *la Fée du Coeur* and break the evil curse.

Issylte glanced back at Kirus, seated beside Tristan and Lancelot. "When I enchant the portal so that Voldurk cannot pass into Malfleur's inner chamber, it will also prevent *la Fée des Ombres* from crossing the portal to reach the wizard. She will not be able to help him, for the crystal barrier I create with *la pierre de l'étoile* will block her as well." Her eyes locked onto Tristan, then sought Darius, Kjetil, and the rest of the Tribe. "Perhaps we can even prevent the human sacrifice, if Voldurk does bring the victim with him to the cave."

"It will undoubtedly weaken Malfleur if he cannot perform the required sacrifice. And perhaps—if we block the entrance to the cave—she will wither and die, with no one able to sacrifice a victim for her ever again." Tristan's warrior eyes washed her in brilliant waves of blue.

She held his steadfast gaze, hoping that courage and conviction shone in her loving regard. They would eliminate the evil wizard. And save countless future victims from Malfleur's abhorrent appetite.

The Tribe exchanged hearty nods of agreement and shared looks of encouragement. Now that the plan to eliminate the wizard had been formulated, the next strategy to finalize was the infiltration of the castle of Tintagel.

To save Tristan's uncle, King Marke of Cornwall.

And capture the wicked Black Widow Queen.

Gwennol, seated beside Viviane, addressed the group at last. "Warriors of the Tribe of Dana," she began hesitantly, seemingly nervous around so many enormous knights. "My name is Gwennol, and I have information which I believe will be most useful as you plan the siege of Tintagel. "

Everyone turned to the gray-haired woman whose wise, patient eyes twinkled in the candlelight.

"I served at the Castle of Tintagel for many years," Gwennol began. "Until my husband and sons were captured in a Viking slave raid on Cornwall four years ago. I came here after that attack, and that is how I met Princess Issylte." The older woman smiled at Issylte, who squeezed Gwennol's hand under the table, offering strength and support. "There is a stream—we call it *le ruisseau*—which flows directly into the keep, from a lake behind the castle. A network of rivers and streams converges at the lake, then flows through *le ruisseau* beneath Tintagel, emptying into the ocean. That is how supplies are floated in, for the castle is perched high on a cliff facing the open sea, and delivery of goods is impossible from the west."

Gwennol met the intrigued looks of the Tribe. "I worked among the kitchen staff, accepting deliveries of provisions such as fresh fish and grain. The barge arrives every Friday morning at nine o'clock." With a pointed look at Lancelot and Tristan, Gwennol grinned. "If we could intercept the delivery of goods...we could hide several armed knights among the supplies. And float right in!"

With a gesture to Issylte, Gwennol proposed, "We women can disguise ourselves as servants. A few of the men can pose as merchants, delivering the goods to the castle, hiding their weapons under heavy cloaks." The warriors of the Tribe exchanged hearty grins. "We float into the keep on the scheduled supply barge and hitch it onto the dock at the base of the castle. When the servants open the door to receive the supplies, you overpower them, and we're in."

Lancelot's eyes widened in apparent delight as he glanced around the table. Gwennol's idea was perfect.

Kjetil embellished the plan. "We cannot all arrive at once, in the same ship, to the coast of Cornwall. Nor can we sail to the same port. We would attract too much unwanted attention. I have an idea." The burly Viking grinned from ear to ear. "As you know, I produce delectable cheeses from my pastures in Normandy, which I frequently ship, along with cases of sweet and hard cider from my apple orchards. And, of course, the exquisite *eau-de-vie de pommes*—the renowned apple brandy for which I am famous...my *Calvados.*"

A hush of anticipation spread over the table as all eyes were glued on the Norman Viking.

"Lancelot—you, Tristan, Issylte, Darius, Kirus, and Nolwenn will sail to the harbor of Polperro, on one of our Avalonian ships posing as a commercial vessel. Kirus will be the shipping merchant, as planned, with Tristan, Lancelot, and Gorvenal hidden in the supplies. Your ship will fly my banner from Normandy to deflect suspicion, transporting wares from France to Cornwall. You disembark, ride to the Forest of Morois, and establish the hidden encampments around the cave portal as the ship returns to Avalon."

With a glance at Dagur, Kjetil elaborated further. "You and I—with Erwann, Bahja, a dozen Vikings, and

Kaherdin's knights from *le Château Rose*—will sail on a different ship and dock at Penzance, a seaport to the west of Polperro. As if we're delivering a shipment of cheese, cider, and Calvados from Normandy to the castle of Tintagel."

Kjetil returned his attention to Kirus, Lancelot, Darius, and Tristan. "The men with me will wear chain mail and weapons, for they'll pose as my armed guards, protecting a valuable shipment. It will appear as if I employ them to package, deliver, and ensure that the products I ship from Normandy are delivered directly to the castle of Tintagel."

A few eyes widened in disbelief. Kjetil chortled, his laugh husky and deep. "Sometimes the best way to remain hidden is to be concealed in plain sight." He took a long pull from his goblet of wine, then wiped his chin with his sleeve. "We unload at the port of Penzance, procure a carriage to transport our goods, and ride directly to the castle."

The Viking grinned at Gwennol. "You sail with us, posing as my mother. You're accompanying me on this shipping voyage so that you can visit a dear friend who serves at the castle."

Kjetil leaned back in his chair, crossing his arms upon his broad chest, a sly grin spreading across his scarred, rugged face. "Prince Kaherdin regrets being unable to sail with us. However, he is most anxious to exact revenge on the wizard and queen who murdered his sister."

Reaching into his cloak, the Viking withdrew several bags of silver, which he placed heartily upon the table, grinning broadly at the members of the Tribe of Dana. "His gift will finance the carriage—for the delivery of our goods to the castle—and procure horses for the men on our ship. We coordinate the delivery of our shipment of Norman cheese, cider, and Calvados—so that it coincides with the arrival of the supply barge."

Wicked delight shone on the faces of the warriors seated at the table. Lancelot quipped, "We overtake the barge and hide among the wheels of cheese and cases of Calvados. We float right into the keep, as scheduled. Take out the guards in the kitchen. Infiltrate the castle. Don the armor of the knights we overtake and position our men to replace them. Little by little, until the entire castle is ours."

Everyone was grinning, clearly delighted with the strategy. Kirus summarized the two-pronged assault on Cornwall. "Our group arrives in Polperro, flying your banner, Kjetil. We ride to the Forest of Morois and—Goddess willing—eliminate the wizard. We seal the cave of *la Porte des Ombres*, then—we ride to the dense woods northeast of the castle. And wait for you to arrive with the supply barge."

The leader of the Tribe of Dana spoke solemnly to Tristan and Lancelot. "Tristan slays the wizard, and you ride across the forest to set up camp that evening. We'll overtake the barge as they load up—early Friday morning." Glances darted around the table as the Tribe responded in agreement.

Dagur had been pensive and quiet throughout the discussion. Tugging on his dark beard in contemplation, he raised his calculating, serious gaze to Kirus. "If we imprison the wicked queen, rather than execute her outright," he suggested, his voice deep and gravelly, "we could bring her with us as a political pawn when we sail to Ireland." Pushing the black curly hair away from his face, Dagur glanced at Lancelot, then at Issylte. "The Emerald Princess would be able to reclaim her kingdom by exposing the truth—that the Black Widow Queen poisoned her first husband, King Donnchadh. That Morag has been denying Issylte the right to her father's crown. That the queen issued orders to assassinate Issylte—the rightful heir to the throne of Ireland. *Twice*." Dagur paused, allowing his words to reach the Tribe.

Kirus nodded fiercely, endorsing Dagur's suggestion. The brutal scar across his feral face emblazoned his heated words. "The wicked queen who married Tristan's uncle through evil enchantment by the wizard Voldurk. The Black Widow who wishes to become sole sovereign of Cornwall as she did Ireland. By *poisoning her husband*."

Tristan locked eyes with Issylte in a private, intimate exchange. Through the *mating bond*, his soul flowed into hers in deep blue waves; her spirit unfurled into his with the verdant magic of the sacred forest. *Mates* whose destinies were entwined, whose kingdoms were threatened, whose marriage and love formed a powerful political alliance that would prevail.

"We capture the queen and bring her with us to Ireland. Issylte formally challenges her in Castle Connaught, in front of her father's royal court. Issylte exposes the truth, reclaims her father's throne, and is crowned the rightful queen. She then executes Morag for conspiracy, treason, and murder." Tristan's deep voice echoed through the silent dining hall.

"Agreed." Lancelot met the resolute expressions of each member of the Tribe seated around the table. "We infiltrate Tintagel and imprison the queen. Liberate King Marke. And establish the stronghold where our French allies will join us." The White Knight of Avalon locked his brilliant gaze on Issylte. "From Tintagel, we organize and launch the attack on Indulf's Viking fleet in Dubh Linn. Once we've taken the seaport, we'll ride to Connaught. Your father's castle. For you to finally reclaim your throne."

Tristan lifted her trembling hand to his lips. "And be crowned *the Emerald Queen*."

The wings of the little white dove fluttered wildly as she soared in the sky-blue gaze of her sea raven *mate*.

Gorvenal spoke next. "Tristan, you served as a squire at your uncle's castle for many years. And I've been the First Knight of Tintagel since you were a boy. We both know the castle like the back of our hands. We know where the guards are posted, how they've been trained, when the shift changes…all of which gives us a distinct advantage." Gorvenal's intelligent gaze gleamed with challenge. "Some of the men have sworn allegiance to me as their First Knight. They might even be swayed to join us, once they learn that our goal is to free King Marke from the wicked queen and her evil wizard."

Tristan and Lancelot locked warrior eyes, their battle strategies forming.

"Any knights who oppose us must be dealt with *decisively*." Lancelot fixed Gorvenal with a commanding stare. "We replace any fallen knights that we are forced to dispatch with our own men, donning the armor of Tintagel. We start with the kitchen, then infiltrate each level, securing every post, until the castle is ours."

Gorvenal would have to kill some of the very same knights he'd trained. The men he'd fought beside and bled with.

His own men.

The gaze of the First Knight of Tintagel blazed with desperation—then somber acceptance—as he returned Lancelot's powerful stare. Gorvenal ducked his chin in silent, solemn agreement.

"Once we've taken the castle, we storm the throne room." Tristan's impassioned eyes blazed into hers. "And capture the queen."

Issylte's commanding voice was regal as she held Tristan's gaze. "We lock her in chains. Throw her in the dungeon of Tintagel. Where they imprisoned and *tortured you.*"

Remembering how the little white dove had found him—his flayed back a raw, bloody mess, his warrior body and spirit broken, drugged into a stupor with thick black liquid oozing from the mating mark—Issylte wanted to torture the wicked queen who had nearly killed Tristan. Who had murdered her father, Gigi, and *Tatie.* Who had sent huntsmen to kill her. And who now threatened Tristan's last remaining family member. The uncle he loved like a father.

Issylte wanted to thrust *Emeraldfire* deep into that wicked heart.

But no. Morag would face formal charges and be publicly executed in Ireland. Exposing the Black Widow's crimes would authenticate Issylte's right to the throne as the legitimate heir to her father's kingdom. Her sovereignty would be strengthened, and her reign would begin honorably, just as her father would have wanted. The Emerald Princess would become a noble and respected queen, the fair and just ruler that the King of Ireland had raised her to be. A queen who would have made her cherished father, adored Gigi, and beloved *Tatie* burst with pride.

Issylte drew her attention back to Tristan. "Once the queen is captured, we'll rush to your uncle's side. We'll remove the enchanted ring that I saw in a *sighting* on the Mirrored Lake. The one Voldurk gave the queen to control King Marke." She smiled at her beloved *mate*. "I'll also bring my healing herbs to treat him—in case they have drugged or poisoned him. Perhaps the *Rose Elder* in my blood can cleanse his as well. As it did yours, when I came to you in the dungeon of Tintagel."

She smiled at the intimate memory of the little white dove with *le cheveu d'or* in her beak, drawing Tristan's blood and mingling it with her own through the *mating mark*. A ripple of pleasure flowed from the teardrop shaped tattoo on her neck throughout her entire body. Tristan's intense look told her he'd felt it, too.

"And my uncle, when he discovers the truth, will join our effort and support us as we sail to Ireland." Tristan brought Issylte's hand to his lips, bestowing a reverent kiss. "For you to claim your father's throne." Her soul entwined with his through the *mating bond,* his eyes dancing with hers.

Ronan interrupted Tristan and Issylte's private reverie. "Once you've taken Tintagel, your allies can sail from France and join you there. You can establish a command center at King Marke's castle, to plan and launch the attack on Ireland."

The Tribe indicated agreement. Tristan responded, "If all goes according to plan, once we've taken the castle, we can send word to Audric, Abélard, and Bénézet. Each has promised at least fifty knights, two hundred men-at-arms. Weapons, horses, and ships." With a glance at Lancelot, he added, "And Kaherdin's giving us a small fleet, with two hundred armored knights. Wielding Elven swords forged by Ronan himself." Tristan cast a respectful nod to the enormous blond Elf. Ronan ducked his chin in silent acknowledgement of the accolade.

Viviane's esteemed voice carried across the table. "The Little Folk are a reliable means of communication throughout the realm. You can send messages, just as Maiwenn did when she sent Issylte here to Avalon." The Lady of the Lake smiled softly at Issylte, love for *Tatie* glimmering in the depths of her lake-blue eyes. At Viviane's gesture, four short, muscular males with long, black hair and skin the color of toasted almonds approached the assembled group. "Allow me to present Benoît, Clovik, Pierrot, and Koraz. They have agreed to travel with you as messengers, should you need them. They are part of a vast network of forest creatures with *otherworldly* communication skills."

Lancelot greeted the woodland inhabitants with a friendly grin as the Tribe shook hands with the mysterious beings. To Kjetil, he suggested, "Two should sail with you, and two with us. If either group encounters unforeseen difficulties, we'll be able to send messages to one another."

Kjetil concurred, then addressed Benoît. "You and Clovik will sail with Dagur and me to Penzance." To Pierrot, he announced, "You and Koraz will sail with Kirus, Tristan, Darius, and Lancelot to Polperro." The forest fairies communicated wordlessly with each other, their enigmatic black eyes gleaming with support of Kjetil's proposal.

Issylte glanced around the table at the determined, courageous faces of her beloved Tribe. In their valiant eyes, she glimpsed the grim acceptance of the risk of death, the simmering fury and nervous tension of impending battle, and the fragile, furtive hope of victory.

In three days, it would all begin.

****

As agreed, the Tribe of Dana, their knights, and the priestesses of Avalon met with Ronan and his Elven warriors in the banquet room of *Le Centre* three nights later for the formal presentation of the inimitable sword *Azeldraig.*

A magnificent farewell feast had been prepared, for Tristan and Issylte would depart with the members of the Tribe and set sail for Cornwall on the morrow. With the dining concluded, the serving staff cleared the area for the ceremony. Ronan rose to his feet and strode to a table which had been prepared for him. He shook out a white cloth and laid it carefully upon the floor before him, then unwrapped a parcel which he had tucked under his arm, placing it upon the tabletop. Issylte's heart caught in her throat. She gulped a swallow of water to quench her suddenly dry mouth.

When at last Ronan faced the throng of friends gathered to witness this unprecedented event, a hush fell over the crowd as he called Tristan to his side.

"Sir Tristan of Lyonesse, the Blue Knight of Cornwall, please approach. That I may bequeath the weapon I have forged for you."

Tristan rose from the table where he sat with Issylte, Lancelot, and the other members of the Tribe of Dana. His deep blue velvet tunic gleamed in the candlelight, enhancing the azure brilliance of his eyes. Issylte held her breath as she beheld her handsome husband. Her warrior. Her *mate.* Her heart.

Tristan wove through the assembled tables until he

reached Ronan, who was facing the crowd, positioned purposefully so that all could witness the entire ceremony.

Ronan's deep voice resonated throughout the hall. "Although I am not a king, I feel this occasion merits the same reverence as a knighting ceremony." Smiling broadly, he made a swooping, gallant gesture. "Please kneel, Sir Tristan."

Tristan knelt onto the white cloth, his head bowed in homage. *He must be remembering how his uncle knighted him years ago in Tintagel, bestowing upon him the title of the Blue Knight of Cornwall. How King Arthur dubbed him a Knight of the Round Table. And now, he will receive an even more prestigious gift. A sword to surpass even Excalibur—the legendary sword Azeldraig.* The wings of the white dove fluttered wildly in her heart.

"Sir Tristan of Lyonesse," Ronan's powerful baritone rang out, "the Blue Knight of Cornwall. Knight of the Round Table of King Arthur in Camelot. Slayer of the Morholt, the Black Knight of Ireland. Warrior of the Tribe of the Goddess Dana. I have crafted this magnificent sword for *you*."

Issylte's breath was shallow, her heart pounding in her chest as she watched the two men who had shared her heart and her body—her former lover and her *mate*—in this sacred ceremony that entwined their destinies with hers.

"A weapon of extraordinary power," Ronan's deep, reverent voice reverberated through the hushed hall. "Forged in *dragonfire*. On this enchanted island of Avalon." His towering presence shone like a beacon of light. "A sword crafted from the molten ore of a fallen star. Mined from the sacred cave. *La Grotte de l' Étoile.*"

Ronan reached for the *otherworldly* Elven blade. Holding the sword reverently across his flattened palms, he extended his outstretched arms to Tristan. "Rise, Sir Tristan, and accept this sword which I bestow upon you. The most magnificent weapon I have ever forged. The Avalonian sword, *Azeldraig.* "

Tristan rose from his kneeling position. Ronan placed the sword in Tristan's chivalrous hands, then stepped back. Placing his right arm across his stomach, he lowered his silvery-blond head in reverence. Ronan then rose to his full astonishing height—an inch or two taller than her towering Tristan. He fisted his heart with his right hand and bowed his head in homage to her *mate*, the incomparable Blue Knight of Cornwall. Ronan lifted his rugged Elven face, and the two seasoned warriors locked eyes in mutual respect.

Ronan then gestured to Viviane, who was seated at Issylte's table near her son Lancelot. "The Lady of the Lake has a gift to bestow upon you as well, Tristan," Ronan announced, his face exuberant with expectation. Issylte's heart fluttered. *A gift from Viviane? What could this be?*

The High Priestess of Avalon rose from her seat, strode up to Ronan, and motioned to two Elves standing along the wall at the edge of the room. At Viviane's signal, they brought to the table a set of dark green armor that exuded an aura of radiant power. A chorus of verdant magic resounded in Issylte's soul.

Viviane whispered something in Ronan's ear. He picked up the enchanted armor to display as Viviane spoke publicly to Tristan. "Years ago, I cast spells upon my son's armor so that he would be invincible in battle and become the legendary First Knight of King Arthur Pendragon. And now, Sir Tristan of Lyonesse, the Blue Knight of Cornwall, I have enchanted this Elven armor and shield which Ronan has crafted for you."

Excitement rippled through the throng as the Lady of the Lake caressed the extraordinary armor which Ronan displayed before Tristan. Of the same deep emerald green as the beast Mordrac himself, the Elven armor was molded in the shape of Tristan's body. A huge dragon scale extended downward over each shoulder, evoking the clawed wings of the beast Tristan had described to her in detail. Sculpted scales covered the cuirass of the torso as well as the vambraces, greaves and cuisses covering the limbs. Metal gauntlets and sabatons seemed as supple and flexible as the softest deep green leather. And the helmet, which covered the sides of the face like curved wings and formed a protective dip over the nose, was shaped like the head of a dragon with two powerfully spiked horns and two blazing blue topaz stones as eyes.

The shield, crafted from the same deep green dragon scales, was formed like a double headed spade, curving to a peak at both top and bottom, boldly emblazoned with the massive head of the dragon Mordrac. A shiver ran up Issylte's spine. It was without a doubt the most magnificent armor she had ever seen.

Ronan addressed Tristan, his deep voice resonating over the captivated crowd. "With the dragon scales you retrieved in Mordrac's cave, I created this armor and shield. Forged in *dragonfire*. Crafted with dragon scales. Enchanted by the fairy Viviane, the Lady of the Lake of Avalon."

Viviane extended her slender, elegant hands, the

long sleeves of her white gown gracing the floor like gossamer wings as a hushed silence filled the air. The little white dove fluttered wildly in Issylte's soaring heart. "Please give me your sword. Azeldraig. And kneel, Sir Tristan."

Tristan offered the High Priestess his majestic sword and knelt at her feet. With the pointed tip of the *otherworldly* blade, Viviane touched each of his shoulders and head with great reverence. Her lilting voice regal and solemn, she announced proudly: "With this legendary Elven sword, inimitable Elven armor, and unparalleled Elven shield, I, Viviane—the Lady of the Lake—dub thee, Sir Tristan. *The Dragon Knight of Avalon.*"

Applause erupted as the audience leapt to its feet, cheers of congratulations rippling through the crowd. Exuberant faces and jubilant smiles greeted Tristan, filling Issylte's heart with endless joy and immeasurable gratitude.

Avalon.

Where she had become a gifted *guérisseuse*.

Where she'd healed the critically wounded Tristan.

Where the Goddess had entwined their fates.

Ronan searched the crowd. He called out, "Princess Issylte of Ireland. *Guérisseuse* of Avalon and Priestess of Dana. Wife and *mate* of Tristan, the Dragon Knight of Avalon. Please come forward."

Issylte clutched the sacred scabbard as she wove through the spectators to join Ronan, Viviane, and Tristan before the hushed crowd. Her husband's brilliant blue eyes blazed with power and pride as he held her loving gaze. Ronan gestured for her to stand at his own side as she prepared to present the protective sheath to

Jennifer Ivy Walker

her *mate*. The warrior who would wield *Azeldraig*.

The Dragon Knight of Avalon.

Positioning herself so that she faced the audience and Tristan simultaneously, Issylte flashed her most brilliant smile at the man she loved with all her heart.

Her articulate, eloquent voice carried across the crowd. "Tristan, my husband. I learned from *Morgane la Fée* how to craft a sacred scabbard which will shield you against the evil which threatens our realm." Hoping he could see in her face the pride and love that filled her heart, Issylte offered the gem-encrusted sheath to her *mate*. "Please accept this enchanted scabbard for your magnificent sword. May it always protect you in battle."

Tristan took the leather scabbard, glittering with sacred gemstones, and belted it around his waist. With chivalresque *panache*, he sheathed the exquisite sword *Azeldraig*, grinning from ear to ear. He then pulled Issylte toward him, dipped her back in his arms, and kissed her deeply before the enthusiastic crowd. Wild cheers and riotous applause wafted through the festive air.

Ronan turned back to the preparation table, where intricately carved silver goblets had been placed. Offering a chalice each to Viviane, Issylte, and Tristan and reserving one for himself, Ronan faced the acclaimed knight at his side. The elated crowd quieted in anticipation. Raising his goblet high, candlelight illuminating his magnificent silvery-blond head, Ronan roared, "Let us congratulate Sir Tristan. The Dragon Knight of Avalon!"

The ecstatic throng jumped up in approval to toast their anointed champion. Verdant magic flooded Issylte's joyous heart.

Viviane hugged Tristan, kissing him on both cheeks with *la bise française* as Kirus and Lancelot rushed over to congratulate him. Gorvenal, Kjetil, Darius, and Dagur pressed in from behind, smiling faces and *félicitations* from all. Everyone conveyed enthusiastic approval of Tristan's esteemed title and magnificent Avalonian adornments, ogling the shining splendor of the *otherworldly* Elven blade and the pulsating power of the dragon scale armor and shield. As the crowd admired the glittering, enchanted gemstones of the sacred scabbard, Issylte captivated quite a few listeners as she related the story behind the emeralds, blue topaz gems, and *la pierre de l' étoile.* Tristan's brilliant gaze basked her in lovelight and pride.

Lancelot, Gorvenal, Kirus, and the members of the Tribe took turns examining the Elven sword, its hilt adorned with the same three enchanted gemstones as the sacred scabbard. The blue topaz eyes of the dragon on the Avalonian helmet were the same sacred gems as Tristan's beloved—and greatly missed—sea raven ring. Indeed, the Elven blade, armor, and shield formed a trinity of *otherworldly* protection for the newly dubbed Dragon Knight of Avalon.

Later, after much revelry and joyous celebration, the evening of merriment concluded, with toasts for a safe voyage to Britain and best wishes for success in their arduous quest.

In the morning, as the early spring sun rose over the enchanted island of Avalon, the Tribe of Dana loaded weapons, armor, horses, and supplies, setting sail for the rocky, craggy coast of Cornwall, armed with a triple trinity of powerful alliances.

A shapeshifting trio of *otherworldly* allies. *La Tribu*

des Loups—the Wolf Tribe. *Le Clan des Ours*—the Bear Clan. And *les Dragons de Mer*—the mermaid sea dragon warriors of the *Gallizenae* priestesses.

A trinity of human allies from France. Armorique, Aquitaine, and Anjou.

And a trio of formidable warriors. The legendary Tribe of Dana, defending the sacred realm of the Goddess. The valiant knights from *la Joyeuse Garde*, with all the prowess of the Elves of Avalon. And Kaherdin's intrepid knights from *le Château Rose.* Clad in Avalonian armor and wielding Elven swords.

Together, she and Tristan would battle the wicked Black Widow Queen, the dark wizard Voldurk, and the malevolent *Fée des Ombres.*

Entwined by the Goddess herself, the *otherworldly* mates would prevail.

Issylte, the Emerald Fairy of the Enchanted Forests.

And Tristan. The Dragon Knight of Avalon.

Coming Soon…
The Emerald Fairy and the Dragon Knight
Book 3 in The Wild Rose and the Sea Raven Series…

Wielding a trio of enchanted Elven weapons to battle a dark wizard and a legion of diabolical dwarves, Tristan is faced with the impossible choice between saving the woman he loves or defending his endangered kingdom. Inexplicably compelled to remain in the sacred forest where he hears the voice of her heart, the heir to the throne of Cornwall incurs the wrath and scorn of his army when he decides to hunt for his captive mate.

Her verdant magic greatly enhanced by the mystical Morgane la Fée, Issylte must summon a coalition of Naiad nymphs and celestial fairies to destroy a nascent evil as she fights to reclaim her rightful crown.

When the Black Widow Queen unites with a malignant menace and a ghost from Tristan's haunted past, the Emerald Fairy and the Dragon Knight must ally with a triad of shapeshifting warrior tribes to defeat a Viking Trident and defend their trinity of Celtic kingdoms.

Interwoven fates. *Otherworldly* mates. Destiny awaits.

A word about the author...

Jennifer Ivy Walker has an MA in French literature and is a professor of French at a state college in Florida. Her debut novel, "The Wild Rose and the Sea Raven," is a dark fantasy, paranormal romance retelling of the medieval French legend of "*Tristan et Yseult*," blended with elements of Arthurian myth, fairy tales, and folklore from the enchanted Forest of *Brocéliande*.

Be sure to follow the thrilling conclusion of "The Wild Rose and the Sea Raven" trilogy with Book 3, "The Emerald Fairy and the Dragon Knight", published by The Wild Rose Press.

Please visit her at the following websites:

https://jenniferivywalker.com/

https://jenniferivywalker.blogspot.com/

https://twitter.com/bohemienneivy

CPSIA information can be obtained
at www.ICGtesting.com
Printed in the USA
BVHW050218190123
656596BV00022B/144